SECRET *of the* SONG

CATHIE HARTIGAN

cwm

Secret of the Song

Copyright © 2015 Cathie Hartigan

Published 2015 by CreativeWritingMatters
www.creativewritingmatters.co.uk

Cover design: Berni Stevens

Acknowledgements

Firstly, huge thanks must go to, Margaret James, Sophie Duffy and Su Bristow, who have championed my work and always given me the most excellent support and guidance.

To Jane Eastgate for her wise editorial suggestions.
To the members of *Exeter Writers* for their support and Dan Knibb of the *Write Group*, for his generous critiquing.
To *Nota Bene*, a wonderful ensemble with whom it is such a privilege to sing.
To my dear sister Jane and brother-in-law Noel, for their continual encouragement and exceedingly sharp eyes.

I should also mention that even if Don Carlo Gesualdo (1560 – 1613) wasn't quite guilty of murder, he was clearly a deeply troubled individual. There is evidence that corroborates both the eccentric behaviour of his early life and the degenerate madness of his later years. A lot of research was undertaken early in the twentieth century by Messers Hesaltine and Gray in their book: *Carlo Gesualdo, Prince of Venosa, Musician and Murderer*. It was here that I first encountered the witness statements, including that of the servant girl, Silvia Albana.

Where I may have done Gesualdo a disservice however, is in the running down of his music. It certainly is neither an easy sing, nor an easy listen, being very short of good tunes, but if you get the chance, listen to his music sung by *I Fagiolini*, under the direction of Robert Hollingworth. Nobody does it better.

Prologue

Gesualdo, near Naples, 1584

'Silvia!' My mother's voice knocked loudly at my thoughts. 'Where are you?'

'Here.' I rose to my feet and hid my sewing behind me. I knew the temper in her only too well.

'Show me,' she said, advancing from the doorway.

'But it is not yet finished.'

'I want to see.'

I placed the garment in her hand. A linen shift.

'It's too good,' said my mother, pulling at the seam. 'Don't make your stitching so neat.'

I protested, of course, having spent many hours trying to make my stitches as fine as I could, and so small they were almost invisible.

'Someone will notice,' she said, 'and none of us want to be noticed.' She threw my work into the basket we were taking to market and told me to go help my father with the olive pressing. 'Be careful, child,' she said, as I dragged my feet towards the door. 'We've all got places in this world. There are no peacocks in the chicken house for a good reason.'

In spite of her warning, I continued to watch the carriages going up the hill and I listened to the curious singing carried back down from the castle on the warm summer breezes. In those tall turrets there were plenty of peacocks. They liked their silks and satins and they liked them stitched well. But finding good needlewomen wasn't easy. It was necessary to look in unlikely places. Even amongst the chickens.

Chapter One

Exeter, October 2014

'Why don't you marry Jon, mummy?' Mollie, Queen of Barbie-land, and resplendent in her twinkly pyjamas, sat up in bed glaring at me. 'Then he'd be here all the time, and you wouldn't need so many minutes on your phone.'

'That's absolutely the worst reason to get married I've ever heard.' I kissed my magenta monster goodnight. 'Now, lie down and go to sleep.'

'It would be nice though, wouldn't it? Wouldn't it?'

'It might, but then again it might not. Besides,' I said, turning the light right down, 'aren't we all happy now?'

She was quiet for a nanosecond. 'But we could be *more* happy.'

'Shh ... that's enough.'

'You wouldn't *have* to get married.'

'Go to sleep!'

Needless to say, I lay awake, staring into the darkness when I went to bed a couple of hours later. Would we be happier? In my mind's eye I saw Jon at our rehearsal earlier that evening. We were all squashed round my kitchen table: *Noteworthy:* Robert and Sophie, Jon and me. Jon sat directly opposite me, his rangy body animated with enthusiasm when he showed us his new arrangement of *Let It Be*.

'Lisa's a proper alto,' Sophie had said to Jon when she introduced me to him at her thirtieth birthday party. 'Fabulous voice.'

Then he held out his hand and said, 'How do you do, fabulous Lisa?'

Well, that was the first time my heart gave a little skip. It wasn't every day a handsome man looked at me with such interest. We'd spent the rest of the evening together and I remember my jaw ached from smiling so much. The wine had something to do with it but he'd made me laugh too. He told one very old joke, and acted it flamboyantly, about altos not being able to change lightbulbs because they couldn't get up that high. Cheek, I'd thought, smitten.

It was at the same party that *Noteworthy's* first rehearsal was arranged. We met the following week, but from then on the music came first. Good for weddings, parties and any other function that needed a bit of music but without all the rigmarole of dancing or a band.

We offer pop, showtunes, light opera, part-songs of the nineteenth and twentieth centuries and our particular favourite genre, Renaissance madrigals. Although to be honest, in the two years we'd been together, there hadn't been any call for those.

Don't try an' fix what ain't broke, I thought, turning over and pulling the duvet around my ears. It's a special thing singing together in a small group and rare to find both voices and personalities that match. Jon and I were good singers and good *friends*. Locally, we were in demand, in spite of our rather niche expertise, and it would be crazy to change the dynamic of the group. In my experience, love brought entanglements and all manner of difficulties not conducive to a professional relationship. Besides, and it was a big besides, the question hadn't arisen. We'd been out, but mostly with Mollie or *Noteworthy*, never on what you'd call a date.

Concentrate on the music, I told myself, snuggling further under the duvet in an effort to get comfortable. *That's the important thing.*

I drifted away thinking about our rehearsal. We were about to sing the first madrigal. It was that moment when everything had settled and we were all focusing our attention into the silent space before us. I'd thought then that we were like synchronised swimmers poised to dive into the water. We weren't about to get wet, but all four of us were launching ourselves away from the safety of solid ground. The music in our hands was a map, that's all, and the crotchets and quavers laced together on lines were symbols, just like a tiny square with a cross on top was a church. It was up to us to make the whole thing real.

Madrigals can be jolly *fa la la* and *hey nonny no* type songs about raunchy love but the one we were about to sing, John Bennet's *Weep, O mine eyes*, celebrated the lovesick drowning in tears. The landscape would only reveal itself if each of us sang our part perfectly. There was no margin of error. As I'd taken a breath, I'd wondered what happened when synchronised swimmers went wrong. Had anybody ever drowned?

Nearly a week went by before I had cause to think about what our next gig might be. It was a Wednesday and my turn to open up the shop. Although it was only part-time, Robert's job offer had saved my life when I'd been at my most desperate. Mollie was small and still launching food missiles around the kitchen when her father rediscovered his libido and took it on a little tour to show anyone who was interested. He was slow to appreciate that my interest in him might be affected by his actions, but he realised soon enough the day he returned to find no Mollie and no me at home.

The phone began ringing as soon as I got inside the shop.

'Good morning,' I said, trying to sound measured, even though I still had one arm in the sleeve of my coat. 'Robert's Classical Music, can I help you?'

'Hello? Are you *Noteworthy* as well?'

The voice was clipped. My old headmistress came to mind and I decided against a smart response. 'Yes, that's right.'

'Excellent. In that case, can you come and see me? Today would be best.'

'Err …'

'We have something of interest.'

'We?' Was this the Queen?

'It's the museum here.'

'Oh?' Not quite the present Queen, but still, there was some sort of association. I assumed the voice was referring to Exeter's principal museum: the Royal Albert Memorial

4

Museum, otherwise known as RAMM.

'We've come across a music manuscript. Italian Renaissance apparently,' she went on, 'which is why I'm calling you. Our initial research suggests it might be previously unknown. Can you come and have a look?'

Yes, most definitely. Exeter is an old city so the chances of finding Roman artefacts are high, but turning up something from the Italian Renaissance was much more intriguing.

When Robert took over manning the shop at lunchtime, I headed off for my meeting with the headmistress/curator.

It seemed to me that Barbie herself might have had a hand in painting the foyer of the museum, and I wondered what Prince Albert, whose statue looked down on every visitor, would have thought of the bright pink décor.

'We're *terribly* excited,' the curator said, staring at a very unexciting volume, somewhat smaller than A4, covered in brown paper.

'Can I have a look?'

'Yes, but prepare yourself, Mrs Barr, the frontispiece engraving is not a pretty sight.'

'Really?' I was surprised. What could possibly be worrying about a four-hundred-year-old Italian song? Gruesome images were everywhere and, in spite of my best efforts to keep the worst web horrors from her, even Mollie, at only ten, had developed a certain resistance to shock.

But when I lifted the cover, I saw exactly what she meant.

'I have absolutely brilliant news,' I said to the others, when we met that evening at Sophie's. Carefully, I slid the precious piece from my case, but somehow it slipped from my fingers and landed next to the roses on the table with a slap. The vase shivered and a few petals fell from the heavy-headed blooms that leant over the brim. Two of the four wine glasses tinged together and I shuddered, the timbre of the sound reminding me of music festivals and exams when the little bell announced *you're next*.

'The museum wants us to sing this.' I went on, nodding at the music, while I fastened my case and leant it against the leg of my chair. 'It's the only copy, so we'd best be careful with it.'

'Good grief,' said Robert, shaking his head and clearly shocked. 'And they let you take it away?'

'Yes, I know. Amazing isn't it? She was quite cavalier about it too. Practically thrust it into my hand.'

He frowned, and muttered something about disgraceful behaviour.

'They're having a big do in December,' I went on. 'It's to open the Renaissance exhibition. It'll be a fantastic opportunity for us, although—'

'Although?' Sophie raised an eyebrow as she gathered up the petals. 'What's the matter?'

'Take a look.'

Jon was quickest. He reached across and picked up the madrigal. Scribbled on the paper cover in a casual diagonal was:

Composer: *Gesualdo, Prince of Venosa*

Title: *Ite Sospiri Ardenti (Burning Sighs)*

'What's he doing in Exeter Museum?' He flipped it open, took one look, then reared back and blew on his fingers as if they'd been scalded. 'Bloody hell!'

The sepia engraving filled the page and instead of the usual cherubs, we were indeed looking at a vision of a bloody hell. Torture, disembowelling, bodies swinging from the gallows, a figure drowning in turbulent waters, another being burnt at the stake. An extraordinary frontispiece – Bosch meets horror comic. You could almost hear the screams.

'How extraordinary,' said Robert. 'They don't come like that very often.'

We all leaned forward for a closer look, ghoulishly intrigued.

'The curator said the same thing,' I told them. 'You'd

6

think a museum curator would be immune to getting the creeps, but she did seem glad to be rid of it.'

'What I'm wondering,' said Sophie, 'is whether it's a warning against going any further?'

'I wouldn't be surprised,' I said, 'but don't let that put us off. Just think of the kudos! We get the chance to sing something nobody's ever done before. The museum has no record of any performance, and the curator said their limited amount of research hadn't found out anything about it. How fantastic is that?'

Robert, ever the one for exactitude, interrupted. 'I expect *someone's* sung it before. Although maybe not for what? Could be four hundred years.'

'The thing is,' I said, waving his comment away, 'there's another problem.' They'd not noticed the Italian inscription. *Madrigal a cinque voci*. Five voices. Two sopranos, alto, tenor, bass.

'Oh well, that's us out then.' Jon sat back.

A muscle in my jaw twitched. 'I did *tell* them we were a quartet.'

'And?' said Jon.

'They thought we could get someone in?'

'I hope you said no.'

'Of course I didn't. It's a good idea. Why can't we?'

'We never have before.' He frowned and folded his arms across his chest with the sort of energy that said there's nothing more to discuss.

I was stunned. 'What kind of a reason is that?'

'Quite a good one, I would have thought.'

Was this going to be an argument? I'd never heard Jon sound quite so truculent, but then, before I could reply, Robert leaned forward and flicked through the pages.

'Good Lord, this isn't easy. We'd have to get someone good enough to cope with all this awkward chromaticism. I *might* know a someone, she's…' he hesitated, frowning. 'I don't know.'

'You don't know?' I said.

We all looked at him, waiting for the something to be

7

revealed, but he shook his head and wouldn't be drawn. 'I'll let you know when I've given it more thought.'

I picked up the Gesualdo manuscript and carefully stowed it back in my case between two fatter volumes. I shivered suddenly. A draught, I told myself, even while remembering that Sophie was very pleased with her new double-glazing.

As I was getting dressed the following morning my phone pinged. A text: *Sorry I was crotchety Jx*

It was during breakfast, that I thought of my reply: *Only minimally :-) x*

I lied. Jon had been worse than crotchety. More like thoroughly negative. It wasn't like him. The Jon I knew relished trying new stuff. What about all the times he'd had a friendly go at Robert for being too stuffy?

When I arrived at work I found the shop door already open even though it was my turn to get in early. 'Hello,' I said. 'This is a surprise.'

'I'm on my way soon,' said Robert. He was thumbing through the box where we kept the names of local musicians and teachers. 'But I wanted to check something. She's in here, I'm sure of it.'

'Do you think it's a good idea?' I said, retrieving the cash float from behind the Beethoven Sonatas.

'Don't you?' Robert picked out an index card. 'Ah, here she is.'

'I think it's a brilliant idea if we can find someone suitable. What do we know about her?'

He looked at me, card held mid-air, with a slight frown. Then having shaken away some flecks of dust he peered at it and read out loud: 'Daniela Alfero. Grad. Conservatori di Milano 2006. LRSM Singing (soprano) London 2008.' He glanced up. 'Impressive enough?'

'Sounds like it,' I said, clattering the coins into the till, 'although we'll have to get her past Jon. You said there was something about her? What sort of something?'

He shrugged. 'I thought she was, a bit … a bit full

on? She's very … oh, I don't know. You'll see. But we're pros, Lisa, and we're talking about one concert, not a lifelong commitment.'

'How do we know her voice will match?'

'We don't. But she's good and it's worth a go. Persuade Jon, will you?'

'I'll try.'

The little bell tinkled as he shut the door behind him.

I fired up the old kettle and equally old PC. I put the cardboard box of names back under the counter, thanked the god of coffee that Robert had embraced cafetières and sat down to email Jon. A minute later I was still looking at the blank screen.

On the back of an old delivery note I made a couple of lists:

YES:

Prestigious gig – could lead to more

Good experience

Will widen our repertoire

Chance to sing in one of the city's prime institutions

NO:

Not audience-friendly music

Have to get someone in

Jon not keen

Hmm … I twiddled my pen on the counter and wondered about Daniela thingy, with diplomas from Milan and London. Was she Italian? Must be.

Greetings from Robert's Classical Music Emporium, I began my email, but then the door opened. Stupidly, I clicked send. Oh well. Jon would laugh. I pictured him in my mind, how attractive he looks when singing and how calm, even though he's usually so lively. Who knows, maybe it's his inability to sit still that's stopping him composing the opera he swears will be his masterpiece. It would be brilliant, but a long way from his day job writing advert jingles.

I sold a violin tutor and two *Messiahs* before receiving a reply.

What?? Sanatorium? Jx

Hah! Robert's 'someone' has very shiny credentials. It's either her or they'll get Exeter Warblers – yuck. Say yes. Lx

Click.

He was bound to agree. Jon was the most easy-going person I knew. The other night was a blip, surely. If anything he was almost too easy going.

Ping – an email. Not Jon. Somebody enquiring about *Nirvana* for easy guitar. I began the reply: *I'm afraid we only stock classical* ... my mind wandered.

There's something very solid about a quartet. Four is good. Four crotchets to a bar is called Common Time. People like groups of four, they're not as intimate as two and less dangerous than three; four is a comfortable number. Unlike five. Five is awkward and unbalanced. I remembered as a kid trying to dance to my mum's vinyl of Dave Brubeck's *Take Five*. Hopeless.

After work and on my way to pick up Mollie from ballet, I nipped into the library. I wanted to find out a bit more about Gesualdo and Robert's computer ran on slug power. I'd read a bit and discovered differing accounts, some really bizarre and others unbelievable, but all were gruesome. Gesualdo lived about the same time as the artist Caravaggio, and apparently was just as crazy.

After the library came Sainsbury's, so I arrived at the church hall with longer arms than usual. Of course, Mollie had her ballet bag, her PE kit and her school rucksack.

'How come you've got all that stuff?' she said.

'This is called "Our Tea",' I said, holding up the right hand bag, 'and this,' I held up the left, 'is because I've been to the library. Hello, darling, had a good day?'

'What's all those books?' A large frown furrowed the otherwise serene forehead of my daughter. She dumped her stuff on the ground and began to wrestle with her rucksack as if she'd never put one on before.

'There's someone I'm interested in, a composer.' I put

my bags down and helped straighten the straps on her back. 'We're going to sing a piece of his music. There. Is that more comfortable?'

'A bit.'

I knew better than to ask how she'd got on at school, so it wasn't until she was full of pizza and recovered from her earlier grumps that she told me her teacher wanted to see me at the end of the week.

'Oh? Do you know why?' I said it lightly, but is there a parent in the land who doesn't have a twang of anxiety when the teacher calls?

She shrugged and still chewing said, 'Not necess … necessarily.'

'What does that mean?'

Mollie slipped from the table, picked up Barbie, who was hanging over the radiator, and sat her on the table facing me. 'You talk to her,' she said to it, before disappearing into the sitting room.

My daughter may be smart, but Barbie I hung from the door handle by her hair.

Chapter Two

Gesualdo 1585

All day the baby screamed. Our ears wearied of the noise that was surely loud enough to be heard in far away Napoli. My mother fretted, but more so when my youngest sister suddenly stopped screaming and her little arms, that had beaten the air for so long, lay still by her sides. Every breath became effortful, sounding like the rasping of my father's saw.

He was away on a forest trip. I had inherited my deft fingers from him, although his skill was in wood. He made furniture but his joy came from being with living trees.

'Go and ask Francesca if you might go to Fontanarosa market with her tomorrow,' my mother said, as the light began to fade. 'Say we can spare a few eggs and if you sell anything we will buy some of her honey.'

Even though I worried about the baby, my heart gave a little lift. It would be the first time I had left our village without my mother. Francesca was old and her eyes were veiled with milk. She would not notice my own eyes roving, or mind if I explored by myself. After all, very soon I would be fifteen.

In the dark of the next morning, I found my mother asleep with the baby in her arms. For a moment I thought the angels had come in the night and taken my sister, but when I put the tip of my finger to her lips, I felt warm breath. The worst had passed. My mother stirred and I hurried away. It would not do for her to have a change of mind.

I carried our two baskets, glad they contained eggs and needlework and not the oil from our three olive trees. By the shrine at the crossroads I hoisted them onto Francesca's cart and prayed her old nag would survive the journey.

We plodded along slowly, but did arrive at last. And what noise! People shouting and singing and all manner of clucks, quacks, bellows and honks from animals. Francesca insisted we set our stall next to the spit roasts.

'Why here?' I said, holding my nose.

'People have to eat,' Francesca said. She smiled and licked her lips, her face crinkling like the skin of the pigs on the spit. 'The smell will bring people here soon enough.'

I became sick of the noise and stench, worrying that my needlework might take on the grease that cloyed the air around us. Francesca's apricots and almonds proved popular and before long we had a little cluster of customers peering into our baskets. My eyes flicked to and fro. I was looking for someone special. Not someone I knew, although I was sure I'd know her when she came.

The sun grew higher, the day hotter and the meat charred. I was beginning to fear that Fontanarosa market was not going to assist in my change of fortune when a woman approached and began looking through my basket of needlework. Yes! I could tell by the way she was dressed. Not in finery, of course, but her apron was white and her cape unmarked, the collar flat and even. She picked up my shirts and aprons, turning them over as if looking for something. Her hands were smooth.

'I have another piece here,' I said, reaching under the straw of the egg basket. I unwrapped the silk chemise from an old, but clean piece of sheeting. 'Perhaps you would like to see?'

The woman sifted the cloth through her fingers, inspecting the seams, the oversewn edges, the invisible working-in of the thread on the reverse. She was no stranger to fine work.

'Did you do this, child?'

I nodded.

She looked at Francesca, who was picking meat from her teeth, then back at me. 'Is this woman your grandmother?'

I shook my head.

'What is your name then?'

I tried to keep my voice steady. *'My name is Silvia Albana and my mother has stayed at home today because my sister is sick.'*

'And where is your home?'

'Gesualdo,' I said. *'My father is the carpenter.'*

The woman reached into her purse. *'It's possible you may see me again,'* she said, *'but for now, I will pay you for this.'*

In my dreaming I had not imagined selling the piece, but merely showing it as an example of my work. Now I had no silk but an enormous amount of money in my hand. My father could earn as much but not my mother, even if we had fifty chickens. I turned to Francesca. She had taken the bone pick from her teeth and was looking at me as if I had magic powers.

'I have to buy more cloth,' I told her. *'My mother said so.'* I put the coins deep in a pocket. *'I'll be back soon.'*

I didn't wait for a reply but left her with the rest of the eggs and two shirts. She would be honest in dealing with them but not too honest with my mother if I bought her a little wine. It would be a coin well spent. How I would explain my newfound wealth to my mother I didn't know, but once it was converted into cloth she could only give it to me to sew. Once, I looked back, but the fabric of the market had already fastened around me.

I hid the length of crimson silk bought for my next garment, a nightgown that would be even finer than the last. My needle flew faster than a flame licks a stick. I prayed at the crossroads shrine too, but not for the forgiveness of my sins. I put all my faith in a woman with an unremarkable face but whose collar lay flat and even all the way round.

14

Chapter Three

I was soaked by the time I arrived for *Noteworthy's* next rehearsal after leaving Mollie at her dad's. Michael and I maintained a delicate truce, but I imagined he would already be interrogating her for anecdotes to add to his Bad Mother file.

Robert's kitchen table was too small for five so he put us in the dining room.

'Is there anything I've forgotten?' he asked.

'What about another lamp?' I said looking round. 'It's a bit dim in here.' The ceiling shade, brown with beige fringing, cast a frilly circle of light on the table. 'Are we having a séance?'

'Perhaps we should,' said Robert. 'We could call up Gesualdo and ask him how he'd like us to sing *Ite sospiri*.'

'Oh don't,' I said, shoving my fingers in my ears. 'He's the last person I'd want to get in touch with. He was completely nuts.'

Robert laughed. 'I'll see if I can find another light.' He said it as if the contents of the house were a mystery to him.

My jeans were still wet from the rain and clung to my legs. Oh well. I sat down, and slid about trying to get comfortable on the leatherette seat. I wasn't comfortable on the inside either. Why the creeping trepidation? As I flicked through the pages of the Gesualdo madrigal, all sorts of negative scenarios began presenting themselves in my mind: the concert would go badly, nobody would come, our reputation would be in tatters.

I took a deep breath and told myself not to be stupid.

Reading the old square notes would have been more than challenging, so I'd played through the parts on the keyboard then printed each one out in modern notation. We'd just have to contend with having no score to read from. It would be much more difficult to keep together but we'd manage.

As for the sound, my experience at the keyboard left me thinking that if I'd picked a handful of notes, like Scrabble letters from a bag, then hung them on the five lines of the music stave at random, it might have been more tuneful. Maybe, when we were all singing, it would be better.

The doorbell chimed something lengthy and portentous.

'Can you get that?' Robert called down from upstairs, amidst much thumping. 'I'm just finding an extension lead.'

I could see through the stained glass panel in the door that two tall people stood on the step under one umbrella. The figure of Jon, I knew immediately. The other had to be Daniela. I set my face to smile mode and opened the door.

Jon gave me a quick kiss on the cheek. 'I met Daniela looking lost.'

'Oh dear,' I said, brightly. I looked at the woman before me: shiny coat the colour of Victoria plums, pillar-box red silk scarf and long black hair, that in spite of the wind and rain retained its knife-like edge down the side of her face. I also took in large sparkly earrings, sparkly brown eyes and equally dazzling teeth smiling down at me. This isn't a woman who gets lost, I thought. This is a woman whom the world turns to find.

'Not lost,' she said, shaking her head. 'But it is hard when there are no numbers on the doors. Hello, is it Lisa, I think?' She held out her hand.

'Yes,' I said. 'Hello.' I added some sort of platitude as well. Nice to meet you, it might have been, but I'm not entirely sure. My mind was taken up with the image of my nail-bitten hand in hers. The painted nails. Coordinated accessories. Make up. Groomed, that was the word, with added shed-loads of style. She turned away and her padded shoulder grazed my nose.

Robert's hall isn't very big and the parquet flooring and brown floral wallpaper combination make it very dark. When he came down stairs carrying an old bedside lamp I found myself trapped in the corner by the hat stand.

The doorbell clanged again an inch from my left ear. 'Can we all move along, please.' I shooed them into the dining room, not meaning to sound quite so like a bus driver.

'Phew,' Sophie said, when I let her in. 'I thought I'd never get here. The builders say I need a new roof and the guttering done. There's something up with the boiler and...' She shook the rain off her coat, gave her hair a rake through with her fingers and groaned. 'Oh, stop me, please.'

In the reflection of the hall mirror, I pointed towards the dining room and mouthed. 'She's here.'

Sophie stopped raking and mouthed back. 'And?'

'Think goddess.'

'Oh dear.'

We both sighed. The mirror, pink-tinted and slightly distorting, didn't do either of us any favours.

'*Salute.*' Daniela nodded at each of us as we clinked our glasses in welcome. 'Thank you for having me.'

Jon coughed. Had he been closer I'd have kicked him. Sophie caught my eye.

'So where's home?' Jon asked.

She leant towards him. 'Novara. It is halfway between Milan and Turin.'

Milan and Turin. That's what she said, but it felt like *Here* and the *Bedroom*. Bloody hell. How did she do that?

'See what you think of this.' I handed round the copied Gesualdo.

'How *thrilling* it is,' Daniela said, breathily, and she sort of quivered all over. A nicer me would not have thought: a bit like a spider when a fly lands on her web.

'Are we sure it's unknown?' asked Robert, glancing through the copy as if it might say so somewhere.

'No,' I said, 'I'm still trying to find out. One of the books I've borrowed has a reference to a bass line being the only surviving part of *Ite sospiri ardenti*. But we've got the whole thing here.'

It was both a marvel and yet a mountain to climb. We all went quiet, frowning as we each tried to make sense of our own part.

'Shall we start with something else?' I suggested. 'Daniela, I don't know whether you've ever sung any of these.' I handed her the *Oxford Book of English Madrigals*.

'Why, yes!' she said. 'I used to sing them at school.'

'Really?'

'Oh, I remember them very well. We all loved to *hey nonny nonny* as children.'

Had I offered Egon Ronay a chicken nugget, I would not have felt quite so patronised. Daniela's English was good but the inflection is everything. Be nice, I told myself.

'How about *Weep, O mine eyes*?' said Sophie. 'Oh no, not that. The next one. *Weep, weep mine eyes*. That's got five parts.'

We all turned to the page. I glanced at her and she twitched an eyebrow. There were no *hey nonnies* in that one.

The opening of John Wilbye's poignant madrigal is quite low for the alto and the second soprano, so it wasn't until about halfway through when Daniela reached higher notes with the words, *weep eyes, weep heart*, that I could hear the quality of her voice. When she sang, *a thousand deaths I die*, the hairs stood up on the back of my neck and for the rest of the evening they absolutely refused to lie down. Perhaps that's why I was so rubbish when we tackled the Gesualdo. Actually, none of us were brilliant. We had a number of false starts, and some of the harmonies were so discordant that we had to stop and check each part to see if we were singing the correct notes. It was hard to tell. In the end we agreed to take it away and get to grips with it on our own. I wasn't convinced that would help, having already tried it, but I was outnumbered, and it was decided to leave it till next time.

Robert was positively perky the next day but I brooded. It wasn't just the Gesualdo. Five is not an easy number to sit round an oblong table even if it is big enough. Sophie and I sat at either end while Robert and Jon looked directly at Daniela. Which, of course, they did. All evening. And who could blame them?

When I got to the bridge, on my way home, I saw how much the river had swollen from all the previous day's rain. The subway on the far side was flooded so I climbed back up the steps. It had happened before, I guessed the drain had blocked …

I heard shouting suddenly, a man and a woman. Over the noise of the traffic and the river too. I couldn't make it out. More shouting, cars braking. I carried on up the steps, the sun in my eyes. A prang probably. There, a car hooting, and another. The junction was busy, buses were nose to tail … but then a shadow was cast, in between me and the sun. A man? No, a boy, really … more shouting, and not a prang at all.

'Hey! Hey, stop him.' The man's voice, booming, and a rather screechy female. 'Look out. Look out!'

We met at the top of the steps. Me, slightly breathless. Him, very breathless, panting noisily as if air were in short supply. He was wearing a T-shirt, black, *eff off* scrawled in red. His arms were … no, not a tattoo, bruised blue here and there. He had something in his hand. I couldn't quite see. I couldn't look either. His eyes were too arresting. Too wild. Too scary. I think I gasped or moaned. I don't know. All I do know is that there was the slightest moment of pause, a twitch or a blink, then he pushed past me and I was knocked back.

Fortunately I still had my hand on the rail and didn't fall, but the boy …

There's a place halfway down the steps where the bank rises up on one side. The earth is worn smooth where everyone clambers over to get down to the river. Usually there's a path along the water's edge, but when the river's up, it floods too.

I don't know what the boy was thinking. Was he thinking? Perhaps he thought the path would be on the other side and he would escape from whatever it was he was running from so desperately. But it wasn't. When the boy jumped from the bank it was into the water. The swirling brown water that took a full-grown tree and waltzed it downstream. I saw the boy's arm above the water just the one time.

The couple chasing him finally made it across the road. I couldn't take my eyes from the water. I think the man phoned the police.

'Are you all right, love?' The woman put her hand on my arm.

'Yes,' I said. 'I'm fine. I think so. Yes, fine.'

'He didn't get you did he?'

'Get me?'

'He was running about in the shop waving a needle.' She gestured in the direction of TK Maxx. 'Kept saying he was going to stick someone. Course, drugs and diseases is the worry, isn't it? I don't know. What can you do? He didn't though, did he?' She looked worried suddenly. 'Did he? Did he stick you?'

I looked down at my right arm. I was wearing a thin shirt underneath my coat. Duck egg blue with cuffs that roll up and you can button them down with a loop. I'd undone them though and the sleeve being a bit long, protruded at the wrist. There was a rip in the fabric. Not a long one, a couple of inches, but not yet frayed. Beneath, a dark stain was spreading.

Chapter Four

Gesualdo 1585

She didn't come. For days the memory of the silver in my hands remained clear, each coin a piece of my bright future. But gradually it dulled. The days cooled. My baby sister was well again and getting everywhere on her hands and knees. I hid my silks in a box out in the woodshed behind a stack my father was saving till next year. I still sewed the seams of my crimson nightgown and I knew it was the best I had ever made but I worked with ever decreasing speed. The following spring, it was done. I held the garment up by the shoulders, first at arm's length, then I put it against my body, against my clean apron, imagining the softness of it next to my skin.

'Hey, you,' said a voice. 'Are you the girl that does sewing?'

'Who's asking?' I said, thrusting the cloud of crimson silk back into its pillowslip.

A boy stood at the door. 'I am,' he said. 'My name is Salvo Carlino and it's taken me a while to find you, Silvia Albana.' He sat on my father's chopping block. When he spoke his voice jumped back and forth from boy to man, but he betrayed no bother about it. 'I've been all over. The old woman with the bees told me where you'd be. Here.' He pulled something from his pocket, stamped on it with his heel, then threw it upwards, caught it in his mouth and began chewing. Then he threw another something at me. I caught it and found a large almond in my hand.

'You stole from Francesca?' He didn't look like a thief. Clean clothes and hands. I didn't recognise him from the village. He stole the light from inside the shed too, so I went to the door better to look at him.

'I didn't exactly steal—'

'Who sent you?' I interrupted, as now I could see what I suspected. The workmanship of his jerkin, the placing on

21

the yoke around the shirt collar. I'd seen it before. 'Your mother?'

He looked me up and down. 'You're a sharp one. Pretty too.'

Heat burst into my cheeks and I would have run back home had he not been the bearer of a message I was keen to hear. 'So who is your mother and why are you looking for me?'

'My mother,' he said, 'is needlewoman to Donna Maria d'Avalos.'

At this, I gasped. Donna Maria D'Avalos! She was to marry the Lord of Gesualdo himself, Don Carlo.

'She needs an assistant,' he went on, 'and thinks you'd be suitable. I'm supposed to speak to your mother and then take you to the castle.'

'The castle?' My heart jumped as I glanced towards its high walls on the skyline. The decision was already made. 'We don't need to speak to my mother,' I lied. 'Besides, she's away today. Wait here.'

Only once in my life had I felt the earth shaking and the panic of everyone leaving their beds and fleeing to safety. The feeling I had as I rushed back home to fetch my few things seemed somehow akin to that. I would leave a message with Francesca for my mother. Quickly, I dashed some water across my face and pulled at my apron strings, wiping my hands on its coarse cloth. There was something in the pocket, the almond tossed at me by the boy. Its shell like pigskin, large and perfect. The trouble with almonds is they often look like that and yet when you open them, the nut is shrivelled, its taste bitter. You can never tell though, and once cracked open there is no repairing the shell.

There were many things to get used to at the castle of Gesualdo, but I was kindly treated. Salvo would speak with me, too often I thought, but his mother, Signora Carlino, said nothing. She said nothing a lot. We would sit together without speaking, but listening to the strange music that echoed around the castle when the master was at home. I was yet to see any more than a glimpse of him in that first year after his wedding to Donna Maria. There'd been a flurry of excitement in the village and up at the castle when we heard that Don Carlo's father had conceded his royal titles to the happy couple. Pietro, Don Carlo's personal man, informed all the servants that the Prince and Princess would not take it ill, however, if we continued to address them as Don Carlo and Donna Maria. Not that it made any difference to me. I'd never seen either of them.

For several months I sewed nothing but undergarments, but even to those I gave my full attention. I doubt there were neater seams to be found. Three of us sat opposite each other at a large table used for cutting and the laying out of clothes for pressing. Laura was a little older than me but useless with a needle. It was her job to edge and darn the bedlinen. Apart from the strangled cough uttered every few minutes, she too was silent. I did smile at her, whenever she looked up, but never received anything except a sullen stare in return.

Then one day, Signora Carlino handed me a velvet jerkin the colour of a midnight sky.

'Let me see you put the lining in this, child.'

The main seams had already been sewn with large stitches. I knew this would be testament to my skills but I had never sewn silk to velvet before. I stroked the fabric to check the way of the nap and found that to smooth the pile required my hand to rise from waist to neck.

'Signora,' I ventured. 'Excuse me, but is this the usual way of the fabric?' I held the jacket up. 'Does my lady smooth her clothes like this? Or like that? I showed her both.

She gave me a long look. 'Bring it here.'

I wondered whether she would be angry. Was it insolent to ask? Signora Carlino ran her finger over the velvet, this way and that, then gave a slight laugh. 'You have sharp eyes, Silvia and a good feeling for cloth. I'm glad you spotted this.' To my surprise, she gripped one

23

side of the front and with great force, tore it from the back. 'This was my mistake,' she said. 'I have cut the velvet upside down.'

Through the small window sunlight suddenly glanced, shedding light across the split seam. The face of the Signora was lit too, and her expression and something in her eyes reminded me of old Fransceca. It took me by surprise.

'Come,' she said, rising from her seat and beckoning me to go with her. 'We shall cut a new piece. Or rather, you will cut a new piece. Here.' She handed me the useless front of the jacket. 'Do what you will with this. I'm sure you will think of something.'

I squirreled it away.

The Princess had regained her figure after the birth of her baby boy and was demanding new clothes. I had yet to meet her but as the garment neared completion I asked what should be done about a fitting. A few days later the Signora announced it would be the next morning.

'Is there anything I should know about the Princess, Laura?' I asked her as we prepared for bed.

'How do I know?' she said, with a sharp breath that immediately set her coughing violently. It was my misfortune to share with Laura, who when she wasn't coughing, wheezed all night long.

'I just thought—'

'It's you she wants to see, not me.' She shook her head with the same violence as she coughed, then muttered under her breath: 'Even though I've been here much longer.'

So that was it.

'I am sorry, Laura.' I said.

She didn't reply. If there was anything curious about the Princess, I would have to find it out for myself.

Perhaps I should not have been surprised that at my first sighting, my lady was in a state of total undress. After all, it was important that I knew her figure exactly. No one

24

person is the same as the next, unless they are twins. Signora Carlino had taken many measurements, but the best fit was made from trying on the body. And for the undergarments, well, it wouldn't do for them to be so big they ruckled the outer garments or so small they split under stress.

'Silvia Albana, my lady. The child I told you about.'

I curtsied at once and studied the pair of feet that were all I could see with my head bowed. They looked new, just like a baby's, although two or three times the size. Unblemished and smooth; I didn't think my lady had done a lot of walking. They stepped nearer and a sweet perfume enveloped me as she leaned down, gently placed a finger under my chin and raised me to my feet. I thought it best to close my eyes but curiosity would not obey, and I took in her nakedness at close quarters.

'So,' she said, as I reached my full height and felt her gaze on my face. 'You come with high recommendation, my pretty Silvia. Shall we get on well?'

Such honey in her voice, as warm and smooth as her skin.

'I...I hope so, my Lady.' I could hardly speak for the constriction in my throat. To be asked such a question!

She laughed and my knees trembled. 'That's very good,' she whispered. And with her fingertip traced a soft line up to my lips. 'Do you know when to speak and when to stay silent, I wonder?' I said nothing and she laughed, turning away and beckoning towards a shift that lay over the bed.

'Can you read and write, Silvia?'

'Yes, my lady. I was sent for tutoring to Father Vincentino's with my brother.'

'That was very generous of your parents. Did they not need your help at home?' She held up her arms and I slipped the shift over her head.

'Yes, but ...' I hesitated, not knowing if I should tell her about all the arguments. How I'd pleaded and wept, how my mother wouldn't hear of it and how eventually ... 'my

father took my part.'

'Your father?'

'Yes.' I pulled on the hem to straighten it. 'He thought some learning would be of help to me if I were to better myself.'

'Did he now?' Donna Maria raised her eyebrows and I saw that her eyes were not brown like mine but a dark blue, like the sky in late evening or just before dawn. I had never seen eyes like that before, and I stared for a long moment until Donna Maria laughed again. 'What a very sensible man your father must be,' she said.

'He is, my lady.' And I missed him suddenly.

Later, when Laura and I were undressing for bed, I glanced across at her and into my mind came Francesca's old nag. Poor Laura wasn't old but coughing had already bent her body. Her skin had no bloom and there was no lustrous quality to her slack hair. I did try to befriend her, but only once, when I shared my roasted almonds with her, did she thank me. She coughed worse than ever afterwards, so I half wished I hadn't.

As I undid my cap and shook out my own curls, I stroked a lock between my finger and thumb while remembering Maria D'Avalos. So beautiful, I thought. And in a moment of fancy, another thought presented itself: what would be the result of mixing such beauty with an equal part of power? My skin smarted under a wave of goosebumps.

I visited my family when I could and although disapproving of my disobedience, my mother and father recovered their good will towards me a little more each time. They were glad of the money I brought and the small items I made for the baby from the fabric remnants. No other child in Gesualdo was so well dressed.

Often, Salvo would happen to be going to the village at the same time, and one day we were approaching the edge of the first olive grove when, without warning, he grabbed me around the waist and pulled me to the side of the track.

'How dare ...' I started, but he shushed me, and I could tell by the look in his eye that he meant no harm.

'The Prince is coming!' he hissed, 'and he will ride straight over us if we are in the way. Be quiet.'

Sure enough, apart from the sound of a few small birds, startled by our disturbance of the undergrowth beneath them, I could hear the sound of horses coming. Moments later, they were in clear view, and I had my first proper sighting of Don Carlo Gesualdo, husband of my lady. Perhaps it was the same birds that we had put up which unsettled the horses, for they shied suddenly.

Don Carlo looked sharply in our direction.

'Who is there?' he said. 'Show yourself.'

'Stay here,' Salvo whispered to me, and I prayed the holly thicket I knelt behind was sufficient hiding place. It would not do for us to be found together. I'd be shamed back into sewing sheets faster than a stork stabs a snake.

'Forgive me, Prince Carlo,' I heard Salvo say. 'It was not my intention to startle the horses. I was hoping not to impede your Highness on his journey home.'

Easing a twig aside, I looked through a narrow window straight into the face of the Prince. It was as much as I could do to keep silent. I thought at once of the honeyed skin of my mistress. The golden landscape of her body with its smooth mounds and darker, hidden places. How would it be to lie with this grey-fleshed fish? He was not old, and I wondered for a moment if he were poor in health, like Laura, for it was as if the day's bright sunshine failed in its shining when it arrived on the face of Don Carlo. From the side, his profile was not so bad for his nose was straight and not too large, but when he turned ... there was the fish again, the eyes set narrow and the cheeks falling away to the smallest point of a chin, hardly wide enough to support the silvery lips, thin as splinters. A shudder passed through me from top to toe as I thought of them pressed in earnest against those of my lady.

Salvo's convincing worked well, and in a few moments

the Prince's troop rode on, and the cart bearing the corpses of the unfortunate victims of the hunt creaked and clattered away up the hill behind them.

'You look like you've seen a ghost,' Salvo said when I crept out from behind the holly.

'Not a ghost,' I said, 'but I do not see any virtue in the Prince's face.'

Salvo's expression darkened with derision. 'Virtue? What need do Princes have for virtue? Nothing can touch them.' He reached towards me and cupped my chin in his hand. 'It is the likes of us who have to be virtuous, Silvia, for we are vulnerable to the vagaries of the wealthy.'

There was a bitter harshness about his voice that I hadn't heard before. It had been in my mind to merely say that Don Carlo was not a handsome man, but I couldn't deny my fear. No, I had not seen a ghost, but the shadow cast across the Prince's face seemed to me an omen, a portent of something a lot more sinister than a cloud on a clear day.

Chapter Five

Larks should never get together with owls. It ought to be written down somewhere. If they do, there's a fifty-fifty chance that a mummy owl might have a lark baby. That's only all right if the daddy lark stays around to oversee the mornings.

Mollie bounced into the kitchen, *singing*. I made her sandwiches with my eyes still closed. Of course, she wasn't the only one with a tune in her head. Mine was *Weep, O mine eyes and cease not ... that I may drown me in you.*

I kept seeing the boy who drowned. A flashback, I suppose, is the proper term. I had two; firstly the crazed expression on his face and then his arm, a pale periscope briefly surfacing above all that dreadful water. Dreadful, *dreadful* ... I leaned against the kitchen table, weak suddenly. My arm was pale too, but perfectly smooth apart from a square inch of plaster. I did think about repairing the tear in my shirt, but when I took it off later, I knew I would never wear it again. Four hours I'd spent in A&E, thinking about mortality. I'd rung Michael and he'd picked up Mollie from school but by his tone, it was obviously very inconsiderate of me to be in danger of death.

I told Michael not to tell anyone, and definitely not Mollie. When I finally went home from the hospital, I had been told that the test results so far indicated that I was *most likely* negative. They couldn't be one hundred percent sure for another four weeks, but I should try not to worry. I was almost fine.

What a difference a word makes.

'*Miss Price said, Miss Price said,*' Mollie sang to the tune of *Three Blind Mice*, '*if you like ... if you like ... you could see her before school ... you could see her before school ...*' She swallowed a few mouthfuls of Ribena and sang it all over again.

At last. Miss Price had put off my calling in for a whole

week. 'Now let me see,' I said. Do you think I should see her before school?' As if I didn't know. She put her hands on her hips and looked at me crossly for a second, but then we both laughed.

My quirky, funny daughter. My heart skipped with love for her. Thank God she had not been with me at the river.

While I'd been sitting in A&E, I thought about telling everyone what had happened but then decided it would be ghastly. Mum and Mollie would be frightened and anxious and I'd feel even worse. There was no reason for Noteworthy to know, although I did think I might let on to Sophie. She was my oldest friend. In my mind I saw her face when I told her and how it would crumple into concern. No, I wouldn't do it. For the next four weeks I would keep quiet.

Mollie continued to sing one song to the tune of another all the way to school and I wondered if I'd been asked to go in because they were fed up with this latest expression of her good moods. Mollie worshipped at the shrine of Jon and was a willing player of his musical games. But there was no denying she had talent. I felt a little swell of pride.

'Mrs Barr.' Miss Price approached me smiling. 'I'm so glad you could drop in.'

She was a happy teacher, nothing like the severe, humourless primary school teacher I'd had. 'No problem,' I said. 'Is everything okay? Has Mollie …'

I must have looked anxious as she waved her hand dismissively. 'Mollie? Good Heavens no. The thing is,' she leaned towards me, voice lowered so the children couldn't hear, 'Mrs Brown had a teeny accident.'

Mrs Brown was the school music teacher.

'Oh dear,' I said. 'How teeny?'

'She's broken her ankle rather badly, so is off for a couple of months at least, and what with Christmas coming…' Miss Price put her hands together and directed her prayers at me. 'The best I can do,' she went on, 'is *Jingle Bells* with one finger.'

It was only October. That anyone could even *say* the word Christmas so soon gave me the heebie-jeebies.

'Well …' I said. 'I expect I could help a little. Did you have anything in mind?'

She clutched my arm. 'That would be marvellous. I can't tell you how … *marvellous*! Let me show you what's in the cupboard. We've just had a delivery. It's why I didn't see you last week. I did so want to show you. Mrs Brown is very keen. Personally,' she said, 'I don't know what to think, but I'm sure someone like you will have lots of ideas.'

Someone like me have lots of ideas about what? The cupboard contained several mysterious boxes.

Half an hour later, I walked through town carrying an extra bag.

'Lisa … Lisa!' A glimpse of Jon before a bus came between us. He reappeared on my side of the road. 'What's that?' he said, nodding at the instrument shaped bag under my arm.

'I don't think I ought to tell you,' I said, turning away from him. 'You'll only want to play it.'

'I'll buy you a coffee.'

'So?' he said, reaching towards the bag that lay between us on one of Costa's leather sofas. 'Are you going to let me see?'

I swapped it to my other side and he moved a little closer. 'No,' I said.

'What?' He raised his hands in protest. 'After such a major outlay?'

'Even so.' I smiled. 'You have to guess.'

'Excellent,' he said, enthusiastically. 'Now let me see.'

No, it wasn't a cornet or a quarter-sized violin. It was when he suggested a didgerydoo and a set of tubular bells that I relented and opened the bag. 'Mollie's teacher wants me to organise some music for Christmas. They had twenty-five of these delivered yesterday and I think she'd like me to use them.'

'Hah!' he said, lifting the ukulele out of my hands. 'If I remember rightly, this is in your top three least favourite instruments, alongside bagpipes and accordions.' He began tuning it at once, then plinked through a few scales.

'I don't mind them one at a time, but a whole classful? I'd rather sing stark naked at the last night of the Proms.'

'Oh really?' He sat up. 'Perhaps that could be arranged.'

'Don't even go there! No, I've already told Miss Price that I'm going to put all my efforts into the choir.'

'Rather you than me,' he said. 'Unless it's a choir of Mollies. That might not be so bad. Does she want to do music? You know, in the future?'

I thought about Mollie pirouetting round the room with ballet Barbie, but most of all lately, the relentless – but because I'm her mummy, endearing – singing.

'She might,' I said, 'if she ever falls out of love with ballet. Her voice is good. I can see her on a stage but I can't imagine her ever being tragic; she'd probably make a good Valkyrie.'

'I'll ask her next time I see her. Hello, little girl,' he said, in a high sing-song voice. 'What do you want to be when you grow up?'

'She'll probably stab you with a Barbie, if you call her that.'

'Pity she's not old enough for *Noteworthy*,' he said, twanging the strings. The girl clearing the next table glanced over and Jon caught her eye. Would she have smiled like that if it had been me playing? Unlikely.

'Did people used to ask you what you wanted to be?' Jon asked. 'They did me.' He yawned at the memory.

'And did you tell them you were going to write jingles?'

'Now, now, come on,' he said, looking hurt. 'I don't *only* write jingles. But no, I didn't. I used to say I wanted to be the Master of the Queen's Music. It must be the best paid music job in the land, I thought. Turns out, the money's rubbish. Not that I'd turn it down.' He tipped back the rest of his espresso. I tried to imagine what sort of music Jon might have composed for William and Kate's wedding. I felt sure he *could* do gravitas. 'I suppose,' he went on, 'you wanted to be an opera singer.'

'Me? An opera singer? No, I wanted to marry Freddie Mercury.' I laughed at Jon's surprise. 'Yes, I know … so wrong and in so many ways.'

'No, I mean *really*, when you were at college.' Jon was looking at me rather intently. Something I found disconcerting. I felt more at ease with the restless, jokey Jon. The one I didn't have to be serious with.

'Yes,' I said, 'perhaps I did back then.' I remembered my final recital. Elgar's *Sea Pictures* and the first alto solo from the *St John Passion*. Meeting Michael, the charming journalist, at the party afterwards, getting married, being domestic … 'But then Mollie came along.'

'Oh, yes. Yes, of course.' He pushed his cup and saucer around the table while I finished my cappuccino. Without warning the drowned lad was in my head again, swallowing water. I coughed, struggling to clear my throat.

'All right there?' Jon slapped me on the back.

'Yes, I think so,' I gasped for air and tried to keep calm. Was I all right? I didn't know. Should I tell Jon? I felt if I did the whole horrible incident would come back, and there'd be another flood of sympathy and concern. Looking at Jon, the way his expression rested in a smile. Life was a warm, light-hearted thing for him. Could I tell him?

I very nearly did, but he spoke first.

'So,' he said, 'what did you think of Daniela?'

'Daniela?' I sounded sharp. Perhaps it was the sudden change of subject.

'Yeah.' He stroked a non-existent beard. 'I thought she was rather good.'

Oh no, no, no, Jon. She wasn't rather good. She was absolutely bloody brilliant.

'Mmm,' I said. 'I thought she was rather good too.'

'I wish we didn't have to sing that sodding Gesualdo.'

33

He sang the opening phrase of *Ite sospiri* while plinking an entirely inappropriate accompaniment.

'Oh, please,' I said, giggling at the ridiculousness. 'If you're not careful, Gesualdo'll be after us.'

'You reckon?' Jon looked over his shoulder. 'We'd best watch out for a four-hundred-year old man in tights bearing a lute and horsewhip then. Do you think he could play the lute and whip us at the same time?'

His impersonation made me laugh even harder.

'Now, stop it,' I said, 'or it just might come true.'

Jon sighed. 'You're right. One should never speak ill of the dead. But seeing as how we're all very alive, I was thinking we ought to do some other five-part stuff as well. We'll have to put together a whole programme for the museum and it seems a waste not to take advantage of Daniela while we've got her.

'Mmm.' It did. It did seem a waste. Agree with him, woman. 'Mmm.' I looked at my watch. 'I'd better go.' It was a shameless avoidance ploy but Robert did pay me money for being in the shop. I put my hand out for the ukulele and he only let it go after the first verse of *Twinkle Twinkle Little Star* and a stare of death from the woman on the next table when her toddler started to cry.

We would be going in opposite directions, so we stood for a moment outside the cafe being slightly dithery with our goodbyes. Yes, I'd see him soon. Err ... umm ... an enquiry about Mollie. How was she? He'd like to see her.

'Do you want to come and have something to eat with us on Friday evening?'

Yeah, brilliant! He would. A big smile. Not only that, he'd collect her from ballet. Very brilliant.

We turned away from each other but after two or three steps I looked back. I saw Jon had done the same. But then, almost in slow motion, I saw his arm rising and his expression change. The smile sinking away. That was just before I saw the bus, but it was too late by then and there was nothing I could do about it.

Chapter Six

Napoli 1587

Napoli! I was going to Napoli. My heart beat faster merely at the thought. Laura was to go as well, unfortunately, although her reaction was to start weeping! Signora Carlino would have been my choice of companion, but I knew why she was not to go.

It perplexed me why all about me were so afraid of the city. After all, we were to stay at the Palazzo San Severo, hardly cheap lodgings. My two years at the castle of Gesualdo had been uneventful, and occasionally almost as tedious as when I was sewing at home. Even then, we went to market once a week.

The castle only came alive when the master and mistress were there. I worked almost always on Donna Maria's clothing, her nightwear in particular. It seemed to me that she must twist and turn a lot in her sleep for there were often seams to re-sew even if they were double stitched.

We had to put up with the discordant voices of the singers that Don Carlo brought in to perform his compositions too, but then, I had no ear for music. That's not to say I didn't like singing myself, but only when I was out walking alone, a rare thing since Salvo appeared whenever I took the path home. I have to say, his attention made me a little nervous. I liked him well enough, but at seventeen I couldn't help feeling there was a bit of world yet to see.

'You will be careful, won't you, Silvia?' Salvo said as the carriages and wagons were being loaded.

Well, perhaps I did have a pang after all. He looked so unhappy at my leaving. As I sat down on the wagon bench I felt the lucky charm in my pouch that always reminded me of the first time I met Salvo. I pulled it out and tossed it high in the air. Salvo saw what it was straight away and caught it cleanly by hand, but I wondered if he would know it was the very same almond.

'I did keep it, Salvo,' I said.

'And I made this for you,' he replied, and he clambered up the side of the wagon and put a small object into my hand. In my palm, no bigger than the almond, lay a sleeping cat whose tail curled all round its body so that the fingertips stroked it like a smooth pebble. Only close inspection revealed the little nose and ears. I was reminded of my father's woodwork but it was crude and rough compared to this. I was amazed.

'It's so beautiful,' I said and my hand closed around it. 'Thank you, Salvo.'

I could feel a tear pricking the corner of my eye. The pull towards Napoli did not feel so strong suddenly but then the wagon jolted in motion.

'Look after yourself,' he called as we pulled away, 'as well as I shall care for this.' And much to my consternation he kissed my lucky almond and clutched it to his breast!

We waved at each other until the the wagon went amongst the trees. Oh Salvo, I would miss him.

I turned back to Laura who was sitting opposite and found her staring at me.

'Isn't this exciting?' I said, trying to raise my own spirits, but she looked away.

It would be a long journey.

The sea! I was giddy with the sight and scent of it. All the misery of two days travelling fell away in a twinkling moment when I saw the sun shining over the blue bay. Even Laura came slightly more alive at the sight. Perhaps she would breathe more easily in the sea air. Everything about the city was brighter, louder and bigger than in Gesualdo. The smell too, unfortunately. A lot of people close together makes for a lot of stink. I pulled my cap down over my face to avoid any mischievous remarks from the men attending to their fishing boats, then jumped down from the wagon so that I could feel the stone of the city's streets beneath my feet.

'Ah, Silvia,' said Donna Maria, when we reached the palazzo. 'I am glad you are here at last. There is much to be done. I want something for the New Year feast. Don Carlo has invited half the court of Ferrara and I have no wish to be outshone.'

'I cannot believe it would ever be possible, Donna Maria,' I said.

She laughed at that. 'I like your earnestness. Come, Laura can unload. Let us look at the fabric samples the merchant brought. We will choose together and then you shall make me something wonderful.'

'I shall do my very best, Donna Maria.'

'I know you will, Silvia.' She took my hand and held it to her cheek. 'That's why you're here.'

Truth be told, even wrapped in an old cheesecloth, Donna Maria would outshine every woman in Italy. It made me shiver, the touch of her, and I couldn't tell whether it was with alarm or delight. What I did see though, was that with beauty and power come certain gifts. Like charms they are, or the honeyed flytraps that hang from the ceiling. And just like flies, some get stuck on them sooner than they know.

Donna Maria's apartment was on the second floor right above Don Carlo's. When I looked out of the window, I could see to the palazzo one way and as far as the corner of the street in the other. My duties were to make and care for all my lady's clothes that hung in the large carved closet and those more intimate garments, alongside the sleeves, cuffs and ruffs that lay in the cedar chest. I was to sleep in the adjoining room to her chamber.

'It is quite a heavy door between us, is it not, Silvia?' my lady asked me as I unhooked her sleeves that night. She waved her hand towards the door and I turned to look, having not given it much thought at all until that moment.

'I would say so, my lady, yes. It looks as sturdy as a door might be for the indoors.' I assumed that was a good

thing.

'Do you think you shall hear me when I call?'

'I should think so, my lady. My ears have never been a trouble to me. Nor my eyes ... why, this lace is coming away.' I held up the offending trim. She didn't even look, but frowned instead.

'That is of no matter, Silvia. Now listen to me. You are to pay no attention to any shouts or cries that come from this room at any time when my husband is present.'

I took a small step backwards with surprise and knocked into the closet that bore the water jug. The blow set it rocking but I was glad to turn away and steady it. What a thing to say! *'Why no, my lady,'* I said, mumbling a little in embarrassment.

'Not on any account, do you understand me? These palace walls are not like those of Castle Gesualdo and Don Carlo is ...' she faltered for a moment, then took a deep breath. *'You must not think anything is untoward, even if it may sound so.'*

'Yes, my lady. I understand.'

That's what I said, but I have to admit I was alarmed. While not having Laura's wheezing to accompany my sleeping pleased me no end, I soon began to see and hear why the seams of my mistress's nightwear might not hold so well.

'Perhaps it's a good thing the Prince does not visit the bedchamber so very often,' I said, having been woken at the darkest hour of night by footsteps and then my mistress calling. In the candlelight she held out a nightdress rent from neck to hem. I couldn't help but see the dark spots that stained the pale silk. *'Oh, my lady ... are you hurt?'*

'No, no,' she said, running her hands through her unbound hair. *'It isn't* my *blood. Here, fetch me another nightdress, and bring me some water to wash with too.'*

'But ...' I must have looked a little alarmed for Donna Maria smiled. To my amazement, she patted the bed and bade me sit beside her. I perched the best I could, but did not find it easy to be so familiar.

'Do you know,' she said, 'that the Prince is not my first husband?'

'I did ...'

'He is my third. I have had three husbands. Three!' She sighed. 'Shall I tell you a secret, Silvia?'

Oh please don't, I thought. 'If you wish, Donna Maria.'

'I am beginning to think that I might have preferred a life of contemplation.'

I did not mean to laugh and quickly cleared my throat to disguise it. In my mind's eye I saw Donna Maria dressed as one of the sisters of Mercy that crossed the piazza every morning. The habit could not disguise the grace of her steps or full sweetness of her lips. 'Surely not,' I began, but she interrupted.

'It is not always ... pleasant, being married. But I think I have tried to accommodate all my husbands.' She began to twist the sheet between her thumb and forefinger, sighing with enough vigour for the candle to flicker. 'But Don Carlo is ... well ... I think the best thing to say is, he is ... he is the most violent.'

I kept quiet and held my breath. What did that mean? She screwed the sheet tighter and tighter almost to rope.

'I think he means well,' she went on. 'He certainly used to ... at first. I thought he was pleased with me. The others were too, they liked to do all sorts of things. I tried, I did try. I decided when I was first married ...' she looked at me, and with the fingers that weren't tied in a knot, stroked the side of my cheek, 'I was younger than you are now, Silvia. My mother gave me little warning, but I decided that a wife should ... should ...' she hunted for the right word ... 'participate fully.'

'Of course, Donna Maria, I see.' But I didn't really see. I did know what happened between man and wife, and between many that weren't. But still, knowing there's a church round the corner isn't the same as sitting through mass.

'But more and more, he is troubled.' She pulled the sheet between two hands, as if testing its strength, then *went on, her voice lower, almost a whisper. 'It is in his nature to seek the edge of the abyss – the glorious moment where life, love and death become one. Think of his music, Silvia, think of how he stretches our understanding of the dance between Heaven and Hell.' I swallowed. Truth was, I had no idea what she was talking about. 'And then,' she went on, turning the sheet into a noose and twisting it round her neck, 'afterwards ... he likes me to hurt him.'*

Ah. This was affirmation for what I had heard lying next door in the dark. I coughed a little and thought to say something bland. 'It isn't a sin for man and wife to—'

'Isn't it?' She laughed grimly. 'I don't think Don Carlo would agree with you. He says he must do penance.'

'But surely ...' I fell silent, being at a loss. What did I know about such things?

'I don't understand it,' she said, holding up her hand and letting the sheet fall away. 'But we should say no more. Enough of this now. Fetch me the water, Silvia. We must get some sleep before the guests arrive tomorrow.' The tone in her voice was firm, but then, as an afterthought, she said: 'Have you ever known love, Silvia?'

'Not yet, my lady.'

She sighed again and I left her to fetch the water. That the Prince was strange was no news to me. That he might be becoming more so, seeded fear within me and much as I tried to keep my thoughts on the feasting of the next day, that fear would keep bobbing back up, like drowned things do, their corpses bloated and rotten. In my mind all of them had the grey fishy face of Don Carlo Gesualdo.

Chapter Seven

I showed Robert the tyre marks on the bag and his eyebrows wiggled up and down. It's the nearest he gets to laughing.

'It's not funny,' I said, emptying the pieces onto the counter. The ukulele was a heap of kindling knotted together with nylon. 'It's brand new. I'll have to replace it.'

'Good job it's not a Stradivarius then.'

The irritating thing, and what I didn't tell Robert, was that the breakage had been my own fault. I hadn't been looking. Why not? Because I'd turned back to wave at Jon. The bag was whisked out of my hand by the low-slung mirror on the door of the bus, and there was a pop and a crunch as if the bus had driven over a huge packet of crisps. I doubt the driver noticed. He didn't stop.

Shock is so odd. It was rather like when the boy drowned. At first I kept saying I was fine. After all, the bus hadn't hit me, although I did feel a ricochet from the impact. Fine, fine, I could still hear my voice in my mind, loud and determined, but then I wasn't fine and started to cry. Jon had rushed back, retrieved the bag and when he saw me wobble, wrapped me in his arms. Part of me wanted to stay there forever. Not the sensible part though.

Robert said something that while dreaming, I hadn't heard. 'So? What did Jon think of Daniela?'

'He said he thought she was rather good.'

'Did he?' Robert snorted. 'That's an understatement. He'd probably say the same about Maria Callas.'

'Now that really would be a coup. I've heard of music being discovered or published after death, but actual *performance* from beyond the grave?'

I chose not to tell Mollie about the ukulele. It occurred to me that the children might not know they even existed. They could wait until Mrs Brown returned; in the meantime, improving the choir was a far better idea. I remembered the summer concert and the choir's feeble singing. All the children twitchily miming, except for Mollie, of course. Her voice had soared over the rest. Not really appropriate for choral singing, but without her I don't think the others would have made any headway over Mrs Brown's idiosyncratic piano playing.

I would take a regular choir practice and get the kids to look up and open their mouths rather than mumble into their chins. Singing was something everyone should do, wasn't it? At least, they should be given the opportunity. My own school choir had been fun but then, I'd been fortunate that the teacher had been new and enthusiastic, and had given us songs that we wanted to sing. I took in a deep, reviving breath and hopped smartly across the road, avoiding a bus turning into Cheeke Street. Yes, a choir. The important thing was to keep it fun and inspire them with the right music.

'So you think a choir's a good idea?' I asked. Mollie, Jon and I were finishing supper, squeezed round my kitchen table.

'Oh definitely,' said Jon, 'much better than—'

'Do you want some more strudel?'

He looked surprised, then down at his nearly full plate, and said: 'Oh yes, go on. I mean, what were you going to do with a load of—'

'Cream on it?' I interrupted, glaring at him and nodding towards Mollie who was purposefully sawing at the pastry with her spoon.

'Mmm, thanks.' He held out his plate. 'Are you all right there, Mollie?'

'Yes,' She tilted her chin up. 'I think a choir is a much better idea than giving out all those ukuleles. 'Specially as you can't even play one.'

Every now and again there's a certain disdain in her eye that I hope doesn't come from me. It was her turn for a glare.

'Does everyone know about them?'

'No,' she said, 'only me. I saw them when Miss Price asked me to fetch the lighty-up globe from the cupboard.'

'Oh, good. Don't tell anyone then.'

'Can we do *The Lion King*?'

When did she become so skilful at this trading business?

Jon did offer to do the washing-up, and if I hadn't been my mum's daughter I would have left the kitchen in chaos and gone in the other room to play as well. So I only had myself to blame when I resented the subsequent music and laughter.

Mollie's keyboard skills were coming on even though she refused to have lessons. When she wanted to know something – 'it would be cheaper if she asked mummy' – that's what she told the piano teacher I'd found. Now she asked Jon. After all, he was much more fun.

I watched them from the doorway, their backs to me, two heads bobbing to the beat of the reggae number Jon had taught her. Behind them, the city's streetlights glistened thousand-fold in the raindrops slipping down the window, their sparkly stage backdrop. It was a happy scene and really, I should have been glad and I would have been, had it not been for the mammoth that stood quietly in the middle of the room. It had been there in the cafe, at the last rehearsal, in fact every rehearsal for I don't know how many years. How had it grown so huge? Once upon a time, it was a baby mammoth, but steadily and on *no food at all*, there was this monster.

'Bedtime, Mollie,' I said, when the neighbours began falling heavily and at regular intervals against the party wall.

'No, not yet,' she said, confidently. 'Jon's got to show me the beginning of *The Lion King*.'

I wondered if there might be a scene but perhaps *because* Jon was there, she was reasonable and went with

43

only mild protest. I tucked her in and went to kiss her forehead but she put her hand up to stop me.

'I wish you and Jon would get together,' she said. 'Then he wouldn't have to go home.'

'Mmm,' I said. 'Well, you know … it's not that easy. We're good friends.'

'Then why aren't you *very* good friends? It's *obvious*.'

Children. They will keep learning things. New vocabulary. How to spot mammoths.

Lying on the sofa, with Horse-Riding Barbie under his elbow, Jon was reading one of the books about Gesualdo I'd left in a heap on the coffee table.

'Bloody business, wasn't it?'

'Was it?' I said. 'I haven't got past Gesualdo's list of titles. Best is yet to come then?'

'Sort of, although I doubt the bit about the monk ravishing the corpse was true.'

'Good grief, I —' He looked up and I sensed the mammoth begin to shuffle about behind me. I swallowed. 'Do you want tea? Coffee?'

'Nope, neither. I want you to sit down and I'll tell you what I've learnt so far.' He clapped the book shut and drummed his fingers on the cover. 'You know me, I can't be bothered to read all this, but I think I've got the outline. And you know what? I might write the opera.'

'It's been done.'

'Oh.'

'Several times, and a ballet.'

'What about a musical?'

'I don't think so.'

'That's a relief.'

I sat down on the arm of the sofa, but Jon swivelled round and put his feet on the coffee table. 'Come and sit here,' he said, patting the space next to him, 'then you can put your feet up too.'

So I did.

'It was a dark and stormy night,' he began.

'Does it say that?'

'No, but it might have been. Besides, I thought you'd be too old for *Once upon a time*.'

'Too old?' I said. 'How can anyone be too old for a good story? Off you go, I'm all ears.'

Except I wasn't. Immediately, I glanced at his ears. They were perfectly nice, flat to the head and with proper lobes …

'Hello?' He waved at me. 'Earth to Lisa.'

Did I blush? Probably, but I got comfortable and he began.

'Okay then, once upon a time, there was—'

'Sorry,' I said, 'I can't let that go. When are we talking? Approximately?

'1580s?'

'That'll do.'

'Right. So there was a young man called Carlo Gesualdo, who came into a mega number of titles when his older brother died. Duke of this, Prince of that. Seems to have been called Don Carlo mostly. The family seat is at a place called, guess what?'

'Gesualdo?'

'Got it in one. So, now he's got titles and land, Gesualdo needs to get himself a wife.'

Fancy, I thought.

'So straight away, Gesualdo married his cousin Maria D'Avalos. She's already been married twice and has two children.'

'That's going some. What happened to the husbands?'

'Well …' He took a breath. 'It seems Maria was quite a girl. Because she was still in mourning for the last husband, they bothered to get a Papal annulment of the marriage so that she could marry Gesualdo.'

'Probably pregnant.'

'Maybe, but from what I gather, she was *very* attractive.'

'Is there a picture?'

'Hmm,' he said, having found a fuzzy black and white

enlargement of the only surviving image in the background of a large portrait of the Madonna and Child. 'She looks like a nun in that headgear.' He gave the book to me. 'Seen one nun, seen 'em all?'

I laughed.

'She was definitely no nun though,' he said. 'Rumour has it the husbands died of exhaustion.'

We both had another look and tried to invest the blandly demure features with some allure. Perhaps it was the big eyes that made me think of *Who Framed Roger Rabbit*.

'She's not exactly Jessica Rabbit, is she?' I said.

'Maybe if she let her hair down?' Jon suddenly turned and looked at me. 'Who knows what …' He slowed then stopped.

For some reason my heart gave one of those awkward hoppy-skippy things it does sometimes. He was so close. There was a moment, a fleeting still sort of moment, as if a frame in a film had got stuck but then, slicing through the silence, came a frightened cry.

'Jesus Christ,' he said, sitting bolt upright. 'Is that Mollie?'

I was already on my way. In the amber glow of her nightlight, my little girl was thrashing about, fighting her imaginary demons with clenched fists. I gathered her to me, making soothing there-there noises, rocking her back and forth as I used to when she was tiny.

'They're coming,' she hiccuped. 'I can hear them.' Her voice was shot through with fright.

'It's all right, Mollie. It's just a bad dream. Everything's all right.' I tightened my grip on her and gradually she relaxed and pulled away from me and opened her eyes. I wasn't prepared for the searing and almost deafening scream that came next, her whole body suddenly tense as piano wire.

'It's him! He's here!' she screamed even louder. 'No! Nooo …' Her eyes were wide and wild as she stared over my shoulder and for a moment I felt her fear and a great shiver passed through me. I looked behind me and saw Jon, a black shadow, standing in the doorway.

'It's me, Mollie,' he said. 'Only me. Don't be scared.'

He stepped into the light and at once she flopped into my arms again. A second later, she was fast asleep. Had she ever been awake? I laid her back down and pulled the duvet up round her shoulders. Even the shaft of bright light from the hallway that fell across her face didn't disturb her. She looked completely untroubled.

The same couldn't be said for Jon. Out in the hall, the shock on his face was clear.

'Bloody hell, Lisa.' He swiped his hand over his forehead as if trying to erase something. 'What's going on there?'

'I don't know. She used to have nightmares when she was little, but never with that screaming and—'

'Being scared of me?'

'Oh it isn't you, Jon. She was really asleep even though her eyes were open. As soon as you came in and spoke to her, she was fine. You know the brain can do funny things.'

'Poor Mollie. It's not funny for her.'

'No, it certainly isn't.' I sighed and felt the long outward breath take all my energy away with it. It was as much as I could do to stand.

'I'd better go.' He smiled albeit thinly. 'Perhaps she won't remember.'

'Yeah,' I said. 'That's what I'm hoping.'

My front door shared a landing with the flat next door and as Jon was saying goodbye, the other door opened. It was my first sighting of the new neighbours, a balding, burly man and glimpsed behind him a very elderly woman. His mother?

'Everything all right?' said the man, 'only we heard …'

That was all I needed. Social services and the police would be round next.

Once they'd been reassured and Jon had left, I checked on Mollie again then had a quick tidy up. When I got to the books about Gesualdo I noticed something rather odd. Also on the heap was my copy of the Gesualdo madrigal. I remembered it having a dark red stain on the back and thinking someone must have spilt a drop of wine on it years ago. Now there were two blots. Both Jon and I had had a glass of red with our supper, but I didn't remember either of us bringing the glass into the sitting room. I thought I'd washed both glasses at the same time but Jon must have had another while I was saying goodnight to Mollie. Strange though. Especially as that meant he must have drunk the wine, then washed, dried and put the glass away all in the space of five minutes.

I didn't know what to think, so wiped my hand across the paper to see if it was dry. Yes, quite dry. Of course it is, you numpty, I murmured. Get a bloody grip. And then, even as the thought entered my head, the music fell from my hand. Just like that. Bam ... straight down onto the coffee table and open at the frontispiece.

God, it gave me the creeps. I'd made a copy of it when ghoulish curiosity had forced my hand at the photocopier. I had another look at it. Whoever did the engraving was certainly skilled. It reminded me of those weird drawings where the more you look, the more you discover. Your perspective alters. For instance, when I'd looked at it before, I'd thought it merely fantastical but as I focused on the drowning figure disappearing beneath the waves, what was real and what imagined began to merge in my mind. There was the boy. He looked exactly like the boy.

A belligerent siren began wailing loudly out in the night and I snapped the music shut and shoved it in the bag, breaking what seemed almost like a spell. You must be tired, I told myself, tired and fanciful. That's the trouble.

Even so, I found myself flexing my hands and fingers after I turned out the lights. Yep, there was nothing wrong with my grip so I don't know why I'd dropped the music. And the drop of blood? Blood? Why did I say blood? It was wine. Of course, it was.

Chapter Eight

Napoli 1588

Napoli was the noisiest place! And at the Palazzo preparations for the feast meant no peace in or out. I remembered the afternoons I sat sewing in my father's wood store, listening to nothing but the wind in our olive trees and the petulant conversation of the chickens, and almost felt homesick. But only for a moment.

There was much consternation in the kitchen as the Prince had insisted that all the guests were equipped with forks at the table. The cook had let us try them out and there had been so much laughter that Pietro had come to quell the noise.

Laura and I attended Donna Maria in the morning and apart from the slightest lift of an eyebrow and the touch of her hand to her lips, there was no mention of the noises I'd heard during the night. Laura padded around behind me, making a nuisance of herself, but she could press a linen undergarment better than most and I was far too busy to do such a task. Donna Maria had chosen to appear in turquoise silk trimmed with gold braid. I was sorry that we did not trim with fur, but my lady insisted the wine and company would warm her well enough.

My heart beat faster to see her in the finished gown. My own work on the most beautiful woman at the feast. All eyes would be upon her. But Donna Maria was not a painting or a statue. She would seek out a splash of sunlight in a cool room, sigh with delight as I pulled the silk nightdress over her body each night, and would sometimes pour the water in her washing bowl from one cupped hand to another. 'I like how it feels,' she said to me, laughing. She was a one for touching – people and things – and there was something about the way she did it that made me feel uncomfortable.

Everyone was excited and I had a particular reason to

*be so, for I was to be present at the feast. Yes! In the sala.
Not at the table, of course, but my mistress wanted me in
attendance, so I was to take a seat near Pietro behind the
screen near the door to the kitchen. The carving of the
screen was very ornate and there were plenty of places
through which we would have a good view.*

*Pietro liked me, mercifully. He said I reminded him of
his dead little sister. It wasn't the most flattering
compliment I'd ever received; but I thanked him as best as
I could manage. He was powerful amongst the servants
and although the Palazzo was grand, we were in far closer
quarters than in the castle back at Gesualdo.*

*Don Carlo played the lute after the first and second
course. I glanced sideways at Pietro but if he thought
anything untoward, his face did not admit it. The idea that
we might have to listen to him play between all eighteen
courses was not a happy one. It seemed to me that the long
solos, and the having to listen so carefully, lowered the
spirits of the guests.*

*The tables had been put together in two rows, with one
table to join them at the top for Don Carlo, Donna Maria
and his very special guests. Directly in my view was Don
Giulio Gesualdo, Don Carlo's uncle. He had come to the
castle on many occasions. I couldn't quite see who Donna
Maria was next to. She was obviously very pleased with
the person because she smiled often and bent her head
repeatedly in that direction.*

*During yet another lute interlude, when we all had to
sit so quietly and still, Don Giulio's face passed through
many expressions. At first, I wondered if he might be in
pain but then I saw where he rested his gaze and it was as
I thought. Had I not said that all eyes would be upon her?*

*'Laura ... Laura!' I whispered loudly to her as she
passed us on her way back to the kitchen. All the servants
had been pressed into waiting at the tables. She ducked
behind the screen and Pietro and I helped ourselves to a
pigeon breast each. Probably the skinniest, as they'd been
left, but we were very happy with them.*

Of course, it was while I had a mouth full and grease slicked my lips and chin that my mistress turned and called my name. Stupidly, I found myself with no cloth so I wiped my mouth on the hem of my petticoat and hurried from my chair.

'Oh, Silvia.' Donna Maria beckoned that I should lean close to her. 'I need a handkerchief,' she whispered. 'Something fine. And I'd like it dipped in flower water, rose, I think, but orange blossom will do.'

Now I knew perfectly well that Donna Maria already had a very fine embroidered handkerchief in the pouch that hung from her waist because I put it there myself, so I was a little surprised as I hadn't seen her make use of it at all. When I took in the features of the guest next to her, however, her request made sudden and awful sense.

In the linen chest there was a pile of handkerchiefs, newly pressed by Laura only the day before. I chose one that had some rather fine cutwork in each corner. I unfolded it, sprinkled it with rosewater then folded it back up again, taking care to align with the previous creases. As I was doing so, the face of the man sitting next to Donna Maria remained clear in my mind. That he was the handsomest man in the room was without question. I did not know his name but I did know the name of the look in his eyes when they dwelt on my mistress. I had seen it before, in Salvo's eyes the day I left Gesualdo.

I had not been forced to make any response then, but being flattered by Salvo's attention, my hand had found the little almond and with its spinning through the air into his hand, I had seeded a hope in his mind.

The earnestness of Donna Maria's voice when she asked for the scented handkerchief filled me with dread. I remembered Salvo's bitter response to my remark about Don Carlo's virtue. He may have been right about a Prince having no need of virtue, but what about a Princess?

Down in the sala, the courses kept coming. The heat, wine and excitement had reddened the faces of nearly all the guests, so the pink spots that so attractively adorned the cheeks of my mistress were not revealing of her feelings. To me, though, they were clear.

'Ah, Fabrizio,' she said to the moon when we were finally alone at almost the hour before dawn. She said it once, twice, ten times after that as well. I was very glad that everyone was exhausted and Don Carlo had gone to his own chamber, for Donna Maria was quite beside herself. I slipped the nightgown over her head and she shivered with pleasure, but it wasn't for the touch of silk, I was sure. In her mind another's hand caressed her flesh.

'Don Giulio was very much looking in your direction, my lady,' I said.

'Don Giulio?' She looked at me as if I were mad, then scoffed. 'Oh, he always does.'

Once she had taken to her bed – which wasn't for a while, despite the moon and me not being very conversational – I took her clothes out into my own chamber and put aside the sleeves and undergarments for washing. The fan and pouch I removed from the jewelled girdle and laid them in their right places. When I drew the handkerchief with the floral embroidered border from within the pouch, I found it untouched. Of the other, there was no sign.

Chapter Nine

The next morning, I asked Robert about the blot on the cover.

'Blot?' he said, without looking up from checking the invoice against the contents of a large parcel of violin music.

'Yes, I wondered if you'd noticed how many there were.'

'How *many*? I don't remember any.'

'What none?'

Then he looked up. 'Why?'

I opened my mouth to tell him, but was thankfully ambushed by the tinkling bell of the door opening. Just as well, because the more I thought about it, the dafter it seemed.

'Hello, you two.' Sophie stood in the doorway. 'I thought I'd be cheeky and see if you'd got the coffee pot on.'

How I wish I had Sophie's style. Daniela might be all straight lines and polish but Sophie was theatre. It was hardly surprising as her job was wardrobe mistress at the theatre, but I did wonder if half of the costumes ended up in her own wardrobe. Today she was wearing Aladdin's harem pants in lime green and a maroon velvet topcoat straight from something by Oscar Wilde. Not an obvious combination but she looked stunning.

Over coffee we chatted about the madrigal.

'Is it just me that finds it so difficult?' I asked. 'I can sing my part perfectly okay when I'm on my own, but when we're together, I keep doubting myself.'

They both nodded vigorously and we were all relieved to find we'd had the same experience.

'Well,' said Sophie, 'we'll have to look convincing on the night even if we aren't, otherwise the audience will think we're singing wrong notes all over the place.

'Jon's all for talking to the audience first,' I said, 'and

singing a selection of madrigals from the period that aren't so hard on the ears.'

'Good idea,' said Robert. 'Especially now we've got Daniela.'

Sophie and I sipped our coffee and exchanged glances across the top of our mugs.

'Imagine living in those times,' I said.

'Fabulous clothes,' said Sophie. 'Valuable too. Everything got re-made several times.'

'I think,' said Robert, 'we should all thank our lucky stars we're alive now and not then. We'd probably all be dead of the plague.'

'Yes, or come to one of a number of sticky ends,' I said. 'Jon and I were reading up on the life of Gesualdo last night. Tut, tut.' I shook my head. 'Henry VIII wasn't the only one with wife trouble at the time. Maria D'Avalos was having her way with reputedly the most handsome man in Italy, Fabrizio Carafa, the Duke of Andria, right under Gesualdo's very nose.'

'Oh dear.' said Sophie. 'What happened?

I was about to say, when the shop clock announced it was midday by playing the opening bars of Beethoven's Fifth Symphony.

'Oh heck,' I said. 'You'll have to wait. I've got to go. The school choir will be waiting.'

My stomach churned with more nerves than if I was about to walk out in front of a few hundred paying punters, not twenty ten year olds. I was determined to keep it simple and be pleased with everything they did, however rough.

I had filled in the DBS form but the school had yet to receive a response so Miss Price would have to be in the room with me. Part of me was glad. One child vexed me often enough. Who knew how I'd be with twenty?

In the event, the half hour I imagined standing in front of them, was more like twenty minutes. I had no idea that moving small chairs could be so effortful and lining them up in two rows of ten almost impossible. What a good thing I hadn't decided on three. Miss Price introduced me. They all knew that I was Mollie's mum but even I didn't know that I was so famous or, indeed, related to Gareth Malone. Mollie appeared cheerfully determined in her guile.

'Hello, choir,' I said, once the shuffling had died down. A bad start. The shuffling increased at once. 'Hi, guys!' I yelled almost at the top of my voice. Silence. In the front row a small round-faced girl with a red hairband began to cry.

'No need for that, Emily,' called Miss Price from the back of the classroom.

Emily continued to wimper.

'First of all,' I said, 'we're going to sing the one song we all know off by heart. Do you know what that is?'

A voice from the back said loud and clear: '*Can You Feel The Love Tonight*?'

'No, Mollie. Not everyone knows *The Lion King*. Miss Price,' I went on, without leaving pause enough for a reply, 'has already told me that it's Toby's birthday today, so what do we sing?'

'*Can You Feel The Love …*'

Everyone laughed including me. Note to self: never patronise children again.

I played the last line of *Happy Birthday* on the keyboard just to get us going then stood up to sing with them. It was a bit all over the place but not terrible. 'Great,' I said. 'Now let's give Toby a second helping and this time, we are going to clap once at the end of each line.' I gave them a quick demo, played the chord on the piano to put them in the vicinity of the correct note and began again.

I was hoping the clapping would show up those whose sense of rhythm wasn't strong, but it turned out there was only the slightest of stutters at the end of each line. Everyone sang approximately in tune. Hooray!

It wasn't until the evening that I realised my mobile was

still on silent.

'Give me a ring as soon as you get this.' I listened to Mum's phone message again. She didn't say what it was about, but I detected excitement.

'We're going to Italy,' she announced, when I rang her back. 'Sorrento. Can you think of anywhere more romantic?'

Of course, she wasn't meaning me when she said 'we'. Thomas was my mother's new beau and the reason why she'd upped sticks and gone to live in Glastonbury. 'Umm…'

'And he said we can go to Capri, and Pompeii. The Amalfi Coast. I've heard they have lemons the size of grapefruits there.'

'And G and T's to match?'

She wouldn't be visiting at half-term. Mollie was going to her father's and I would be all on my own. For a whole delicious week.

When I switched off the phone I began planning. London for a couple of days or more. I could even do some decorating. Less than a minute later, the phone rang again.

Michael.

'I'll come straight to it, Lisa,' he said, without even a how are you. 'Greta and I have been offered tickets for the Bayreuth Festival at the end of October. We'd like to make it a proper break.'

'Oh, that's nice,' I said. 'I expect Mollie will really enjoy that.'

He coughed. He didn't have a cough, I could tell, but he coughed anyway. 'Err, no,' he said. 'Not Mollie. That's why I'm ringing. I was hoping she could stay with you at half-term. Perhaps I could have her the week after?'

'When she's back at school.'

'Yes.'

I sensed a semblance of contrition in his voice. A trip to Bayreuth. Lucky bastard. Even though Wagner wearied me there were certain places and performances in the musical canon that would be impossible to turn down. 'Can I think about it?'

I could hear him frowning. 'I'll phone you tomorrow, we have to book the flight.'

Poor Michael. Greta would harangue him for not getting a definite answer. Being a lawyer specialising in international law gave her clout in most social situations, but I couldn't help being a bit pleased when I had the chance to wield my smidgeon of power.

Mollie was watching *The Princess Bride* again, which gave me some quiet coffee time. I picked up the book about Gesualdo, but I hadn't even opened it before the phone rang yet again.

'Hi, Lisa, I'm so glad you're in.' Sophie sounded rather flustered.

'Are you okay?'

'Yes, yes, fine. I'm just a bit excited.'

'Oh?'

'Listen,' she paused and I could hear her swallow something so I drank some coffee of my own. After another swallow, she carried on: 'I've bought the most amazing thing. It'll be perfect.'

'What will? Perfect for what?'

'For the publicity shot.'

'Oh! Are we having one?'

'Of course! We absolutely must now there are five of us. I had an idea the other day, and then I saw it. The scythe. It's fantastic. Not one of those little sickle things. This is huge! You could swish your way through a field of wheat in no time—'

'Hang on a minute,' I interrupted. 'You've lost me, Sophie. Why on earth—'

'Don't you see?' she interrupted back. 'It's for the Grim Reaper.'

'Right … are we expecting him?'

It was meant to be a joke.

When I switched off the phone, I sat with it on my lap trying to imagine why Sophie could possibly think a scythe was a good idea. She wouldn't say, but I was to meet her the next day and she'd show me.

Without thinking, I slid the Gesualdo madrigal out from the heap of music on the table and opened it. There was the Grim Reaper leaning on his scythe and right by the point of the blade cavorted a band of devilish figures. The room was dim as I'd only got one lamp lit but when I held the frontispiece closer to the light I thought the group were perhaps the damned, forced to dance on hot coals. It was difficult to tell. I did notice a new figure though; next to the group stood a young man holding an instrument that resembled a lute. He appeared to be playing, but then I saw that all the strings were broken, and his face was stricken.

Chapter Ten

Napoli 1589

I was dressing myself the day after the banquet when Laura sidled round the door of my little room.

'Silvia? Can I ask you something?'

'That depends on what it is.'

She looked uncomfortable, even more mournful and pathetic than usual.

'I'm not sleeping.'

'Well, that's not news, Laura. When did you ever?'

'It's worse here. It's too hot and the others don't like my coughing.'

'Are you sure it's just that? I heard they didn't like the way you kicked the cook's cat.'

She looked at me and said nothing.

I sighed. 'Have they been mean to you?'

'Very mean,' she said, sniffing. 'I thought perhaps maybe,' she hesitated, then said all in a rush, 'please, Silvia, please will you let me sleep here?'

I looked at her. Was she mad? I swept my hand round the room. 'Where exactly were you thinking of, Laura? Were you planning to sleep standing up?'

'There's enough room on the floor. I'm not very big.'

Having Laura next to me was nearly the worst thing I could think of, but I have to say I was touched to be asked. How desperate must she be? Even so ... 'It's not up to me, Laura. Donna Maria said I should be near her, not you.'

'But can you ask her if it would be all right?'

'I—'

'Please, Silvia.'

'I'll see.'

Donna Maria met my request for Laura to come and sleep in with me with surprise, but she did agree. In respect of the coughing, Laura was a little better for living by the sea so I hoped her sleeping might have improved too.

'Can't you at least try not to snore, Laura?' I said, after the first night.

'I can't help it if I'm asleep.'

'Don't sleep on your back then.'

'But I don't mean to.'

'Pity your husband,' I said. 'It's like sleeping in a sty of suckling piglets.' The chance of Laura finding a husband was about as likely as a snuffling piglet dying of old age. She knew that as well as I.

'Here' I said, taking one of the lavender bags from the closet. 'Put this under your pillow. It might help.'

I meant it kindly, and she thanked me, but as usual, I felt mean. As if Laura was the cook's cat and I'd kicked it.

In the days following the feast, I reported to Pietro that my mistress was unwell with a malady that required several trips to the nessessario every night. The half-truth had the required effect and we saw nothing of Don Carlo in his wife's bedchamber. The fact was that if Donna Maria rose in the night, it was with love-sickness, and she had that very badly. So what with Laura's snoring and Donna Maria's loud and lengthy sighing, my own temper frayed worse than the stupid piece of silk I was edging with lace.

The months passed, spring became summer and a hot one too. I missed the cool of the hills. Outside, the piazza was a furnace. Eventually we became prisoners, shut in the dark. The shutters were closed through the day of course, but still the heat would seep through the slats so we could do nothing but wait for evening. I couldn't sew anything of merit as the needle slipped about in my fingers and the only beading I could manage was from the droplets of my own sweat. A smell of bad eggs rose from the ground and lodged in the back of the nose. Everyone was bad tempered.

One morning during this very hot spell, I went down to the courtyard early. It was necessary to cross this

*courtyard to reach the stables, and usually there was much
coming and going, but perhaps all the horses were being
fed or groomed indoors because there was no one about.*

*Donna Maria was still asleep and I'd set Laura to
mending. It was the time of the month for laundering the
linen, and sheets hung limp and heavy on their lines. They
would soon dry once the sun rose over the wall. I sat
myself down in a corner and enjoyed a little peace. Not
that it was quiet; the city was awake early too. Swifts
screamed, cutting through the air in clouds of little black
scythes. Horses pulled squeaky-wheeled wagons, clopping
by on the other side of the wall, and as the hour struck,
first the deep clang of the cathedral bell and then a chorus
of lighter bells chimed all about me.*

*I thought of home. I hadn't been back for more than a
year and wondered if my youngest sister was growing
well. She would certainly be running around. I imagined
her chubby hands picking up the warm eggs from the
straw. Had she watched a chick tap its way out from the
shell yet? I saw her running in and out of the sheds, hiding
from her older brothers and sisters and not knowing who I
was, if I ever did go back.*

*Then I thought of Salvo. I still kept the carved kitten in
my pouch and the thought of it made me seek it out right
then. He'd probably forgotten me by now. I ran my fingers
over the warm wood then put it away and went back to my
sewing. Perhaps I too would be like Laura and never have
a husband ...*

*It made me sad to think like that and I determined to be
happier. The tune of a catch that Salvo and I had warbled
together when we had walked along the path between the
castle and the village came into my mind and I began to
sing:*

*'Buon giorno mia cara, bambina, molti baci, molti
baci...'*

*The tune was light and quick and, of course, repetitive
but soon, singing 'molti baci' – many kisses – so many
times began to make me feel rather sad again and I*

faltered. But when I fell silent, the sheet nearest me was suddenly swept aside and Don Carlo himself stood only an arm's length in front of me, his horsewhip holding back the cloth. I jumped up in fright, dropping my work on the ground.

'Do you sing, girl?' he said.

'N-n-not really, sir.'

He came closer and looked me up and down. I'd never been so near to him before and my eye was at his ruff height. His breath stank but I dared not move. It was just at the moment when the sun came over the wall and everywhere took on its brightness. Everywhere except Don Carlo, that is, whose shape grew as dark as my mistress's secret.

'There was something,' he said as if he'd forgotten what and spoke to himself. 'Yes, something in the tone.' He stepped away and I was straight ways blinded by the sun, full in my eyes. 'Go, ready yourself,' he said. 'We leave in an hour. Tell Donna Maria you are coming with me to Gesualdo. That other girl can look after her.' He walked away to the stables and a minute later I heard him shouting to make ready for the journey.

Gesualdo! I couldn't believe I was to be going back. And so near on my thinking about it! I nearly forgot my sewing in my haste and when I ran back for it, discovered a streak of black dirt across the middle. On the sheet that Don Carlo had swept aside, his whip had left a similar mark. I hurried away, afraid I might be falsely accused by the housekeeper.

'What?' said Donna Maria, sitting straight up in bed. 'How long for?'

'I don't know. I'm so sorry, my lady. I do hope Laura will be able to manage.'

'He should have told me before. Besides,' she looked at me from the side of her eyes, 'I have been not in the best of health.' I smiled and helped her from her nightgown – one of my better efforts, flesh-coloured, silk-trimmed with black braid, the effect of which was very startling. It was

one of Donna Maria's favourites. 'You did say,' she said, standing before me without a scrap on, 'he wanted you for the singing, didn't you?'

As I ran down the stairs from Donna Maria's quarters, the more pressing fear of Don Carlo held sway. It seemed advisable to develop a bad throat as soon as possible. I began with coughing quietly. Gradually it would develop into something really quite sore.

The journey home did not seem so far as I remembered, but then the roads were baked hard and the wagon rolled over them easily. I was alone in the back and, without the distraction of conversation, looked all about at the landscape. We rode round Mount Somma to the North. Some say the mountain once spewed fire but, rather like Noah's flood and Moses making the sea part, it was difficult to imagine. The day was calm. As we left the city, we left behind the noise. The screaming swifts and irritable gulls were replaced by a more gentle twittering amongst the groves and vineyards. High in the sky, I'd see a lonely eagle or falcon circling and all the way to Gesualdo, I only saw three snakes basking by the road, although one of them was probably as long as I am tall.

It was nearly dark when we arrived, for Don Carlo had been determined to spend only one day on the road. A rider had been sent on ahead and as we neared the castle, lamps were sent out, and the first face I saw beneath the glow was that of Salvo's. His happy expression at the sight of me suggested he hadn't forgotten who I was at all. Don Carlo pushed on up the hill quickly, but the wagon slowed.

'Jump down,' Salvo called to me. 'Here ...' and he held out his hand. I gathered up my skirts and jumped. My mistress would have been horrified at the inelegance of my leap and the way I arrived, or rather, fell into Salvo's arms. 'Well, Silvia,' he said, while helping me to stand upright, 'you are pleased to see me.'

'Now, now, Salvo, don't you go misreading a slight unevenness in the ground for anything improper.' Closer *too, I realised how much he had changed. My memory recalled the boy in my father's woodshed, but before me in the half-light stood a taller and broader person: Salvo the man. Why, he even had a neat line of growth about his chin. I smoothed my skirt hoping to smooth a little fluster at the same time.*

He bowed low, laughing. 'Would I?'

'I think you might.'

'So, why have you come back? And where is Donna Maria?' He lowered his voice, 'You're not in disgrace are you?'

'Salvo! That's a terrible thing to say. No, of course not.'

'Well, it is odd. Don Carlo doesn't usually bring a girl with him. Unless,' his voice caught in his throat, 'don't say—'

'No, no, not that. But I am fearful. He's brought me here because of my singing.' I walked on, not realising Salvo had stopped. When I looked back his chin had dropped almost to his chest. It was a funny sight and although the worry of Don Carlo was alive in me, I couldn't help laughing.

The castle, unlike Salvo, was much the same as when I left. His mother greeted me fondly and had put fresh linen on my bed too, but when I lay down I felt lonely without my mistress in the next room. I even missed Laura. The castle walls were thick and the heat of summer hadn't penetrated them. I shivered and drew back from blowing out my little lamp. The light flickered and sometimes even in my drowsy state, I would start wide awake, for the shadows cast would take on shapes, some human, some grotesque. Eventually, I listened to my courage and with a large breath, blew out the light.

Pietro found me early next morning. Don Carlo would remain in bed until midday, but I was to be in the music room once he had breakfasted.

As I hurried along the road to the village, I wondered

whether other Princes kept such curious hours. What a good thing for their servants when they did. The morning was mine! Signora Carlino let me go and bade me wish my family well from her. I knew what was behind this, of course, so I decided to hold back with her wishes rather than fuel expectations.

By the time I reached my home, I had fallen in love again and was in exceptional spirits. The blue hills were as beautiful as the sea, the scent of honey in the air much nicer than the city stink which we only kept at bay with lavender bags and rosewater. A hoopoe came along with me too, flitting from branch to branch. Its 'hoo, hoo, hoop – sigh' of a cry, rather a one-sided conversation but company all the same.

It was a shock, though, when I reached my family home. How mean it seemed after the palazzo and the castle. A vivid memory came back to me of carriages winding their way up the hill and in my heart, the sharp desire to be amongst those who went with them. How easy it was to become accustomed to such things.

'Silvia! Is that you?'

I looked towards the chicken house and saw my nearest sister with the egg basket in her hand.

'Agnola!' I ran over and kissed her. The scent of chickens was very strong and I laughed. I must have smelt the same once. 'How are you? How is everyone? Where are they?'

'Silvia?'

My mother stood at the doorway of the house. All our past differences were forgotten at once. We embraced and I do believe I saw a tear in the corner of her eye.

'Fetch your father,' she said to Agnola. 'He's at Francesca's.'

'Francesca?' I hadn't thought of her for years. 'Is she still alive?'

'Yes, just about. Your father is fixing one of her hives.' My mother turned to Agnola, who stood stroking my sleeve in wonder – it was silk after all. 'Off you go, Agnola.

Don't just stand there. Silvia will still be here when you get back and I'll see if I can do something with some of these eggs.' She turned back to me. 'You can stay, can't you?'

'For a little while, yes,' I said.

Together, we carried the trestle table to the little spot between our three olive trees where we celebrated birthdays and saints days. The morning was to be enjoyed. My later appointment with Don Carlo lay upon me like the heavy mist that at times would obscure the Mount Somma, but even then, the city of Napoli shimmered in sunlight.

Chapter Eleven

'We ran into the museum curator at the cinema,' Sophie began to explain as soon as she opened her door. It was the day after her phone call and I had nipped round after work and before picking up Mollie from ghastly ballet.

'We?'

'*The Imitation Game.* It was jolly good.'

'We?'

'Yes, Robert and I. Anyway, we met—'

'You went to the cinema with Robert?' I was so surprised that I sat down without checking whether there was a seat to sit on. Luckily I made contact with a corner and caught the edge of the table to steady myself. The vase of bright pink nerines in the centre of the table fared worse though and tipped over.

'Yes, that's right.' She said it so lightly, as if they went to the cinema every week.

I put more water in the vase while she mopped up.

'And you both just happened not to mention it? I've been at the shop with Robert all day. He never said—'

She laughed. 'You're making too much of it, Lisa. It was quite casual.'

'Really. Robert hasn't been to the cinema in all the time I've known him. If it was that casual, he'd have told me.'

'Listen,' she said, 'forget that. Let me tell you about what we should do for the publicity shot. The curator said they needed a photo of *Noteworthy*.'

'Did she,' I said, vaguely, still trying to see Robert and Sophie sitting next to each other in the cinema. Sophie, exotic in her jewelled-coloured robes, with Robert. Mr Taupe.

'It was the scythe that gave me the idea of a tableau.'

'A what?'

'A tableau. The Victorians did them all the time. Dressed up in classical poses and what not, then had their photo taken.'

I imagined us all draped in togas. 'Classical poses?'

'Well, we wouldn't, obviously. I thought we could do something more appropriate.'

'What sort of something?'

'Here, let me show you.'

'This is ridiculous,' Robert said at *Noteworthy's* next rehearsal. 'I'm certainly not going to dress up like that.' His finger trembled above the figure of Duke Fabrizio.

'Dress down rather,' Jon said. 'He doesn't appear to be wearing anything at all.'

I put on my imaginary high definition love-detection glasses. There may have been something between them, but Robert didn't look that much like a man smitten with anything, and definitely not with Sophie's mock-up design for the tableau. We were in my kitchen, which could just about accommodate five. It meant sitting very close together, not ideal for singing and to my mind, Daniela being so particularly close to Jon was not ideal either.

Sophie frowned. 'But what do you think of the idea?'

We all looked at each other.

'Brilliant, Sophie,' said Jon. 'A damn sight better than the usual stuff you see, where everyone's in black and gawping straight at the camera.'

'*Che divertimento!*' Daniela clapped her hands together and beamed at all of us in turn. '*Molto buon!*'

We got the message.

I was taken with it too, the way Sophie had arranged us reminded me of something, but I couldn't put my finger on it. The tableau had four figures in action posed at the front: Don Carlo, Donna Maria, the Duke and the maid. To one side, a little apart, was a figure all in black holding a large scythe. 'So how are we going to decide who's who?' I asked.

'Okay, Robert, heads or tails?' Jon tossed a coin, slapping it on to the back of his hand. 'Which one of us gets to be Gesualdo?'

Mercifully, Robert lost. While it was possible Gesualdo was rotund, all my research had given me the impression Don Carlo was a gaunt figure, not exactly compatible with Robert's rather portly frame. There again, I couldn't really see him as the Duke either, especially not in such a revealing costume.

That left the three women. I put two brown Smarties and one red one into a cup and covered it with my hand. 'Whoever gets the red one gets first pick.' And to my amazement, when both Sophie and Daniela pulled one from the cup, they were brown.

It was an easy choice for me, almost a cop-out. 'I'll be Silvia Albana, the maid.'

Daniela had the next go and decided Death was better than Donna Maria. I was surprised at her choice, imagining she'd prefer the tragic heroine role. Perhaps I'd got her wrong, or maybe she didn't fancy appearing quite so undressed. That led me to a mean thought. Her underwear, especially in the bra department, had to be quite substantial. Who knew what might happen when she took it off?

'Oh dear.' Sophie laughed. 'It looks like my petard has been well and truly hoisted.'

The theatre was chosen for the venue. Being wardrobe mistress meant Sophie was a key-holder. She would sort our costumes and, with luck, Jon would persuade a photographer who owed him a favour to come along and do the deed.

I looked at Sophie's drawing again.

'Oh!' My stomach lurched with the shock of realisation.

The others looked at me. 'What?' said Jon.

'I know where I've seen this before. The group. Us. The figures.' I rifled through my music, looking for the frontispiece. I looked twice but it wasn't there. 'Damn.'

I got up and went into the sitting room. Could I find it? 'Mollie?'

No response. She sat at the keyboard wearing

headphones so I went and lifted one from her ear.

'Have you been messing about with my music?'

She looked aggrieved. 'No. Why should *I* want to do *that*?'

'Okay, never mind. But while I'm here, I think you'd better get to bed.'

'Can Jon come and say goodnight?'

'Not right now, we're about to sing.'

'Later then.'

'All right.'

Back in the kitchen the others looked at me as if I were about to produce a rabbit out of a hat, but the frontispiece wasn't anywhere obvious, and I couldn't spend all evening turning the place upside down so I left it.

Jon looked nervous when I asked him to say goodnight to Mollie. 'She's not going to start screaming again, is she?'

'I doubt it, she hasn't gone to bed yet. Tell her sleeping is good for her voice. She's got choir practice tomorrow.'

'Does Jon often make Mollie scream?' Daniela asked, when he'd gone out of the kitchen. Her expression was the usual blank screen and for a moment I felt a touch of anxiety, as if she was some sort of secret abuse police. I explained about the nightmare.

'It sounds as if Mollie is dreaming about Gesualdo,' she said.

'Oh?' I was surprised and immediately felt stupid for not thinking the same thing myself. Perhaps Mollie *had* read one of the books I'd got from the library and had been frightened. It was possible although I'd never seen her look remotely interested in them. 'I don't think so. It's more likely she's seen something frightening on the television or the web.'

'Yes,' she said. 'You are probably right. It is funny that Jon is going to be our Don Carlo, isn't it?'

I looked at her. She wasn't smiling and neither was I. 'Mmm,' I said. 'Maybe.' I took a rather large gulp of wine and focused my attention rather fiercely on the music, although it didn't escape me that Robert and Sophie had been discussing the latest Picturehouse programme.

Chapter Twelve

Gesualdo 1589

'I have some news, Silvia.' Salvo greeted me in the castle courtyard.

'I do hope it is good, for I am in desperate need of cheering up.'

'Oh?' His concern for me was immediate. *'What is it?'*

'My appointment with Don Carlo. I am in dread of him.'

Salvo sighed. *'We all are, Silvia. It is something we have to live with. The best thing is not to get noticed.'*

I remembered my mother's advice all over again. How chickens do not thrive when cooped with peacocks.

'But I have been noticed, and for something I didn't even know I had.' Tears pricked in the corner of my eyes. *'And Salvo, I am afraid ... for I confess I'm not altogether sure that my voice is the Prince's real interest.'*

Salvo pulled me into a pool of dark shadow cast where the castle wall blocked the sun. *'Listen, Silvia, when Pietro tells you to go to the music room I will hide myself in the gallery. If anything happens, I will make a loud noise and disturb him.'*

'But Salvo, you will get into trouble then.'

'Better that than ...'

I put my finger to his lips. *'Shh ... don't say it.'*

Salvo smiled, and taking hold of my hand, kissed it gently. For the first time, I felt no desire to pull away. But I was afraid for him, and an idea pressed itself into my mind that might help us both: *'Is the Prince already in the music room?'*

'I don't know. He wasn't when I passed by a little while ago.'

'Perhaps if you were to take something from the room up to the gallery and drop it over the edge, he would not know it came from above and you would be safe.'

'Ah, Silvia.' Salvo laughed. 'I always knew you were clever as well as beautiful. Why yes, he will think it a portent. Don Carlo is most superstitious and fearful of anything that might be magic.'

'Quickly then, let us find something for you to drop.'

'Of course, there is one difficulty with your plan, Silvia.'

'Oh?'

'You will have to make sure he doesn't see whatever I drop fall through the air.'

'Oh.' I was downcast at once. How could I make Don Carlo do anything? The answer seemed to me exactly what we were trying to avoid.

Salvo looked a little rueful. 'It still is a plan, Silvia, and better than no plan at all. Let's go and—'

As we stepped out into the sunshine, Pietro appeared at the castle door.

'Ah, there you are,' he said. 'And both together. How convenient for me as I have come to take you to the music room, Silvia, and for you, Salvo, an errand. Don Carlo wishes you to go to the papermakers.'

In spite of the sun, I felt a chill run through my flesh right into my heart. Salvo and I looked at each other. We were chickens once again.

I didn't hear Pietro's instructions for Salvo. All was darkness in my head as Pietro and I climbed the castle steps. When we reached the music room door, I remembered that Salvo said he had news. He had looked pleased too. I hoped whatever it was would be good enough to cheer me later.

Pietro entered first, the door hinges complaining as they opened and closed. I stood outside and tried to determine whether it would be a good thing to sing very well or very badly. Perhaps having a good voice might keep me respectable but would retain Don Carlo's interest in me. Being a poor singer might give him a reason to pursue another desire.

It was fruitless for me to even think I had any choice,

for when I finally entered the room, I was too afraid to make any sort of noise at all. Don Carlo sat tuning his archlute. I stood quietly although my heart danced a tarantella to a beat nearly as loud as the instrument. I looked up at the gallery and must have made a slight murmur or sigh as Don Carlo stopped playing at once and turned his gaze upon me.

'Ah, girl. Come here.' I walked over and stood a little way off from him. 'No,' he said, pointing at the floor, 'here.'

I did as directed, quivering quietly. The place he'd chosen was in the centre of a shaft of sunlight that sliced the room in two. Then he walked away, not turning until he stood beneath the gallery. 'Sing now,' he ordered.

Nothing happened. I did open my mouth. Honestly, I did. I had thought the Prince to be fishlike but it was me that gulped, opening and closing my mouth as if the air about us were in short supply.

'Sing as you did before,' he called. 'The same thing will do. Start now.'

I cleared my throat and prayed I would not wet myself with fear, but I was able to manage half of the first line without a gasp for breath. Bbuon gggiorno ... The sound was very thin to my ear.

'Again.'

I tried once more. It was a little better. 'Buon giorno mia cara ...'

'And again.'

I sang the first line several more times and then the whole song over and over until I began to feel rather faint. For the entire time Don Carlo stood beneath the gallery and I was very happy that he was so far away. Then he poured himself a glass of wine and came to sit on the chair nearest to me.

'Look at me,' he said.

I turned towards him but could hardly see anything for the bright sun, and my heart, which had settled somewhat, began to tumble all over again. He picked up the lute and strummed a chord or two as if I wasn't there. I had no idea as to success or failure, but I had not been dismissed.

'My lord.' I curtsied, and cleared my throat. Quietly, I stepped out of the sunlight, in order to see his expression.

He did look up and about but not directly at me, as if he thought the voice had come from elsewhere. I curtsied again.

'May I go now, my lord?'

Then he looked at me and I wished I'd kept silent.

'Go?' he said. 'Go? Oh, no.'

He didn't sound cross or shocked that I'd spoken. If I'd been a dog that barked suddenly, I suspect he would have sounded thus. A slight irritation, that's all.

So I just kept on standing there with only thoughts to keep me upright. Being so near to the Prince set me thinking about my mistress. I hoped Laura didn't get herself dismissed in my absence and was looking after Donna Maria well. Not too well though. I did not want her usurping my place. I began to wonder about the missing handkerchief. There's only one reason a married lady might give her handkerchief to a man who was not her husband, and it had nothing to do with blowing noses. Fabrizio Carafa, Duke of Andria and father of four or was it five? I had no memory of his wife, another Maria, sitting on the far side of him, and I wondered if she might have glimpsed the moment when my best cut-work handkerchief changed hands. I hoped not.

The sound of Don Carlo knocking over his glass made me jump. I reached for it at once. 'Leave it,' he said. 'Now, begin again. Here ...' He struck a chord. 'I wish you to start higher.'

So, off I went again. And again. It was more of an effort to sing so high but I could do it. Once I was let from that room I would never sing that song again unless on pain of death.

'Again!' Don Carlo commanded over and over.

'Please, my lord,' I said, eventually when desperate and almost hoarse, 'a little water?'

Abruptly, he picked up the fallen glass that had lain precariously on the edge of the table and filled it to more than half. 'Drink,' he said. 'All of it. Wine is more restorative than water.'

For some that may be true, but shortly after I downed the glass, I felt a great need to hold the edge of the spinet. After two more verses I began to sway and the third time, I sat on the empty stool unbidden. At once Don Carlo stood up, laid his lute upon the ground and came to where I sat almost weeping.

'Come now. There is no need for fuss,' he said, as if I were a small child. 'Do you not know how to work? The musician has to practise and keep on practising if he is to improve.'

I did not like him, frowning so and berating me. Perhaps the wine had altered him too, for instead of a cold gaze, he now stared at me with a strange determination. He came closer as I stood, teetering precariously from the wine and faintness.

'Your voice has an unusual timbre, girl. And there is much breath in you.' He drew even closer and bent his face to mine, peering as if to find a witch sign on my face. I tried to lean away, to avoid his breath, the look in his eye. 'Stamina too,' he said, and his lips peeled apart into a thin smile.

I felt his hands on my body then, like two monstrous spiders finding their way about me. I took a breath to scream but his fingers were at my throat. They crushed my neck so that no air could come forth at all. With a great crash, the world I knew slipped sideways from its usual course and grew black before my eyes.

Chapter Thirteen

Once Mollie had let Jon go, we finally set about singing. I'd made a bit of an effort with my part but the minute I opened my mouth, I began coughing. If I'd swallowed a fly, it couldn't have been worse. A sip of wine didn't help and neither did half a glass of water.

'Sorry, sorry ...' I spluttered, and went into the sitting room. I couldn't seem to clear whatever it was and at risk of throwing up I went into the bathroom. There was a spray somewhere I'd bought for a sore throat ages ago. I thought it might help.

'What's the matter?' Mollie called out.

'A frog,' I said, wheezing slightly.

'Some frog.'

'A bullfrog probably.'

She stood at the bathroom door. 'You can't do that at the concert, Mummy.'

'No, I know,' I rasped. 'And you'd better get back to bed.'

The spray did help and when we finally got round to singing again, it went okay. Nothing special but no coughing fits or spilt wine. The weather accompanied us with loud gusts biffing the kitchen window.

Later, I inspected my throat for signs of inflammation but couldn't see anything amiss. Perhaps it was just a crumb or a fragment of Smartie shell. Daniela had no such trouble, her voice as rich and as wonderfully warm as her personality, but even so, I couldn't stop feeling that I was an object being observed. Like being in a music exam or taking the driving test, and for someone so gushing with her smiles, she was very held back about her own life. We'd had a few rehearsals together and yet I knew no more about her than was written on the card at the shop. I'd served a few balls in her direction, but nothing ever came back, and I began to feel as if I was an interrogator.

'Oh, Jon,' said Daniela, when they were all getting

ready to leave. 'Would you be a lovely man and give me a lift? It is so raining?' She did that leaning thing again and smiled at him as if he were Mr Special.

His smile was pretty impressive too. With effort, I set my face to neutral.

'I can hardly breathe in this, let alone sing,' I said, as Sophie pulled at the corset during my first fitting.

'You're too short in the waist.' She spoke through a mouthful of pins.

'So I keep telling myself,' I said. 'You should hear me when I'm in a changing room.'

'There. You can take it off now. Go carefully, it's pinned all the way round.'

My costume involved the most complicated fitting even though I was only the maid. I'd met Sophie at the theatre and was doing a tree impersonation while she tried not to stab me. She was clever with her pins though. I eased my way past them and stepped away from the pool of fabric.

'Thanks,' I said, shaking my arms to get the blood circulating again. 'I'm very glad to be Silvia Albana and not centre stage. Even so, poor girl, it must have been awful.'

'And Gesualdo got away with it. That was really awful.'

'One of the many perks of being a prince, I suppose.' I struggled back into my jeans and felt very drab amongst the finery of all the theatre costumes. 'What about you, Sophie? Surely you're going to wear *something*, aren't you? Or are you going to do a proper *Calendar Girls* stunt and be demure behind your music.'

Sophie laughed. 'I think there's a bit too much of me to hide behind a piece of music. Don't worry, I've sorted a few props that'll help.'

'They'll have to be pretty extensive to please Robert.'

'You'll see.'

'Phew,' I said, pulling my sweater on. 'That feels better.'

Sophie gathered up the dress, or rather the over-dress, as it went on top of the bodice and skirt, and hung it over the ironing board. 'Have you got time for a cup of tea?'

'Yes, if you have. Mollie's at her dad's. I have all the live long day.'

'Tell you what,' Sophie looked at her watch. 'There's not much day left, it's nearly evening. Why don't we go to the new place on Queen Street? I could just do with something nice and cold with bubbles in.'

'Oh yes! And when was the last time you and I had a chat?' I wondered if Robert might figure in Sophie's news. 'We're not celebrating anything are we?'

'No. Not particularly. Only …' She snapped the lid back on the pin box. 'That's exactly it. You and I haven't had a proper chat for ages. Is it me or do *Noteworthy* rehearsals feel completely different with Daniela there? We sound different, the conversation's different … she's got a lovely voice and there's nothing I can put my finger on to dislike about her, but …' She shook her head and stuffed the box into her sewing bag. 'What do you think, Lisa. Am I mad?'

Relief propelled me across the room to give her a hug. 'Oh, Sophie, I'm so glad you said that! I thought it was just me.'

She laughed. 'And I thought it was just me. Or having to sing that Gesualdo.'

'Yes, definitely that.' I remembered the last rehearsal and my struggles.

We walked down the hill in the first real chill of the year. Cold, damp air and leaves were everywhere, slippery and rotting like a month old salad in the bottom of the fridge. I heard all about Sophie's house on the way. Not that we were avoiding anything, but there was a comfort in the certainty of new guttering. *Noteworthy* had felt certain but things change. Get old. Stuff happens. No, wait … stuff happens then things *have* to change.

I was glad to hear about Sophie's roof repairs and especially about the impending new central heating boiler, but once we sat in the comfort of an emerald green plush velvet booth we looked at each other and went quiet.

'Cheers,' I said, clinking glasses. 'I was thinking it was because I was jealous.'

'Aren't we all? Who wouldn't want a voice like Daniela's?'

I laughed rather ruefully. 'I didn't mean her voice.'

'Oh, *that* … well, yes.' Sophie sighed and a cluster of little lines fanned around her mouth. 'Do we know anything about her?' she went on. 'What's she doing in Exeter? It's a long way from Milan.'

'Especially as she used to sing at La Scala.'

'Did she? Wow.'

'That's the only thing she's said about her past. God knows what she's doing here. I asked her once, but she changed the subject. Then I blamed myself for being too nosy. I thought she'd think I was interrogating her.'

'That's typical of you,' Sophie said, between swigs.

'What is?'

'To think you're at fault.'

'Is it? Do I?' This was news to me.

'Not all the time, but if you're given half the chance. Don't look so appalled. Better that than assuming nothing is ever your fault.'

'I suppose not.' I tried thinking of other times I may have taken false responsibility. 'You've got me worried now.'

'Don't be. I think Daniela is making us all feel nervous.'

I remembered the way she smiled at Jon and the look on his face. 'I don't think *all* of us do. Did you notice that Jon took her home last time?' It didn't come out quite as nonchalantly as I'd hoped.

'Did I *notice*? Of course, I noticed! Who could fail to?'

I gulped back the rest of my wine as a shiver of fear ran through me. 'Do you want another one?'

'Yes,' said Sophie, 'that would be very nice. But listen,' she put her hand on my arm as I stood up, 'you should say something.'

'What do you mean?'

'You should speak to Jon.

'And say what?'

Sophie tutted then shooed me away. 'Go and get the drinks. We'll talk about it when you get back.'

At the bar a cluster of sparkly girls wound themselves into a frenzy in readiness for the evening. They giggled behind their hands and adjusted their clothes; tops downwards and skirts up. I remembered something similar at college. How old is it possible to feel at thirty? Through speakers, Sam Smith warbled *I'm not the only one*. It wasn't reassuring.

'You and Jon ought to be together,' Sophie announced when I put our drinks on the table.

'Oh, not you too. That's what Mollie says.'

'And she's absolutely right. What's stopping you?'

'Well …' I hesitated. This was looking the mammoth right in the eye. Like elephants, mammoths have eyes that are quite small and with all that wool in the way it can be difficult to see them. When I left Michael, I made vehement noises about how I'd had it with men. A toddler is enough, especially one as delightfully demanding as Mollie was. But a couple of years ago, when Sophie's party invite had arrived out of the blue, it was Mollie's excitement about her mummy being invited to a party that made me go. My own mummy had been pretty excited too, but then she wasn't like me. When her husband left, although it took her a while, she did find another one – the caretaker at my school.

'But he died …' I said out loud, startling both myself and Sophie.

'Who died?'

'My stepdad.' I waved my hand, somehow trying to wave away the past. A useless gesture, of course, so I gulped a mouthful of Prosecco instead. Alcohol is better at that sort of thing.

'I didn't know you had one.'

'He died a year after my mum married him. It was such a shame. He was so lovely.' I felt the prick of tears just thinking about him. 'You see, Sophie, that's the trouble with me and men. They either leave or die.' I could hear it sounded a bit over the top but it was as if something deep down wanted to be said. Perhaps a herd of mammoths lurked just over the horizon.

'That's not really true, Lisa.' It was said mildly and I knew she was right, but I couldn't shed the feeling that I might cry at any moment. The mammoths were pressing forward. 'Let's face it,' she went on, 'Jon's not gone anywhere and he's looking pretty healthy.' She picked up her handbag and began rummaging in its depths.

'But he's never said anything.' I remembered the moment I thought we might kiss, the night he came to supper. There was something in that moment, but nothing was said. I saw him playing with Mollie, messing about and having fun. 'Besides,' I said, 'let's face it, he's like an overgrown schoolboy.'

Sophie looked shocked and I was shocked I'd said it. The tears were shocked forth too and filled my eyes. Sophie handed me the tissue she produced from her bag, almost like the rabbit of a magic trick.

'Thank you.' I sniffed. 'It's just that … for goodness sake, he's so … so … so not *serious* about anything.'

'But that's his charm, isn't it? You don't want another misery like Michael.'

'God, no. But he's always messing about … all those games—'

'Excuse me,' Sophie interrupted me, 'who is it that always joins in? Certainly not Robert, and I do only occasionally. You like all that stuff, Lisa.'

'But …' It was true, I did enjoy it. Jon made me laugh. 'But I don't want it to change things, Sophie. What about *Noteworthy*?'

'What about it?' She began to plait the long fringes of her scarf.

The nap of the velvet upholstery was making my legs

itch, and I wriggled about trying to get comfortable, although comfort wasn't on offer. 'I'm scared it'll all go wrong and then he'll leave.' I retrieved the tissue from my sleeve and wiped my eyes again.

'He might, but nothing ventured, nothing gained. And supposing Robert and I fall out, or Robert and Jon?' She flicked the plait undone. 'That's much more likely. What would happen to *Noteworthy* then?'

I didn't know what to say. She was absolutely right, of course. What did I sound like? I knew the world went round; it wasn't sunny every day.

'Let's just hope,' she said, 'that Ms Voluptress has not yet got her claws into Jon.' Sophie flexed her own fingers and with her scarlet nails they looked quite menacing. Not that she would ever have need of them.

'So you and Robert,' I said. 'Any more movies lined up?'

'Umm.' She looked at the ceiling, then the table, then at me with an expression that was definitely mischievous but with a few big spoonfuls of wicked. 'I think so.'

I wanted to know where, when and what, but Mozart's fortieth symphony began playing in my handbag. I fished out my phone, pressing answer before I checked who it was.

'Oh, Lisa, thank God you've answered.'

'Hi, Mum,' I said, keeping it light even though her tone suggested disaster.

'I tried your landline,' she said, 'and you're obviously out.' Disaster with tears. 'I'm on my way to your place now. Will you be back soon?'

'What is it, Mum? Are you all right?'

'It's Thomas,' she said with a hiccup, then began to weep in earnest.

'I'll be about twenty minutes,' I said. 'Where on earth are you?' Background noise whizzed and whooped like an amusement arcade.

'Taunton Deane Services.'

She'd be half an hour at most.

Having run for a hundred yards, I began to feel the onset of a stitch in my side. The Prosecco was jiggling about in my stomach, so I slowed to a stroll. My thoughts slowed down too and became more coherent. I assumed that something had happened to Thomas. Mum hadn't had much luck with men after my stepdad died until Thomas came along. He was Saint Thomas after all. Thomas the Good, the Calm – he had to be to put up with my mother – and also Thomas the Deeply Romantic. Or was he?

'I couldn't stay another minute,' Mum said. She sat on the sofa, box of tissues on one side, bin to throw the tear-sodden in on the other. I'd made her a cup of tea that she cradled but didn't drink.

'So what happened?'

'He lied to me, Lisa. A huge horrid lie.' She shook her head. 'How *could* he?'

She kept repeating this but I was yet to know what this terrible lie was. 'But Mum, what did he actually *say*?'

'He didn't say,' she said with a sniff. 'I found out.'

'Found out *what*?' It was getting tortuous.

'His wife,' she said in a thin whisper. 'He told me she was dead! And all the while she's alive and well and living in *whoopee*.' This last word arrived with a loud hiccup.

'A wife?' I said, incredulous.

'Yes,' she said. 'In Wookey.'

'And they're not divorced?'

She shook her head.

The bastard. He'd set Mum up in a little love nest in Glastonbury and told her he worked away from home half the week. Did he say the same thing to his wife? What a pillock. Wookey was only up the road.

Eventually, I did get Mum to drink a cup of tea and later, when she was limp with the exhausting business of weeping, I put some clean sheets on Mollie's bed for her. What we'd do the next day, I couldn't imagine. Mum had let out her flat, and she could hardly turf the tenants out at a moment's notice. It seemed incredible to me that Thomas had been so disingenuous. He must have had a lot of practice.

'I'm glad you're so sensible, Lisa,' Mum said when I poked my head round the door and asked if she wanted anything else.

'What do you mean?'

'Not getting mixed up with anyone. It always ends badly, one way or another.'

'Mmm,' I said. 'Maybe. 'Night, Mum. I hope you sleep all right.'

I thought of the conversation with Sophie. I thought of Jon. I couldn't help my feelings for him but I could help what I did about them. Was 'being sensible' sensible?

The bit I didn't understand about my mum was that she sought love over and over again, even though it let her down every time. The fallout always landed on my head, of course, and I wouldn't wish that on Mollie. I resolved to do nothing. If Jon was really interested in me, then he'd have to show it. If he could be so easily seduced by Daniela, then I'd be better off without him. Who knew how many more hot-bloodied temptresses might hap along in the future?

Mum stirred her Weetabix into a beige soup at breakfast the next morning. I don't think anything passed her lips but she did manage three cups of coffee. I made the last two with decaff without her noticing. I know she didn't sleep much because I kept hearing the bedroom door open and close. Being programmed to believe Mollie was next door, I woke up too. I imagined both of us would be feeling it later but didn't fancy the half-crazed, eye-popping effect of too much caffeine as well.

'Umm,' I said, stirring my coffee rather intently. 'Mollie's home this afternoon.'

Mum sighed a sigh of doom but followed it up with: 'Would you like me to pick her up from school?'

'Oh!' What an offer. It would give me the opportunity

to go back to the library. 'Yes, please. If you don't mind.'

She sighed again. 'I might as well.'

'The thing is, Mum …'

'I know,' she said. 'I can't stay here for ever.'

'It'll be okay for a bit,' I said, and then surprised myself by suggesting that she had my room and I slept on the sofa.

'Oh, darling, that would be wonderful. I can't quite face going back to Mother's. Not just yet.' Queen Victoria was a liberal leftie in comparison with my eighty-year-old grandmother, and her bungalow made Robert's house look shockingly *à la mode.* Mum reached across and squeezed my hand. 'It's so lovely that you and I can really *talk* to each other.'

I didn't say anything.

'So much for Sorrento.' She began to sniff again.

'Never mind. Better find out beforehand rather than halfway along the Amalfi coast.' I passed her the kitchen roll as the sniffing was getting more serious. 'I hope the bastard never gets his money back.'

Mum shook her head. 'No …'

The look on her face. I knew at once. 'Oh, no, Mum. You *didn't*!'

'He was going to pay *me* back,' she wailed.

'Yeah, yeah …' God. I knew what would happen. I'd have to sort it all. The chance that she would get her money back was about as likely as Mollie offering to sleep on the sofa instead of me. I checked the calendar even though I knew perfectly well that from Thursday to Tuesday's departure date was less than a week's notice.

'Did it cost loads?' I said.

She nodded. 'He said it would be nice to go first class… a real treat.'

I'd never really thought of myself as violent but it was a good job Thomas the Snake didn't live round the corner. 'Bloody hell, Mum. It's—'

'Lisa!' she interrupted me. Big Idea was written across her forehead. 'I've had a brilliant idea!'

Chapter Fourteen

Gesualdo 1588

Lavender. When the small blue buds are just about to burst open it is harvested and much time is spent refilling the little linen bags that freshen the closets. The scent is so strong at the beginning that we would work out in the open air if the weather allowed.

It was this scent that first roused me from my swoon, or maybe it was the sound of familiar voices. When I opened my eyes, I found I was lying in my old room. Signora Carlino was speaking.

'Don't fret so,' she said. 'She will be awake soon.'

'But how do you know?'

Ahh ... Salvo! Such delight coursed through me.

'It is only a little shock,' said his mother. 'She's young and strong. You'll see.'

I cleared my throat and found it sore, but the sound alerted them and Salvo was by my side in a second.

'Silvia, you are awake!'

'Yes, yes. So I am.' And I laughed to see his expression, although in truth I could not have been more pleased. I began to raise myself to sitting but found my neck to be very stiff and lay back down. The pain of it reminded me why I was there and I put my hand to my throat. 'What happened?' I said. ' I remember Don Carlo ... I thought ...'

Salvo's face darkened. 'Don't think of it.'

'Help me up, Salvo. I would rather sit than lie.'

For some reason we both looked towards his mother, but her head was turned away. Salvo smiled and slid his arm under my shoulders. Sudden heat in my cheeks betrayed me, for I liked the feeling of his arm around me very much and found it hard to look directly at his handsome face. I felt his lips press softly against my forehead. Of course, I would have jumped away at once had I not such a stiffness in my neck.

'There was a great noise when I fell,' I said, once upright on the edge of the bed. 'A clattering and the sound of clashing notes. Did I break the spinet?'

'No, you didn't break anything.' He smiled. 'But it was most fortuitous for you that the wooden crucifix fastened to the front of the gallery should choose to fall on the harpsichord underneath at that very moment.'

'Oh!' I realised his meaning in an equal moment. 'But...'

He put his finger to his lips. 'Perhaps it was a sign,' he said, sounding very serious. 'And it may be that Don Carlo believes so too, for I know he has been much at prayer since.'

'Well,' I said. 'I am very glad of that.' Signora Carlino and Salvo both laughed in similar fashion, for I spoke with great feeling. 'But, Salvo,' I said, remembering our earlier meeting. 'You have some news. What is it?'

Signora Carlino approached and gave Salvo a light cuff to the ear. 'What? You have not told her yet?'

He looked aggrieved. 'And exactly when was I supposed to?'

'I think you should tell me now,' I said, 'as I'd like to go and see my family again.' I stood up rather sharply and felt the ache in my neck once more.

'I shall escort you,' said Salvo, catching my arm beneath the elbow, 'and tell you on the way. We can sing that song too. How did it go?'

Really! Could anyone be more vexing?

'Well?' I said, once we'd left the castle's shadow. 'Will you tell me?'

'I might,' he said. 'If I may steal another kiss.'

This time I sidestepped his attention. 'Now, now, Salvo Carlino, I won't have you making free in such a way. I was in a weakened state earlier, but now I am quite recovered.'

He looked crestfallen but it was not in his nature to stay that way for long. We had only walked a couple of steps before he spoke again. 'You are to go back to Napoli tomorrow,' he said. And then, sounding extremely pleased with himself, added, 'and I am to take you in the wagon.'

'Oh!' I was surprised, early the next morning, when only Salvo appeared. 'Just you?'

'Yes, just me. How fortunate that I was going anyway, for I do believe Don Carlo might have sent you by yourself on a mule. After yesterday he is quite anxious for you to be gone.' Salvo jumped down, picked up my box and put it in the wagon. 'What a good thing it was that a crucifix came to hand! The Prince is so very concerned for his immortal soul.'

'Salvo! That is a very wicked thing to say. Are you not concerned for yours?'

'Of course, but when did I ever do anyone harm?' He took my arm and helped me up so I could sit beside him. Not that I needed help, but why refuse it? 'Although,' he said, 'I should say that Pietro told me the Prince was merely trying to find the source of your voice's quality.'

'Quality! Of a demented dove, perhaps. I could hardly make a sound by the end.' I shivered, even though the day was bright and warm. 'So why are you going?' I asked, not wanting to think back. 'If not just to take me.'

The wagon swayed from side to side. My small box knocked against the two other, larger boxes, first one, then the other, time and again. After a while I began to believe a phantom drummer travelled along with us and I wondered what it was that Salvo was taking all the way to Napoli. 'What are we carrying?'

'All that I possess,' he said, cheerily, and as if quite normal.

'But why?'

'I am going to live with my uncle in Chiaia.'

'But why?'

'My mother thinks it is a good idea,' he said with a shrug, 'and now that she is going to live with her sister—'

'Is she?'

'Yes, didn't she tell you?'

89

'No,' I said. *Signora Carlino had been more than kind to me after Don Carlo had been so keen to explore my 'quality'. I think she felt responsible for bringing me to the castle in the first place, although I had put myself square in front of the idea. 'Is it because of her eyes?'*

Now Salvo was surprised. 'I thought she hadn't told anyone.'

'It is not difficult to see if you are looking. Both at her eyes and at her sewing. And, Salvo, while I think your mother likes me, if nothing was amiss she would already be in Napoli with Donna Maria, not mending the linen back at Gesualdo.'

The wagon jolted suddenly on a dip in the road and Salvo's arm was the only thing I found to steady myself. His hand closed over mine. 'But what will you do at your uncle's? Has Don Carlo no need for you at the castle anymore?'

'He may have, but it is time I made the most of my talents. Pietro isn't going anywhere else and his is the only position I would desire. Besides, I don't like Don Carlo. He is more strange and demanding than most and after yesterday ...' He squeezed my hand and my heart gave a little skip. 'So I am going to Napoli. My uncle is a stonemason and he thinks I have a little talent in the arts myself.'

'A little?' I searched amongst the oddments in my pouch and brought out the carving he had given me. 'This shows more than a little talent.'

'Ah,' he said. 'I'm glad to see you have it still. My uncle is to have me as an apprentice. I'm too old really but he is kind and my mother's brother. I want to make something of myself, Silvia, especially if I am to one day take a wife.'

He looked at me very earnestly then and I felt the heat of a blush.

'How hot the sun is now,' I said.

The wagon slowed our journey almost to a crawl and we

did the poor pony a favour by walking beside her. I was reminded of the times Salvo accompanied me from the castle to the village, and I put my mind to working out exactly how long ago it was. But then, glancing sideways, I took in the neat trim of his beard, and realised that there was no true measure for the turning of children into adults.

The road near Gesualdo was very quiet but as we approached the city, more horses and merchants clogged the way ahead. I knew we were close when the swifts and seagulls began to wheel above.

'We shall see the sea soon.' I clambered back up onto the wagon to get a better view, trying to stand, although the swaying was precarious. 'Have you ever seen it, Salvo?'

'Take care, Silvia! Do not stand like that! You'll ...'

And I did. Perhaps one of the wheels hit a large stone or fell in a rut, I don't know, but the next thing I was tumbling through the air. Most fortunately in the direction of Salvo's strong arms.

'Tut tut, my dear,' he said as if to a child. 'How many more times am I going to have to save you?'

I was quite without breath so could not immediately reply. He clasped me firmly and there was no slight hiccup of my heart, but a wild knocking in my chest – perhaps from the fall – but it did not abate when I looked up into his eyes, for their usual twinkling had changed and was now charged with something far more fiery.

'Ah, Silvia,' he said, his voice serious and urgent. 'Am I worthy of reward?'

I could not speak but neither could I turn away from his gaze. His face came closer and closer and all sense of myself was lost as he put his lips to mine.

I would remember that day for all of my life. So soon after the horror of Don Carlo when I thought my life was done, it began afresh and full of possibility. But who does not remember their first kiss? When the space between each narrows, thirsting with delight. I would remember that I was wearing my favourite crimson bodice that I had embroidered with daisies. Salvo's jerkin was rough against my skin but his undershirt was fine cotton, its stitching as neat as anything I could do.

But as we descended into the city, all the day's joy began to leach away from me. Salvo grew quiet too. The charm of the day was over. By the time we reached Palazzo San Severo the night had come. Salvo's new life lay ahead, though we parted with promises. I had thought little of Donna Maria while I was away but when I arrived at the palace, Laura came to greet me with the news that Don Fabrizio Carafa, Duke of Andria was in attendance on my mistress.

I looked over my shoulder to where the wagon was turning a corner. Salvo was already out of sight. I took a deep breath as a shiver passed through me from head to foot, the cause of which, I was quite sure, had nothing to do with the chill in the evening air.

Chapter Fifteen

If ever I am in need of any marble, then I will go to Naples.

We landed in the dark so missed seeing the bay spread out beneath us. In 'Arrivals' the first thing I saw was a huge billboard picturing the statue of David. He had a few bits missing and the slogan underneath written, for some inexplicable reason, in English: *For all your marble needs.* I imagined him sitting beside me on the plane home.

The lack of sleep, large amounts of coffee and brandy – to get me on any plane – all contributed nicely to my feeling that the world was a surreal place and I was in it, in a very out of it, sort of way. Perfect for accompanying my mother on her little holiday for I would float over the top of any difficulties. The warmth of the air was delicious. I stood at the luggage carousel and marvelled at the soothing nature of circling suitcases.

'Lisa! Over here.' My mother already had our luggage by her feet and stood with a clutch of elderly folk clustered round a young man waving a red flag.

'Am I being sent off so soon?' I said. Blank faces all round.

My mother hissed,' I hope you're going to behave,' as we were loaded onto the coach, 'and what the blazes have you got in your suitcase? It weighs a ton.'

I didn't start singing and I wasn't sick either. To be honest, our fellow holidaymakers weren't very inspiring and I dozed on the coach only to feel truly terrible when we were turfed out an hour or so later. I had that horrible shivery feeling, mouth like a mouldy flannel and stiff as hell from too much sitting. But even in that state, I caught the scent of lavender and lemons in the air and, once the coach's engine was turned off, a blissful quiet.

Whether I thought of Mollie before I passed out between some very welcome clean sheets, I can't honestly remember.

'Wake up! Come on, Lisa. Wake up.'

Mum stood over me and I had a sudden worry that I should be getting ready for school. A second later and she'd ripped back the curtains.

'Oh, my,' she gasped. 'Oh, my … oh, my goodness!'

I had to get up then. She used to do that a lot when I was little and couldn't see over walls. It's really irritating. But when I got to the window, what did I find myself saying? 'Oh, my …'

Breathtaking? Splendid? Tremendous? Yes, our view was all of those things. Sorrento is almost at one end of the Bay of Naples and we looked directly across the sea to where the most thrilling feature in the area, Vesuvius, rose up to the right of the distant city. My first sighting of a proper volcano, and from grey and rainy Exeter to this sparkly blue place in one night. Wow!

I had a sharp pang of Mollie-missing. She'd want us to go there at once and climb to the top. My mother wasn't decrepit yet, and she was one of the youngest in our party. I couldn't imagine the others would be up to climbing a mountain.

'It is on the itinerary,' Mum said. She held it out. 'Of course, it's all voluntary. We could just sit on the terrace and sip Limoncello if we wanted to.'

I didn't want to. One of the reasons my case was so heavy was that I had bought a couple of books about Gesualdo with me. It was the opportunity to pay a visit to the scene of the crime that finally made me agree to come. That, Mollie's insistence and the way everything had slid so very smoothly into the correct slots. Michael was away in Bayreuth but Mollie suggested Jon might like to come and stay in the flat while I was away.

Of course, I said no. The conversation about Jon I'd had with Sophie was pushed way back in my mind, especially since two-faced Thomas had erected a few more props under my suspicions about men. But after a few hours badgering by both Mollie and Mum, I rang Sophie.

'It's only for four nights,' I said.

'Me?' she said. 'Have Mollie to stay? Yes. That's lovely. Of course, I will. I'm very flattered, Lisa.'

'Oh, phew,' I said. 'That's fantastic. Problem solved.'

'But,' she sounded anxious, 'I don't think I can take her to work every day.'

'I'm going to ring Jon,' I said. 'And there's, Jessica, her schoolfriend too. I expect she can go there for a day.'

'Jessie is going to Weymouth,' Mollie said, when I'd put the phone down.

'Is she? Oh well. Let's see what Jon has to say.'

He thought it not only a 'cool' thing to do, but also a 'gas'. He'd take her to Paignton Zoo, the movies, busking...

'What?'

'Only kidding.'

His apparent pleasure at being asked meant I mentally removed one prop, that's all, but the plan was going from strength to strength. Even more so when Sophie rang back.

'How about I come and stay in your flat?' she said. 'Only next week is when they're coming to replace the central heating. I'll have floorboards up and no water or heating. God knows how long it'll take.'

Brilliant. Mollie was a bit disappointed but I was glad. If you asked me, Sophie's house full of workmen meant many accidents not just waiting to happen but eagerly jostling in the queue.

I prayed the nightmare was an isolated incident. Newspaper headlines that read *Nightmare Child Abandoned By Mother*, and *Neighbours in Screaming Child Rescue*, flashed across my mind, but I was outnumbered three to one. It was Mollie's idea that I record a voice message on her iPod. She suggested that we played that bloody *Lion King* song in the background, then if she got upset in the night, Sophie should put it on. It would be sure to soothe her. We were all impressed by this idea. Perhaps instead of being an opera singer, my daughter might grow up to be a psychiatrist or behavioural psycho-whatsit.

After a couple of paracetamol at breakfast, I felt altogether better. While Mum and I drank coffee on the terrace under the mimosa trees, Mollie replied to my vastly expensive text. *Having the best time! Mxxx.* In that case, I would not feel guilty and I thrust the nagging anxiety about my HIV test results into a far corner at the back of my mind.

The package bit of the holiday was a whole new experience for me. I hadn't been on holiday proper since Michael days and then we usually self-catered in England or camped in France. When I actually read the itinerary that Mum had waved at me, it struck me as punishing for someone of my age, let alone those with dodgy hips and high blood pressure. On the other hand there was a lot to see and if another trip wouldn't be along for some time – or even, ever – then why not pack in as much as possible? Pompeii, Capri, Vesuvius, the Amalfi Coast … Naples, however, wasn't on the list. I would have to make my own way there.

I'm not sure I could describe the holiday as relaxing. Mum could talk for England and to begin with Thomas's name cropped up frequently, but after a couple of days and due to a budding friendship with Charles – *Lisa, you don't mind sitting behind us on the coach, do you?* – Thomas was signed off. Charles was from Yorkshire. I couldn't decide whether that was a good thing or not. His wife had definitely died a while ago, and while it sounds like a callous thing to say, I was glad.

Missing out on a trip to Pompeii was out of the question. Seen from where we pootled about the ruins, Vesuvius had two peaks. Mum and Charles chatted together, pointing at this and that, reading their guidebook.

I wandered off. It struck me that there were two varieties of tourist: those who were happily amazed by how civilised our forebears were, exclaiming at their cleverness, artistry, and architectural skills. Then there were those who would pause, and whose eyes would turn towards the mountain every third or fourth step. Not with anxiety for their own safety but as if seeking comprehension about how the seemingly impossible had happened, that that over there, could do this over here. I was one of them.

My personal volcano slept uneasily. The letter from the hospital containing my test results was yet to arrive, but there was nothing more powerful than seeing an entire town wiped out in a few hours to remind me of the transience of life.

The trip to Herculaneum the next day began with the trip to the summit of Vesuvius. My Italian is non-existent except for a comprehensive knowledge of musical terms. Piano duettists play either the *primo* (first) part or the *secondo* (second) so I was able to persuade the coach driver that *primo*, I would go to the volcano, but *secondo*, I wanted to go to Naples not Herculaneum. This departure from the norm troubled him. He frowned and gesticulated considerably but eventually agreed to drop me at the *stazione*. So, after two days in Italy, I was beginning to think I could get by.

'Are we really going to the *summit* of Vesuvius?' I said through the gap in the seats, once we were back on the coach.

'That's what it says here. I *told* you.' Mum waved her piece of paper at me and Charles nodded too.

Most of our party looked as if they would find a ladder challenging let alone a mountain. In the event, the coach park was six hundred meters from the summit – a stroll up a clinker path. Walking sticks were for hire. I trusted my youthful legs might be up to it without.

More enterprising even than the walking sticks was the turnstile at the top. Why was I surprised? After all, it is a major tourist attraction. Charitably I thought that maybe they didn't want everyone rushing at once and then tipping over into the crater although I knew that idea was way up high on the naïve/stupid scale. Once we'd parted with considerable euros and gone through, Vesuvius revealed its vertiginous hand. On one side, it spread the world beneath us while on the other we looked down into the crater. No smoke, just steep scree and a few spindly shrubs making an effort.

I felt very insecure, and in attempting to acclimatise to the altitude, found comfort in focusing on the postcards clamped to a stand as wobbly as my knees. They were nearly all bent, because of the feisty breeze that we walked into once through the turnstile. The 1944 eruption taken by an American Air Force pilot was the most impressive even though it was in black and white. It looked up at the mountain as monstrous grey clouds of ash rose above the summit. The strange thing was that snow appeared halfway down the volcano, below the hot rock above.

'Look.' I showed it to Mum. 'I think Mollie will like this one, don't you?'

She shuddered. 'Only if it arrives after we've got home. You'd scare her to death otherwise.'

'I thought I could draw a little arrow saying *We Were Here.*'

'Don't,' she said. 'I don't want to think about it like that.'

Neither did I, but I didn't know how not to.

Charles took Mum's arm and they picked their way round the rim of the crater. I followed, equally gingerly, wishing I had an arm to hold. I was on top of a volcano and my little girl and my little life, for that matter, felt an awfully long way away.

I picked up a fragment of the clinker and thought of all the people that had lived on the slopes of Vesuvius prior to 1631. I'd read more about Gesualdo in the books I'd brought with me. After the murders, two servants had made statements, and a third was mentioned in passing. I wondered what had happened to them all. Another thing I wondered about was the repeated mention of the silk nightdress with the black cuffs and fringing at the bottom. My character in the tableau, Silvia Albana was in charge of the wardrobe. Had she made it?

I put the clinker in my pocket, anxious to do a different sort of digging that afternoon. A copy of the frontispiece was in my bag and I was hoping to find something out about its provenance and how on earth it ended up in a museum in Exeter.

At the Tourist Information Office at Naples central station I bought a little street map and was told it was about a twenty-minute walk to Palazzo Sansevero. It was right next to the church in Piazza San Domenico Maggiore. I suppose in my mind, I thought Naples would be a bit like Florence, the only other Italian city I had visited.

'Walk?' The assistant looked shocked. 'Taxi are outside.'

She tried again, pointing this time to a row of buses. I shook my head and smiled but she tutted, shaking her head much more vigorously. Then she patted my bag and wagged a finger. 'Be careful,' she said. 'Take care.'

Had she filled a syringe with anxiety and shoved it in a vein, her warning could not have been more effective. I left the office with a mind to get a taxi but the sun was shining, the street was broad and the deafening noise of hooters and squealing brakes made me more fearful of wheels than my own feet and an imaginary miscreant. But vehicles can be dangerous to pedestrians as well as passengers. How to get across the road in one piece was a mystery. On a large billboard on the building opposite, I saw the same advert I'd seen at the airport. Wasn't it odd that Italians had adverts in English? *For all your marble needs*. What marble needs? I could only think of gravestones.

The traffic slowed amidst much hooting, shouting and the appearance of raised fists through car windows. I decided to take a chance. But, as my foot left the pavement, both of my arms were gripped tightly from behind. Before I had breath to scream I was dragged back into one of the narrow dark alleys between the shopfronts.

A man's voice growled rapid Italian in my ear. Only two words made any sense.

'*Silenzio*' and *'morte!'*

Chapter Sixteen

Napoli 1588

In Napoli the world had changed. Not for the better either. I could hardly question Donna Maria, so my source of information had to be Laura.

'He arrived here only a little while after you had left for Gesualdo.'

'But how did he know we'd gone?'

Her gaze slid away from mine. 'She sent me,' she said, in a low voice. 'Donna Maria sent me to their house.'

I could hardly believe it. 'What?' *I took both her shoulders in my hands and looked directly in her face.* 'She announced it to Fabrizio's household? To his wife?'

'No!' *She shook me off.* 'They were to borrow the forks.'

Those stupid forks; they should never have been invented. 'And? That's no reason for the Duke to come galloping over.'

'I was told to deliver them to the mistress of the house with a message to say that the children were invited to come and play with Emmanuel now that Don Carlo was away.'

'She invited the children to come and ... play?'

'Yes, that's what I had to say.'

It was an extraordinary strategy, but it had obviously worked. I was surprised she sent Laura though, as witless as ever and even more unkempt since I hadn't been there to straighten her up.

'But why did you go and not a kitchen maid or the nurse?'

Laura's face froze and her jaw twitched near to the ears. She said nothing but shook her head.

'Well?'

'Donna Maria said I looked too stupid not to be believed.'

'I see.' And I did. My mistress had been wise in that regard but only that. 'Now look, Laura,' I said. 'Have you said anything to anyone about this?'

'No, I haven't. But everyone knows he came here.'

'Has she seen him since?'

She said nothing but yes was written all over her face. A chill ran through me and I wished more than anything that I could be with Salvo, riding back and forth between Gesualdo and Napoli without ever arriving at either place.

'Don't say a word, Laura. Not to anyone. Not even me... unless I say so. Now, where is she?'

'Silvia, how glad I am to see you.' Donna Maria greeted me warmly as she alighted from her carriage. 'How was your singing?'

'Not worthy, my lady,' I said. 'Don Carlo was afraid I lacked stamina in that direction.'

'Is that so?'

'Yes, my lady.' I told her the story of the crucifix falling down, but left out the hand behind it.

She gave me a long look, perhaps to see if I had sprouted horns or grown a serpent's tail. But then she laughed and shone the light of her smile upon me as usual. We climbed the stairs to her chamber and found Laura wrestling with a ruff which had been sat upon by one of the house dogs.

'Will Don Carlo be staying at Gesualdo for long?' Donna Maria's offhand tone was no disguise as to the purpose of her remark.

'I don't know. He was much at prayer when I left.'

She laughed and it wasn't pleasant. 'Perhaps we should send him Laura. They could pray for better things together.'

I didn't reply but suggested to Laura that she took the ruff down to the press.

'My lady,' I said, once she had left the room. 'I have heard—'

'Yes? What have you heard?'

'It's just that ...' What could I say? Salvo was right. We were vulnerable to the vagaries of the wealthy. It also seemed to me, however, that women were equally vulnerable to men, whatever their wealth.

'Don't look so worried, Silvia.' Her voice was silk. 'You have nothing to fear.'

'But what about Don Carlo?' I said. 'What if he finds out?'

'Why should he? We shall be very careful. Fabrizio is no fool and neither am I. Besides, Silvia, you shall help us.'

Something cold crawled over my flesh then, almost worse than the hands of Don Carlo.

Later, I found Laura weeping with frustration over the ruff. It was beyond repair and I set her to unpick the stitching. The fabric needed to be washed and re-starched for it was a fact that every piece of cloth Laura touched wearied from the experience. She was very good at bed linen and hangings, but I always pressed my own clothes and those of Donna Maria.

'Tell me everything,' I said, 'and don't leave out the slightest detail. If we are to keep this secret, there should be no discrepancy in what we say.'

'She hates me anyway,' Laura sulked. 'Why should I care if Don Carlo does find out?'

'Laura! Are you mad? Don't ever say such a thing. Would you put your hand in a fire and not expect to be burnt? You would be turned out of this house in a trice. Imagine,' I pointed to the door. 'Imagine walking through there with nothing but your own possessions. No food, no roof when it rains ...'

She began to cry, so I think she got the idea.

'We went to Chiaia.' She blew her nose wetly into her handkerchief. 'The Duke had found somewhere for them to go – the pavilion in Don Garzia's garden.'

The name wasn't entirely unknown to me but I couldn't place the man in my mind. 'Who's he?'

'He's a Spaniard. That's why there's nobody there. I heard the Duke say he'd gone back to Toledo.'

'That's something to be thankful for, I suppose. I wish Don Carlo had gone with him.'

It wasn't until the following week that a further visit to Chiaia was made. A servant of Don Fabizio's was the go-between and we set out in the carriage with a view to inspecting the gardens that Donna Maria was so enamoured with. I persuaded my lady that Laura should accompany us, although neither was keen, but I was determined that I shouldn't be left alone in a strange garden with no one but the carriage driver and Don Fabrizio's servant for company.

I'd heard all about Don Fabrizio by then for Donna Maria could think of nothing else. He was fierce but tender, the way he undressed her, so slowly, he too shivering with the sensation of silk against flesh. She'd never known a man whose whole body was as sensitive.

Where did my thoughts go when she carried on so? There was only one place. Salvo. I had not seen him since we came back from Gesualdo even though he promised he would come and visit.

'Is it not a fine garden, Silvia?' Donna Maria said, hurrying us through the scented groves and past a group of stone cherubs frolicking in a water trough.

'Yes, my lady. It would merit a gentle stroll rather than a run.'

'You may both stroll all you like, for the next hour at least. Just as long as you do not stray from within site of the pavilion. It would not do for us to be disturbed.'

The pavilion was a much grander place than I had imagined, and the pillars across the front gave it the appearance of an ancient temple.

I was to enter first to check that all was well. I did not question this, but had a moment of hesitation when my hand pressed against the door. Perhaps Don Fabrizio was not the god I had been led to believe but, in fact, a demon.

I had to push hard for the door was heavy and the hinges stiff but then, with a loud creak, the handle flew from my grasp and I fell forward into the arms of the handsomest man in the whole of Italy.

Even in the sudden gloom and even though I had already had sight of Don Fabrizio at the feast, it was a new wonder. For here, close to, was a man with apparent and considerable expectations. At that moment, had my lady not been with me, I might have found myself in danger, for I am not made of stone.

He lacked Salvo's sweetness of expression, as the broad brow and downward gaze spoke only of authority and power, but the air about him was as if he were bathed in honey and I was an unfortunate fly. Later, I thought it must have been the quality of his gaping doublet. The gold threads shining so; I must have been dazzled.

When Donna Maria entered behind me, the air fairly shook with anticipation and quickly I left them, imagining their greeting almost as if two great forces were joining in battle rather than love, for both were formidable.

Laura and I did stroll about, but there was no settlement in the heart for me. Even the sweet scent of the frangipani could not please, for we were party to a folly of colossal proportions and I was more afraid than even in the moment when Don Carlo had pressed his cold fingers about my neck. For then the real fear had been brief, and if my demise had been the outcome, a few people might have been sad for a while, but no household would have been upset, no marriages torn asunder, no revenge sought.

'We must never speak of this, Laura,' I said. 'Do you understand how important it is that we keep these meetings to ourselves?' She merely shrugged and I had to take her by the shoulders in order to give her a little shake. 'I mean it,' I said, trying to get her to look me in the eye. 'This is the biggest secret you will ever hold and if you're not careful, it may even be your last. That's how important it is.' She looked at me stupidly and I reached into my pouch for a handkerchief. As far as I could tell, that time I'd only

managed to make myself cry.

I lay awake at night listening to Laura. The familiarity of her snoring now something of a comfort rather than a trial. The only thing to look forward to was a visit from Salvo. The note from him, which Pietro had delivered, was in the hand-sized fold I had stitched into the seam of my skirt. I'd made it especially for the little kitten that Salvo had carved for me. I liked that both were hidden away, although the contents of the note I couldn't keep secret. Donna Maria depended on my presence more and more. There was no one of her ilk that she could confide in, and I prayed hard every day that when Father Strozzi took confession he would be as blinded by her beauty as every other man in Napoli. Not that she considered her love for Fabrizio sinful at all, although she knew its danger.

It seemed to me that love was the worst of illnesses. If only she would come out in spots or be raging in a delirium then we could all have a little peace.

'Yes, yes,' she murmured when I asked if I could go and see the street singers that were to perform on the quay. 'Don't be long though.'

'I may be some hours, my lady.'

She looked up from her book of poems. 'You're not going alone, are you?'

'No. Salvo Carlino has asked me to accompany him.'

'Salvo?' A frown creased her forehead, then cleared. 'Oh, yes, that boy. I remember. Very well. Make sure you are back by evening prayers.'

I saw him first. We had arranged to meet on the steps of San Domenico and he was sitting near the top. My heart lifted at once and I couldn't stop smiling. The stretch of it felt quite strange. I ran up the steps almost laughing, for I had been set free! What a relief it was to be out from underneath the roof of San Severo. The day was fine, the sky blue and when he saw me, Salvo looked so happy I nearly cried.

'There you are,' he said, catching my arm beneath the elbow and leading me across the piazza. 'I was worried you might not come.'

'Sorry,' I said. 'There was an argument about who should refill the pillows. I didn't want Laura to do it as it will only make her ill.'

'Laura Scala? I'm surprised that cough hasn't been the death of her.'

'It might be one day, and soon if she has to deal with all those feathers, but the cook didn't want the kitchen girl doing it either.'

Salvo squeezed my arm. 'That's very kind, Silvia. I remember you being rather impatient with Laura.'

'Yes, I was, but now I think she's my only friend,' I said, miserably. 'Oh please, let's not talk about her. I don't want to think about any of them this afternoon.' I waved my arm in the direction of the palazzo.

'What? Not even the illustrious Donna Maria?'

'Especially not her, Salvo. For I swear she will undo us all. Don Carlo is not a man to be easy and forgiving, is he? I began to be afraid he wished me harm after that day with the singing. Then I thought Donna Maria might protect me, but ... but—' I broke off, as the true terror of my situation became too much.

Salvo pulled me close to him for we were in a narrow and crowded street. There were many people going to the quay for the entertainments and they came on wagons, donkeys and by foot in great numbers. Groups of young men with too much wine inside them. Sailors from foreign lands with black faces, old women in black with sticks, cursing at being jostled by noisy children dressed in costumes: a fox, a bear and a small duck girl. We were all pushed along past stalls with bright blue and yellow awnings selling everything to fill the stomach with deliciousness, judging by the aromas. There was shouting of names and news, both good and bad, and then a scent of flowers and for a coin, Salvo bought a sprig of mimosa

*and lavender. We slipped into a small pool of sunshine
between two high walls, just to one side of the crowds, and
he tucked the stems into my bodice.*

*'Listen, Silvia,' he said. 'I want you to promise me
something.'*

*Perhaps it was the perfume that made me feel a little
lightheaded. The touch of Salvo's fingertip and his
nearness, the scent of him. I was reminded of the bright
clean smell of the cedar linen chests but there was
something spicy about it, exotic and compelling. I didn't
want to draw away. For a moment, when I looked up into
his face I thought he might be about to kiss me but his
expression was earnest and there was much anxiety in his
tawny eyes.*

'Yes?'

*'If there's any trouble or you feel in danger, I want you
to go straight to the nuns of San Domenico. Don't stop to
go back for anything. They will be kind. I will mention it to
Sister Caterina when I go there next.'*

*'No, don't,' I said, alarmed. 'Don't say anything.
Nobody must suspect anything is wrong.'*

*'It's too late for that, my dearest, there are already
little voices in the air that Donna Maria is behaving as
badly as her husband is strange.' His hand flew about in a
flapping, chattering gesture till it dived towards me,
opened out and gently stroked my cheek. 'Promise me?'
And he leaned forward and kissed me lightly on the lips.*

*I might have promised him almost anything then for the
whole of me lit with pleasure. 'Yes,' I said, my voice
catching, 'only ...'*

'Only?'

'Only if you kiss me again.'

*At prayers, I could only think of Salvo and our afternoon
of freedom. In my hand I cradled a small carving of a
swan, with its neck curling behind to rest on its feathery
back, a companion for my little kitten.*

*'Once you were as jumpy as a kitten,' Salvo had said,
when he gave me the parting gift, 'but now you are a*

beautiful swan. Don't forget to fly, Silvia, if the water becomes dangerous.'

He had carved the swan in olive wood such that a tiny knot appeared like a small eye that followed wherever you went, and I thought that in some way I might be looked after if I kept it with me. The singers we heard down on the quayside sang of a gentle white swan: Il bianco e dolce cigno, *by Signor Arcadelt, about how it died singing. It was beautiful but gave me the shudders. They sang of dying repeatedly, but I knew your body can't die more than once. They really meant the peak of pleasure that happens in the act of love. Everyone knew it, but nobody said anything.*

I thought of Salvo again and my heart skipped a beat. Loving was dangerous, it seemed to me. Whatever the singers meant, love and death were far too intertwined for my liking.

Chapter Seventeen

It wasn't *silenzio* the man kept saying, but I couldn't quite hear correctly because of the truck that had mounted the pavement in order to overtake on the inside. It thundered past the entrance to the alley, over the exact spot where I'd been standing only a second ago.

'*Attento! Stia attento!*' The grip on my arms fell away and I turned to find an elderly man shaking his head with an expression full of concern.

'*Stia attento,*' he said. Be careful – a phrase I'd learnt from the woman in the tourist office.

I thanked him profusely and he escorted me to the crossing and made sure I was safely across. He smiled then disappeared into another of the alleys whose mouths seemed so menacing, but perhaps acted as refuges more often than not. Okay, I was on the right side of the road and apart from feeling a little shaken, it was time to get my bearings.

From the summit of Vesuvius, the city of Naples had appeared as an unfolded map. Lucky for me that it had been a clear day, because I could also make out Sorrento at the far point on the opposite side of the bay. And what a difference a stretch of sea made. When we were lounging in the first class luxury of our hotel, I kept thinking of the old song, *Come Back to Sorrento* – especially as I couldn't decide between the languid and sexy Dean Martin recording and Mario Lanza's, the more authentic and spine-tingling operatic rendition. Who wouldn't want to come back? Everywhere was beautiful, scented with citrus blossom, stylish and clean.

The only thing I had in my head once I left the broad road on my way to Piazza San Domenico Maggiore was 'See Naples and die!' My understanding of the phrase was that Naples was so beautiful, your life was fulfilled by the mere fact of seeing it. But if you died before you'd seen it, well ... your life was a poor thin thing. I was sure that *bits* of Naples must be beautiful but with the ribbon of blue sky above the high buildings getting ever narrower, and graffiti becoming the decoration of choice on every door and wall, in spite of the heat, I didn't feel warm towards the city.

I'd been glad to leave Mum with Charles, thinking that I wouldn't have to keep an eye on her, but began to wish she was here to keep an eye on me. Both of them would have been even better. Whiney two and three-wheeled scooters zipped about and I clutched my bag to my chest. At a fork, I dithered and thought to look at the map, only to have two men appear from the gloom of a doorway and approach. I set off with renewed purpose and a prayer, having no clue whether I was going in the right direction or not. But lo! Out of the dark and into a dazzling sun-lit piazza with a sign on the wall that read Piazza San Domenico Maggiore. Hallelujah!

It wasn't exactly a square of grace and beauty. The frontage of San Domenico Maggiore, which took up the whole of one side, was the most peculiar mishmash of styles, as if a child had been in charge of works, and had stuck together bits of other churches and thrown in a few castellations and a cinema hoarding. At the bottom of the steps, café tables huddled in the shade of half a dozen large brollies. I put on my sunglasses, pulled my hat down almost to my nose and thought I'd risk a cappuccino.

All Italian waiters are handsome and all cappuccinos drunk under an Italian sun are actually intoxicating. Some things are self-evident. On the table next to me a couple of elderly women sipped espressos and talked rapid incomprehensible Italian, all the while gesticulating acts of what appeared to be murder. I felt very safe in their vicinity and rummaged in my bag for the photocopies from the book about Gesualdo that I had brought with me.

The Palazzo Sangro di Sansevero, where Gesualdo and Donna Maria D'Avalos spent so much of their time, isn't obvious. But when I looked at the picture – an old blurry photo – I realised I was sitting only a couple of metres from the front door, which was just round the corner in a narrow street. Every single window in the palace looked onto a blank wall, although I supposed that behind the tall but closed doors under the arch, was the usual courtyard. A tranquil haven away from the busy street. I wondered if San Severo was ever tranquil. Like so many of the grander houses, it had been converted into a hotel.

There was no mention of Gesualdo anywhere, which rather surprised me. I would have thought a gruesome tale would make a good tourist attraction. I'd read one account that said the bodies were thrown down onto the church steps and a little later, walking into the church, I checked the steps but there were no four-hundred-year-old blood stains to be seen. I looked over my shoulder too for some reason, perhaps thinking of *A Room with a View* fleetingly, but nobody was being stabbed. Just as well, it would have been more than freaky if they were.

San Domenico Maggiore wasn't exactly the Tardis, but I did get a hell of a surprise when I went in. Rather like splitting a rock and finding it full of sparkling crystals; the interior made me gasp. Not that it really sparkled, but it was of cathedral proportions and glowed with gold. I was beginning to get neck ache from admiring the gold-framed bosses on the ceiling above the nave when I bumped into something. A somebody, actually.

'I'm so sor—' I began. A man. Older than me by quite a bit, not a great deal of hair and with a corduroy jacket and a stick, but a nice face. Or at least, not a face that appeared hostile.

'No, no,' he said. 'My fault entirely.'

Thank goodness. 'English!' I blurted for some reason. It felt like such a relief.

'Well, I don't know about that.' He laughed. 'I'm from the wrong side of Hadrian's Wall to be called English.'

'Oh, yes,' I said. There was no mistaking the Scottish burr. 'But I'm still sorry, it wasn't your fault at all.'

'I wouldn't dream of arguing with such a pretty lady,' he said, so very charmingly that I couldn't help blushing.

We were both whispering and suddenly there was an

awkward moment. It was rather like seeing an acquaintance walking towards you in Sainsbury's and realising that you're going to keep meeting them in every aisle after that. Would this man be round every pillar in San Domenico Maggiore?

'I wonder though,' he said, looking almost embarrassed, 'would you mind if we had a chat? Can I buy you a wee coffee or something to eat?' He said it so earnestly I took a step back, but then he smiled. 'Don't get me wrong, but it's such a joy to be able to talk to someone without the dreadfully exhausting effort of translating it into Italian. The name's Duncan. Duncan Grant.' He held out his hand and I shook it.

'Lisa Barr.'

'Oh, a *Barr*. There's a few of them in Scotland.'

'Aberdeen, I'm told. My ex-husband's family.'

We did a tour of the church first. I was still slightly fizzing from the cappuccino I'd had, and also didn't want to get too distracted from my quest.

'I have only *heard* of Gesualdo,' said Duncan, when I told him why I was there, 'and know nothing about him.'

'It's quite a story: lust, betrayal, murder, the usual ingredients. But quite honestly,' I shrugged and gestured vaguely at the various chapels on either side of the nave as we strolled along, 'I'm on a fool's errand here. This was where Gesualdo married Maria D'Avalos but there's no record of where she was buried and Gesualdo is in the church of the Gesù Nuovo.'

'I'm surprised you didn't go there instead of here.'

I laughed and it echoed a bit too loudly. There weren't that many people about, but we happened to be passing one of the church officials. He frowned and put his finger to his lips.

'Oh, no, I had to come here,' I whispered. 'We're only a few feet from where the murder took place. And there's a story – made up I'm sure – that a monk committed necrophilia on the church steps.'

'Good grief.'

'Didn't you feel a cold shiver as you walked up them?'

We'd been walking side by side, but he turned towards me and I could see he was wondering if I was serious.

'Don't look so worried,' I said. 'I didn't either. If anywhere is haunted then it's the palace round the corner, but I'm not one for that sort of th … ow!' I'd smacked the corner of a pew. 'Bloody hell.'

'Oh dear.' Duncan took my elbow. 'Is it all right?'

'Yes, yes. No problem.' I rubbed my arm vigorously. 'Probably those vengeful spirits I offended.' We sauntered on, past the Chapel of St Martin, which housed the Carafa family monument and where Fabrizio was buried.

'Shall we get that coffee now?' I suggested, tired of the church's lofty oppression. 'You can tell me what you're doing in this part of the world.'

I liked Duncan. Not in a like *like* way, but he was easy to be with and relaxed even though I'd only just met him. There was no angst about him, none apparent anyway. Speaking poor Italian hardly counted.

'Me?' he said. 'I'm on a mission too as it happens, although nobody got murdered in my chap's story. Same era as yours though and surprising really as the Inquisition had it in for him for a long time.'

We left the piazza on the opposite side from where I had arrived, and immediately I got the impression of being in a better part of town. The air had taken on a balmy quality, not as sweet as Sorrento but not smelly either. There was less graffiti and rubbish and we sat outside a little cafe in the shade, tacitly agreeing not to mind the heart-stopping roar from the scooters that regularly screamed around the corner only a few feet from our table.

We were so engrossed with each other's stories that two coffees and a glass of wine went by. Then, as another noisy bike almost clipped the leg of my chair, it occurred to me that I had no idea what the time was and in a sudden panic, I looked at my watch.

Duncan raised an eyebrow. 'Meeting someone?'

'Only the hydrofoil back to Sorrento. It's okay though, I have an hour and a half. I need to get back for dinner, otherwise my mother will alert Interpol.'

Duncan was researching the life of Giambattista Della Porta, a Neapolitan scientist, dramatist, and writer of books on just about everything, including cryptography, horticulture and optics.

'He lived to eighty?' I put my cup down on its saucer. 'That's ancient for then. I wonder if Gesualdo knew him.'

'I wouldn't be surprised. Della Porta certainly came to San Domenico Maggiore. He was part of an academy that met there in 1589. Chances are your man saw one of his plays.'

'Probably did. The murders took place in 1590.' We were delighted at the coincidence. 'Did he publish anything, your man?' I brought out the photocopies from my bag. 'Look at this. It's the frontispiece of a madrigal book that's turned up in Exeter Museum.'

'Good Lord,' said Duncan. 'That's one of the best I've ever seen.'

'Have you seen many like this then?'

'I've seen a few, yes. Della Porta published all sorts of things but the frontispieces have always been benign. Fanciful, yes but not macabre like this.'

'I'm trying to find out about it. Who, why and how did it end up in Exeter?'

'Well, what a good job it is you've met me!' Duncan said, not a little pleased.

'Really? You know about this sort of thing?'

'Nothing at all, but I know a man who does. There's a little shop in the Piazzetta Nilo that specialises in antiquarian books. I went there only this morning. Why don't you take it to show them? We can go now.' He swallowed the last of his coffee, wiped his mouth with a quick flourish of his napkin and waved at the waiter. 'Although,' he said, looking sheepish, 'I'm afraid you'll have to do all the talking.'

The man in the shop was suspicious. It was as if I'd taken in an old sketch to an art expert and it turned out to be by Leonardo. I felt rather glad I'd only taken a photocopy otherwise I might have feared for our lives. Communication was tortuous and there was much arm waving and repeated phrases that meant nothing to me. Eventually, he phoned a friend.

'*Cinque minuti,*' he said, holding up five fingers so even I got it.

While waiting, Duncan and I browsed and found a small volume of madrigals by Monteverdi, but the frontispiece was a melee of cherubs and muses, no demons at all.

The friend turned out to be the boss, Signor Pace – more Al Pacino than Marlon Brando – a man in his sixties. He spoke measured English with a very attractive accent. When he saw the frontispiece, he was as taken aback as everyone else.

'You have the original?'

'Yes. Well, not me, Exeter Museum in England has it.'

He nodded, took a small eyeglass from his pocket and began an examination. Duncan and I exchanged glances. A solemn turn had been taken and I could feel my heart beating faster than usual. All that coffee. Signor Pace muttered under his breath, in Italian of course, and every now and then the assistant, who had busied himself shuffling a few bits of paper, gave us a sharp look. I felt like jumping up and down and shouting: Well? Well? Tell us …

The atmosphere in the shop reminded me of Robert's house, musty and bookish, due to the rows of leather bound volumes that lined the walls. It didn't look as if Signor Pace and his assistant had opened some of them for a long time. A clock on the wall struck the half past. I had another hour before the boat.

After five interminable minutes, Signor Pace offered me the eyeglass. 'Look here,' he said pointing, 'at the flames of hell. The letters *C*, the ampersand and *P*?'

What a difference magnification made! The workmanship was truly astonishing. A tiny pile of books being consumed by the flames, and various musical instruments, a lute and a viol. I hadn't even noticed them before, let alone the letters.

'Yes, yes. I see.'

He pointed to the bottom of the *C*, 'this say it is from after 1600. Before this date, we know the *C* is plain. Here, the letter surface is not quite flat and the ink makes a little pool.'

We were talking about a millimetre at most but still, I could see what he meant.

'Do you know who did the engraving?'

'Ah …' he shrugged. 'The quality? Yes, I make a guess. But the subject? I don't know.' He sighed deeply and turned to his assistant. They spoke together in extremely rapid Italian. I looked at the clock again and at Duncan.

'I'll have to go soon.'

Duncan looked at his watch and frowned. 'Ask him if he could find out more for you?'

'Good idea.' But before I got the chance, Signor Pace asked if he could photocopy my photocopy. If I left him my email address, he would do some research and let me know the results. There was a photocopier in the back room, it would not take long. Of course I agreed, and wrote down my address for both Signor Pace and Duncan, who produced a well-thumbed reporter's notebook for the purpose.

There were some high decibel curses from the back room. Perhaps the paper was jammed? After much thumping, whirring and the manic percussion solo most printers and copiers perform when they're getting ready, I heard the sound of a successful print.

I was ready to run, but Signor Pace put his hand on my arm when I picked up the copy from the counter.

'Please,' he said, his eyes flicking around from my face, the shop, the street. 'I'm wondering if you have had any …' he seemed to search for the word, '… troubles lately?'

'Troubles?' It was out of the blue, as if someone had told me I looked ill, when I felt perfectly well. 'What do you mean?'

The assistant said something under his breath but Signor Pace hushed him. 'I am not alarming you,' he said, although that was exactly what he'd done, 'but a frontispiece like this, is not at all, how you say, everyday?'

'I should think not.' I said it louder than I meant.

'It may be nothing …' He spoke so hesitantly, I thought I might explode. The clock was ticking away but I knew I needed to hear what he had to say.

'Please,' I said, putting my bag down on the floor. 'Do tell me.'

I arrived at the ferry in time to see its wake still washing against the quay. I couldn't blame Duncan; he could limp as fast as I could run.

'Damn,' I said. 'Damn and bloody bollocks. Now what?'

'Ouch, that sounds painful,' he said. 'Well then, the way I see it, you have two options: catch a train – there's bound to be one sometime this evening. Though I have to warn you, all the guide books beware bandits and ne'er do wells on that line, or—'

'Or?' I said, gloomily. 'What other choice is there?'

'Or you could phone your mother to tell her you're all right, then come back to my hotel and spend the night there. What do you think?'

Chapter Eighteen

Napoli 1590

'Fabrizio will come here at four hours of the night,' Donna Maria said as if it were perfectly normal for another woman's husband to visit so late. *'I want you to keep a lookout.'*

We sat at opposite sides of a chessboard on a small table at one end of the sala, away from all the commotions of the kitchen. She folded the note that Laura had delivered and gave it to me so that I could burn it. The evenings were cooling down now that we were into October, and Donna Maria liked a fire. I did too, such luxury! It also meant I didn't have to keep singeing my fingers burning the notes in a candle flame.

Don Carlo still didn't know about Donna Maria and Fabrizio. Right under his long dank nose they were, and not quiet. True, he spent most of his time with the musicians that came from as far away as England to benefit from cook's talent and the comfortable beds at the palazzo. When no one was visiting, he'd spend hours by himself in the music room plucking away on his lutes, of which he had many. And of course he'd go off hunting at a moment's notice. But even so! I never expected the secret to remain intact for one year, let alone two.

When the weather was fine, we went to Chiaia in the carriage, but rain was coming more frequently. Sadly it did nothing to quench the ardour of my lady and Don Fabrizio.

'Is ... is that wise, my lady?'

'Wise, Silvia? Wise?' She stood up, knocking several of the pieces over. *'There is nothing wise in this world!'* Her cheeks flushed, she began to pace up and down, offering a mixture of prayers and curses to the air. I said nothing and replaced her king and queen on what I believed were the correct squares. *'Isn't it quite clear,'* she went on,

adjusting her bodice in the sort of manner that I'm sure Fabrizio, and probably every man in Italy, would enjoy, 'that he and I are meant to be together?'

'I don't know, my lady.'

'Of course, we are! Beauty is a gift, Silvia. A gift from God. Is it not His purpose that two such blessed people should love one another?'

'Err ...' A cold hand thrust itself into my chest and began squeezing. I'd often wondered why fat and leery Father Strozzi could be considered holy, but if the church said so, I wasn't going to argue. And Donna Maria was a princess. I remembered one of the English musicians telling me their Queen's father, King Henry, had taken on the role of Holy Father in England. He wasn't struck down by a thunderbolt, so perhaps royalty did have an ear to the Lord's purposes.

The puddles in the street below glistened in the moonlight. It was a breezy night and my lamp's little flame jumped back and forth, threatening to go out. I had to keep standing up to stop myself from falling asleep so I leaned out of the window and caught any conversation that was passing. Being so late, it was mostly the songs and complaints of those with too much wine inside them. At one point a couple came by, and they stopped in the doorway opposite, right by the church. The shadow deepened as a cloud crossed the moon, but I saw the flick of a red skirt rising and it wasn't difficult to know what happened next.

Then, as the night bells tolled four, I heard the clip clop of hooves. Two horses stopped at the end of the street but only one rider dismounted, giving the reins to the other. The Duke strode towards me, face turned up, searching for the flame that signalled all was well. I covered the light, once, twice, three times, then ran down the spiral staircase in my cloth slippers. I'd oiled the lock on the side door especially and it slipped back without the slightest sound.

'Silvia!' Fabrizio whispered, too loudly for my liking,

and I put my finger to my lips. He put his arm round my shoulders and gave me a kiss on the forehead. 'You are a good girl.'

I felt his breath on my face and I must say that it wasn't at all unpleasant. He hastened up the stairs to Donna Maria's chamber. I followed much more slowly, for it is quite something to be kissed by the handsomest man in Italy, however fleetingly. Laura was already asleep even though she was supposed to be guarding the door that led into the outer chamber. I had half a mind to shake her awake but could think of no sensible reason for doing so.

While Don Carlo was away, the night visits weren't too bad, except that Laura and I became gradually more and more cross and distracted through lack of sleep. Donna Maria stayed late in her bed but we were up as usual with our work to do. The afternoons were set aside for Donna Maria to receive visitors once prayers were said, and the most fraught visit of all was that of the Duke's wife.

'Let's have a birthday party for Emmanuele!' Donna Maria clapped her hands together and turned to me. 'That's a good idea. Don't you think so, Silvia?'

'Yes, my lady.' I said, as demurely as I could under the circumstances.

Fabrizo's wife, Donna Maria Carafa sat opposite us. Her face, which I remembered was apt to crease into laughter, remained composed. At the other end of the sala her four children, our Margarita and little Emmanuele, asleep in his cradle, were all watched over by his nurse. They had the board and dice on the table and every now and then we would hear cheering from one and complaints from the others as luck made its choice.

I shouldn't have been there at all. In the room, perhaps, sewing quietly on a bench a little way behind, but not sitting beside her. This was another of Donna Maria's madnesses. She had it in her head that if she behaved outrageously in lots of ways then no one would notice her one huge outrage. It was only when Donna Maria Carafa left that the painful tangle in my stomach began to ease.

For the visit, Donna Maria made sure all the serving dishes were changed for the beautiful blue ones that came from Firenze and were only used at feasts. She'd also instructed that the fine tapestries hanging in her chamber should be moved to the sala, and she had me dress her in a gown that was trimmed with silver thread and white fur at the neck and wrist. The purpose of all this care made me even more uncomfortable. It was quite usual for things to be moved about the place, but the particular and unnecessary show, plus the elevating of servants such as myself, would be greeted very badly by the other ladies Donna Maria visited.

Don Carlo was often away hunting and I was extremely glad of it. He'd looked at me coolly ever since returning to Napoli, and Laura told me that she'd heard a remark by him that mentioned my name and the word 'witch' close together. Nothing could be more dreadful. She was lying, I told myself, although I'd seen the gleam of triumph in her eyes. I avoided Don Carlo if I could, but when Donna Maria took it into her head to give me status that I wasn't due and certainly didn't want, I knew that he would come to a very unfavourable conclusion. If Salvo had had something apart from a crucifix nearby to drop into the castle's music room, Don Carlo might have sought the ear of the Inquisition.

The only people excited about the party were Donna Maria and Margarita, who was a little cross that her birthday had gone by without such a celebration, but she was given promises and I was to sew new sleeves and a bodice for her. The menu and matter of who was going to be seated where at the table for the evening feast took much discussion. Don Carlo would be on one side of his wife, but who would be on the other?

'Do you remember the last feast?' I said to Donna Maria after she'd agreed on only eleven courses and I'd

given the Cook a long list of requirements.

'Oh, Silvia. How could I forget?' She laughed like a gleeful child. 'Did I tell you that Fabrizio grasped my hand under the tablecloth?'

'Many times, my lady. Shall we try the new way with your hair now?' I was determined that her unruly hair should be plaited and pinned into the new net, and it wasn't easy. And probably I pulled too hard.

'Ow!' she said. 'Take care.'

'I'm sorry, but ...'

'Oh, what is it, Silvia? You seem so vexed this morning.'

I hesitated but could not hold back. 'Please don't sit with Don Fabrizio again, my lady. I beg you. It would be a terrible mistake. It really would.' I stood quite still with one of her braids in my hand.

For a while she was silent and I could not tell her feelings, but then she reached up and took my hand, holding it against her cheek.

'I'm glad you're here, Silvia,' she said, with the catch of tears in her voice. 'Please don't think badly of me. I hardly know what to do these days.'

'Then perhaps will you think about it?'

'No, Silvia,' she said. 'I won't think about it. Fetch me a glass of wine.'

If the sun were never to shine again I wouldn't have felt more miserable. I poured out the wine slowly, blinking back tears. When I gave it to Donna Maria, she looked into my face, then, to my surprise, after taking a sip she gave the glass back to me.

'Here,' she said, 'swallow a little of this. I think we both have need.'

I remembered Don Carlo and his glasses of wine sending me into a swoon, so I shook my head. 'It doesn't agree with me, my lady.'

'Have just a sip then, to celebrate. For you are right, Silvia. I will not sit with Don Fabrizio at the party.'

What a difference I felt then! So much so, that I did

take the glass and have a little sip after all.

We decided that Don Carlo's own father would sit next to his daughter-in-law, and I took care not to place Don Fabrizio on the opposite side of the table so the lovers couldn't trap themselves in each other's gaze. But on the morning of the party, Pietro came to see me.

'You have one less for the table. Don Carlo's father is ill.'

'Oh, no.' I said. 'But that means ...' I shut my mouth so suddenly my teeth came together with the click of a mousetrap.

Pietro looked surprised. 'Means what?'

'Nothing. It's just that I'll have to put Don Giulio in his place.'

'Is that a problem?'

'No, no. Not really.' I forced a laugh, 'I'd best find a bigger chair, that's all.'

Don Carlo's blood uncle, Don Giulio. Oh dear. Praying that Donna Maria would be sensible was about as useful as sewing a seam with no thread. She didn't like Don Giulio at all, but he liked her more than enough for both of them.

I pinned a smile to my face before the guests arrived and kept it there the whole time. It made me look simple, but that was all to the good. Donna Maria had turned the contents of the palazzo upside down once again and brought out the best cutwork tablecloths, but she did not insist that I sat with her. Of course not. With Don Carlo home it was back behind the screen for me.

If Don Carlo suspected his wife then he did not show it, even though she'd asked to move from her apartment above his to the opposite end of the palazzo. Her excuse was to complain about the night-time noise of the young swifts in their nests outside her window. Personally, I enjoyed the squabbly conversations of the baby birds at any time of day or night. They didn't have fears that their *behaviour might betray them. Perhaps their parents did, for they could have nested anywhere under the building's eaves, but they didn't, choosing the corner open to the piazza rather than the narrow street, where there was less room for their swooping flight.*

When Don Carlo refused my lady's request, I thought he must suspect, but I was there when he responded with a wave of his hand, as if some slight nuisance or a fly troubled him, rather than a rival for his wife's affection. He didn't want to hear the noise of such an unpheaval whilst composing his latest lute pieces. At least, that's what he said. I was there and heard him clearly.

How Don Fabrizio came to sit diagonally opposite Don Giulio I don't know. Men never take any notice of what women say – except perhaps when the woman is the Queen of England – and I could hardly insist he moved.

'You look like you're at a funeral, not a party, Silvia.' Pietro slapped me on the knee. 'Cheer up, girl.'

'I've had a little bad news,' I lied. 'My aunt.'

'Oh dear,' he said. 'I'm sorry to hear that. Is she ...?'

I shook my head, not saying anything more about my imaginary aunt. Of course, he thought she'd died. That's what happens when you stay silent, people make up something instead. Pietro was kind, but he was Don Carlo's man, and I was my lady's maid. If we'd been in another household we might have been able to speak freely to each other, but to do so here would be fatal.

Through the screen I could see Don Giulio laughing and leaning his fat bulk towards my lady. She leaned away, managing to maintain her polite face. Opposite, Don Fabrizio had one hand on the table and was indicating something extravagant with the other. It might have been the noise that meant his voice couldn't be heard, but I think he meant to interrupt any conversation between them.

Don Carlo played the lute, of course, but fortunately with other musicians and singers. And my lady asked

Torquato Tasso to recite quite early, straight after the little herb tartlets, while everyone's digestions were still strong and not too much wine had been drunk. Wine. Several times that evening, I swore I would never touch it again. Once the children were taken to bed, the noise in the sala grew louder as the wine in the jugs ran out and was replenished more and more often. Everyone laughed at unfunny jokes and the singers sang unseemly words with gestures to match.

'Silvia. Silvia!' Donna Maria's voice called. I ran over, taking care to appear at the opposite side from Don Giulio. She pushed back her chair and stood up. 'Come with me,' she said.

We ran up the two spiral staircases to her apartment at such speed that I was almost giddy when we reached the top.

'I cannot bear that hideous man and his vile breath a moment longer,' she said, her face flushed with anger, wine and exertion. 'First of all he is patting my hand, then my arm, then ...' she paused for breath, 'then Silvia, under the cloth, he has the audacity to not only place his hand on my knee, but then, he ... he began to go further up!' She shook her head.

I poured some water, rinsed a cloth and began to wipe her brow, all the while making soothing remarks, but she pushed my hand away.

'It's truly terrible, Silvia. Not only Giulio's hideous slobbering, but to see Fabrizio so close! I can hardly look at him, but I feel his gaze. It is like fire!' She sat down on the chair beneath the window, then stood up, crossed the chamber and threw herself down on the bed.

'It's good that Don Carlo is so taken up with his friends,' I said, trying to find something to be glad about.

'Pfft ... Don Carlo? He's such a—'

There was noise on the stairs and we both stiffened. Surely Don Giulio could not move so fast.

'Fabrizio!' My lady jumped up at the sight of the Duke. 'My love ...'

126

And they were in each other's arms. Keeping my eyes firmly on the floor, I left them. Once alone in the antechamber, I tried to breathe normally, but it was as if I were wearing a girdle of iron, I was so afraid. How long before they were both missed? And who would miss them? Don Giulio for sure.

In the distance I could hear laughter and voices and told myself there were always comings and goings of people at parties. But then I heard something that set icy fingers clawing at the back of my neck. Holding my breath, I listened again. Silence. I began to relax, I must have imag— but there! I had heard correctly. Terrified, I fell back against the door, my heart thumping in my chest more loudly than the slow footsteps that were, for sure, ascending the stairs.

Chapter Nineteen

'Charles said he might visit in a few weeks.' My mother sighed, then wriggled around in the spacious comfort that only first class air travel can provide.

'That's nice,' I said, distracted by the glistening Alps beneath us. 'You did tell him he couldn't stay with us, I hope.' I swallowed another mouthful of brandy. Charles was apparently a nice man, but then Thomas had hoodwinked us all.

'Oh, Lisa, listen to you putting obstacles in the way of everything. We can sort it somehow.'

'Mum, I am not having him stay in my flat and that's the end of it. He can book into a hotel. For heaven's sake, if he can afford to go on a first class jolly to Sorrento then that shouldn't be a problem.'

She went quiet. But not for long. 'What about Duncan? Will you let him stay?'

'Oh, Mum. I keep telling you, it wasn't like that. He's married.'

Silence.

'So was Thomas.'

'Yes, but Duncan told me. Besides, it wasn't like that.'

She gave one of those I-don't-believe-you-for-a-moment shrugs before flicking through her week old copy of *Woman and Home* that she'd brought from England in case she felt homesick. Home. How was Mollie? According to her texts she was having the best of times. Sophie was lovely and every minute with Jon was fun and he didn't worry about stuff like I did – all of which translated in my mind as: he'd been totally irresponsible, wrecked the flat and they'd all nearly died after setting fire to amaretti biscuit wrappers. I could see the tall tin in my mind's eye. It was at the back of the cupboard … Stupid, I told myself. They won't even know they're there. Nobody I knew liked them except me, but I'd managed to squeeze a tin into my suitcase. A souvenir, I told myself, and when

I'd eaten all the biscuits, it would be a good place to entomb a Barbie.

I thought about Duncan. It wasn't like 'that' at all. But he was funny, kind and as far as I knew, honest. He did tell me about his wife, and when he spoke about her and his grown up daughter, it was fondly. He missed them and showed me their photographs. The family was obviously wealthy and well travelled – Sydney, New York, Paris.

Duncan's hotel was way beyond my means and although tempted by his offer to pay half, with the feeble excuse of being half responsible for my missing the ferry, there was only one place I wanted to stay. Actually, *wanted* wasn't the proper word. I knew that the Palazzo San Severo, where Gesualdo once lived, had been converted into apartments, but most of the building was a hotel. So, when the opportunity to spend a night at Hotel San Severo suddenly presented itself, I'd felt compelled.

Duncan did talk me into dinner at his hotel though. It was heady, to be in such splendour. The food was fantastic. I had gnocchi for starters because it was a word I recognised, but shrink-wrapped potato wodges from Tesco they were not: spinach and parmesan little spheres of deliciousness they were. The monkfish was equally amazing and as for that white chocolate and pistachio panna cotta …

But although I'd really enjoyed the fabulous food, and said so, it wasn't the main topic of conversation. That had been about the Renaissance, the Spanish Inquisition and Signor Pace's warning. The frontispiece appeared to be the work of the most talented engraver working in Naples at the end of the century. Salvo Carlino was the nephew of the printer, Giovanni Giacomo Carlino. Salvo worked for *Carlino & Pace* but nothing was heard of him after 1597. It was assumed he had died, although there was no evidence for that.

Which is why my frontispiece was such a surprise for Signor Pace, and the first reaction of his sidekick was to cross himself very vigorously. But then everyone crossed themselves in Naples.

In hindsight, I wondered why on earth I was so keen to stay in Gesualdo's old palace. Inside, the stone treads were worn down badly and while going up wasn't too bad, coming down felt quite treacherous. Here was a job for the company whose advert I'd seen at the airport. It wasn't only *my* marble needs that needed fulfilling, anyone could take a tumble.

The room I had on the second floor was very contemporary and rather soulless. It could have been in any European city, especially given the Ikea furniture and waiting room décor in cream and brown. Dividing walls chopped through the moulding on the ceiling and the view from the window was of a featureless wall. When I leaned out over the balcony, I could just about see into the square.

I wasn't there for the view though. Teeth, bed, sleep, I thought, and that's exactly what I did.

Voices out in the street woke me. Whether violence was imminent was hard to tell. All Italian spoken at high speed and loud volume sounded threatening to me, but I was surprised when I heard the clip clop of hooves. Whining scooters yes, but horses? I thought about getting up to look, but found I had no energy to move.

It wasn't a nice feeling. I lay in the dark somehow weighted down, every breath hard work. You're still asleep, I told myself. That must be it, although it seemed then as if a part of me did get out of bed and did go over to the window. How could that be?

Listen, said a voice in my head. Listen…

Although I knew I was warm beneath the bedclothes, there was also a me standing shivery and cold. What I saw from the window I had no idea. Everywhere was dark and gloomy and the atmosphere heavy. The voices faded into the distance. But as they did so, I became aware of another noise, getting closer and much more menacing. Somebody was coming up the stone staircase and their footsteps echoed round the stairwell. They were slow and sometimes stopped, as if whoever it was didn't find the stairs easy. I lay rigid, telling myself it was just another guest, but as they came ever nearer, I heard a the rasp of someone's breath.

That was it. I began trembling, no, rattling, in the bed. With what felt like Herculean strength I forced my arm from under the covers and leaned across to switch on the light. Whoosh! Bang! Light filled the room and I couldn't see a thing. I struggled to sit up and then opened my eyes. Ah. That's what made the noise: my book on Gesualdo was on the floor. Everything else was just as it was. Not only that, everywhere was quiet. No footsteps. I got out of bed and went to look out of the window. The shutters creaked and up above me birds squabbled in the eves. One by one, they flew off into the pale grey light of dawn.

I went back to bed and slept like a baby till eight.

When Duncan and I met for breakfast I told him about the night's noises.

'You think I was dreaming,' I said. 'I can tell by your expression.'

He laughed and hid behind the coffee menu. 'I don't know what you mean. But,' he said, 'if you were me, what would you think?'

'I'd think you were mad.' I sighed. 'Oh well, there's no proving it, either way. Are you going to have the High Mountain or the Single Estate Colombian?' We really were in very particular surroundings. It was a little too chilly to sit outside on the balcony, but the sun was bright, and through the window, I watched a couple of sparrows hopping about under the outdoor tables. 'It's a shame birds can't talk, otherwise I could ask the swifts.'

Duncan lowered the menu. 'I beg your pardon?'

'I disturbed the swifts nesting under the eaves last night. They were all awake, so could have been witnesses.'

He shook his head. 'No, they couldn't.'

'Couldn't?'

'Well, all the swifts have migrated south by now. They leave in September. Hmm,' he scratched his chin. 'I think I might have tea.'

I looked at him for a while, then out at the sparrows. The memory of the birds fluttering away into the dawn was clear in my mind.

I was replaying my time with Duncan when the plane began its descent. The sudden change of engine noise always made me jump and I had to tell myself to keep calm. I couldn't stop my thoughts turning back to Signor Pace's suggestion that the frontispiece I had was the equivalent of a curse.

Certainly, *Noteworthy* hadn't been its usual happy self since we had been asked to sing the Gesualdo, but I put that down to Daniela disturbing the equilibrium. Then I remembered my close shave with the bus and the poor man who drowned. In my mind's eye, I saw the brown paper cover of the madrigal and the red spot of wine, that I kept thinking looked like blood. Somehow one spot had become two.

I shook my head. Out of the window, I could see rooftops. Both Mum and I held our breath as the wheels of the plane touched down.

Amongst the mosaic of faces in 'Arrivals', I saw Jon's first. I'd been looking for Mollie but Jon, with his hair tufted up as if he'd drawn his hand through it, was taller than the rest. He was frowning as he scanned the crowds. A huge wash of gladness rushed through me. Glad to be down on the ground, glad to see him, in fact very glad to see him, and there was Mollie! Tears came to my eyes as she rushed towards me.

'Mum, Mum!' She flung her arms round my neck. Had she grown in less than a week? 'Me and Jon,' she said, as I squashed her against me. 'We've had the best time without you. It's been brilliant.'

'Shall I get back on the plane then?'

'Only if we can come too,' Jon said, rather quickly. He looked a little fraught, and I wondered if Mollie's 'brilliant' was Jon's 'completely exhausted'. His smile was very slightly tight at the corners … he was a darling. Any anxiety I'd had about leaving him with Mollie fell away.

'That would be lovely,' I said, meaning it, 'but I think we'd have to busk our way on and hope everyone was very generous.'

Mum sat in the back of the car with Mollie, who talked non-stop about her trips to the zoo (baby tigers!), Exmouth beach (they had to climb the escape ladder when the tide came in!), Dartmoor (got right to the top of Hay Tor!) and Birmingham.

'Birmingham?'

'Last minute job,' Jon said. 'I was going to turn it down but—'

'We went on the train,' Mollie interrupted, 'and everyone thought Jon was my Dad. How cool is that?'

'Err …'

'They were ever so nice to me,' she galloped on, 'and I was allowed to go on their computer.'

'Really?'

'Yeah, great people. A software design company,' Jon said. 'Mollie was a test driver. I'm supposed to write something for a radio ad.'

'That's good.' I was a little too sleepy to think about computer software. The brandy and gradual easing of the tension I'd held onto during the flight didn't help. As I nodded off, I kept thinking about Mollie calling Jon 'Dad'. It sounded cool to me too.

I woke to the motorway rumble in my ears accompanying Mozart. The car radio glowed in the dark. My head was on Jon's shoulder. 'Oh, sorry,' I said, straightening up. 'I didn't mean …'

'That's all right,' he said. 'You were spark out.' I glanced over my shoulder to check on Mum and Mollie – also both out for the count – and he shifted away from me. I hoped he didn't think I was shrugging him off. It wasn't long before we lit up a bright blue motorway sign. Bath and Stroud. Still the wrong side of Bristol.

'Any *Noteworthy* news?' I asked.

'Well …' he hesitated.

'Yes?'

'It's just that …' We were fast approaching a lorry apparently doing about two miles an hour. It was a hill but even so. Jon indicated and moved out into the middle lane.

'It's just that what?' I said, once we were safely past.

'I didn't text you,' he said, breezily, 'because really, there was nothing to worry about.'

A gale force ten type of breeze. My stomach turned over.

'What's happened? Tell me.'

'It's okay—'

'Now!'

'Sophie's had a bit of an accident.'

'What! Why? What happened?'

'All right, all right,' he said, reaching across to pat my arm. 'She's fine. They've put her in a cast.'

Immediately I pictured Sophie with a broken leg. 'Oh, no. Poor thing. But what …' Then it sank in. 'When was this? Where was Mollie?

'Mollie was with me,' he said. 'Robert texted me about Sophie from the hospital. And we all thought the best thing would be for me to stay over at your place. Mollie was fine. I think she thought it all very exciting.'

'Oh?' I glanced over my shoulder again. They were both still asleep. 'She didn't say anything.' I didn't know what to think. After all my efforts to get Sophie to stay. I was glad Mollie had been looked after, but it felt weird that they hadn't even sent me a text.

'No, I know,' Jon said, 'that's because I told her not to. Honestly, we didn't want you to worry.'

Men. I could just imagine Robert and Jon deciding between them what I should and shouldn't know about my daughter's well-being. If Sophie …

'So how is Sophie?' I said. 'Will she be able to get about?'

'I expect so, although driving might be tricky.'

134

I remembered when Mum had broken her leg. She couldn't even get in a car, let alone drive. The cast went right up to her hip. 'Where is it broken?'

'About here, I think.' He demonstrated with the side of his hand, sawing just below the elbow.

'Oh?' I felt stupid for jumping to conclusions. Perhaps it was the memory of Mum's fall down the stairs that made me think Sophie had done the same. We were crossing the Avon gorge, high above the river. Not that it was visible in the dark, but I could see the lights of Avonmouth in the distance and, further away, a twinkling necklace along the Welsh coast. 'So, what happened?' I said. 'How did she do it?'

I was about to find out, but a plaintive voice from the back said, 'Have we got anything to eat?'

When we got home, Mollie – even though she was almost asleep – insisted on giving Jon a big hug and whispering urgently in his ear, before she would go to bed.

'What was all that about?' I asked him, after I'd shooed her into the bathroom for teeth cleaning.

'That? Oh, nothing. You know what she is.' He quickly leant forward and kissed me on the cheek. The suddenness of it, his nearness and the jolt that ran through me made me gasp, otherwise I would have pressed him on what he meant. As it was, we stood looking at each other and for some reason the image of a weather house came into my mind. The figures, never touching, doomed to spend their lives apart. 'I'm glad you're back safe,' he said, softly.

'I'm glad I am too,' I said and without a thought, put my hand up to his chest, the imperative to feel the beat of his heart irresistible.

'What shall I do with these sheets?' Mum stood at the door with a bundle in her arms. Both Jon and I jumped apart. 'Oh, sorry,' she said, 'you carry on. I'll leave them here.' She dumped them on the sofa and went back into my bedroom, shutting the door behind her.

'I'd better go,' Jon said. 'You have a house full and it's

late.'

'Yes, I suppose you must,' I said, wishing it early and the flat empty. 'Thanks, Jon. For meeting us, looking after Mollie ... everything. I really appreciate it.'

He waved away my thanks. 'It was an education being with Mollie. She's great company and funny. Like you. I even enjoyed ...' he paused, smiling rather ruefully, 'I even enjoyed the responsibility.'

'Well, well,' I said. 'Who'd have thought it? Perhaps I ought to go away more often.'

'God no, don't do that. We'll all go next time.'

We both laughed and then checked it with a sort of happy but embarrassed, spluttery cough.

'I'd better go,' he said. 'Don't forget it's the tableau photo tomorrow.'

I groaned. 'God yes, tomorrow. But what about Sophie?'

Jon shrugged. 'She says it's amazing what you can do with the right props.'

My tomorrow began with Mollie clattering around in the kitchen. My gran's kitchen has a door, my mum's flat has a hatch through to the lounge-diner, I have an arch in my lounge-kitchen-diner. Soon, bedrooms and bathrooms will be under threat. I knew it was Mollie by the sound of Coco Pops filling a cereal bowl, a delicate shower compared to the clunking of Mum's Weetabix. The trouble with sleeping on the sofa is that there's no privacy. In fact, the sofa is the heart of the home it seems to me, not the hearth – who said that? – I haven't even got a hearth, unless you count a storage heater. Mollie came and told me to 'shove over', then clambered onto the sofa, holding the telly remote in one hand and the cereal bowl, waving directly above my face, in the other.

'Oh, no, Mollie.' I hid under the duvet. 'Not the telly. It's too early.'

'It's ten past eight. That's not early.'

I almost wished for adolescence. 'Can't you talk to me

136

instead?'

She shook her head, pointing the spoon at her mouth full of cereal.

Defeated, I threw back the duvet and tried standing. Ten past eight wasn't early, not if I was going to be at the studio by ten thirty. Urgent: coffee.

In the kitchen I grumbled loudly enough for Mollie to hear me. 'Where is everything? What's happened to the mugs?'

Above the jagged whines and crashes of the cartoon soundtrack, Mollie shouted back. She loved cartoons, they were her absolute favourite and commanded her total attention. So when Mummy asked her something, she didn't give much thought to her reply.

'I don't know. Daniela put awa—'

Daniela? Not a sharp shock sort of a name, but that's what I felt. How quiet it was suddenly, in spite of the noisy whizz-bangs. I put down the coffee jar and went and stood in the archway.

'What did you say?' I needed her to repeat it, just in the slightest case I'd misheard. She was silent, eyes still fixed on the telly, so I went and stood in front of the screen. She looked up at me, eyes shifting and scared.

'Tell me,' I said. My voice came out taut as a tightrope.

She shook her head violently and scooped another spoonful of cereal into her mouth. I could feel my own heart beating faster but not in a good way, not in the way it did only hours ago when Jon was saying goodnight.

'So,' I said, trying to keep my voice light, 'was Daniela here then?' About as light as a lead feather it turned out.

Mollie said nothing.

Remain calm, I told myself. Be reasonable. There's no point in getting angry. She'll only clam up.

'Just bloody tell me!' I shouted.

Mollie jumped and a few Coco Pops hopped out of the dish and polka-dotted across the duvet. Her face went white.

'I can't,' she said, chin wobbling.

'Yes, you can.' I stomped into the kitchen and brought back a cloth but Mollie was picking up the little brown droppings one by one and pushing them in between her closed lips, the only way she could deal with such a conflict of interest.

'I *promised* I wouldn't,' she said.

'Did you now. And why was that?'

'Why was what?' said Mum, coming in with her glass of water that she always took to bed and never drank and exactly the last person I wanted to be there while I interrogated Mollie.

'Oh ... *nothing*,' I said.

In the kitchen I smacked the switch on the kettle and stomped about, opening and shutting the cupboard doors. Now I could see she must have stayed for supper. Three dinner plates resting on top of the frying pan. And two wine glasses ... who the hell would put wine glasses in the same cupboard as saucepans? And there was an empty bottle of red wine behind the bin. So they'd had a whole bottle? The bin was empty apart from a tea bag. A takeaway then, boxes straight in the bin downstairs. A ghoulish curiosity would have sent me to have a look if I hadn't still been in my pyjamas. God, Daniela in my flat, with my daughter, with my man ... except he wasn't my man. Almost, but not really. I pulled too hard on the cutlery drawer, nearly emptying it on the floor. The kettle's irritation seemed to increase with mine but it went quiet on boiling. I did not. The coffee got made somehow.

'Are you all right, dear?' Mum put her glass on the table. 'I think you've probably stirred that enough, don't you?'

I threw the spoon and regretted the noise as it ricocheted round the sink. Suddenly, I felt as limp as the dishrag it settled on.

'I'm going to have a shower.'

Such sanctuary is to be had in a shower. No one can hear you. Especially if the radio's on. It was only when I got out, lobster pink and suffering to all intents and purposes from an excess of soap in the eyes, that I realised the radio was set to a channel I never listen to.

Another couple of hours and we'd all be in costume pretending to be other people. If only I *could* be someone else.

Chapter Twenty

Gesualdo 1590

I held my breath, listening to the footsteps coming up the stairs. They were slow and laboured, like the sound of a fat old man with too much food and wine inside him. I ran back and knocked on the door of the chamber.

'My lady, be quick, someone is coming!'

There was a good deal of rustling and then Donna Maria appeared, her skirts and bodice very much awry.

'Help me, Silvia,' she said. 'I shall go to greet whoever it is. Pray to God it is not Don Carlo!'

We were on the second floor, and although the main staircase in the middle of the house had fewer treads and was not so effortful to climb, the spiral stairs led directly to the outer chamber. I pinned back her hair as best I could and pulled her bodice laces tighter while she straightened her petticoat. Sometimes I wished we all walked about in sheets like the people in ancient times.

'Go and meet them, Silvia. Delay them if you can. Fall down and block the way if you have to.'

I ran to the door. For one happy moment, I thought that maybe the owner of the noisy feet had stopped at the first floor and was wandering the rooms there. But no, another footstep and then another. I started down the stairs and, after the first turn, thumped the stair with my heel and gave a shriek. Then I sat down, tilted my cap to one side and rubbed my ankle. In truth I wished I really could be knocked out cold and therefore not come face to face with…

'Laura!'

I couldn't believe it. She looked absolutely terrible. White as the best linen, no, grey as the worst and clammy too. 'In the name of God, what …?' No wonder she was making such a row. In her arms she carried one of the large blue two-handled pitchers full to the brim with water. It would be heavy for a strong man, let alone Laura. 'Here, let me help.' I took hold of one handle and braced myself to receive the weight. 'You half frightened me to death.'

'Who's there? Who is it?' Above us stood Donna Maria. She took one look at Laura and her beautiful face shrivelled into ugliness. 'You! Have I been disturbed because of you?' One more step and we set the pitcher down on the floor. Laura tried to stand behind me but Donna Maria took hold of her ear and dragged her forward. 'How dare you!' she hissed into Laura's face. 'Get out of my sight at once and don't come back.'

And with that she went back to Fabrizio, slamming the door behind her.

'Laura,' I said, 'what possessed you to carry this all the way up here?'

'Don Giulio,' she said, whilst both snivelling and panting for breath. 'It was him. He saw you both go, and Don Fabrizio too. That's when he called me over.'

I knew it. Soon everything would be known.

'But why this, Laura?' I knocked on the side of the pitcher. It was one of the palazzo's treasures. 'Didn't Don Carlo see you with it?'

'Don Carlo? Pfft ... he was busy with the musicians as usual. Don Giulio was furious with everyone. He said Donna Maria looked feverish and needed to be cooled down. That's what he said. He didn't care that I could only just lift it.'

'Cooled down? He said that?'

'Yes. And about time too, if you ask me.'

'Oh, Laura,' I groaned. 'You've no idea what might happen if she was found out.'

'I do know, Silvia. I know that I've got to go.' Laura's shoulders drooped. 'She won't let me stay here now, and it wasn't my fault. If she wasn't messing ...'

'Stop it. Don't say another word.' I glared at her, whispering loudly. 'She'll hear you.'

'So what?'

'Look,' I said. I made her sit down on the top stair, then dipped my handkerchief into the pitcher and wiped her brow. 'Just keep out of Donna Maria's way for the time being and I'll see what I can do.'

She gave a scornful laugh and I wiped my own brow. We both knew there was nothing I could do.

Laura gathered her things from under my bed. It was a sad bundle in the finish. A few clothes, and her little wooden box of sewing things, one of my father's rejects I'd given her. 'Go and see cook. Tell her I said you could sleep in the laundry.'

I sat on the top step after she'd gone and put my head in my hands. From downstairs came the sound of singing, one of Don Carlo's pieces I'd heard a few times before. The trouble with his music was that bits of it sounded pleasing, but they'd be surrounded by strange sections that rambled on and on, clashing unpleasantly, as if the singers were having an argument.

From the inner chamber came a different duet, another that I was very familiar with and wished I wasn't. I went to look out of the window, thinking that the noises of the street might drown out all the noise from inside the house. The air outside had remained heavy all day and rain was yet to fall. I hoped it would hurry up, for the next day I'd arranged to meet Salvo.

Thinking about him made me feel much better; but then, beneath me, I saw Laura slip out of the door. For the life of me I couldn't understand what she was doing because she didn't walk away, but crossed the street, set her bundle down and stood leaning against the wall. After a little while she sat on the ground looking even more pathetic than her bundle. I was about to call down when I heard a man's voice say her name and she jumped to her feet. Then, to my horror, Don Giulio walked towards her. Although their voices were too quiet for me to hear, I could see very clearly, and there was no mistaking the bright coins that Don Giulio trickled into Laura's hand.

Why was he paying her? Had she lied about him being

142

angry and making her carry the pitcher upstairs? Perhaps he'd offered to pay her and she'd found it heavier than she'd expected. She must have been waiting for him, so it wasn't a passing tip. He'd come out to find her especially and now they were speaking.

I jumped back from the window and rushed to the door of Donna Maria's chamber. What was happening inside didn't matter a jot. Laura had lied.

'My lady, my lady!' I banged on the door. 'Please... it is very, very urgent. Don Giulio—'

'Don Giulio?' Donna Maria appeared clad only in a sheet. 'Damn that man. What does he want?'

All the pity I'd ever felt for Laura was entirely washed away. As I told Donna Maria everything that had passed, Don Fabrizio rose from the bed. On any other occasion this would be a most interesting sight, but I was too anxious to pay heed. Once he had pulled on his breeches and arranged himself within, he came and placed a hand on my lady's shoulder. A glance at his face and I knew he understood the danger of our situation. If Don Carlo should find him there...

'Maria,' he said, 'Maria.' I could see his hand was squeezing more and more tightly. He kept shaking his head too, and if I wasn't mistaken, his eyes took on the glaze of early tears. 'We are fools to love.' He kissed her neck but she reared away from him.

'Fools, Fabrizio? You say we are fools?' Fire was in her eyes then and I stepped back a little. 'There is nothing about our love which is foolish! How can you say such a thing? Are you not a duke, and I, a princess?'

She knew how to pierce a man to the heart, and Fabrizio raised himself up to his full height. I was reminded of when I saw a pair of lions being carried through the city by a group of travelling jugglers and acrobats. Even though they were caged, a hush went through the crowds when they went by. A full-grown boar or a bull is a fine animal and to be admired, but none of us had seen so much power contained in such sinuous beauty.

I remember looking at the male lion's paw, then down at my own hand, and feeling a little faint. As Fabrizio and Maria faced each other, I felt similarly feeble.

'Where is your courage, Fabrizio?' she went on. 'Has it deserted you? Must I have strength enough for both of us?'

The Duke paled at this insult. 'Princess,' he said through clenched jaws and with taut fury in his voice. 'I have no lack of courage. If I should die, it will not be with cowardly pleadings for mercy. It is only when I contemplate what harm may befall you, my fairest love, that I quail.'

It did not seem to me that there was any quailing going on between the two of them. But I was quivering enough for the whole city.

'Then let us be as one, Fabrizio,' said my lady. She placed both her hands on his chest, allowing the sheet to fall away from her breasts. 'For without you what is courage? What is our life without passion?'

I swallowed and wished that passion had never been invented. Strewn across the coverlet of the bed lay a crimson night dress almost identical to the one I'd made before I became keeper of Donna Maria's wardrobe. How I'd dreamed of the position, desiring the smooth hands of a seamstress, to sew silk instead of coarse linen. I was the fool in the room.

It was much as he could do not to renew his ardour but once he had finished dressing, Don Fabrizio, after many kisses, left to rejoin the party. I wondered about his wife, Donna Maria Carafa. She would know, surely. Perhaps he would eat enough of cook's garlic pastry pom-poms to quell the smell of sex.

Donna Maria remained in her chamber, still 'unwell'. She picked up the nightdress from the bed and held it to her like a baby. How I wish she held her real baby in the same manner. Donna Maria seemed to care so little for her children.

'Here,' she said, passing it to me. 'Help me with this.'

She stood with her arms up, almost like a child and I passed it over her head. It was then I noticed the tear.

'Oh, my lady. Shall I fetch another? The seam is split here.'

'Is it? No, don't bother. I like this one. Besides,' she said, putting her nose to the fabric and inhaling deeply, 'it will be as if he is still here.' She lay down and I straightened the sheets and coverlet. 'Read to me, Silvia dear. Something soothing.'

I did not want to fetch a book from the study downstairs in case I was seen and questioned by Don Giulio or Don Carlo. Instead, I chose from those we had in the chamber; my favourite. Everybody loved Ariosto's Orlando Furioso. *Even those who couldn't read knew the story. It was so exciting! Orlando, the hero, goes mad when he discovers that his love, Angelica, has run off with a Saracen. The people are worried because Orlando destroys everything in sight. Eventually, an English knight comes to try and find a cure. He flies to the moon, which is where everything that is lost is kept (I love that part) and he comes back with Orlando's wits in a bottle.*

I sat next to the bed, and by chance the book opened at that page. Was it fate? Or perhaps the English knight had come to help me. Either way, Donna Maria wasn't listening as I read the passage where Orlando sniffs the bottle and recovers his sanity by falling out of love with Angelica. If only we could all do such a thing.

'Shall I read more, my lady?' Her face was turned away and I wondered if she were asleep, but with a big sigh she turned her head. Tears streaked this way and that across her cheeks. With my handkerchief I dabbed them dry.

'You will help me, Silvia,' she said, in a smaller voice than usual. 'When ... when it ... when the worst comes. For I fear it will.'

'If I can, my lady.' I smoothed her forehead with my hand and sat with her in the quiet until I was sure she'd fallen into sleep. Then I went out onto the landing. There

was still music being played downstairs but the raucous time had passed. From the window I saw Don Fabrizio leaving in a carriage with his wife. He held her hand to his lips at one point but as the carriage pulled away, he glanced back and up at the window. There was no doubt in my mind he would return.

I stepped back almost into the pitcher full of water. It wobbled dangerously for a moment, but I steadied it and plunged my hand into the cool water. Scooping it up, I drank several mouthfuls, all the while wondering how on earth I could be of help to Donna Maria. And what would 'the worst' be when it came?

Don Carlo did not like me, and ever since the singing session at Castle Gesualdo, I worried that he might take it into his mind that I should be tried as a witch. Then what could I do? I looked down at the water as a shaft of moonlight brightened the room, my face was in shadow and the interior of the pitcher oily dark. Why had Don Giulio sent up the pitcher? Danger came in many guises. A sharp blade, a blow ... or a simple swallow of something unknown. I put my hand up to my throat, fearing there was something more deadly in the pitcher than water.

Chapter Twenty-One

Mollie retreated into web-land. Short of wrenching the headphones from her ears, there was no communication. Even when I stood directly in front of her with my arms folded and sporting my best determined-and-fierce-mother expression, she merely closed her eyes and began to hum. I knew that if she knew how upset I was, she would be at least twice as upset, but still wouldn't tell me. There are times when admirable qualities are really ... really ... actually, there are times when admirable qualities are a total pain in the arse.

My mobile rang as I was putting my shoes on.

'The shoot's off,' said Jon.

'What?'

'Ted's just rung me. He can't come.'

'For heaven's sake,' I said, crossly. 'That's rather short notice.'

'He's got to go and shoot butterflies hatching.'

'It's the wrong time of year for that.' Are any men truthful?

'It might have been sea horses.'

'Really.' Yeah, yeah ...

'Are you all right, Lisa?'

He sounded concerned. Why hadn't he told me about Daniela? I almost asked him. Almost. And I might have if Mum hadn't chosen that very moment to mouth something incomprehensible at me.

'... thought we might have a rehearsal instead,' he was saying. 'I've rung Robert. He says they're okay with that.'

'They?' I said, shrugging at Mum.

'Who is it?' she whispered, loudly.

'Jon,' I mouthed back.

'Yes, Sophie's at Robert's,' he said.

'Is she?'

'Yes. So is it all right with you? You sound pissed off.'

'No, I'm not,' I said, meaning yes, I am. 'I'm perfectly

147

all right. See you later.' I didn't wait for him to say goodbye.

'Why don't you ask him to lunch?' said Mum. 'I'm sure Mollie would like that.'

'Mollie saw enough of him while we were away.'

'If you say so.' She sniffed and went into her bedroom. Now Mum had the hump. What was I saying? It wasn't her bedroom; it was mine! God. We were all pissed off now.

I got my music together, waved at Mollie and called out goodbye to Mum. Neither responded.

After Naples, October in Exeter felt chilly. The wind had a sharp edge to it. I didn't feel like a rehearsal, but there again staying in the flat wasn't much of an option. I took a deep breath. The world seemed to have shifted after being away only a few days. Sophie would tell me what had happened. At least, she might have something sensible to say.

I had to fight my way into the drama studio. Somehow I got tangled up in the long black curtain that hung just the other side of the door, and for a moment I thought I might end up in Narnia or another perhaps more spooky world that required cloaks rather than fur coats. Once I'd wrestled my way through, I found myself alone in a large space lit by one small bulb.

'Hello?' Silence. My voice sounded flat. I walked into the puddle of light and peered into the gloom, turning slowly round a full three hundred and sixty degrees. There was no one. My shadow stretched out on the floor. It wasn't every day I stood alone in the middle of a large empty space like that. Black curtains draped across every wall, and even the ceiling was painted black, so it seemed as if there were no edges to the world. It was like being outside on a dark night. The air pressed down on my head like a weight.

I sang a few notes to test the acoustics. Not good, but maybe it wouldn't be too bad when we were all together.

A bang, a whoosh of air, and one of the curtains drew back to reveal Sophie in a bright turquoise kaftan. A butterfly in a dark forest. Robert stood behind her in the gloom.

'Ah, Lisa. Hello. How lovely. Gosh, a bit dim in here.' She let the curtain drop and all was drab again. 'Let me find the lights.' The curtains bulged and billowed as she fought her way through, then suddenly I was engulfed in light. Not quite Wembley stadium, but I'd been looking up when they first came on and was completely blinded.

'That's better,' Robert said, nodding hello to me. 'We'll be able to see the music now.'

'Maybe,' I said, and rubbed my eyes in exactly the way you're not supposed to. One day, I'd probably be counting the crow's feet and buying special cream for the eye area, but there was something very satisfying about giving them a good rub, especially when trying to restore any sort of vision.

'How was Italy?' Sophie said, when she reappeared from behind a curtain on the other side of the studio, dragging a chair with her good arm. 'Don't tell me … wonderful. I bet it was. Did you meet any nice Italians? How's your mother? Better? Robert, I left a bottle of water in the car. Would you mind fetching it? There's a love.'

'She's fine,' I said, 'and yes, it was wonderful. But, Sophie, I want to know what happened. How did you do this?' I knocked gently on her cast. 'Mollie said something about a fire as well as a fall. But she wasn't clear. And "there's a love"? Robert? Has the world turned upside down since I've been away?'

Sophie laughed as we went back behind the curtains to fetch another couple of chairs. 'Oh, you,' she said, giving me a friendly biff on the arm. 'It's just a figure of speech. And as for what happened …'

The door banged again but it wasn't Robert. I could hear Daniela laughing – high and singsong, a naughty giggle – and felt a cross between anger and distress, then the beginnings of a slow churning sensation in my stomach.

'Oh, look, Jon,' Daniela said. 'We're all alone.'

I rammed the legs of my chair against the curtains, pushing through them like a bull with its head down but with somewhat less grace. Unfortunately my effort didn't find a gap in the fabric, and I ended up carrying the curtain with me and making my entrance from beneath it as if I was wearing a long black train. It did terrible things to my hair.

'Hi,' I said, swivelling my eyes from one surprised face to the other and then putting my chair down rather too particularly and taking a while to get comfortable.

'Oh, hello, you two,' Sophie said. I felt a stab. You two? Were they a two? Robert came back and handed Sophie her water.

'Is that it?' said Jon. 'No wine?'

It was a joke and I felt a riposte begin to form that on another day might have resulted in a little banter, but I squashed it at once. 'Someone could go out for coffee later.'

'Good idea, Lisa,' he said.

His use of my name made me glance in his direction long enough to see concern on his face, but I quickly turned back to my music. 'Let's do some singing first. How about *Languisco e moro*?'

It had been agreed that we would sing two madrigals by Gesualdo, one already in the public domain and the newly-discovered *Ite sospiri ardenti.*

There was a flapping of pages before we all stood up.

We stood in a circle and cast the spell; notes seemed almost solid. I looked at the music on the page. Sophie began, her opening phrase falling step by step as she sang '*Languisco e moro*', then Daniela and Jon joined her in a similar descending cascade, '*I languish and die*'. Robert and I would begin later. How reassuring, how reliable he was, steady … you needed a steady bass in this sort of thing. It could so easily go off the rails. Come apart. Soon, we'd be in. In fact, we already were, although we hadn't

150

sung a note. We'd acclimatised to the pulse of the music, consciously at first, following the slight raise of Jon's hand. It had slipped into our subconscious once Sophie had started singing. Now it resided deep in our bodies, firm and reliable as our bones. Four bars, five … I heard Robert's quiet intake of breath at the same moment as mine and we were there.

My entry was on the same note as one being held by Daniela, so I had to sing as quietly as possible to begin with, gradually getting louder as she faded, otherwise there'd be a sudden jolt in the sound. I remembered Jon saying it was like passing on a baton and the overlap should be almost imperceptible.

It was as if we opened a portal into the distant past. All the emotional torment of the mad Gesualdo poured out into the drama studio and his strange, unworldly harmonies rocked the reality of that Sunday morning. Everything felt different. '*Ma tu, fera cagion de la mia sorte*', the words filled my mouth with the taste of lemons before they poured out into the fray. Our voices swirled around the room, *but you, savage cause of my death, for pity's sake, comfort so painful a death with a single tear.* We all pleaded with equal sorrow, with equal pain, with equal intensity. Single threads wove together in an ever more complex twine, twisting and turning until the agonies were over, the knot was tied and the resolution made. '*Now that you be merciful, sweet it is to die.*'

Phew.

'That wasn't bad, was it?' Jon said, and I couldn't help smiling to myself at the outrageous understatement. 'Shall we go straight into the other one?'

We all focussed once again.

Well… you win some, you lose some, I suppose. If we were a relay team then we'd have been disqualified for false starts, changing lanes and not just dropping the baton, but lobbing it into the crowd. It can happen, but not usually with an ensemble as experienced as we were. It's the sign of an amateur group if they lose confidence when one part goes astray. Usually the others will cover the error and the perpetrator joins back in, hopefully without any of the audience noticing, but halfway through singing *Ite sospiri ardenti*, we fell completely apart.

I was listening to Daniela in order to pick up a note for my next entry only to find she wasn't singing it. There was a hole where a sound should have been. That didn't matter terribly as I did know my part, but when it came to it, instead of hearing something recognisable from the others, it was if they were singing some other madrigal, one I'd never seen or heard before. Gesualdo's harmonies were challenging but it was the oddest thing, like walking in the front door and discovering your house had been redecorated, and instead of your own furniture there was nothing but junk. I felt irritated, then completely overcome with doubt. I missed my entry.

We all began talking.

'You should have sung a G sharp in bar twenty-eight ...'

'It wasn't my fault ...'

'They're *quavers*, not crotchets ...'

'You completely cocked that bit up ...'

'Bollocks ...'

I looked round at everyone's faces, hardly recognising my friends, their expressions were so bad-tempered and accusatory. How did that happen? Daniela spoke rapid Italian to the air above our heads. Apparently, knitting an imaginary cat's cradle was her out of sorts response.

'All of you,' she said, thrusting her chin at each of us in turn. 'You are all very bad with the accent. Italian is the language of lovers, is it not?'

'Isn't that French?' murmured Sophie.

Daniela smacked the challenge away. 'You must listen to *me*. The way you say *sospiri*, it is terrible. The *sos* is like in *sock*,' she waved her hands at Robert's ankle. 'Not *soap*.'

There was something hilarious about the way she began

vigorously rubbing her face but I couldn't access sufficient light-heartedness to go there.

A chill wrapped itself round my neck, and I remembered the very first time we opened the museum's copy at Sophie's house. It was a warning, this draught, I was sure of it, like a spectre from the past lurking just behind my ear. The notes of the madrigal seemed to shift before my eyes.

'Nooooo,' they whispered. 'Nooooo.'

Choir practice at Mollie's school the next day couldn't have been a more different experience. Yes, there were tears, but they were Emily's, a child of the highest snivelly order. I was all sympathy, every time. There were no cross words though. I'd moved Jonah, whose pathological wriggling had irritated those all around him, to the end of the back row next to the sizeable Connor. Jonah and Connor were now friends, and any whale jokes I may have thought of never reached their ears.

The sound made by the choir had improved so much I began to think I might be distantly related to Gareth Malone after all. Miss Price said that they'd taken my pronunciation advice so much to heart that they corrected each other. 'It's MOVE-munt, not move-MEANT, bum-face…'

It wasn't like *Noteworthy*; the simplicity of the relationship – you choir, me conductor – enabled a lot of songs to be sung and improved upon. Halfway through the wretchedly premature *Away in a Manger*, it occurred to me that they should enter the local music festival. It would be good experience for them and lovely for the school if they won.

'Do you fancy that?' I asked Mollie, when I picked her up later.

'Could do,' she said, airily.

She meant yes, but I haven't forgiven you for the incident with the Coco Pops yet. I didn't point out that I might be the one doing the forgiving.

'Can I have a muffin?'

We were passing a Costa and I had a weakness-of-will attack.

Mollie did the obvious and correct thing by ordering the double chocolate muffin while I made a mistake and chose the raspberry and white chocolate. If only raspberries came without pips. I was mulling over the thought that they should come supplied with floss when Daniela walked through the door. It was quite a big café and she didn't see us, I suppose because we were mostly concealed both by a pillar, and the large sofa we were sitting on.

'Eat up,' I said to Mollie.

'Why?' She looked up, saw Daniela standing at the counter, and immediately her expression changed. Guarded would be a word for it. Shifty might be another. She grabbed one of the large cushions and put it on her lap, so that the only bit of her visible was from the knees down.

'You've got some explaining to do, Mollie,' I said in my best and fiercest cushion-penetrating whisper.

The cushion trembled but stayed put. I decided that I would be perfectly nice and friendly to Daniela, steering the conversation round to what the bloody hell was she doing in my flat, in a reasonable, measured way.

That's what I was going to do, and had half raised myself from the sofa when the door of the café opened again and Jon walked in. He saw Daniela, she saw him. They didn't see me. He smiled; she smiled. He kissed her on the cheek. I sat down again. His arrival was clearly not a coincidence.

'So what happened?' Sophie said, when I told her. We were sitting at Robert's dining room table, although now that Sophie had commandeered most of the surfaces in the room with her bright fabrics and sewing boxes, it looked a vastly more cheery place. She was holding the fabric in place with the arm in plaster, and sewing with the other.

I'd been called upon to thread the needle. 'Has Daniela really got her teeth into him?'

'Teeth and claws it looked like it from where we were sitting. But …' I had a sudden moment of horrid clarity. There was my friend with her arm in plaster and a house about to cost thousands, and I was bleating on about Jon and Daniela meeting for a cappuccino. Or a latte. I bet she had an espresso like Jon … aaargh! I shook my head. 'Oh, Sophie, I am sorry. You should have stopped me. I really want to hear what happened to you.'

'Me?' she said. 'Well, you know what they say about things being a recipe for disaster? Here's mine. One ancient kettle left on the gas, loose floorboards because the boiler man hadn't nailed them back, and one clumsy Welsh woman without her glasses on. See?'

'Almost.'

'It was one thing after another really,' she said. 'A sequence. I'd put on the kettle and gone away, only realising quite a long time later that I'd forgotten to put the whistle back on. So I rush in to rescue it, up comes the floorboard, I fall over, and the next thing, I've got a pain in my arm the likes of which I've never had before.'

'Oh God, Sophie, you poor thing.'

'I was screaming, I'll tell you. Nobody's about though. My phone's in the other room, so somehow I get there and ring 999. But then, I'm clutching my arm in case it falls off and waiting for the ambulance, when I smell smoke.'

I gasped. She nods.

'So I stagger back to the kitchen, where somehow my bashing the kettle has knocked my music into the gas and it's set my *Noteworthy* music on fire. I'd left it on the worktop, right next to it.'

'Oh my God. What did you do?'

She laughed, although I don't suppose she did then. 'Well, I turned off the gas, but you know how I've always got a vase of something on the table?'

'Yes,' I said, 'your lovely roses.'

'Well, I threw them at the music.' With her good arm,

she demonstrated. 'The vase broke, of course, but luckily I'd just filled it up and there was enough water to put out the flames. It had only really caught the top piece of music. Funny thing that …' She frowned.

'What?'

'It was that God-awful Gesualdo. Burnt to a crisp it was, but only the cover. The music underneath wasn't even charred.'

I let this sink in.

'It was right by the curtains too,' Sophie went on. 'It was amazing they didn't go up.'

'Yes,' I said, slowly. 'Amazing.'

In the end, I didn't tell Sophie about how Mollie and I retreated from Costa by way of the fire exit next to the loo. I was distracted by Sophie's Gesualdo manuscript nearly going up in smoke.

On the way home, I told myself that the cover paper was probably more flammable than that of the music, although God knows, it seemed unlikely. Perhaps her curtains were made of something fireproof. The frontispiece appeared in my mind's eye. Ever since I'd looked at it through the magnifying glass in Signor Pace's shop, I saw it with much greater clarity. And I kept seeing it. For a moment, I thought of when Mollie and I had watched *Close Encounters*, and how the people in it were inexorably drawn towards the place where the spaceship landed.

My *Noteworthy* music was still in my case and as soon as I opened the front door, I just had to go and check whether the niggle I was having about it was true. The case was lying on the sofa with the flap open, spilling its innards. I thought of Sophie's kitchen table again. The rose petals falling and the red spot on the cover. That uneasy, shivery feeling. The chill like an imaginary spider strolling across the back of my neck. I remembered finding the spot after that poor boy drowned. It seemed a mad connection but when I took the music out of the case, I realised how badly my hands were shaking.

It was happening again, that feeling, only more magnified. There was a connection between the music and all the bad stuff that was going on. I held the copy in my hands while summoning up the courage to turn it over. Something would be changed on the front cover. I was sure of it.

Chapter Twenty-Two

Napoli 1590

Don Fabrizio did return that same night, as I knew he would. I lay listening to their lovemaking and it sounded to me like the cries of agony rather than joy. Sleep would not come, as I started at every creak. It was a hot night and the sheets felt so damp that I began to imagine my throat was constricted, that my heart beat too fast, that I had a pain in my stomach. Perhaps the water in the pitcher did indeed contain something bad. The night bells tolled and I heard every one. Far away thunder rumbled and flashes of lightning lit the room. I shut my eyes tightly and pulled the sheet over my head.

But morning did come and I dragged myself upright. When I opened the shutters, it was clear that a great deal of rain had fallen while I slept and I stood breathing in the new air for some time. Sparrows had taken up residence in one of the swifts' nests just above me. They chirruped irritably then flew off towards the palazzo. The daylight lessened my night-time fears. I could be wrong about Laura, and the payment from Don Giulio was for something else. What did I care anyway?

The pitcher of water still stood at the top of the stairs so I did not have to go all the way downstairs to fetch water for my lady. I was still alive with no pains, so it must have been sound. I took a sip and then a few more. The world brightened, and even more so when I thought of meeting Salvo in the afternoon.

'Is Donna Maria really wicked?' I asked him. I did not speak too loudly as we were sitting in the back of a wagon. Our plan was to picnic in the hills away from the noisy city, and we'd been thankful for a ride from a farmer on his way home.

Salvo shrugged. 'It depends. I'm sure the Holy Father

would say so. But don't go getting ideas, Silvia, it wouldn't be the same for you. Besides ...' I felt his breath soft against my cheek and I would have had a kiss but the wagon rolled at that moment as we splashed through a puddle deeper than it looked. Instead, his nose crashed against my cheek and, laughing, we hung on to each other and defended ourselves against the toppling fruit crates. I was glad they were empty.

It wasn't so very far to the farmer's home and when we clattered into the yard, a pair of geese set up a loud honking and a little girl of about ten ran out to meet us. She was very curious to find her father with two strangers from the city, and her eyes popped at the sight of us. At once I thought of my little brother and sister and felt horribly homesick.

'Why don't you tell Donna Maria you want to go home? Then you and I could go together?' Salvo said, when I told him. We had found a grassy spot in an old lemon grove and the rain had either dried in the sun or never fallen there. No one had cleared away the tangle of branches or the trees that had died, but there was a clear place for us to spread the cloth I'd brought. 'I would like to see my mother,' he went on, 'and I would like to visit your family too.'

'Oh?' I busied myself with unwrapping the bread and slices of roast meats that I had persuaded Cook to part with. I wondered if Salvo wished to visit my family for more than a polite greeting.

'I have to go away for a while,' he said, 'but when I get back we could go?'

'Away?' I said, startled. 'Where are you going?'

Salvo's smile was shy, almost embarrassed, and my heart jumped as I thought all over again how handsome he was. Not in the same way as Fabrizio, who could crush with a gaze, as well as with his muscular arms, but I much preferred Salvo's slender body and jaunty step. I loved the way his eyes twinkled, teasing and admiring me all at the same time. How I wished for the touch of his lips.

'I'm going to Rome,' he said, reaching up to pull down a branch that had a lone lemon amongst the leaves.

'Rome?' I was amazed. 'But why?'

'Why, Silvia,' he said with a laugh. 'You are full of questions as usual.' He threw the lemon at me and I caught it with one hand.

'And you are throwing things at me, as usual,' I said, inhaling the fresh scent. 'Now, tell me why you are going to Rome, or I'll eat your picnic.' I picked up a crust of bread.

'Oh no you won't.'

Before I knew it, Salvo had leapt across the cloth and wrested the slice away from me. But it was the bread he let fall to the ground and not my hand. He knelt down and put his arms right round me.

'I love you, Silvia,' he said, pulling me closer. 'You know that, don't you?'

'I do, Salvo,' I said, in barely more than a whisper. 'I really do.'

Every bit of me wanted to say that I loved him too, but I had no breath for speaking with so much kissing going on.

A rustle nearby disturbed us. We glanced up as a plump pigeon flapped overheard. Salvo toyed with the lace of my bodice. 'Did you sew this?' he asked and I nodded. He began to pull at it slowly.

To begin with the lace became tighter and tighter, but then, almost with a pop, the bow came undone and my bodice loosened. 'May I?' he said, slipping my chemise down from my shoulder. I was only alive to the line of fire that Salvo's fingertip was drawing down from my neck to where the fabric's edge caught on my nipple. I gasped as he released it and then more so as he kissed it, his lips soft at first, but then with more urgency.

I'd never felt such desire. Had I always lived in the dark? Here was a hot sun on my flesh for the first time. On a fine day, the finest ever day. Oh, Salvo, I moaned, hardly recognising my voice and feeling light as a feather as he wrapped his arms around me and lowered us both down

160

onto the warm grass. There was a soft brightness in his eyes that thrilled me in a way I had never known before.

'You are so very beautiful, Silvia. May I ...' he hesitated. 'May I see?'

Perhaps it was the contact with the ground that gave me weight again, and a thistle with sharp thorns that reminded me that a lot of pain and trouble can come along with pleasure. I pulled away a little and immediately he did too.

'What is it?'

'I ... I'm frightened, Salvo. You are going away so soon, and for a long time. What if ...'

'I want you more than anything, Silvia,' he said, and I could see very clearly that he did not lie. 'But I will also never hurt you.' He sighed but took my hand to his lips. 'Have no fear. You will save your virtue.' He paused, looked at me closely, and smiled with the old familiar and delicious twinkle in his eye, 'We shall make do very well with kisses.'

After very many kisses of all different sorts and in all different places, we lay on the picnic cloth in the late sunshine.

'Rome?' I said, suddenly remembering. 'Why are you going there?'

'It is Signor Carlino's idea, although I must say, Signor Pace is not so keen.' Salvo hesitated. 'The thing is ... wait, let me show you something.' He reached across me to the leather bag he always wore over his shoulder and took out a paper. 'Here.'

I could not help gasping at what I saw. It was a frontispiece, an engraving – the sort I'd seen in all of Donna Maria's books, but none were so lovely as the one I held in my hand.

'But, Salvo ...' Suddenly, I was short of words. I was looking at a pastoral scene not dissimilar to the one we were in. A grove, but well kept, the trees hanging with plentiful fruit. Birds flitted about and sat on the branches,

I could almost hear them singing. In the centre was a small choir, and I could see that the picture I held in my hand was reproduced in miniature for the copy that each of the singers held. They had an audience of both real and imaginary beasts and above the trees, angels cupped their hands to their ears in an effort to hear the music from below.

Tears formed in my eyes. 'Salvo,' I mumbled, 'this is so... so beautiful.'

'Thank you. I'm rather pleased with it. Look,' he pointed at two of the singers, 'did you notice ...'

'Oh!' I laughed and choked on tears all at the same time. 'It's you and me.'

'Yes,' he said, pleased with himself. 'We may never get our portraits painted, Silvia, but we'll have our faces alive in this for some time to come. That's if Signor Marenzio likes it, of course.'

'Signor Marenzio?' I said, impressed. The composer's name was often mentioned by the musicians at the palazzo. 'I'm sure he will. It's nicer than anything I've ever seen, and it's very much better than the one in Orlando Furioso.'

Salvo kissed me on the nose and I inhaled the delicious inky scent of him. 'You can keep that one if you like,' he said. 'I'd like to give you a perfect one but Signor Pace counts the pages and would miss one.'

'But isn't this perfect?'

'There's a smudge in that corner.'

Then I could see, but it was nothing but a small blot. 'I'll treasure it,' I said, and I held it next to my heart.

We'd reached the same door in the palazzo through which Fabrizio came in and Laura had left. Salvo put his arm round me and squeezed. I couldn't resist another kiss even though people were walking by. If there were sniggers, I didn't hear them.

'Let's go in,' Salvo said.

'What?'

'I want to see Pietro.'

'Pietro?'

'You're doing it again, Silvia.' He shook his head and sighed. 'What is to be done about all these questions?'

But I could see the twinkle in his eye and I gave him a playful push, only to have him reel back as if I had used all my force! We both started to laugh. Perhaps it was the jug of wine we'd shared in the village the other side of Chiaia.

'If you really want to see Pietro, then you'd better go through the stables.' I pointed round the back. 'That's where he spends most of his time, and I heard this morning that Don Carlo is preparing for yet another hunting trip.'

'Yet another?'

'He's always going hunting,' I said, 'and a good thing too. I'm much easier in my mind when he's away.'

Salvo caught hold of my arm again. 'I hope you won't be easier in your mind when I'm away.'

I frowned and raised my eyes heavenwards as if wondering what to say, but then he looked so anxious I had to laugh and shook my head, smiling.

'Of course not. I only hope you aren't away for too long.'

He sighed. 'So do I, but I have been told that if Signor Marenzio wishes me to go to Florence, or even Venice, then I am to go. There are many composers that wish to be published and my job is to see their business comes to Carlino and Pace.'

'Everyone will admire your work, you'll see. Perhaps Signor Marenzio will give you all his madrigals to publish, then you will be back home in no time.'

I left him then and climbed very slowly up the spiral stairs to my lady's apartment. Donna Maria wasn't there and I guessed she was at evening prayers. I didn't care that I'd missed them. I didn't care either that I would have quite a few little sins to confess next time.

After a quick splash of water over my face and hands, I glanced at myself in the mirror and couldn't help thinking that kissing did wonders for the complexion and brightness

163

of eye.

'Stop that now,' I said, wagging a finger at myself. 'Put the day out of your mind and pay attention to your work. Besides ...' A small frown creased my forehead and I looked away.

I did love Salvo but I hadn't been entirely truthful with him. It wasn't only that I was afraid of conceiving a child that had made me draw back from him. I was afraid of the act itself, and how it might change me. Would I become like Donna Maria? Reckless and wild in my behaviour? Distracted and forgetful? That would not do at all. Not when Don Carlo held our lives in his hands.

I went down to the sala and found Donna Maria not at prayers but with cheeks puffed out, full of almond lumbolls. No sooner had she swallowed one, than she took another from the bowl. It was a large dish and only a few were left. For a moment, I thought she might be with child, remembering her appetite from last time.

'Have one of these, Silvia,' she mumbled, whilst chewing. 'I do believe Cook has excelled herself.'

I only nibbled the sweet, but the strong flavour of almonds and caraway burst in my mouth. Delicious, even though I didn't usually trust caraway seeds. They always reminded me of mouse droppings and I often saw the flick of a tail in the kitchen.

'Don Carlo is going hunting again,' Donna Maria announced, in between mouthfuls. There was a happy gleam in her eye and once the bowl was empty, she stood up and twirled about laughing. I had seen little Margarita do just the same thing.

'I'm glad, my lady,' I said. And felt so relieved I took hold of her hands and we twirled round like children. Faster we went, throwing our heads back and letting our laughter swirl up to the ceiling. Only part of my joy was for Donna Maria, for I was happy in my love for Salvo. In the little pocket beneath my petticoat, I could feel the kitten and not my olive-wood swan but another swan, made of a smooth wood almost black. It was highly prized and

expensive, according to Salvo.

'Swans are very special,' he'd said when he gave it to me. 'Once they choose a mate, it is for life.' Putting the two side by side, I saw they fitted cleanly, almost like the pieces of a puzzle. 'See? They're meant to be together. But for now, they must be apart. Here, let us exchange. It will gladden my heart when I am away to think how near you this little swan has been.' He'd kissed my swan and made me kiss his. Then he'd kissed me very nicely indeed.

My lady's happy shrieks must have alerted Don Carlo. I looked up and saw his dark figure standing in the doorway. His presence in the sala quietened us at once and our arms fell to our sides. Donna Maria sat down and I made to resume my sewing on the bench under the window where the light was best for embroidery. It would not do to sit by my lady as she usually insisted, but I was not so far away that I couldn't hear the conversation.

The Prince's voice was cold. 'We'll lodge at Astruni tonight.'

'Astruni?' said Donna Maria. 'I am sorry to hear that, it is far away.'

I kept my eyes on my work, but marvelled at her apparent sincerity. Without moving my head I looked towards Don Carlo. He was standing with his back to the great fireplace.

'Will you be entertaining?'

The way he lingered over the word 'entertaining' sent a hot stab of fear through me. If he knew ... but perhaps he did! Why say it at all? I sewed pretend stitches, too busy listening to concentrate.

Donna Maria's reply was all syrup. 'Father Strozzi is taking some refreshment here in the morning. We are to discuss the new altarpiece in the convent chapel.'

Don Carlo said nothing, but stood silent. I was reminded of the first time I saw him on the road to Gesualdo, when I hid and Salvo had kept us from harm. He had been a cloud on a sunny day then, and here he was again, a dark presence in a well-lit room. I swallowed and decided that my imaginary seam needed unpicking. I reached for my sewing kit to find the little bone hook that did the deed so well, but somehow caught my sleeve on the edge of the bench and the box fell, spilling the contents all across the floor.

I swear the noise it made was twice as loud as usual because Don Carlo was in the room.

'Oh, Silvia,' said my lady, 'do take care to pick them all up, won't you? Emmanuele might prick his knees.'

Don Carlo was not so thoughtful. He made a nasty remark about my carelessness, then bid Donna Maria goodbye. If there was any feeling or sorrow in the parting, I didn't hear it. Once he'd left the sala, I glanced across to Donna Maria. There was no disguising the relief we both felt.

'Do you think we should ask Cook for more of those lumbolls?' she said.

I held up the bodice I was embroidering. 'Not if you ever want to wear this, my lady.'

November was only three days away but during the evening it was as if all the day's heat had come indoors. We opened the shutters on both the courtyard and the street side of the palazzo, but failed to create the slightest draught. The trickles of sweat that leached from beneath our clothes may have soaked our handkerchiefs, but nothing could daunt my lady's good mood.

At four hours of the night, Donna Maria decided it really was time to retire and we climbed the main stairs to her apartment, passing the quiet darkness of Don Carlo's apartment on the floor below.

'Do you think we shall have venison or boar for dinner tomorrow?' I said, by way of conversation.

'I'd rather have cook's lumbolls, especially if it meant Don Carlo never came back.' Donna Maria sighed, but then with a flick of her hand she said, 'I shall not think of him. Tonight is for Fabrizio ... ah, Fabrizio.'

How she enjoyed saying his name. I said nothing, but

busied myself with unhooking her sleeves. It was one of my favourite gowns. It had taken me many weeks to embroider the twining wild strawberry pattern. The cuffs needed washing. Some sticky residue from the sweets had found its way onto the linen.

Outside, in the street below, a dog started barking, a large hound by the sound of it, and then another. We heard shouting too and both of us looked towards the window.

'Go and look, Silvia.' We were thinking the same thing, I'm sure. Donna Maria's expression in the flickering lamplight said as much. It was too early for Fabrizio, but was it Don Carlo returning? My mind jumped to Don Giulio as well. Perhaps he had an appointment at Palazzo San Severo we didn't know about.

The street below was lit red by the flames of several torches. I searched through the faces but saw no one I recognised. Two men were being held back from violence by others. Gradually, the party moved off towards the main square and I breathed out.

'It's all right,' I said. 'They're going. Nobody we know.'

Donna Maria laughed almost too loudly. The truth was that, even with Don Carlo away, we were jumpy as new lambs. I slept so little at night that some days the only thing that kept me awake was stabbing myself with the needle. Not sufficient to draw blood, of course, I didn't want any more work than necessary. As it was, every day after Donna Maria went to bed, I checked and hung all her clothes then prepared those for the following morning. It seemed that the minute I lay down, Don Fabrizio arrived, and although I willed it, sleep would not come while he was there. I missed Laura and was yet to find anyone else to take her place. As for Donna Maria, she seemed to think I could do everything without help.

The false alarm set me giggling too and soon we were both needing to wipe tears from our eyes.

'Ah, Silvia,' said Donna Maria, stroking my arm. 'There's such tremendous absurdity about life, isn't there?'

I could only agree, although I did feel uncomfortable at having my own life considered so lightly. She continued to stroke my arm rather absently until suddenly, her hand gripped tighter than my stays.

'It's far too hot to sleep,' she said. 'Bring me something of yours to put on. I'll wait for Fabrizio on the balcony. No one will know it's me. And a shawl too so I can cover my hair.'

'But—'

'Go on, Silvia. I'll find out what it's like to be you,' she said. 'Isn't that a good joke?'

I left her and went back into the antechamber where I kept my clothes in a small wardrobe at the end of my bed. This absurdity of Donna Maria's gave me the jitters. Why did she have to keep turning the world upside down? I pulled at the closet door too briskly and although it opened, the handle came off in my hand. There. Another person might have taken it as a sign not to meddle with the order of things.

'Here, my lady,' I said, holding up a grey skirt and a light shawl of the same hue. 'Are you sure you want to put these on?'

'Oh, yes.' She clapped her hands together. 'What fun. Fabrizio will certainly laugh.'

He'd never struck me as someone with a sense of humour, but you can be wrong about a person. I'd thought Laura silly and she turned out to be devious. And my lady was as changeable as the waves on a stormy day. Often lately I'd been wondering what my life would have been like if I'd stayed at home and helped with the chickens and darned hose instead of going with old Francesca to market that day.

'Go to bed now, Silvia.' Donna Maria picked and smoothed at my skirt and shawl, but seemed pleased with the effect overall. 'No, wait. Go and have a look round the house and the courtyard first. Come back and tell me if all is quiet.'

I was nearly dead on my feet but, taking a lamp, I went down the stairs and looked out into the courtyard. In fact, I stepped outside, for it was cooler and more beautiful than the gloomy house. The moon was pale through the clouds but enough to see by, and the scent of the few late roses did sweeten the city air. But the colour was leeched from all the petals and although some were darker than others, I only knew their rich pinks and crimsons from memory. I heard the night bell strike five. No wonder I was tired.

Back upstairs, I found my lady not on the balcony but sitting on her bed.

'I've changed my mind, Silvia. Shut the window. I will wait for Fabrizio as usual. Take this off and bring me another nightdress.' I helped her step from my skirt and retrieved my shawl from the floor. 'The one with the black collar,' she said. 'Bring me that one.' The favourite. Both my lady's and mine. It wasn't the same crimson nightdress I had made so long ago, but I had copied it since and was particularly proud of the embroidery at the collar, a pattern I had made in white thread against the black silk with two swans, their necks intertwined. I had matched it at the cuffs too. I fetched it, hoping it would be the last task for me that night.

When I went back into her chamber, Donna Maria was already lying down. 'Oh, leave it there,' she said, waving for me to lay the nightdress on the far side of the bed. 'Perhaps later... bring a candle though. That one is nearly gone.'

I dreaded looking in the candle box and finding none, then having to go downstairs again, but there were two left, one of which was short, but substantial. I fitted it to the silver holder and placed it on the chair as my lady told me. I was walking in sleep by then but said to myself that if I lit the other candle and read from Orlando Furioso, *then I would be sure to stay awake enough to hear Don Fabrizio's whistle.*

But if I read any sentences, I don't remember them and it wasn't a whistle that woke me. Nor was the next face I

169

saw that of the handsome Don Fabrizio, Duke of Andria, but, as in the worst of nightmares when death has surely come and stares at you with eyes of fire ... then did I wake. And in noise worse than thunder, amidst crashes, wild shouts and cries as if from beasts, as flames flickered round the walls, I started into sitting and all my whole life welled up and became a little spot before my eyes, for there with a sharp and glittering blade brandished in my face, I saw him. I saw the Devil.

Chapter Twenty-Three

I held the Gesualdo madrigal. It felt strangely damp, as if fresh off the press. Even in the low light, the three blots were quite clear. In fact, they shimmered, as if they too were fresh. There was no wine in the vicinity, but as I put the volume down on the table, a drop of blood fell from my sleeve. Then another, staining the cuff. Soon all around the wrist was sodden and splashes covered the engraving, colouring the white lines deep crimson. Pulling up my sleeve of Silvia's costume, I saw the gash on my arm weeping a great river of blood. There were footsteps outside and a loud thumping on the door.

I woke with a start.

'I've made you a cup of tea.'

Over the duvet I saw Mollie standing there in her Barbie pyjamas clutching my *Best Mum in the World* mug. Nothing could be more suspicious.

'Thank you, darling,' I said, struggling to sit up. Still half in the dream, I couldn't help checking my arm, but the scar from the needle was almost invisible. The tea, however, was lukewarm, mostly milk, and had the tea bag still floating in it, but I did my best. Mollie sat down trapping me where I was. I glanced at the telly. The clock on the display said six-thirty. 'Isn't it a bit early for you?'

She waved away the idea. In a Most Imperious Wave competition, I think the Queen had better watch out.

'I wanted to ask you something,' she said.

'Okay. Ask away.' I sipped my tea and hoped she wouldn't ask anything sufficiently surprising for me to spill it.

'You know in choir?'

'Err …' I hedged my bets. 'Probably.'

'When you say we should all listen to each other.'

'Yes, I do say that.'

'And you say it to me on the way to school on choir day and on the way home?'

'Do I?' She gave me a look. It was a look I knew but couldn't quite place … and then with a burst of recognition, saw myself. She wasn't having me pull the wool over her eyes so I owned up. 'I believe I do.'

'Is that because I sing louder than the rest?'

What could I say? The fact was Mollie sang louder than the rest of the choir put together. She had a fantastic voice with a clear tone and a natural effortless technique. I didn't want to put her off by telling her to be quiet, but I did wish she would meld more with the others. Ideally, they'd all meld their voices with hers but that wasn't likely.

'Umm … well …'

'Okay. I get it,' she said. 'I'll listen better next time.' She remained seated. There was something else. Had to be. Early tea in bed didn't come that cheap.

'That's a good idea,' I said, giving her back the mug. 'Can I get up now?'

That wave again, then: 'You know when …' she hesitated. I waited. 'You know when you have a secret?'

Ah. 'Yes,' I said. 'I do.'

'And you know that you're not supposed to tell.'

'Mmm.'

'If you really, really want to tell …'

'Mmm,' I said, in my best measured tone but meaning God! Hurry up and bloody tell me!

'If you don't tell all of it, is it all right to tell a bit of the secret sometimes?'

I put my arm round her. Reassurance was vital. I wanted to know what her big secret was but at the same time didn't want her to think that blabbing was always okay. 'Well, darling, sometimes it can be a good idea, especially if you feel it would really help someone, or maybe if you thought something had happened that was wrong?'

She frowned and then sighed. Clearly it was a tough decision for her. I gave her a kiss. Big mistake. Obviously far too reassuring because she brightened up almost at once.

'Nope,' she said. 'I think it's all right. I don't have to tell. Anyway, it'll be done soon.' She put my mug on the coffee table then went into the kitchen without taking it with her. I flopped back down on the sofa, defeated. Done soon? What did that mean?

'Oi,' I called out, weakly. 'What about this mug?'

At least she had the decency to come and fetch it. I lay there for a while longer making up my mind. I'd ring Jon, arrange to meet him and ask him to explain. No, not ask – demand he explain. Everything. I'd been a coward that time in Costa. What sort of example was I setting to Mollie? Besides, I wanted to talk to Jon. I wanted to tell him about the frontispiece, what happened in Italy and, more than any of that, I missed him.

Later, when I phoned him, he said he'd drop by the next evening. I suggested then because Mollie would be at Michael's and Mum was going to see Gran. I wanted to be able to speak my mind freely. It was a brief call and there wasn't the usual warmth in his voice. Was I being paranoid? He was in a hurry, that's all. Perhaps someone was there. Somebody in particular?

I got back from work the next day to find a postcard caught halfway through the letter box. It had a serious crease down the middle but the picture was of a familiar scene: the Bay of Naples. Taken from the Sorrento end, it looked back towards Naples, with a snowy peaked Vesuvius cutting its way into the sky to the right. Well, I hadn't sent it, so there was only one person it could be. Somebody old enough to send a postcard rather than send a photo with a text. I turned it over.

Wednesday
Coming to Exeter for your concert.
I have something for you!
Yours, lonely in Naples,
Duncan.

Lord. What was I supposed to make of that? He was coming here? I'd be pleased to see him, certainly, but …

173

God, I hate exclamation marks. Something for me? Why didn't he just say what it was?

I put it on the bookcase in the hall, took my jacket off and carried my shopping into the kitchen. Everywhere was a mess, except my room, which was becoming more and more Mum's room. Gradually, she was moving my stuff out. My little Isle of Lewis chess piece: the Queen, hand on cheek, looking worried; the wooden angel with a bit of her wing missing; the verdigris frog candlestick. I could understand that one as she did have a phobia about frogs. But it meant all my stuff was in the sitting room, along with Barbie's, and while I was secretly pleased the pink pretender was beginning to fall from Mollie's favour, I didn't want her moving in with me. She had sharp feet and far too many accessories.

I put away the shopping, and convinced myself that I would have bought the bottle of red even if Jon hadn't been coming over. And fajitas? They weren't what you could call proper cooking, more like assembly. No trouble at all.

In the sitting room I attempted a tidy up. All the bedding went behind the sofa, Barbie etc filled a large hessian bag-for-life. Writing implements were given a special place all of their own in a Charles and Di mug I'd been given on my third birthday. My music needed a proper sort out, but it would have to wait. I put it in neat piles on the cupboard by the telly. Then I had a little worry that the telly might burst into flames and, like Sophie's kettle, set fire to everything. Except only the Gesualdo cover had been burnt.

And now there was the extra red spot.

A great shiver ran through me and I slumped on the sofa suddenly exhausted. How I wished the bloody piece had remained locked up and lost in some vault somewhere. Ever since it came to light, things had been going wrong. Bad things were happening and everyone I knew was keeping secrets from me. My daughter, Jon, and now Duncan. Was Signor Pace right and it was cursed? I would take a photo of the cover. If something weird was going on, I wanted evidence.

'Hi,' Jon said. He was smiling, not exactly broadly, but a bit more than narrowly. He had his hands rammed into the pockets of his jeans when I opened the door.

I smiled back. 'Hello. Come in.' Not long ago, such politeness wouldn't have existed. He'd have been halfway through a sentence and in the door without an invitation. 'Can I get you anything?'

He hesitated. He did, I swear. I could feel my heart thumping. Please don't be hesitant, I thought. Be springy and careless. Be funny and play games and look me in the eye. But he didn't. He stood in the hall and waited for me to say something. To invite him in to my sitting room. The one he would stroll into and collapse on the sofa in, without a thought. What's happened? Daniela, I thought, and in my mind's eye I pictured her in Costa, all long black hair, big bosoms and laughter. She's what happened.

'Cup of tea would be good,' he said. 'Thing is …' he looked shifty. 'I can't stay long.'

'Oh?' I made my way to the kitchen. Was my face scarlet? It certainly felt like it. I hoped he wouldn't notice. He sat down at the table and I messed about making tea, even getting out the pot. Eventually, I sat opposite him. The table felt half the usual size. I poured the tea and the noise of it, the scale rising as it filled the mug, had never sounded so loud.

'So,' I said, brightly. 'Whatcha been up to?'

'Oh, you know …' He hesitated again, coughed, then sat forward. 'Actually, I've been really busy.'

'Really?'

'Yes, I've got this big work project on.'

Work project? I just stopped myself from choking on a mouthful of tea. 'Oh? What's that all about?'

'I can't really say,' he said, with a pained expression. 'It's a big deal, you see. I'm not supposed to breathe a word.'

'Oh, right. Don't then.' I didn't believe him for a moment. Not even the Official Secrets Act would stop Jon talking about his advertising campaigns in the past. For God's sake, he used to bloody well consult me! Jesus!

'Yes,' he went on. 'I've never done anything like it—'

'The thing is, Jon,' I interrupted. 'The reason I rang you...' My heart was going like the clappers now. I wanted to cry. Wail like a baby. Noooooo ... go away trouble and horribleness. I didn't want to be at odds with him, didn't want to confront him – didn't want to reveal my own feelings – how upset, how angry, how afraid of losing him I was. I put my lips to the edge of the mug but couldn't bring myself to take a sip.

'Yes?' Jon said.

'The thing is, I'm worried about Mollie.'

'Mollie?' He looked surprised. And I'd surprised myself. I wasn't exactly worried. 'Is she all right?'

'No, she's fine ... but whatever it is that she's keeping secret, it's upsetting her,' I said, bluntly and without adding, 'and me'.

A frown creased his forehead. 'But surely ...' I didn't say anything. The ball was better in his court after my wild serve. 'She'll tell you in her own good time, won't she?'

Damn. 'I'm not so sure,' I said. 'She does seem upset.' God, I was lying now.

Jon put his mug down and looked stricken. 'You don't think anybody's ... you know, doing her any harm do you?'

'No, no. It isn't that. But ever since I got back from Italy, she's been so secretive. And apart from that,' I could feel a groundswell of emotion. 'I wasn't at all keen on you staying here, with her.' My voice had got louder. Up, up, up I went, onto my highest horse.

'We thought it was the best—'

'You shouldn't have done so without my permission.' A voice in my head said: are you listening to yourself?

He was shocked. 'What are you saying?' I'd never heard his voice sound so cold.

I regretted what I said immediately. It wasn't Mollie I was cross about, it was nothing to do with her. It was really all about Daniela.

'Listen,' I said, suddenly desperate to mollify. I'd tell the truth. 'It's just that—'

Jon scraped his chair on the floor. A harsh and painful sound to the ears but not as upsetting as the sound of the key in the lock, the front door opening and my mum calling: 'Cooeee ... only me!'

How could that be?

Jon stood up. 'I'd better go.'

'Jon. Well, well,' Mum said, beaming when she saw him. 'How nice to see you. I haven't seen you for a while.'

'Why aren't you at Gran's?' I said.

She was taken aback by my crossness. 'Oh, you know Gran,' she said, mildly. 'She said I had to go because she wanted to watch *The Apprentice* and didn't want me interrupting.'

Awful. It was just awful. Jon gave her a quick kiss on the cheek and went out. I followed him into the hall.

'Listen,' I said.

'No,' he said, turning to face me. 'You've obviously got it into your head that I'm not to be trusted.' He yanked open the door and the sudden draught flipped Duncan's postcard on to the floor picture side down at Jon's feet. We both leant down, almost knocking our heads together. Jon got there first.

Yours, lonely in Naples ...

He handed it to me and left without another word.

Chapter Twenty-Four

Napoli 1590

Surely, I was already dead. My life poised on the point of the Devil's blade, of no more significance than a tack about to be ripped out.

'Traitress,' Don Carlo hissed. 'I shall kill you. You cannot escape me now!'

I had no breath to scream. Amidst the furore it was as if my spirit left my body. I was a floating thing beyond the noise and clamour. My eye remained fixed, gazing at the sharp point of the halberd. I could see the edge quiver from the tension of Don Carlo's grip. The plunge was imminent and in this strangely stretched time I wondered – my heart or my throat? A voice I knew called from far away, but not to me.

'My lord. My lord!'

Like a pebble dropping over the edge of a waterfall I fell from my lofty refuge back to the usual dwelling place within my skin.

'My lord.' Pietro placed his hand on Don Carlo's arm.

Torches flamed, the smell of their burning acrid in my nostrils. Those intent on harm, more than just the Prince and Pietro, three or four at least, panting from their ascent of the stairs, blundered about like bears released from their cages. They growled and swore and smashed down the door to my lady's bedchamber. The noise beat about the walls. Shouts and screams. Oh, my lady! My dear lady. Her hour had come and nothing could be done. I heard her cry out for mercy, for pity, for ...

Two arquebus shots, and then silence. But then, my lady! I could hear her weeping. And in it more hopeless grief than I had ever heard or wished to know.

'They are both there, my lord,' said Pietro, quietly. I looked at him, but he kept his gaze elsewhere.

And with that, Don Carlo straightened from his

crouching over me. 'Don't let her go,' he said, and after jabbing his halberd close to my throat he went to the door of the bedchamber. 'And put a torch here.' He gestured at the portiere.

Then there were terrible screams. Fearful screams and cries, full of terror but full of life. Then the horror of the strikes, the strange gasps and gurgles of pain and finally the heavy quiet thuds of butchery.

The men all came out of the bedchamber. Last of all, Don Carlo. He still held his halberd but now its blade was black with blood, both hands too and the cuffs of his hunting coat. A sickly smell of shot, sweat and flesh pervaded the room and my throat clenched ready for retching.

'Wait!' said Don Carlo. 'I do not believe she is dead.' And with that he went back into the bedchamber! As he turned I saw all the front of his coat was spattered with blood and where he must have wiped his brow too. Then came more dreadful sounds from within, like the breathy gruntings of a dog mad with lust for blood.

I think I swayed but Pietro was there and caught me under the arm. 'This is no time for fainting, Silvia. Go,' he said, under his breath. 'Go now.'

I took a deep breath and was away in a trice. The convent was close, only across the street. But it may as well have been in another country, for I realised I could not get out of the apartment. Two of the men, the murderers of Don Fabrizio, I guessed, had gone on before me and stood at the top of the main staircase. The only other stairs were the ones from the antechamber I'd just left. I was trapped. The nursery was the last place I could go.

Mercifully, Margarita was at her cousin's. Emmanuele slept in his cradle. In the dim flicker of the night oil lamp his nurse stood like a ghost in nothing but her chemise, woken no doubt, by the ghastly cries.

'Save me,' I whispered loud as I dare. Perhaps she was struck dumb with fear, for I got no reply. I glanced about, *then scrambled under the bed and I hid myself there as best I could, pulling down a corner of the sheet till it reached the floor.*

The arrival of Don Carlo in the room only moments later frightened the nurse into voice.

'Spare the baby, my lord!' she squeaked. 'For the love of God!'

From where I lay I could see Don Carlo's boot and the sharp tip of the blade that had so recently been at my throat. A drop of blood hung like a jewel and then splashed on the floor less than an arm's length away. I needed to breathe but dare not. I saw his boots swivel one way and then round towards me. As the drumming of my heart became nearly as loud as thunder, I took a breath. Did he hear? A boot stepped nearer but, by some miracle, at the same moment, the baby woke with a little mewling sound.

'Take him downstairs, woman,' Don Carlo said, his voice its old repellent rasp. At once, the nurse gathered Emmanuele in her arms and ran to the door. 'And Pietro,' he went on, 'lock up the cupboard, then lock the apartment. Silvia Albana is here somewhere. She's a witch and a whore just like her mistress but I'll not waste time on her now.'

I saw his boots move away and then when they'd disappeared through the door, I heard them go down the stairs. Still, l dared not leave my hiding place. In fact, I wondered if I would ever move again for I was stiff with fear.

The key of the closet where my lady's jewels were kept clanked in its lock.

'Pietro?' I whispered.

His boots appeared at the edge of the bed and he lifted the sheet. A lamp shone in my face. 'Silvia? Why are you not away?'

'There were men ...'

He straightened up, went to the door, then came back. 'Don't come out just yet. I must lock you in for now. If I keep the key, the men Don Carlo has left on guard will not be able to come in. They are all strangers to me, Silvia. Stay there, I will be back very soon.'

I lay like the corpse I was surely soon to be. 'I am dead as my ... my lady!' I whispered, and a great and painful blackness washed across my thoughts. Already, I was cold, although my heart still beat. Was this purgatory? My fingers felt towards the underside of the bed, so close. Had the space always been so small? Was it not bearing down on me as I lay? I could only sip the air, the tightest of stays were as gossamer in comparison to the restriction in my chest. In one swift and dreadful notion, I was in my coffin.

In a distant place, it seemed in my mind then, there were scenes of colour and sunshine, the twinkling sea and laughter – my family and the pecking of chickens on the palm of my hand – threading needles with silk, charting patterns for blackwork – my little carved swan, Salvo... Salvo... why are you so very far away?

The sudden rattle of the key in the lock, stopped my breath altogether.

'Silvia?' Pietro's voice and a flicker of lamplight. 'They are all gone. Come out now.'

I breathed again. Movement shocked the deadness in my limbs into trembling, but I crawled out and with effort, hauled myself to sitting up on the bed.

'Oh, Pietro,' I said, hardly recognising the hoarse whisper as my own. 'I am dead. Dead as my lady!' The Princess Donna Maria, lying so close, who'd hoped her beauty might protect her, her screams still echoed in my head. 'Am I not dead, Pietro?'

'No, Silvia. Here you are, very much alive.'

I looked up at him and saw that, although servant to the devil for so long, he still bore kindness in his expression. 'He wants me dead too, Pietro. He said as much.'

'Listen,' he said. 'The house is roused now. I shall send for the officials and the justice. They will protect you.'

'But they will not come in time, Pietro.'

'I think they will, Silvia. Don Carlo has changed his clothes and taken the horses. He said he was going hunting this evening and now he is. I did not know about ...' He looked towards the door, where but a room away, my lady and Fabrizio still lay. 'I didn't know Don Carlo had such a plan. He didn't tell me, Silvia. Are you not surprised? Me...' Pietro slapped himself on the chest, 'of all people, he did not tell me.'

'You have a heart, Pietro. That's why not.' I could feel my body returning to something I knew.

'Although who can be surprised?' he went on, not acknowledging my words. 'We all knew about the Don Fabrizio and Donna Maria.'

'I feared as much, Pietro. Ever since Laura ...'

A noise of footsteps and voices on the main stairs startled us both. I clutched Pietro's arm.

'He has come for me. He has come!'

'Who's there?' shouted a voice I knew, but couldn't at once place. 'Come out so we can see you.'

'Don't be afraid, Silvia,' said Pietro, gently.

But I was very afraid and hid behind him as we went to the door.

'Father Strozzi,' said Pietro. 'I am glad to see you.'

Of course! Father Strozzi! I stepped from my hiding place. He was with another man I did not know but who bore a torch in one hand and an arquebus in the other. Neither were properly dressed but had cloaks to cover their nightgowns. I shrank back as the three of them spoke together. The stranger was an official of the Grand Court of Vicaria. Already, the Master, Royal Councillors, Criminal Judges and even the Magnificent Prosecuting Attorney himself had been sent for.

'You girl,' said the official. 'Who are you?'

'Silvia Albana, my lord,' I stuttered. 'Maidservant to ... to ...'

'Stay there, whoever you are,' he ordered. 'Now, Father Strozzi, would you lead the way?'

When they opened the door to the bedchamber, I heard

182

a cry from Father Strozzi and then the more muffled exclamations of Pietro and the official. My mind's eye struggled to see into the room. I knew it so well, the beautiful emerald green curtains around the bed, the chair with the crimson velvet seat where I had sat so often to read to my lady. Then my mind's ear replayed the noises I'd heard and I shivered, focusing my eyes instead on Emmanuele's cradle and the dent in the pillow where his little head had lain.

The men came back, their faces changed and full of horror; tight about their jaws and their eyes sunk deeper in their sockets as if they had retreated from what they had seen. The official gestured towards the large ring of keys that jangled in Pietro's hand. 'Do you have keys to this apartment?'

'Yes, my lord.'

'Lock it up after us. Nothing must be disturbed.' He looked at me. 'Make sure of that. We'll be back at first light.'

I had time only to glance at Pietro's surprised face before the door was closed and the muffled voice of the official demanded that it be locked.

'There'll be some clearing up to do,' I heard Father Strozzi say, then they'd gone.

Pietro's oil lamp on the small chest under the window flickered from the draught of the door closing, then settled into stillness. I did not move either, but stood stupid as a chopped log. A great silence now pressed around me; surely a chasm had opened in the ground and swallowed all of the sounds in the world.

My lady and Don Fabrizio lay dead in the bedchamber and I was locked in with them.

The terror of lying beneath the bed in the nursery was a real thing. The glittering blade that Don Carlo held would have flipped me into death with a small swish. That I understood. But not this new dread. The one that came over me like a night sea fog, rolling inexorably towards me, dank and dark, and in which I might be forever lost.

That fear overtopped everything I had ever known.

Why had I not said my prayers more fervently? For what other armour could there be against evil? I had seen demons. Several, though they looked like men. I was no witch and had not thought witches any more than women who knew some incantations and liked to play on the weaknesses of others, but now I was not so sure. Perhaps Orlando Furioso *was more true than I had thought. What was my little life but that of a miserable ant stuck fast in a tiny crevice?*

A noise! There ... in the antechamber! Perhaps the creak of old wood, perhaps a mouse scurrying, the splutter of a dying candle. It sounded like none of these things. Oh, how quickly all the little hairs on my flesh rose. How my eyes wished to close but could only bulge with gazing. My ears pricked, sharp as any of the needles in their cushion.

The doorway into the antechamber swallowed all light. The candle was out and Pietro's lamp was the only source. Quickly, I crossed the room and delved into the candle box. At first I thought it was empty, but a short inger-length had fallen across the bottom. I was very fervent in my thanks to Jesus and Holy Mary and several saints. But it seemed doubtful to me that they would hear my quivering little voice. What else could I do though? I knew that beyond that was the door into hell.

With shaking hands, I lit the candle from the oil lamp, but with the flare of light came into my mind the awful thought: who had come to fetch the souls of my lady and Don Fabrizio? And where would they go? Were they really so wicked that they would burn not with passion but with flames licking their flesh instead?

Another noise! Low, like groaning, but getting louder. I ran to the door and beat my fists against it, screaming.

'Let me out! For the love of God.'

Some monstrous thing was coming, I was sure of it. Perhaps the souls had yet to be collected. Or their torment had started even before they reached the furnaces. This noise seemed to shake the door as if it were flimsy cloth.

Trembling worse than a milk pudding turned from its mould, I looked over my shoulder and in a flash the thing itself was lit as if with a thousand moons, bright silver piercing the darkness as easily as Don Carlo's blade sliced through my lady's velvet flesh. The demons had come and I was trapped.

Chapter Twenty-Five

I'd acquired a new demon. A youngster, full of energy. One whose voice interrupted the dull, repetitive conversations of the old crowd who told me I was fat, stupid and boring, and lured me into believing something even more depressing. *He prefers her*, it taunted. *Of course he does. Who wouldn't?*

It was blowing a gale, grey clouds buffeted the finials on top of the cathedral and the river was choppy and brown. I avoided the underpass and the steps where the boy had pushed past me before he jumped. Ever since that day, I'd crossed the road instead. The sneery-voiced demon regaled me all the way into town. It was the day of the photo shoot, but I had to go to the museum first.

'It's a pity,' said the curator stiffly, when I handed her the madrigal, 'that when I let you take the original away, I didn't know how clumsy you were.'

'I'm so sorry,' I said, 'the actual manuscript isn't harmed, only the cover.'

I wished I'd taken the damn thing back sooner. Maybe this would be the end of the curse and we could all get back to normal.

After Jon had gone, leaving me holding Duncan's postcard, I'd opened the bottle of red and put my glass on the coffee table. The Gesualdo was on the top of the heap of music beside it. Next thing, it tipped over. God knows how. The wine puddled in the centre of the cover. When I'd patted it with some kitchen paper there was no sign of any spots; rather, it looked as if the copy itself had haemorrhaged. Luckily, the waxed brown paper, although old, had stopped the wine from seeping through. Of course, it meant there was no chance of acquiring any photographic evidence about the number of spots.

'I've found something out about the provenance of the manuscript,' I said. Immediately, the curator's expression brightened.

'Oh? Really?'

'Yes,' I said, breezily. 'I've just come back from Italy.' I added one of those little offhand waves that implied I went every other weekend, then felt embarrassed and began mumbling about my mother.

'But what did you find out?' the curator interrupted. She had the same intensity in her voice I'd heard when she first showed me the manuscript.

I told her about meeting Signor Pace and his theory about the curse and instead of the derisive laugh I'd expected, she said, 'I'm not at all surprised. But don't worry. Cursed artefacts are the stuff of museums. With all those bad vibes festering away, it's amazing the buildings stay standing.'

'Do you happen to know,' I asked, 'if anything was with this manuscript when you found it?'

'With it?'

'Yes. Any other music or books, artefacts maybe?' It was one thing knowing where the manuscript came from, but I still had no idea how it got to Exeter.

'I'll check,' she said. 'Oh, by the way, I've been told to ask for the photo of you all as soon as possible. I hear it's going to be rather daring.'

We went into the pink foyer.

'Hmm,' I said, looking up at Albert's statue and his disapproving expression. 'I think we're all getting daring these days.'

I walked up the hill to the theatre, holding my music bag with both hands against my body like a sort of breastplate. I'd got fed up with it slapping against my legs. The forecast had said gale force nine, gusting to storm force ten in Portland and Plymouth. A line of newly planted birch trees bent and strained against their ties, a weary chain gang. The mature evergreen oak by the entry to the car park was more stalwart, merely moaning. I imagined it had felt quite a few gales in its time.

'Ted?' I said to the guy huddled against the studio

door. He had a heap of photography paraphernalia at his feet so it wasn't a wild guess. The khaki flak jacket and ravaged look spoke of war, not butterflies and sea horses, but what do I know?

He nodded. 'Don't suppose you have a key, do you?'

'No, sorry. I'm surprised Sophie's not here already.' I looked back down the hill. It wasn't very cold, but the wind was strong enough to grab hold of my words and chuck them away as soon as I'd opened my mouth.

'I wanted to set up before you all got here,' Ted shouted. 'I texted Jon, but he said he had to go and pick someone up.'

Guess who ... said my sneery demon.

I was glad to see Sophie appear from around the corner. With her good hand, she was holding on to her hat, a mob cap made out of emerald green velvet. It looked great on her and I could imagine it looking very well on someone in a Shakespeare production. There were times when I wished I was more theatrical and not quite so High Street.

'Sorry, sorry ...' she said, unlocking the door. 'One of tonight's cast had ripped his blazer, see, and I'm not so quick with this bloody plaster on.'

'It's amazing you can manage at all,' I said.

'Well, I'm thankful it wasn't the other arm.'

Two cars were coming up the hill. Robert first and there, yes, Daniela sat next to Jon. *See? Told you so* ... My stomach lurched and not in a good way. This would be an ordeal. Everything was an ordeal.

I went into the drama studio and welcomed the flat atmosphere, black curtains and dead acoustic. They seemed appropriate. Sophie had all the costumes on a rail and I took mine and went behind a curtain to change. The dress was lovely, not elaborately embroidered like Jon's outfit, but, Silvia Albana was no peasant or kitchen maid. She was a maidservant to a princess. Sophie had given me a lecture on corsets, and eventually I'd given in, because I didn't want to look like a 'comely wench'. On top of the corset I had a straight up and down garment made of fine cotton which, she said, would have been linen in 1590. I made the mistake of calling it a petticoat. Sophie had tutted and said it was a chemise. Petticoats were worn on the top, except for the bodice and skirt and the over-dress, which probably had detachable linen bits for washing; cuffs, sleeves, collars …

She could talk for England about clothes and who wore what, how and when, but I was just glad the outer dress was a nice colour. Blue-grey like my eyes and made in some sort of faux silk. The corset did wonders too. There'd be no bungee jumping for my bosom – and Wonderbra, thou art a feeble thing in comparison. Once I'd got everything on, I sat down on a chair behind the curtain with the wig on my lap and tried to feel more enthusiastic.

Not everything had gone wrong, I told myself. Sophie and Robert seemed happy. My mother was in regular contact with Charles, who so far hadn't shown any signs of being like Thomas the Snake. The school choir was fantastic – that did cheer me. I remembered the last practice and all the lovely expressions on their faces as they focused a hundred per cent on what they were singing. That's the way, I thought. Focus on the music, not yourself. The concert would be over soon and *Noteworthy* could go back to being a happy quartet. *Oh yeah?* Oh, no … the realisation that this wasn't likely hit me in the stomach. I bent forward, groaning.

'Here she is!' The curtain swished back. I was blinded by a spotlight, but I knew it was Daniela by her voice. 'Oh, dear,' she said, 'is it all right?'

I was *it* now, was I?

'Oh!' she said, laughing in that treacly way of hers that made me want to nail her teeth together. 'It's your *wig*. Look everyone, doesn't it look like a pussy cat?'

My eyesight recovered enough to see Jon look embarrassed. Sophie, lovely Sophie, was clearly cross. 'Have you been to the optician lately, Daniela?'

She'd spent some considerable time braiding that wig.

I stood up and picked up the chair I'd been sitting on. 'Let's get on with it then.' God, it was all rather grim. Why had we ever thought it was a good idea? Had we? Back in the old days, when we were young, carefree and laughed a lot. Yes, all of a few weeks ago.

'It's a good job we're not singing this evening, with this gale blowing,' I said. The studio was fairly well soundproofed but I wasn't the only thing moaning. The wind rumbled like a train with an infinite number of carriages.

I liked the wig and thought it looked good on me. There's no way I would have worn it if it hadn't. Sophie had done a fantastic job on all the costumes, and the placing of the music stand with a very large piece of music on it, plus a swathe of black drape from Daniela's Grim Reaper costume, obscured her plaster very well. Jon bore no resemblance to the fish-faced Don Carlo Gesualdo of the portrait in the book, but in his costume I could see him catching the eye of Elizabeth the First as the Earl of Leicester. Or catching anyone's eye, come to that. As for Robert, he might never live it down. I could see the mortification in his eyes, but when he looked at Sophie, it fell away. He was in love. They'd known each other for years and all of a sudden … Quite the opposite of Jon and me. I glanced at Daniela who, even though she'd complained about how black wasn't her colour, somehow was managing to look cool dressed in a shapeless cape. The tableau placed her in the centre behind the two lovers. She held the scythe at a diagonal with the blade at the top. On the right of the picture, Jon held his dagger raised, ready to strike. I was on the opposite side, facing the action and looking upset.

Ted unpacked his paraphernalia – umbrellas, tripods and lights – while we tried to pose like Sophie's tableaux. I tried to imagine the Victorians in the early days of photography, standing like statues for ages during the long exposures. When we saw the first attempts on Ted's laptop, each of us reacted in the same way. With silence.

Except Ted, who laughed.

'Not good?' I ventured.

'I should cocoa,' he said. 'This is why I don't do people. The idea's good but …'

'Yes?' We all wriggled and coughed like children.

'You look as if you've just walked out of a fancy dress shop. None of you mean what you're doing. Isn't this supposed to be a murder scene?'

'I know some drama exercises,' Sophie offered. 'Perhaps they might get us into character.'

Daniela burst into fits of laughter. 'Oh, this is funny. You English are so … what is the word … stiff? Yes. I will enjoy telling this to my friends in Milan.'

Nobody said anything but we reeled with collective offence. Sophie opened her mouth, a knee-jerk reaction to being called English, but she shut it again and frowned instead.

'Let's have another go,' Jon said. He looked grim-faced enough for all of us.

Then I realised that *upset* wasn't the right emotion for me. God knows, I felt upset enough in reality but that was because of my situation, which was a long way from Silvia Albana's. What I needed to feel was shocked, horrified and frightened. Frightened for my life too. Poor Silvia Albana was barely twenty and had expected the tip of a halberd to be plunged into her chest. That would require an entirely different expression on my face.

We took up our positions again and I tried to imagine what it must have been like. A dark night, there'd be shouting, screams probably, footsteps, flickering torches. I closed my eyes and straight away I saw Mollie's face and remembered her nightmare. Heard her cries … the sound of them in my head grew louder and more penetrating, more desperate. It was as if I was there too. And so real … so real! I could almost smell the smoke and the sweat of the men. Hear them shouting, Italian words I knew, so lyrical in music, so violent in anger. My heart began to beat faster and the back of my neck prickled with sweat.

There was something else too … I didn't know what. Some dreadful thing coming closer. The wind thrashed about louder than ever.

The world had become nothing but noise and a high and persistent screaming. I wanted to open my eyes but dared not. No, could not. I heard a voice cry out but couldn't understand it. I'd lost any sense of where I was, when or even who I was. I took a breath but found the air hard to take in.

My whole body began to shake, and then beneath my feet, the floor began to move, slip away. Was I falling? I forced my eyes to open but as I did so, a great firework display of flashing white lights ripped the world apart. I think I saw the others, their arms up, shielding something. I held my hands to my ears but was deafened by something louder than thunder. And then it seemed the sky was falling, falling down on top of us and a monstrous hand came out of nowhere, grabbed hold and took me into the dark.

Chapter Twenty-Six

Napoli 1590

They did not come at first light. They said they would but they did not. I was woken from my swoon by a noisy argument amongst the sparrows. I found myself at the foot of the door in the grey of dawn. For a moment, as I listened, my thoughts flew freely too, up and away over the rooftops, but then the memory of the night's events rushed in faster than a great wave, re-awakening all my fears.

I began to pick myself up from the floor but found my head pounding and sat back down. A little investigation found blood on my forehead. Had I hit myself falling? Perhaps on the corner of the chest? Then I remembered the monstrous 'thing' I had seen, and shuddered. I raised my eyes to the place where I last saw it advancing towards me, but there was only the familiar door curtain and the tapestry-backed chair.

I struggled to standing and crossed to the window. The storm had brought heavy rain in the night and the air smelled fresh when I pushed back the shutter. I breathed deeply and stayed there a while as the light brightened. Still nobody came to unlock the door. It was a strange thing to be in my clothes from the day before, but it meant I could seek out the little carvings that Salvo made. I felt the warmth of the wood in my hand when I found the kitten, the first he gave me. I knew them all by touch now but the sight of it made tears well in my eyes.

It seemed to me that we sewed our lives together as best we could, but if the cloth was weak or a seam had too much to bear, then eventually even the best of mendings might fail.

Into my heart then came a dark curiosity. I wished to see her. Donna Maria Carafa – Princess of Venosa, wife of the Don Carlo Gesualdo. My lady. I had to see her. Swiftly and with purpose, I walked through the antechamber, past my own bed, past Orlando Furioso *which lay face down on the floor. Only when I reached the door to the bedchamber and put my hand forward to push it open, did I pause.*

This was my last chance to see, to really know her fate. The hard truth of it. Soon the apartment would be full of people. They'd come to take my lady and Fabrizio away. Poor Rosa would be sent up to clean. Questions would be asked of me, and at some point Don Carlo would return. At the thought of him, I shuddered, remembering the blade at my throat. I put my hand up to where it had grazed and felt the warm pulse of life beneath my skin.

In daylight, the dead held less sway over me. Those alive were far more dangerous. I reached to push the door panel as I had done so often before, where the wood was slightly worn and where the merest pressure from a fingertip would swing the door wide. But I was not so brave that I didn't shut my eyes as it did so.

'Silvia?' A woman's voice, quiet. 'Silvia,' it insisted, 'you had best wake up now.'

I opened my eyes and sensed by the bright sunlight that the day was far on. Sister Caterina stood in the doorway.

'Yes,' I said. But my limbs refused to move.

'How are you today? Here, let me look.' Her cool hand stroked my forehead. 'I think the swelling is going down now. You must get up, Silvia,' she said. 'Besides, I need your help.'

'My help?'

She smiled but my face wasn't ready for such a bold expression. Half a smile was all I could muster.

'When the Master of the Grand Court came yesterday, I told him you couldn't be woken.' She sighed and shrugged her shoulders. 'Of course, that meant a great many prayers to redeem my untruth. When he returns today, I cannot say the same again, for then I will have no time to water the garden.'

'Oh, of course, I will see him. You have been so kind...'

I felt a tear fall and my voice failed me. Sister Caterina came and sat on the bed, putting her hand on mine. Her touch was cool and soothing.

'I will stay and be with you, Silvia.'

She left me then and I rose and splashed my face in the bowl of water she'd put on the table. I found in my bundle of clothes the same grey skirt worn by Donna Maria for that short while on her last evening and pulled it on. My precious scissors and needle case hung from my belt and as I fastened it about my waist my hands began to tremble. What was going to happen to me? Would Don Carlo have me tried as a witch after all?

I sat on the bed again as my thoughts, swirling with new horrors, made my knees so weak I couldn't stand. What if the Inquisition were to come?

A high bell rang out from somewhere in the convent, and the sisters began singing their prayers. It soothed me and before long I could bear my fears enough to stand again. I couldn't help wondering why anyone should want to compose ugly music when it could be so beautiful.

The grey shawl topped the heap of clothes in my bundle and once I'd recovered enough to continue dressing, I picked it up and held it to my face, breathing deeply in the hope of finding a vestige of her still there, if only in the faintest trace of the rose essence she loved. There was a comfort in the soft wool against my cheek, and I stood for a while with my eyes closed while pictures of her welled up in my memory. The repertoire of her laughter rang through the scenes, from deep and sultry when she was with Fabrizio, to the gurgles of pleasure brought on by a mouth full of lumbolls.

You will help me, Silvia – *I jumped, startled by the sudden change and nearness of her voice. The back of my neck prickled but when I looked over my shoulder there was only the small statue of the other Lady in the room. I pulled the shawl around me and bent my head. Donna Maria had asked for my help and I had failed her. Now I could only pray to the Virgin that she might look after my dear lady. I whispered the words, hoping that the holiness of the place I was in might make up for my feeble faith.*

Although I had received no other injury apart from the bump on my head, my whole body ached, and when I stood up, it was as if I was an old lady. Sister Caterina said that a whole week had gone by since my arrival, when I banged on the door like a madwoman and pleaded to be let in. My memory of that is vague. I have not been keen to turn my thoughts back to that time. But now I must.

Two gentlemen sat on one side of the table and there was a chair opposite for me. Sister Caterina went and stood by the window. My heart beat quickly and I smoothed my skirt repeatedly when I sat down. Don Carlo would have me dead, I was sure of it. Were these men here to do his bidding?

'Now then ... Silvia Albana, isn't it?' said the elder and better dressed of the two. The fur trim of his cloak was impressive, in spite of the stitching being obvious and the wrong colour where mended. 'My name is Master Giovanni Sanchez. By order of the Grand Court and with the assistance of the fiscal advocate, Master Mutio Surgenti,' he gestured towards the other man, 'I have come to hear your account of the events concerning the death of Don Fabrizio Carafa, the Duke of Andria and the Princess of Venosa, Donna Maria d'Avalos.

The advocate's quill on the parchment reminded me of chickens scratching in the dust. I gave my full name and when they asked me my age, I realised that my twentieth birthday had passed that very week. No wonder I felt old.

I proceeded to tell them what had happened during the evening in every detail, even to the point of demonstrating how my lady had worn my shawl about her shoulders.

'Were you Donna Maria's only maidservant?' Master Sanchez interrupted my explanations of how it suited her. He was clearly a thorough man.

'There was Laura Scala but she ...' I nearly said, she betrayed us, but thought in time that it might be better for me not to say much about that. I was a servant that only

did as I was told, and certainly didn't have an opinion ...
'she had left only recently.'

But the truth was, I didn't want to remember what
happened. As I talked, the memories became clearer. I
found myself back in the apartment. Back to the times of
terror, when Don Carlo first threatened my throat with the
tip of his halberd, when the night demons came ... and
when I saw... I saw my lady for the very last time, when I
stood in the doorway of the bed chamber and finally
opened my eyes.

'I'm afraid you will have to tell us what you saw,
Silvia,' said Master Sanchez, not unkindly.

I looked from one to the other and then turned to Sister
Caterina. 'Go on,' she said. 'It's all right.'

'It was Don Fabrizio I saw first,' I whispered. 'He was
on the floor, right there at my feet almost. But I didn't
think it was him. I thought it was my lady.' Everything
began to come out in a rush. 'At first I couldn't tell. He ...
he was in the nightdress, you see. The special one. I'd laid
it out for her, but he was wearing it. Don Fabrizio was
wearing my lady's nightgown! And he was dead on the
floor and it was covered all over in blood.' I began to cry.
I couldn't help it. The memory of Don Fabrizio's brains
coming out of one of his eyes and being all of a mess
against the little swans on the collar was too upsetting.
'Why would he do that?' I said, hiccuping. 'Why would he
be wearing it? I made it for my lady ...' I fumbled in my
pouch for a handkerchief. 'He shouldn't have been. No
wonder the seams gave way.'

Master Sanchez cleared his throat and leaned towards
the man whose name I'd forgotten but was doing all the
scribing. 'I don't think we need to mention any
nightdresses,' he said, under his breath. 'Let's not forget
the Duke's father is still alive.' He waved his hand in a
gesture that made light of it.

'But it's true,' I said, surprised they were not going to
record it. 'It ought to be written down. And that he was
wearing it before the arquebus was fired. The holes went

through the silk. I saw them. There were scorch marks too as well ... and great gashes everywhere. They didn't put the nightdress on him after he was dead. He had it on before.' I sat back, trembling and put my hand to my mouth. The awful sight had sickened me then and did again.

Both men looked at me directly. I could see they didn't want to say anything about the nightdress, but then from behind me, I heard Sister Caterina shift a little, perhaps only from one foot to the other, but enough to remind us all she was there.

'Very well,' said Master Sanchez. 'You'd better put down something to the effect, Mutio. Carry on, Silvia. What of Donna Maria?'

I swallowed. Had the air become sticky and glued itself to my tongue, I wouldn't have found it more difficult to speak.

'My lady ... she ... she was ...' I shook my head.

'Please do try, Silvia,' said Master Sanchez. 'The sooner you tell us, the sooner it will all be over.' He spoke firmly and I tried again to remember the scene.

When I had lifted my eyes from Don Fabrizio's grisly corpse, the next thing I saw were his clothes cast all about the room. He must have walked about as he unbuttoned his yellow and green doublet for it lay on the chest, whereas his gauntlet and glove beckoned from the chair. On the floor by the bed, discarded in haste, no doubt, were his linen drawers. The sleeve of his shirt with the lettuce leaf cuffs hung over the side of the bed, limp and pale in that morning's grey light.

My lady was lying as usual, turned away from the door with her face towards the window, but then I saw how the bed curtains had a great swathe of red-brown spots that reached for more than my arm's length up towards the canopy. The sheet too, I had thought it the bedcover at first glance, but then realised, with wrenching horror, that the sheet was so soaked in my lady's blood that none of its whiteness could be seen.

'Blood was everywhere,' I whispered, putting my hand to my throat. 'He'd cut ...' I demonstrated how that blade must have sliced from one side to the other, remembering the first time I had seen a pig slaughtered and how the blood had bounced and sprayed from its neck.

The quill went on scratching across the page. It was the only noise in the room, almost as if we had all stopped breathing. I remembered Don Carlo coming from the bedchamber looking like a wild beast and covered in blood.

'How could he not believe she was dead?' I said, sounding loud and desperate. 'There was so much blood. So much.' I fanned my arms wide. 'But he did not believe it. That's what he said. I do not believe she is dead. I heard him say it! And he went back into the bedchamber and chopped at her ... with his sword. He had a sword as well. His sword! I saw what he did to her. Who would do such a thing?' I couldn't stop myself. 'Only a wicked person. A demon ... a devil!' I began to cry again.

'Thank you, Silvia.' Master Sanchez held up his hands. 'That's enough.'

I found my handkerchief. Although I willed myself to stop the tears, they would keep coming. Eventually, the other man spoke.

'And in the morning? What happened then?'

'They still wouldn't let me out.'

'Yes, yes,' he said, tapping the quill against the inkpot irritably. 'But who exactly?'

'They came for the Duke first, three from the Jesuits – it took all of them to lift him onto the bed. They sent me out then to get water, but I saw under where he'd been lying, deep dents in the floor full up with blood.'

'Dents?'

'They didn't just shoot him, sir. Whatever weapons they used went right through and made dents in the floor.'

Behind me, Sister Caterina gasped and the gentleman scribe turned to Master Sanchez.

'That explains the crooked halberd that Dominico was

talking about.'

'Yes,' he said. 'I suppose it does.' Then he turned back to me. 'Go on, Silvia. Let's get this done, shall we?'

'After the washing,' I said, 'they put him in black silk hose and a nice overshirt with a black velvet collar and—'

He interrupted me. 'That's enough about the clothes, Silvia.'

'But sir, good fabric and needlework like that is valuable and the collar was hardly worn. Besides,' I said, a little put out, 'clothes are what I know best, sir.'

'Clearly,' he said, sighing to himself, but so I'd notice. 'And did the Jesuits take the body away? Was there no family there?'

'Oh, yes.' I nodded. 'His grandmother, the Countess and two other gentlemen of the church. I don't know who they were, although I think one of them was his uncle, but I wasn't really listening. When they'd gone, Pietro came back with my lady's aunt, the Marchioness of Vico, and I helped her.'

'And the Prince? Was Don Carlo there?'

'No. Pietro said he'd stayed away that night.'

'And ever since,' nodded Master Sanchez. 'Very well, Silvia Albana. That is all. Although,' he looked at me sternly, 'can you shed any light on how the Duke of Andria gained entrance to the Lady Donna Maria's apartment that night?'

A strange thing. If he had asked me about any other night, I would have known, but not that night. 'No, sir,' I said. 'I went to sleep straight after leaving my lady in bed... alone. It was Don Carlo that woke me, not the Duke.'

'I see,' he said. 'Very well. That is all. Have you finished, Mutio?'

Mutio wiped his quill and fastened the lid of the inkpot. 'Yes, I think we have enough.'

'Enough?' I said. What did he mean? All my fear of Don Carlo flooded into me. He'd spared me in his haste to murder my lady. Perhaps he meant to have me tried after

all? 'Enough for what? Have I done wrong, sir? Am I in trouble?'

'Not as far as I am concerned.' He shrugged and turned to Master Sanchez.

'You may go, Silvia,' he said. 'Don Carlo has been to see the Viceroy who advised him to return to Gesualdo. It is understood that he will remain there for the foreseeable future.'

'Go, sir?' I whispered. 'Where should I go?'

He frowned. 'You are in good health, are you not? And young still?' He put an eye-glass on his nose and examined me. 'Get yourself married. That's the best thing. By the looks of you, you'll probably have pretty children.'

I was left alone. At first I felt relieved to hear that Don Carlo had gone to Gesualdo, so far away. As my lady's husband, he was also my lord, and the one person in the world I most feared. I could not return to his service, but now he was living within spitting distance of my home. As I looked to my own future I grew more and more disturbed, for where could I go and what could I do?

Chapter Twenty-Seven

'I remember sirens,' I murmured, peering into my foggy memory. 'And blue flashes. Was there lightning? ' I remembered the smell too: a mixture of new timber and hedge clippings, but there was something burning ... acrid. Was there smoke?

Mollie sat on the bed, jiggling about a little too much for my sore head. I put up with it, for the warmth of her hand holding mine was too much of a joy to let go. I was back in a familiar world, although I'd rather have been in my own bed than in hospital. Mum straightened the sheet and tidied the water jug on the bedside cabinet, going back and forth with the regularity of a cuckoo at midday.

'You were so lucky,' she kept saying. 'I can't believe how lucky you were.'

'Or unlucky,' Mollie said. 'You could look at it both ways.'

'How do you mean?' My mother, ever the optimist.

I closed my eyes while they argued whether life was a glass half full or half empty. They'd be bound to let me know eventually. My head throbbed. I had a bump the size of an egg just above my forehead and was in for observation. They suspected concussion.

You hear about people being crushed under trees during storms, but they're usually in cars. Sometimes there's footage of chimneys missing, upturned caravans and sheds going sideways, but Devon is hardly tornado country. When the old evergreen oak smashed down onto the flat roof of the studio, it went straight through. I sided with my mum. That nobody died felt like much more than luck; it was surely a miracle. The only broken bones were a finger and a toe. Ted and Jon's respectively. Lucky for Jon it wasn't the other way round. The toe was painful but not being able to play any of his various instruments would have been much more upsetting.

I wasn't so concussed that I didn't remember what we

were doing and why, but the doctor began to look at me oddly when I burbled about the manuscript being cursed, so I kept quiet.

Voices, like the sort of sound bites you get when surfing telly with the remote, floated across my mind.

All right, love.

Over here!

I do not believe she is dead.

Is she dead?

We'll need to chop this up.

Blimey, what a mess.

Lisa ... Lisa!

I jumped and felt my head throb. The last voice was familiar.

'Lisa?'

Mum had turned into Jon somehow and Mollie wasn't there either.

'How are you feeling?' he said. There was a warmth in his expression I hadn't seen for a long time.

'Better, thanks. You? How's the toe?'

'Oh, not bad. And look ...' He reached round to the back of the chair. 'You get a free stick for every one broken.' He tried giving it a twirl, but a cry of anxiety from the woman in the next bed prompted a sheepish apology. 'Oh, well,' he whispered. 'You'll have to wait for my Fred Astaire impersonation.'

I began to smile but found the pull of the muscles made my head ache again. 'Ouch,' I said feeling the bump. 'Now I know what it feels like to be an egghead.'

'They say we'll all be right as rain in a couple of weeks.'

'That's good.'

'Everyone's shook up, of course. God, there was such a bloody mess everywhere.'

'Was there? I don't really remember.'

He laughed. 'Daniela gave the ambulance bloke a turn, clutching her scythe and rambling in Italian. You were spark out and Robert had turned into a cross between

Batman and Florence bloody Nightingale around Sophie. All flappy nurse.' He did an impersonation that brought tears to my eyes. 'Did I miss something about those two?' he said. 'How come after all this time?'

'I don't know. They went to the pictures together and next thing ...' I shrugged.

'Makes you wonder what they went to see, doesn't it?'

I nodded gingerly. That the others were okay was important, but I needed to tell someone about the curse. Someone who wouldn't think I was mad, who wasn't my mother or my daughter, who knew and who, I hoped, cared enough to listen. And even more importantly, who might be in danger. 'Jon,' I said, and then hesitated. 'I need to tell you something. About the madrigal. The Gesualdo madrigal ... I don't think we should—'

'Oh bugger!' he interrupted, patting all his pockets. 'I meant to bring it with me. Damn.'

'Bring it with you?' I said, appalled. 'God, I'm glad you didn't. The thing is—'

'No, no, not the *music*.' He dismissed it with a wave. 'The *photo*! It's absolutely perfect.'

'What?'

'Yes.' He leant forward and grabbed my hand, his eyes shining. 'Ted must have pressed the shutter at the exact moment the tree came down. We all look totally terrorised! It's *brilliant*!'

'Brilliant?' I said, weakly. His hand echoed his enthusiasm, alternately squeezing and shaking mine. I let go and reached up to push the hair from my forehead. *Ouch* again.

'Yeah, it's going in the papers. Not just the local either. National. And there's going to be interview spots about it on the radio ... and telly. It's the best advertising we could possibly have. The museum is *thrilled*!' He looked too happy.

'But, Jon,' I said, 'we shouldn't do it.'

'Shouldn't? Why ever not? God, we couldn't have asked for better.'

'Don't you see? We could have been killed.'

'Yes, but we weren't, were we? And why not make the best of it?' He took my hand. This time in both of his. 'Apart from that, Lisa. Don't you see? This is our chance. With all this coverage. As long as we do a good job at the concert, *Noteworthy* could make it big time. Isn't that what you've always wanted? What we've all always wanted?'

Part of me knew he was right. But it was a part that had become veiled in my mind, a dark veil embroidered with black thread. Behind it lay a bright place and the *Noteworthy* of old.

'And there's something else,' he said. He began to twitch about on his chair as if it had suddenly become uncomfortable. 'It's about the secret.'

'The secret?'

'I'm really sorry you were upset,' he went on quickly. 'And Mollie too. Daniela said I should tell you right from the beginning.'

A spasm of fear ran through me. The pounding in my head went from uncomfortable throb to being whacked with a hammer. Not Daniela. Please not Daniela. *It's bound to be, the demon sneered.*

'Oh?' was all I could muster.

'The thing is, I've been writing something.'

I blinked.

'Yes.' He glanced at me, as if guilty. 'Yes, a musical. I know it sounds daft. But do you remember when you first read out that stuff about Gesualdo?'

I nodded carefully. When was he going to get to the bit about Daniela?

'Well, it kind of kept rattling about in my head. And then Mollie was telling me about your school choir …'

School *choir*? I shut my eyes. Did I have concussion after all?

'So I thought, okay, other people have written operas and ballets and musicals for grown-ups … but what about a musical for children? It's such a great story. Beautiful princess, wicked murderer. What's not to like? All that

205

grim stuff, you know how much kids love that kind of thing.' His words tumbled out so fast. 'The more gruesome, the better. Mollie was dead keen. We thought it would be great for your choir. The secret bit was my fault. I wanted to get it mostly down before I told you. Just in case, it went bollocks up. But it's nearly there now.' He sat back, pleased with himself. 'So, Lisa, what do you think? Surprised?'

I couldn't speak. Surprised, bewildered, shocked: a soup of them all swirled about in my head. Once again, I heard the voice of Mollie crying out during her nightmares. Other voices too, men shouting, a snippet of *Noteworthy* singing the madrigal …

'No!' I blurted. 'You can't. You mustn't. It's a *terrible* idea.'

His face freeze-framed.

'It's a horrible story.' I could hear desperation in my voice as it got louder. 'Not at all right for children.' There was a cough from the next bed. 'And Jon …' I put my hand on his arm but he pulled it away. There was more hurt and disappointment in his eyes than when we'd rowed at my flat, a lifetime ago. 'What about the curse?' I whispered.

'Curse?' He looked at me blankly then swallowed. 'Lisa, I—'

'But it is cursed, Jon. Don't you see? All the things that have happened. Ever since that first time. Even the boy drowning—'

'What boy drowning?'

'You know,' I went on, leaning forward in spite of the pain. 'In the river.'

The curtain between me and next door twitched.

'For fuck's sake, Lisa,' Jon said between clenched teeth. He folded his arms and crossed his legs too, retreating into as small a space as possible. 'That was a coincidence.'

'That's what I thought then, but there's everything else. Sophie's arm, the tree—'

206

He shook his head. 'No, no, no. Look, you've had a bang on the head—'

'Ahem,' said a voice from the end of the bed. A nurse stood waving cheerily. 'Sorry to break up the conversation, only there's a reporter out in the corridor.'

Jon pushed his chair back with a searing scrape over the floor. 'I'll go,' he said, looking at me with that ghastly remote expression that made me wish the tree had knocked me out for good. 'We'll talk again.'

The nurse went with him and I felt tears well up. I grabbed a tissue from the box Mum had brought in and squeezed it against my eyes trying to push back the tears. Everything seemed even worse than ever.

'Oh, Jon,' I moaned. A musical! For children. It couldn't be more wrong. The curse was widening its territory. Like a virus infecting everyone it came into contact with. If any harm should come to Mollie …

My head throbbed when I blew my nose. I kept my eyes shut, and as the stars cleared from where I pressed against their lids, I peered through, not a flimsy veil at all, and not embroidery of thread but of substantial wrought iron. The frontispiece appeared before me as great gates and even though I took hold and shook them, they remained locked. When would I ever get through?

Chapter Twenty-Eight

Napoli 1590

'Please let me stay, Sister. I can be helpful. I don't mind hard work and my sewing is good.' I handed her the apron I'd been mending.

Sister Caterina smiled and sat down beside me. We were in the convent cloister. The central courtyard had been planted with lavender and roses in square beds surrounded by box. It was less grand than the courtyard at the palazzo but much tidier. I had noticed that as soon as a petal fell then the first nun to pass would go and pick it up. Everywhere in the convent was kept well, and prayers were happily uttered whilst doing even the dirtiest jobs. I remembered all the squabbles amongst the kitchen maids at Palazzo San Severo, how Laura would complain, how everyone complained about something or other.

'I know that, Silvia.' She tied the strings behind her back then smoothed the fabric over her knees. 'If anything your sewing is too good for us. Why, I can't even see where it was torn.' I could see the patch perfectly well, but I'd done my best in spite of the linen being coarse and old. 'The trouble is,' she said, 'you can't stay if you have no purpose here. This morning Mother asked me about you and I didn't know what to say. You are no longer a child ...' She was interrupted by a hoopoe landing noisily on the roof of the cloister opposite where we sat. A few stones clattered down the tiles. Hoo-hoo-hoo, it called and was answered by another just above our heads.

'There are a lot of those in the woods around Gesualdo,' I said, glad to be distracted from my predicament. 'I used to go to sleep to the nightingales singing and wake up to hoopoes. Before I knew better, I thought they were the same bird with a different song for night and day.'

'I can understand that,' said Sister Caterina. 'I've

never actually seen a nightingale, although I've heard one or two.'

'They aren't much to look at, that's why. Not compared to the hoopoe. You see the way the feathers fan on its head? That lovely honey colour? I always think the black tip looks as if its been dipped in ink.' We both shielded our eyes from the sun and looked again at the bird on the roof. 'I once embroidered all the braid on a dress in a pattern based on those feathers,' I said, remembering the labour, and Donna Maria not thinking much of it in the end. 'Do you think it would be better if we were all nightingales, Sister? It seems to me there's a lot of unhappiness and trouble caused by beautiful things.'

'But the song of the nightingale is one of the most beautiful in the world,' she said, 'and what unhappiness does that cause?'

'It kept me awake sometimes.' I knew I was grumbling over nothing. 'But I suppose I should be thankful you can't embroider a song.'

'Can't you, Silvia? Why I thought you could embroider anything.'

I was startled at this, but knew by the smile in her eyes that she was teasing me. 'Oh, Sister,' I said, shamefaced. 'Am I boastful about my skill? I do not mean to be.'

'No, you are not,' she said. 'Although you should beware of those without your talent, saying as much. Now; there is work to do.' She gave her apron another stroke and stood up. 'What I will do, Silvia, is find out if any of the other convents require a needlewoman. It would not be fine work, of course, but it might be something. Besides, I was thinking that perhaps when Salvo comes back ...' She didn't need to say more.

I did not know what to think about Salvo. He had been away for so many weeks and I had heard nothing. Every day, I took out the little carvings and the copy of the frontispiece with our likenesses etched so finely. Why had he not written to me? As I looked at his work, it seemed to me more beautiful than any of the expensive pictures that

Don Carlo had at the palazzo and the castle. Perhaps his travels had changed him. Or he had acquired a patron who demanded his time? Even so, why not write and say so?

Men. Were they all either wicked or faithless? I wondered about the things men and women did together in private, and how much I had desired Salvo that day. That lovely day. Did everything change with habit, though? It seemed to me it did, and always for the worse. Donna Maria had had no joy with her three husbands. Even I had heard the rumour that the first, Federigo, died of exhaustion from spending too much time in his wife's bed, and the second, old Alfonso, died trying. Donna Maria herself told me that he'd been too feeble to succeed. Don Carlo liked the whip and as for Don Fabrizio ... I remembered the nightdress.

Then, with a start, I remembered all the nightdresses. The ones I had mended even before Don Fabrizio. A warm tear trickled down my cheek; I realised it wasn't only men that had their particular fancies.

More weeks went by and I tried my very best to be useful at the convent, but I could see they didn't need me. Sister Magdalena, in charge of all the needlework, began to complain that I was too quick with my needle. I think she really meant good rather than quick, but I didn't say anything and began to count to three between each stitch.

I was very glad of my little cell when I woke each morning. It could not have been more different from the palazzo. There was no velvet, no silk, no tapestries or embroidered hangings. The chapel would be very ornate when its renovation was finished and while there were frescoes above the doorways and in the refectory, the rest was plain. Everything about the convent soothed me, which was just as well, for the nights were a torment.

Sometimes I could not tell whether I was awake or asleep for my dreams were of people and places very familiar to me. They would begin in happy places, the lemon grove, the quayside, or just quietly sewing, but I would always be drawn back to the horror in the same way.

Donna Maria is seated before her mirror while I stand behind. We are laughing together. She is wearing the nightdress with the black cuffs. On the table, her jewel case lies open and I am offering her different necklaces to try. She has many and we cannot decide. The pearls are lovely, so too is the gold chain and crucifix studded with gems, but we settle on the rope of garnets. I lean down, so that my face is beside hers in the mirror. How beautiful she is, and I confess, I don't look too bad either. We are very pleased with ourselves.

'Yes,' she says to me, 'that's perfect, Silvia. What would I do without you?'

Her voice is as clear as the nightingale's song is sweet. But then something happens to the mirror. It blurs our faces, so I can't tell one from the other. Perhaps it is Don Fabrizio's face I see instead. In my hands I am holding each end of the garnets, for I have yet to fasten them, but for some reason I can't fathom, they feel less than solid. I look down and discover that the stones are slipping through my fingers; in fact they are no longer garnets but great drops of crimson blood. When I look up, I see the jagged slash across my lady's neck and as the blood spurts out and splashes across the mirror, her head tilts to one side and begins to fall.

It was always dark as pitch when I woke. I'd peer into the black, searching for light, but all I'd see were the same scenes wherever I looked. Two figures, one seated and one standing, their outlines crude like poor frescoes. My eyes would be full of tears and the little bed shaking with the hammering of my heart. Gradually, I'd see the outline of the window and on a moonlit night, the silhouette of the crucifix hanging on the adjacent wall. It offered little comfort.

The conversation with Sister Caterina had made me anxious, but it was also good to be reminded that I was no *longer a child. Twenty! It was a very old age to be.*

I realised that while it had pleased Donna Maria to have me by her side nearly all the time, sometimes she would pet me in the same way she petted Margarita who was only ten. When I thought back through the years I had spent in Napoli, the number of times we had left the palazzo apart from going to church were very few. Donna Maria was invited out by other women of her status as a matter of politeness, but she wasn't a popular guest and pleaded illness more often than not, especially after she'd met Don Fabrizio.

The Sisters did not imprison me, but when I ventured out to seek work, I would see evil faces in every door or in the gloom of the narrow alleyways. The noise of men's voices, even if only a sudden greeting, made me jump in fear.

There was no work. Or perhaps there was, but nobody wanted to employ me. Once I mentioned Palazzo San Severo, there'd be frowns, then a shake of the head. I was something to do with the city's great scandal, and just my presence in the house of the murder was enough to place suspicion on my head. That I was in the next room, I did not tell anyone, for I soon realised it would be the equivalent of plunging the knife into dear Donna Maria myself.

I was beginning to give up all hope when Sister Caterina called me to the chapel. Father Strozzi stood with arms crossed and resting on his ample belly, contemplating the altar. He was not praying.

'Ah, Silvia,' he said. 'What a very good thing it is you are still with us.'

I wasn't sure whether he meant in the flesh or in the convent but I smiled anyway. Even though I'd always mistrusted his smiles and gestures of affection, it was cheering to hear that I was of some small worth.

'It is, Father?'

'Yes, yes. You are just who we need. Donna Severina has written to me.'

'Donna Severina?' I said.

'She remembered that your mistress – God rest her soul – was to pay for the new altar cloth and has agreed to honour her wish.'

I was surprised that Donna Maria's mother would wish to remember anything about her daughter at all. They barely spoke to each other, so in the light of the family suffering the shame of her infidelity, this offer was very generous.

'And,' Father Strozzi went on, 'who do you think came to our minds when we thought about who might execute such a task?'

I looked at both Father Strozzi and Sister Caterina and felt a burst of heat rush to my cheeks. Whatever it was that instantly lodged in my throat, it prevented speech. I dropped to my knees and bowed my head. Tears dotted the floor and I wiped them away with the back of my hand.

'Oh, th-thank you,' I said, when I could manage to say anything. 'You have saved my life.'

'I think that might be something of an exaggeration,' said Sister Caterina. She raised me to my feet. 'Your life has not been in peril.'

'But I had nothing to do here and the Mother Superior said—'

'Oh, let's not worry about that. Now you have an excellent reason to stay, and we are all glad.' She swept her arms wide. 'Besides, Silvia - and and I hope our Father in heaven and Father Strozzi here on earth will forgive me for this - but it pleases me a great deal that with you in charge of its making, our altar cloth will be the finest in Napoli.'

It was a good thing I was wearing my apron. A handkerchief would have been no use at all for mopping up so many tears.

Relief was better than any sleeping draught. The next day I woke refreshed and more cheerful than I could remember since … since … No! No looking back. I threw off the *bedclothes and stood up, for unlike on all the mornings since my arrival at the convent, I was keen to rise.*

It was midwinter and the water in my basin was very cold, but I hardly noticed when I splashed my face and hands before dressing. My mind was full of other things. An altar cloth. I would have to source the fabric, the thread, decide on the design. Then there were the colours to consider ... why, it would keep me busy for months and months! I could not resist humming to myself.

There was a sensible pot of money, not a fortune, and the convent was a place of simple calm. It would not do for me to design a gaudy cloth. It would be of the finest linen I could buy, and then I would do my very best embroidery.

I was well acquainted with the cloth merchants, and after a little bread for breakfast, I wrapped my thickest wool shawl about my shoulders and set off. No evil faces leered at me from the shadows and I even enjoyed the sharp sting of sleet on my cheeks.

My head was full of thoughts about the design. Both Father Strozzi and Mother Superior assumed that I would depict the story of Christ, but after my conversation with Sister Caterina in the cloister garden, and also, truth be told, because of the frontispiece that Salvo had given me, I suggested Adam and Eve in the Garden of Eden might be my subject. They were surprised, but after a short discussion without me present, I was told that I could go ahead with some samples for them to see.

The streets weren't very crowded for it was still early when I left the convent. The quickest way to get to the cloth merchant meant passing the front door of Palazzo San Severo. If Don Carlo was back ... I hesitated, but then thought he'd most likely use the entrance by the stables, so I would risk it. I pulled the shawl down low over my forehead and hurried along, past the place where I'd seen Laura talking to Don Giulio. I could not bring myself to look up at the window where I'd been standing.

In fact, I was so busy inspecting my boots that I did not

see the figure approaching until it was altogether too late. Before I could do anything to save myself, I felt the full force of him strike and a moment later, the ground was rushing up to greet me.

Chapter Twenty-Nine

The hospital let me out later that afternoon with a box of painkillers and an assurance from Mum that I wouldn't be left alone for twenty-four hours. The flat was amazingly tidy, all the washing up not only done, but put away, and my theory that I had too many mugs to go in the cupboard was clearly not proven. The music had been patted into straight-sided heaps and there wasn't a Barbie in sight. Mum had magicked all the bedding away from the sofa too.

'You're a star, Mum,' I said, easing down onto it. I was a bit surprised and hurt that Mollie had opted to go to her dad's instead of coming with Mum to get me, but his telly could get loads more channels than mine.

I was even more surprised when Michael phoned later and said that Mollie wanted to stay with him for the next few days.

'Can I speak to her?'

'Erm ...' He held his hand over the phone so I could only hear muffled noises. 'She's in the bath,' he said, eventually.

'Don't be ridiculous,' I said. 'She doesn't do baths.' God knows, it's difficult enough to get her into the shower. There was another pause and more indistinct conversation. I knew it was her voice though. 'For goodness sake, Michael,' I said. 'Whatever's the matter?'

Mum hovered over me. 'Do you want a cup of tea, dear?'

'Yes.' I mouthed at her. She looked worried but then Michael coughed loudly in my ear.

'She says she'll ring you.'

'Oh really? Well, tell her to make it soon.' I switched off the phone and felt a renewed and enthusiastic throbbing in my head.

'Mollie's a bit upset,' Mum said, handing me the tea. 'So she thought she'd stay at her dad's for a few days. But the good thing is,' she went on brightly, 'I've made your bed up in her room.'

'What's she upset about? She was all right when she came to the hospital with you.'

'That was before Jon's visit though, wasn't it?' She had fetched the biscuit tin and offered it to me, looking down so as not to catch my eye.

'But ...' I was going to say, what's that got to do with it, when everything dropped into place. Of course, Mollie knew all about Jon's musical. It was the big secret and she would have the starring role. If Jon had said it was all off, Mollie would be livid, not cross. I put my hand in the tin, pulled out the first thing I came to and bit into a pink wafer. Mollie's favourite and my last choice. Sweet sawdust that turns to glue once combined with saliva.

'Are you sure you said the right thing to Jon, dear?'

I shrugged, feeling exceedingly miserable.

All evening the phone kept ringing, or at least, that's what it seemed like. None of the calls were from Mollie though. Or Jon. Gran phoned to complain about her neighbours. Sophie phoned to see if I was all right, but couldn't stop because she was about to serve up Robert's dinner. That depressed me on all sorts of levels.

Mum flirted with Charles for a good twenty minutes on her mobile, during which time the doorbell rang. I opened it and found that my disapproving neighbours had bought me a get-well poinsettia. They'd heard about the tree coming down while listening to the news on Radio Devon. Was this new warmth because I was an object of pity, or because I was a celebrity? I couldn't decide. It was a kind gesture, I told myself firmly, when I closed the door. Don't be horrid.

I felt horrid though. Slumped at the bottom of the self-esteem ladder with a bad head, estranged from my daughter and my... my *friend*, Jon, I had to endure listening to my mother's coy, one-sided wittering with Charles. It was not the best time to take the last call.

'Lisa?' The voice on my mobile was familiar but I

217

couldn't place it immediately.

'Yes?'

'It's Daniela.'

'Oh?' Yes, of course it was. The sofa was the nearest thing to sit on, but I perched on the edge. There was nothing comfortable about a call from Daniela.

'You are home?'

'Yes, thank you. You survived then?' I felt nervous suddenly. Why was she ringing? I was pretty damn sure it wouldn't be to enquire about my health.

'Yes, I am well.'

'That's good.' I meant what I said. Although she was hardly my favourite person, I wouldn't wish her any harm.

'I have some news, Lisa.' My anxiety ratcheted upwards. Her voice always sounded cool but there was an edge to it I hadn't heard before, a sort of vibrato that meant either the demise of someone close or very good news indeed. Winning the lottery, passing an exam, or perhaps going public about a new relationship.

'Oh?'

'Can I come and see you in the morning?'

No, I thought. But I couldn't think of an excuse fast enough, especially as I'd just told her I was all right. 'Of course. You know where I live, don't you?' I wondered if her command of English was good enough to appreciate my heavy irony. Actually irony didn't do it. Lead-ery more like.

It was getting close to Mollie's bedtime, so I sent her an email wishing her goodnight. Nothing came back.

At breakfast next morning, I told Mum she had to go out. She grumbled and looked at the clock, saying that the twenty-four hours wasn't up. But as I pointed out, I wouldn't be alone.

'You will tell her, won't you?' she said, while I patted flat the hood of her new coat. We were looking at each other in the mirror by the front door. In spite of the bruise, a purple splodge that was making its slow way down my forehead, I could see the resemblance between us more clearly than ever before. I could even imagine wearing her coat. It's Per Una and a sort of sexy parka. God … was I so middle-aged?

'Tell her what?'

'That he's yours.'

'For heaven's sake, Mum.'

Sneery demon popped up. *Fat chance you've got.*

I imagined that Daniela would look exactly the same whether she was twenty or fifty. A crow might land but I doubted if its feet would make any kind of impact round her eyes. I imagined her skin made of the same bronze as its colour, and thought of those Renaissance sculptors and their voluptuous goddesses. And gods too. Perhaps early Briton women were secretly pleased when the Romans invaded.

She sat on the sofa and I perched on the keyboard stool, which gave me an altitude advantage of several crucial inches. My stomach rumbled. I hadn't fancied Coco Pops or Weetabix for breakfast and it was complaining about my drinking a third cup of coffee with nothing to soak it up.

'I don't think you will like what I have to say,' she said, 'but I must tell you.'

'Okay,' I said. 'Go on then.'

'I've been asked to sing at La Scala.'

I let the words roll about in my head. They performed something like an impromptu maracas solo. Interesting but lacking any depth or meaning. So, she'd been asked to go back to La Scala. In Milan. I quite liked the sound of that.

'Didn't you used to sing there?'

'I had an audition before I came to England last year.'

Her face acquired a whole new expression. Instead of the usual lush and smiley confidence, two deep frown marks dented her forehead. She looked almost pale. I didn't take in what the transformation meant.

'Last year?'

'I was put on the reserve list.'

'But didn't you say you—'

She interrupted me. 'I lied.'

'Oh …' I said, carefully. 'I see.' So that was it. She was embarrassed. Ashamed even. Fancy that. She *lied*.

'That is why I left Italy. Everybody thought I would get in and I did not.' She shook her head. 'I was humiliated at being refused and when I came to England, I thought, why should I tell anyone? What does it matter to them?' She flicked the air. 'But now I discover they want me after all.'

I was hearing the words, but mostly I was reacting badly to her being quite so dismissive of the population of England. Why was she telling me this?

'Lucky you,' I said.

'Yes, it is. But …' she hesitated.

The room was quiet. Be a stone, I told myself. Don't react.

'I have to go back right now, otherwise they will ask someone else who is on the reserve list.'

Now. She had to go *right now*. The significance hit me with a force that jerked half of my coffee up and over the top of the mug straight onto my lap.

'Now?' I said, mopping it up with the bottom of my jumper and making a worse mess. 'When's now?'

'The day after tomorrow. They start rehearsals for Tosca then.'

'But … but you aren't serious, surely?'

'I'm sorry,' she said, not looking at me. 'I thought you wouldn't be happy.'

'Happy? The concert's the week after next. You can't let us down like this. It's … it's …' I couldn't think of a word that would do. That would express how outraged I felt. 'It's outrageous! Daniela, you can't go *now*.'

'I am sorry.'

She shifted to the edge of the sofa so all her weight was on the balls of her feet, ready for flight, although she wouldn't get far in those heels. I thought of how much Mollie would like the silver bows – but only for a millisecond, because crashing down behind that was a great cascade of thoughts about what a shitty thing it was to drop us in the … in the total, utter *shit* like that. It was the most unprofessional thing anyone could do! And she was swanning off to La-bloody-Scala …

'How could you?' I said, spluttering. 'What the hell are we supposed to do now?'

'I have told Jon,' she said, in a sort of meekly penitent voice, as if that was supposed to make me feel somehow better. 'And he was cross too but we talked and he thought it best.'

'He thought it *best*?' I said, slowly. 'Well, there's a thing. Why am I not surprised?'

She looked at me and frowned. 'Surprised?'

'Yes, surprised,' I said, aware that sarcasm didn't suit me. 'You've been sucking up to Jon ever since the first time you met.'

'But—'

'I've seen how you give him the eye, don't deny it.' I didn't give her the chance. 'And you've managed to wheedle Mollie over to your side.'

'Wheedle …' she said to herself, as if searching through her English/Italian dictionary. She shook her head. 'What is that?'

'Talked her round. Persuaded. Inveigled.' Ha! I doubt she knew that word either. She looked blank, face like a mask. 'Yes,' I went on, my voice trembling, 'you've lured them both right over to the Dark Side!'

There was a silence while we both took this in. Okay, you're sounding deranged now, I told myself. My head felt sore again and it wasn't helped by my whacking the bruise when I put my hand up to sweep the hair out of my eyes. I stood up and Daniela sprang up too. Bloody hell, she was loads taller than me. The best I could do was fold my arms and sniff. Pathetic.

'I'm sure you will find someone to sing the part,' she said, gesturing towards the music heap on the table. 'After all, *Noteworthy* is very good.'

'Thank you very much,' I said, with the same tart sarcasm as before. 'If we'd known someone else, we would have asked them.'

Now I was being mean, but it was that or weeping, and I couldn't bear the humiliation of tears.

'Listen, Lisa,' she said. 'I understand how you feel but Jon thought—'

I snorted. Horribly pig-like.

Daniela stood firm. In fact, she put her hand on my arm and gripped it rather tightly. I got a nose-full of hefty perfume. 'Jon thought,' she hesitated only for a nanosecond, 'that Mollie should sing my part.'

'*Mollie*?' Had I heard right?

'Yes, Mollie. She could certainly do it. And as Jon …' she glanced at me, probably in fear of a slap. 'As Jon said, her voice has a similar quality to yours and therefore would match very well. Perhaps even better than mine. Although of course, my voice is—'

'*Mollie*?' I was staggered; more of a hyena than a pig now.

'Yes, of course. Why not? We thought it a good idea.'

I sat back down, weak suddenly. 'Have you said anything to her?'

'No. Jon thought you—'

'Okay, I can imagine what Jon thought.' But could I? I was beginning to think I didn't know anything anymore.

Daniela headed for the door. Once we'd said goodbye, which I managed very civilly, I went into my bedroom and lay down. The black web of the frontispiece appeared once again when I shut my eyes, so I opened them and stared at the ceiling.

Oh, piss off then, Daniela, I thought. I can't say I'm sorry you're going.

Sneery Demon snorted. *But she's dropped you well in it, hasn't she?*

I sniffed irritably. Yes, she had.

Perhaps it would be best to cancel the concert altogether.

Perhaps it would.

Admit defeat.

That possibility swelled my mind as I imagined the outcome of cancelling. I thought of the others: Sophie, Robert, Jon and finally, Mollie. What would their reactions be?

Midday. The clock of St Mary Steps announced the hour. The bell has more of a clank than a clang, and it jarred me into a new line of thinking.

I sat up and swung my feet down to the floor. If I left straight away, I'd get there in time. The fact that I wasn't expected wouldn't matter. If there was a decision to be made, then best get on with it.

Chapter Thirty

Napoli 1591

'Ow!' I rubbed my knee where it had struck the ground with considerable force. 'You should be more care—'

'Silvia!'

'Oh!'

He was wearing a magnificent cloak. Dark green with a silk lining the colour of limes, and trimmed with rabbit fur all the way round. All that I took in with a glance. For it was the merry twinkle in his eyes that really caught me, just as it had all those years ago.

'Well, come on then,' he said, helping me up. 'You can't sit there all day long.'

'Salvo Carlino!' I said, grimacing with pain. 'You should look where you're going.'

'Me? Why, I couldn't avoid you. Who's that hiding away and looking so suspicious? I thought. They must have done something very bad.' He was laughing at me.

'Why just you stop that!' I said, frowning. I straightened up and put my shawl to rights. 'For I am very cross with you and won't be teased.'

'Cross with me? But why?'

'Because I have not heard a single word from you in all these months.'

'But—'

'And especially after... after... all that's happened.'

Then he saw that I was truly upset and his expression changed at once to concern. 'Silvia,' he said, taking my arm and stroking my hand. 'I was so very happy to see your lovely face just now, and happy that I hadn't missed you, for I was on my way to the palazzo.'

I shook my head. 'But I am not at the palazzo now,' I said, pulling him along the street. 'Haven't you heard what happened?'

'Happened? No? I arrived very late last night. What's

happened?'

Was it my doom to keep reliving the horror over and over? The memory drenched me from top to toe and all my earlier joy ran along the gutter and joined the rubbish making its way down to the sea. That Salvo had not sent word to me had bruised me badly, but I had over-laid the pain of it with something like a bandage made, not of soft cloth, but of thick linen heavily starched. It could stand up by itself if need be, much like a soldier's armoured breastplate. Strong enough to protect the heart.

'Oh, Salvo,' I said, pulling away from him so I could hide my face beneath the shawl again. 'I can hardly bear to tell you and certainly cannot so near to where it happened. Please,' I looked over my shoulder expecting to see Don Carlo's face appear at every window. 'Let's go away from here. We'll go to the harbour. Maybe the breeze from the sea will blow away my fears.'

'Fears, Silvia? What do you have to fear?'

I didn't answer but walked quickly away, ignoring his pestering questions. Soon we were both out of breath, but rounding the last corner, I stopped still. The bay spread before us and the sea glistened in the morning sun. The shock of its sudden brightness after the dark streets hurt my eyes and I put my hand up to shield them.

'Well?' said Salvo. 'Here we are. Are you going to tell me now?'

To the accompaniment of screeching gulls, I began. Fishermen interrupted, beseeching us to buy their various catches, each better than their neighbours. I stopped to admire the crabs and lobsters, glad to be taken away from my story. The fish I wasn't so keen on though. Their eyes stared at me, pale and shiny, and just as in the windows of San Severo Palazzo, I saw Don Carlo in every one.

Do all stories change when told repeatedly? An entertainer might embellish to make his audience laugh or if he wished to scare them half to death, but I kept such embroidery for cloth. My tale needed none of it. In fact, for some reason, there were things I didn't tell Salvo. I didn't

225

tell him about the wounds on the bodies, or how scared I'd been of the night demon, but why did I not mention that Don Fabrizio was wearing my lady's nightdress when it had seemed so important that Master Sanchez should know?

Eventually, I neared the end and told him how I'd gathered all my belongings together and fled to the convent once my lady and the Duke had been taken away. I was reminded that I'd met Rosa on the stairs carrying a pitcher and scrubbing brush. Nothing was said, even though we both stopped. A nod was enough and an understanding passed between us. The world had grown far more fearful as a result of the previous night.

'Oh my dearest,' Salvo almost moaned as he took my hand and kissed it. 'My sweetheart. I wish I had not been away so long. My poor love.' His face was grey with worry and sorrow.

'I am not so poor now, Salvo,' I said, managing a smile. 'The sisters have been very kind to me and I like it at the convent. Besides ...' I was about to tell him about the altar cloth but hesitated. The conversation I had with Sister Caterina in the garden came back to me. Salvo and I had an understanding. Didn't we? If we were to marry, what then? This little bit of freedom would disappear.

'Besides?'

'Oh, nothing.' I lied, pointing towards a woman selling dried peaches and apricots. 'Look, they must be worth the eating.'

We sat on a wall further along and beyond the smell of fish. The sweetness of the fruit exploded in my mouth and I felt better.

'It's a good thing that Don Carlo is not here,' said Salvo, his voice almost like the fearsome growl of the gate dog at Castle Gesualdo. 'I wonder how he would like to have a halberd pointed at his throat.'

I was shocked. 'No, Salvo! Don't say such a thing. It was you that told me we were vulnerable to the vagaries of the wealthy. I remember you saying exactly that. Don

Carlo will not be punished, the Viceroy has said as much, but you would be punished ... horribly.' I shuddered. 'You'd probably be han—'

'Yes! Yes, you're right. Of course you are. But that doesn't stop me thinking it. Curse the man.'

We finished the fruits in silence but I barely tasted them, my own mind too full of ghastly thoughts.

'Besides,' I said, offering Salvo an escape. 'I've heard that the Carafas wanted revenge. That's why Don Carlo went to Gesualdo.'

'Well, I hope they get their revenge, and if not, then I hope Don Carlo remains a prisoner in his castle for ever and ever.'

I shook my head, gloomily. 'I don't think there's much chance of that. I've also heard that he is to marry again.'

Rosa was my source of information. She came to the convent from time to time with left over offerings from cook or old cloth that the sisters would re-make but I didn't want to think about Don Carlo or Gesualdo any more.

'Tell me about your travels, Salvo,' I said. 'Where have you been all this time?' I fingered the fur on his cloak. 'And where did you get this finery? Why, it's nearly as good as I could do.'

He grasped my hand and wouldn't let it go. 'Surely not,' he said, and then he kissed the ends of my fingers in turn. My heart began to skip. I did love him. There was no doubt in my mind, and every part of my body said so too.

'Now you stop that,' I said, pulling away rather half-heartedly. 'I won't have everyone thinking I behave badly.'

'Who gives a fig, Silvia? You're my girl. You know that.'

I should have been overjoyed to hear him say so but something gnawed away at my heart. Why could I not feel entirely happy?

'So?' I said, trying to distract myself from such thoughts. 'Where have you been then? Did Signor

Marenzio like your frontispiece?'

'Like it?' Salvo looked coy but only for a moment. He jumped down from the wall and turned to me, laughing. 'He loved it! That's why I've been away so long. He wanted to show it off to all his friends and let me tell you, Silvia, Luca Marenzio has a great many friends in a great many places. I've been to Rome and Florence and ...' he counted the places on his fingers '... and Ferrara and Venice and I've met people from all over Europe, Silvia ... Denmark, even as far away as England!'

I was very impressed. But this was Salvo I was talking to.

'Oh, England,' I said, waving my hand as if to swipe away a wasp. 'I know all about England. They have a Queen there who tells everyone what to do.' The truth was that Don Carlo had once invited a trio of musicians from England to San Severo, and they'd told me about Queen Elizabeth. They had been nice enough if rather too pink in the skin for my liking.

'It sounds the perfect place.' Salvo laughed. 'I wouldn't mind being ruled by a woman one little bit. Although ...'

'Although what?'

'I'd want to get my own way some of the time.' He reached towards me but I jumped down from the wall and ducked away.

'Signors Carlino and Pace must be very happy with your success. Does it mean that they have a lot of printing work as a result?'

'Much too much to do by themselves. Since I have been sending them work they have employed three more boys.'

'Oh,' I said. 'That's good.'

But the news didn't make me feel good. Salvo had been sending work back to Napoli quite regularly it seemed. Why had he not written to me? We walked a little further and I heard all about the wonderful cities that he had visited, the deliciousness of their food, wines and something called grappa, that he liked particularly. It occurred to me that I was hearing how it came about that

Salvo was nearly twice the man he was.

'Why didn't you write to me?' I interrupted another tale.

He stopped dead. 'But I did.'

'Oh!'

'And you never replied.' He looked aggrieved.

I didn't know what to say. Certainly I had never received a letter and I always looked when Laura brought the letters to my mis ... I groaned. Laura. Had she kept it from me?

'Well, Salvo, you are here now.' I couldn't help smiling when I looked at him, for I was very happy to see him. 'But I have to be getting back to the convent soon, and I have yet to go to the merchant's. If I'm much later, the sisters will begin to wonder where I am.'

'Yes, and I have to meet with Signor Pace before the morning is over,' said Salvo. 'So let's walk back together and on the way we can make some plans.' Before I could protest, he had taken hold of the edge of his cloak and cast it about my shoulders so that like children playing amongst curtains, we were both trapped inside. I felt his heart beating as he pulled me to him and when I looked into his eyes, the world outside our velvet tent fell away.

'Oh Salvo, I—'

'Shh ...' he said.

If the sting of a nettle could be a sweet and pleasurable thing, then that was how I felt the tingle of his whisper against my lips. The soft warmth of his kisses, the shivers of delight. The power of them. I felt ... oh, what did I care about the time or the place?

I don't know how long we remained by the wall at the far end of the harbour, but it was a sudden squall that eventually interrupted our enjoyment. We huddled together a while longer but the wall was no shelter at all, so we ran back, jumping over the ropes that fastened the boats, until we reached a stall that sold succulent boiled crab and squid.

'Can I see you later today?' Salvo asked.

I thought of how my days had been in all the months he had been away. The early days of terror, how Sister Caterina had been so kind, how I was looking forward to embroidering the altar cloth.

'Tomorrow, Salvo,' I said. 'I have things to do today.'

He was taken aback at this, I could see. But I was resolved, even though inside, I could feel much of me would have liked to say yes! As soon as possible!

'Silvia Albana! How is my favourite seamstress of all? I haven't seen you for a while.' The cloth merchant's broad smile revealed that he had lost yet another tooth. Even though he was old enough to be my father's father, and I'd had to put up with his being a little too friendly at times, I'd always been glad of his kindness and his appreciation of my skills.

'I have some beautiful silks for you,' he went on, pointing at the bolts of cloth stacked one on top of another. 'All colours. A ship docked from the Orient only last week.'

Seeing such riches, I sighed a little, and told him I was living with the sisters at San Domenico. 'So now you know why it isn't silks I need anymore, Vitore.'

'What? You are wasted there. Didn't the Carafas want to keep you?'

'Not after what happened. It isn't surprising to me, but I did wonder whether any of the other families who value their clothes might have employed me.' I shook my head. 'But I suppose they think I might be unlucky, or worse I had some part in ... in—'

'Oh nonsense! Now, now, don't upset yourself. Tell me what I can do for you today instead.'

I didn't tell him exactly what I wanted the linen for, but he was happy for me to choose, and I went back to the convent with two pieces that I could make into samples to show the sisters. On the way back the rain fell relentlessly and I arrived at San Domenico wet through. When I took off my clothes all the little hairs on my body stood up. The sight of them on the back of my bare arms reminded me of the afternoon with Salvo in the lemon grove. I'd had the same reaction then, but for quite a different reason.

I wondered what it would be like to be with Salvo. Really be with him. His travels had broadened not only his girth, I was sure. When he took me in his arms it was with a surety he had not had before. A shiver went through me and, even though I was sure I really did love him, it wasn't one of pleasure. It seemed to me that strange things happened to people when they became lovers. I thought of Donna Maria and her three husbands. I thought of my own mother and father. His absences and her struggles without him. Salvo's father was unknown to him. The act of love changed people, and not always for the better.

The sisters began singing at the mid hour of night. It was a devotion they undertook once a month, and as I lay somewhere halfway between sleeping and waking, I found that my heart was full of both joy and sorrow. I turned from side to side until the pillow was wet through with tears of one sort or another.

I was sure that at our next meeting Salvo would ask me to marry him. He'd be sure that I'd accept. Certainty abounded. A simple yes, that's all I had to say. It would be madness to say anything else.

Chapter Thirty-One

I almost knocked over the postman on my way out of the block.

'Quick getaway, is it?' he said. 'Hope he's not a big bloke.'

'Pardon?'

'Or is it a dog?'

'A dog? Oh … no. I'm in a rush, that's all.'

He handed me a couple of fliers and the sort of envelope that can only be a bill. I shoved them in my bag and gave him my best non-invitational smile. Another time, I might have stopped for a chat.

At the school gate I pressed the bell. It was nearly a quarter past twelve. Don't go to lunch. Don't go to lunch … I willed the secretary to be in her office, to answer.

Crackle … crackle … 'Hello?'

Phew.

'Hello, Lisa,' she said, once I'd got in. 'We weren't expecting you today. Mollie said you were still recovering.' She frowned, her gaze flicking from one side of my head to the other, as if checking for something unsavoury. I wondered what else Mollie had said. Mum's bang on the head had turned her into a nutcase?

'She's been at her dad's,' I said, all syrup and smiles. 'So not quite up to speed.'

Worry turned to relief. 'Oh, I see. Miss Price will be pleased,' she said. 'They've badgered her into taking choir practice, but she's not at all keen.'

'Umm… I was *wondering*,' I said, my voice higher than usual, 'if I might have a word with Mollie first. Do you think that would be all right?' I kept nodding, hoping she might get a subliminal message.

'I'll fetch her for you. No problem.' The secretary nodded back. Ah, body language, subtle as a wall.

'Brilliant. I'll go and start setting up.'

Fortunately, the hall was empty. I'd put out the first

row of chairs when Mollie appeared. She stood at the door, clearly anticipating the need for an escape route.

'I thought you were still ill,' she said.

'Did you?' I said, brightly. 'Well, you'll be glad to hear I'm better. Especially as that means I can take choir practice.' She didn't say anything. 'I could do with a hand with these chairs though.' I went on. All the nodding in the world wouldn't move Mollie if she didn't want to, but slowly she dragged herself across the floor and picked up a chair.

I looked at the clock. There wasn't really time for the usual negotiations.

'Listen, Mollie.' Urgency put an unexpected vibrato in my voice.

She stood still, holding the chair to her chest.

'Daniela dropped us all in the sh—' I checked over my shoulder. 'Right in the shit. She's going back to Milan.'

Inscrutable is my daughter's middle name, I swear. It must be written in invisible ink on her birth certificate in between Mollie and Susan (Michael's mother). She looked straight at me, eyes like moons, and said nothing.

'You already know, don't you?'

Still silence. I knew the answer anyway.

'Have you been in touch with Jon?'

There. The tiniest of nods.

'And did he say you could sing with us instead?'

Damn. That surprised her. The chair hit the floor with a bang and her jaw dropped almost as far. I regretted saying it at once, for the next second, I caught sight of a familiar gleam in her eye.

'We'll have to talk about it when you come home,' I said, as the rest of the choir jumbled through the door.

I was completely knackered afterwards. My intention had been to phone Jon the minute I left the school, but couldn't raise the energy for an argument. At home I sprawled on the sofa with a cup of tea and plumped for the comfort of junk mail. The postcard dropped out of the free newspaper from Lidl. A picture of the Colosseum. It fell just too far away for me to reach and my mobile rang before I could pick it up.

'Lisa?'

Oh God. 'Jon.'

'Listen, I'm sorry …'

Perhaps he thought I was going to interrupt. I *definitely* thought I was going to interrupt and opened my mouth to do so, but I don't know where the words went.

'I'm *very* sorry,' he went on, in the silence where I should have been, 'that Mollie knew about Daniela before you did. I didn't mean that to happen.'

'Oh?' I managed a sound at last. 'And what did you mean to happen? You know what Mollie's like when she's got the bit between her teeth. She'll be hell.'

'Then let her do it.'

'What? That's madness. She's a child.'

There was a short silence, then a sigh. 'It isn't madness, Lisa, it is our best option by a very long way.'

'We … we could get someone else?'

I heard the clatter of crockery and Jon cursing. 'I don't think so. There's not enough time … and besides, we're not going through all that palaver again.'

'What do you mean?' My voice sounded thin and whiny, almost like Sneery Demon's.

'You know exactly what I mean. *Noteworthy* didn't work with Daniela. She probably showed the rest of us up and not just in the voice department. Come on, Lisa, we both know it.'

My heart jumped about even more loudly. Worse than any stage fright I'd ever had. Jon wasn't only cross. This was a moment of decision and it wasn't about the concert, it was about us. Him, me, and the mammoth. I shut my eyes. Perhaps it wouldn't be there when I opened them. I took a deep breath.

When I did open my eyes, the first thing I saw was the Gesualdo madrigal. It lay on the table, open at the frontispiece and facing me. I didn't leave it like that, I was sure. Mum hadn't been back. There was only me in the flat…

'Lisa? Are you still there?'

'I'm frightened, Jon.'

'What?'

'I'm frightened.' The faces on the frontispiece leered at me. 'It's the frontispiece. I'm sure it's cursed.'

I heard John groan. A small sound, like the drawing back of a bow. The arrow wasn't far behind. 'Oh, no no *no*, Lisa, what the bloody hell's got into you? I know you've just had a bash on the head, but even before that you were being really weird.'

'It keeps changing. I see different things.'

'Give me strength—'

'And now it's open on the table and I know I didn't leave it there like that. I know it.'

Perhaps he heard the fear in my voice for there was an abrupt change in his. At half the previous volume he said, 'Okay, I'm coming over.'

I kept gazing fixedly at the frontispiece. There was much I remembered that didn't seem to be there at all. I could have sworn I had seen a row of hanging bodies, but now the gibbets contained only the bones. Worse things drew me in, especially a child being buried alive. I shuddered but couldn't stop staring.

It wasn't long before I heard him. The car door slammed, feet on gravel. Up the steps, two at a time and then the bell. Its jarring buzz broke the spell and I stood up.

'God, Lisa' Jon said, examining my face as if he'd never seen it before. 'Whatever the hell is up? You look absolutely bloody terrible.'

'Thanks.' I felt my chin begin to wobble. Just like Mollie's did before she cried. I couldn't stop it – wibble-wobble, chin-jelly.

And the next thing, Jon reached out, pulled me close and put his arms right round me. That's when I did cry, the horrible, heaving hiccupy sort that sticks eyelids together and leaves plague-like blotches all over your face. Jon rocked me like a baby, crooning nice soothing things like, *it's all right, you have nothing to fear, I'm here now.*

Eventually, I calmed down.

'Okay now?' he said, peering at my hideous face.

I nodded.

'Good. Now show me the frontispiece and tell me everything about the curse. I promise I'll listen, although…' he looked at his watch, 'I have a six o'clock deadline and so far all I've got is two chords and a duck call for the vitamin pills ad.'

I managed half a smile. 'Have you quack to health in no time?'

'Ha! That's brilliant!' Jon hugged me tightly. 'See? That's my lovely Lisa. You're better already.'

I did feel better. How could I not? But the frontispiece still sat open on the table. That hadn't gone away. Jon sat and listened while I made my case.

'Ever since we started singing this,' I jabbed my finger towards the Gesualdo, 'things have been going wrong. We've been at odds—'

'Robert and Sophie haven't.'

'No, but you and I have. And there's been so many bad things happening. The boy drowning—'

'But that hasn't got anything to do with us.'

The knot of anxiety at the back of my mind flared into pain just then. I still hadn't told anyone about the HIV test. The result would come any day. The temptation to say something was huge but the temptation itself felt malelovent, the same feeling I had when I looked at the frontispiece. It was as if it wanted me to distract Jon.

But I wouldn't. *After* the result came was the time for revelation, not before.

'Sophie's fire and her arm, your toe, the whole tree thing, then there was the nightmares – both Mollie's and mine.'

Each of the elements: water, fire and air had been

236

roused, that seemed to me. Would we have an earthquake next? I knew there was precious little hard evidence,

'Look at it carefully,' I said. 'Try the bottom right hand corner. Just sit and look at it. I'll make tea.'

Jon grabbed the madrigal, sat back and got comfy. I left him to it. What I hoped for, I wasn't quite sure. Vindication that I wasn't seeing things was one thing, but equally, who in their right mind would wish for any sort of curse to be true?

I hadn't said anything about Daniela. Except that without the madrigal, we'd never have met. But *not* talking about her made me realise how much she'd occupied my thinking. As I squeezed the teabag between finger and spoon, I realised I could put a name to Sneery Demon. *Jealousy*. And he wasn't a demon; he was a horrible monster. Ouch... I threw the teabag in the bin. And he'd burnt my finger.

Jon was still staring at the frontispiece when I took him his tea and only when I put the mug down did he look up. His face was strained.

'I don't know, Lisa,' he said. 'It's weird.' He snapped the copy shut and threw it on to the table. 'God knows, we've all seen enough grim pictures to last us a lifetime. Why should this one have such an effect?'

'So you noticed something, did you?'

He shrugged. 'Something, yeah. But difficult to describe. I'm looking at it, thinking, oh, that's not very nice and God, that must be painful, when all of a sudden, I'm sort of anxious, scared even. I'm actually *feeling* bad and I don't get that when I'm looking at real horror on the telly.'

'But you didn't want to stop looking?'

'No, I didn't. But I reckon I've sussed why you think it keeps changing. Look ...' He pointed at a figure being squashed in something like a mangle. 'Keep your eye on it.'

Gradually he turned it round, until, by the time it was upside down, the figure looked completely different. When

237

part of a bigger scene, legs became horns, and the mangle disappeared into the coil of a snake.

'Oh, yes,' I said, and I kept on looking at the snake, following the coils round and round and somehow down and down …

'Mmm.' John sat back suddenly, and I jumped. He nodded then took a slurp of tea. 'The thing is, it's so interesting. All those little hands reaching out for help and all the time they're trying to pull you in … brrr!' He shivered all over. 'Whoever did it was a genius.'

'That's what Signor Pace said. It's by Salvo Carlino, one of the finest engravers of the Renaissance.'

'Poor guy, he must have had a very bad day.'

I nibbled my way though half a choc-chip cookie while Jon put away three.

'But …' I hesitated, 'can you see why I'm worried?'

He sighed. 'Yes and no. I'll grant you it's creepy, but I don't see why this has anything to do with Mollie singing in the concert.'

'But what about all the bad things that have happened? I wouldn't be human if I wasn't worried for her.' Although, it dawned on me – at the speed of a racing slug – that ever since the tree came down, I was the dotty one.

He looked at me without saying anything but his eyes spoke loud enough to get through my thick skull.

'The thing is, Lisa, we both know that if we tried hard enough we could get someone to replace Daniela. Exeter isn't a small town, it's a city. But we've made one mistake. Let's not make another.'

'But Mollie—'

'Mollie is perfect. She's one of us and we'll all look after her. Curse or no curse. Let's face it, Lisa, ' he looked at me straight, with no lies or weirdness, 'you, me and her… we're practically a family.'

At that moment, I swear I heard from somewhere in another room the sound of a mammoth trumpeting. Perhaps that was why I found myself smiling; a curious sensation if you haven't done it for a while.

'You're right,' I said. 'Of course, you are. I'll tell her later.' People talk about waves of relief washing over them but for me it was like standing on the prom and watching the shingle take away all the crap and rubbish that had built up on the shore. Not so much the wave but the washing bit. Cleansed. Yes, that's what I felt.

I picked up the Gesualdo and put it face down at the bottom of the heap. 'And you, my friend,' I said to it, 'are staying right there.'

'Phew! Thank God for that.' Jon jumped up and for the second time, gave me a big delicious hug and this one really did lift me off my feet. It didn't last that long though. 'Right,' he said, putting me down. 'I'm out of here. The ducks are calling.'

I could still hear the mammoth. 'Bloody hell, we live in a menagerie.'

'A what?'

'Oh, nothing,' I said, laughing. 'It really doesn't matter.'

Mum put her key in the lock at the precise moment we went out into the hall. Of course she did. Her face was a picture of trepidation when she saw us, but a quick glance from one to the other and she turned up her smile volume to maximum.

Jon extracted himself very promptly so I had to go through the full interrogation. In the end I couldn't bear her ecstatic wittering any longer, and I decided to leave earlier than was necessary to fetch Mollie from school. It meant I could pop into the shop to tell Robert: a, I'd be back at work the following day and b, the good news about Mollie singing with us.

When I checked in my bag to see if I'd got my keys, I found the bundle of post. Out from the fliers fell a postcard of Buckingham Palace. Duncan had got as far as London.

Will be there for the concert.
You'll be amazed.
Can't wait!
Duncan

I frowned. He was a nice man, but I wish I knew what what was so amazing that he couldn't wait.

The rest of the post I thought I'd look at later. I put the heap down on the hall table, and it was then that something amazing really did happen. I caught sight of a couple of letters – not even a whole word – on the frank of one of the envelopes, and they sent a huge shockwave through me. R D &

The hospital, and most probably the final result of my HIV test.

Mum was in the kitchen. I could hear her opening the cutlery drawer, putting on the kettle, doing ordinary things. She was humming.

I opened the door and went out. I made it down the stairs, out into the street and as far as the bench by the postbox at the end of the road. The rush of adrenalin whined in my ears and the world seem all too bright. I sat down and looked at the envelope, badly crumpled in the corner where I had been clutching it so tightly.

Open it. I told myself. Open it now.

Should I go home? I sat on the bench for quite a long time while the hem of my shirt soaked up the tears I shed. I'd not taken Mum's advice; always carry a hankie or a tissue. A whole box might have done, I don't know. Who can know what will be adequate for such situations?

Another amazing thing, the world can be turned upside down, or in my case, turned the right way up, in just a short sentence. The test was negative. I need not worry anymore.

Hence the soaked shirt. I hadn't done up my coat and rather than soaking my sleeves with tears I wiped my eyes on the bottom of my shirt. I could have gone home and changed, but explanations would be required, I wouldn't get to the shop to see Robert, and then I'd be late for Mollie.

I sat appreciating the traffic and marvelling at the fallen leaves skipping along the pavement in the breeze. The world was a good place after all. Jon and I were happy, Daniela had gone for good, *Noteworthy* was back on course. The concert would be brilliant and as for the curse... it was ridiculous.

A smidgen of unease muscled in on my euphoria. I stood up, tucked my damp shirt in, and began walking into town. There was no curse. I had imagined it. After all, this was the twenty-first century. If curses were real, then everyone would be casting spells and drinking love potions.

Even so, I thought, it was a good thing that the concert was soon and we'd get it over with. As for Jon's musical, it was a nice idea but completely mis-guided. Performance was out of the question.

When I arrived at the shop and told Robert about Mollie taking Daniela's place, he was surprised, but pleased. I knew Jon was pleased, and Sophie would be. I was pleased, everyone was pleased, so when I got to Mollie's school I was completely confident that she would be pleased too.

Except she wasn't. She was pleased to be asked, but no, she wouldn't do it. Or rather, she *would* do it, but only on one condition.

Chapter Thirty-Two

Napoli 1591

In the morning, I sat for a while in the chapel, having told Sister Caterina that I wanted to think about the altar cloth. Certainly, I was keen to start. My fingers twitched as I imagined pulling the thread through the needle, how I would plot the pattern repeats, how in a thousand stitches, the Garden of Eden would take shape.

Salvo would want an answer.

The cloth wouldn't be gaudy though. Unlike the show that my sewing achieved with my lady's clothes of silk and brightly coloured velvet brocade, I wanted all sense of my endeavour to be hidden, so that only its beauty was remarked on. Perhaps I was influenced by the simplicity of the convent, although for some reason, into my mind came the memory of Signora Carlino and her collar that lay so perfectly flat.

What would I say to him?

How I had hankered after his mother's skill. And how determined I had been. Disobeying my mother – when I remembered the day I went to market with old Francesca, my cheeks became hot with shame. But I had got what I wanted, for now I could sew a flat collar better than anyone, although it was a great pity that nobody wore flat collars any more.

Salvo – darling Salvo. I loved him so, but ...

Sitting for so long without activity had made me cold. Outside I could hear two of the sisters sweeping the cloisters; they were laughing together although I could not hear their conversation.

I wished I had someone to talk to. Someone who might understand.

Father Strozzi took confession and while I knew I shouldn't think of him as the man who leered at my lady, I couldn't help it. What could I ask him about the act of love? Love. Even as I thought the word, I wondered at its meaning, for it seemed to me that with love came violence and fear. Did it make men mad? And women, come to that. I remembered my lady's shivers of pleasure and how she toyed with death at every meeting with Fabrizio. I thought of Don Carlo's need for the whip.

I didn't think Sister Caterina would be able to help me. She had made her choice a long while ago.

My mother was far away and nothing would induce me to go to Gesualdo while Don Carlo was there, although Rosa said that he was definitely to marry a lady from Ferrara. Heaven help her, I thought. She probably has no choice in the matter. Donna Maria never had any choice about her husbands and had been married at thirteen. Thirteen – at that age, I was still feeding the chickens and wishing they were peacocks.

As I left the chapel I looked back over my shoulder at the altar, and imagined it draped in my cloth of fine white linen. The embroidery would be in silk thread the colour of wine. To remind us of the blood of Christ, Sister Caterina said, although I preferred thinking of the wine. I would appliqué a border possibly across the whole in thin strips ... or maybe I would keep the body plain but have a weft cut fringe.

Unlike Donna Maria, I did have a choice.

The wind blew straight from the sea and forced its way round every pleat and fold.

'It's far too cold for a walk, Silvia,' Salvo said when I met him on the quayside. 'Besides,' he hesitated, 'my uncle has invited his colleagues and their families for a party this afternoon. There is to be dancing. Would you like that?'

'Dancing?' I hardly knew whether I liked it or not.

'Yes, wouldn't you like to dance with me?' And before I could draw breath, he had picked me up and swung me right round. When I landed on my feet, he wouldn't let go.

'But I can't let you go,' he said, 'look.' He pretended

243

that we were indeed stuck together. Pushing me a little and then falling towards me. 'See?'

'I do see,' I said, laughing with him. 'How terrible! What is to be done?'

'Why, I believe the key may well be a kiss,' he said, frowning. 'Shall we try it and find out?'

What could I say?

At first, his lips brushed lightly over mine. But it wasn't enough and not just for him. Once again he wrapped me in his cloak. The thrill of his nearness and warm breath was enough to unlock any resistance I might have felt. My lips parted. At once, Salvo pulled me closer and his kisses became deeper and more urgent until, had he let me go suddenly, I would have fallen straight to the ground.

A shout of laughter and a lewd remark from a passer-by intruded on our little world. I opened my eyes and found Salvo looking down at me; the familiar twinkle in his eyes so close and much brighter than I had ever seen before. My heart was beating as rapidly as if I had run up a mountain. In fact, I was so overwhelmed with powerful sensations all over, that I hardly recognised my body as my own.

'Come, Silvia,' Salvo said, drawing away. 'Let's go. I'm looking forward to dancing with you. Do you know the sfessania?'

'No.' I shook my head vigorously. 'Please don't ask me to dance. I learnt the saltarello as a child but I haven't danced it since.' Sometimes the servants at San Severo would hold dances in the kitchens or the courtyard when Don Carlo was away, but Donna Maria always kept me with her.

'I'm sure there will be lots of saltarellos this afternoon. Everyone knows that.'

By the time we arrived the music and dancing had already started, but Giovanni Carlino, Salvo's uncle, greeted us effusively.

'Here you are at last, Silvia,' he said. 'I was hoping

that my nephew wasn't going to persuade you to keep away. You are quite right, Salvo – she is a lot prettier than most.'

Then he put an arm round my shoulder and gave me a kiss. I flustered an answer, amazed by such audacity, but when he drew back there was nothing in his expression but friendly warmth.

I hadn't expected such a wealthy household. Obviously it wasn't as grand as San Severo Palazzo, but the sala was very spacious and with the tables cleared to one side there was just room enough for six couples, as long as the musicians stayed squashed in the corner. Salvo was right. The steps of the saltarello came back to me with more ease than I expected.

Everyone knew Salvo and as we danced, I received nods and smiles from them all. Who would not be flattered? Never in my life had I received such attention from so many! And while I accepted a little wine to quench my thirst, it wasn't the cause of my intoxication.

I did refuse to dance the sfessania. When the musicians struck up such a quick and lively rhythm, I knew I would be falling over in no time if I'd tried. Salvo looked disappointed so I shooed him away to find another partner, and couldn't help smiling when a small crowd formed the moment he stepped away from me.

The music made not tapping a foot impossible but I was glad of a seat, especially as it meant I could watch Salvo from a little distance. Everyone had their eyes on him. He was, without doubt, the handsomest man there, and we were all mesmerised by his dancing of the sfessania. I decided it was a good thing that he wasn't as skinny as he used to be. It suited him as a boy, but a man needed dignity and a little flesh on his bones.

His doublet was very fine and I wondered who had made it. After a little while, I wondered who had taught him the sfessania too.

When the dancing was done, the tables were put back out and two serving girls brought food for us all. Much to

245

my amazement there were forks on the trays. I couldn't help being reminded of San Severo then. I wonder what my lady would have said, if she knew I was a guest at such a party. My lady. In spite of the lively music, I couldn't help sighing at the thought of her and then into my head came the dream I had of us both looking in the mirror before ... before ...

'Silvia, why so sad all of a sudden?' Salvo leant towards me and beneath the table I felt his hand on my knee. The shock of his touch made me jump and he laughed. Perhaps I had had more wine than I thought for when I turned to face him, it was Fabrizio's face I saw. I did not jump then, but almost fainted and poor Salvo looked very worried.

'What is it?' he said. 'Are you ill?'

'No, no.' I managed to smile. 'I'm all right.'

'Are you sure? We could go outside.'

'No, there's no need.'

There was no need, I told myself firmly. The Duke was dead and buried. It was silly imaginings, the result of too much wine and dancing.

We were both distracted by a huge cheer from the other end of the sala. Dessert was arriving, a biancomangiare so huge I thought it would wobble off the dish. The mere sight of it made me feel considerably better, and when everybody laughed at the rude noise it made as the serving spoon scooped out the portions, I couldn't help joining in.

Sitting so close to the host, we were served quite quickly. The spoon was almost in my mouth when Signor Pace stood up and called for silence. Out of politeness I put my spoon back down, and hoped his speech would not be as long as one of Don Carlo's lute solos.

There was much thanking of people I didn't know and clapping of hands.

'And now, my good friends,' Signor Pace said, 'let me show you the source of our good fortune today.' He held up something covered in a velvet cloth. 'Silvia!' he said, making me half jump out of my skin and setting the

biancomangiare all a-quiver. 'Please do me the honour of revealing our latest publication.'

There was considerable clapping when I pulled the corner of the velvet and it tumbled away. Signor Pace held up a large volume. The cover was tooled in dark red leather and embossed in gold with the name of Luca Marenzio.

'Thanks to the talent and charm of Salvo here, Signor Marenzio has allowed the printing of this book for general sale at the price of eight lire.'

There was a general murmur of surprise from the company. That was a lot of money.

'And already we have orders for ...' Signor Pace paused and beckoned us to guess. *'Six? Ten?'*

Everyone shook their heads. I did not have a number in my head at all. How many people could afford to pay so much?

'Thirty twoooo! And that is before they have even seen it.' He opened the volume and laid it on the table out of the way of the *biancomangiare*. Salvo's frontispiece brought gasps of pleasure from those who could see it, and soon everyone was crowding round.

I sat back while Salvo was being congratulated and stole a mouthful of pudding. Never had I tasted such an excellent dessert. Smooth, creamy and sweet with honey, I went to take a second mouthful, but the speech wasn't over, so I laid my spoon down once again.

'We should all congratulate ourselves,' said Signor Pace. *'For, ten, twenty years ago, who could have imagined that we should receive commissions from so far away? At last we can show those in Venezia and Firenze a thing or two.'* Everyone laughed at this. *'And looking to the future, who knows what young Salvo will bring back from his next trip when he goes to the royal court in Denmark? He has told me that Herr Borchgrevinck, the court organist there, is especially keen for him to go.'*

My ears stumbled over the last bit. The name sounded like a sudden coughing fit and meant nothing to me, but I had heard of Denmark. I wasn't exactly sure where it was, but did know it was a long way away. If Salvo was going there, then I wouldn't see him for a very long time.

Why hadn't he told me? In a daze I picked up the spoonful of biancomangiare and put it in my mouth, but it tasted too sweet, too cloying. Everything about it was wrong.

Signor Pace signalled to the musicians to start again. Straight away Salvo took my hand and held it to his lips.

'Forgive me, Silvia. I was going to tell you.'

'Oh?' I said. 'When exactly? The day before you left?' I stood up, then swayed, feeling muzzy and overwhelmed. 'I think perhaps I do need to go outside after all.'

My manners did not desert me and I thanked Signor Pace as quickly as I could without appearing rude. Whether he noticed the glaze of tears in my eyes, I don't know. There isn't a great deal of difference to be seen between tears of pain and those of too much wine.

Salvo followed me out of the sala but then stood between me and the door. 'Please, Silvia. Let me explain.' A maid was lurking behind a pillar and by her expression, I knew she was after some gossip. With a stare from me, she slid away, no doubt to listen from somewhere more discreet.

I spoke quietly, but my voice quivered with anger. 'What is there to explain?'

'It's too good an opportunity for me to refuse. I might even meet the King of Denmark.'

'That's very nice for you. Now, will you let me out?'

'Not yet,' he said. 'Silvia, please. If I go to Denmark, I will come back a wealthy man. Then you and I ... we will be able to live comfortably. I would be my own master. Not in service to the likes of Don Carlo.' He spat the name with disgust. 'Wouldn't you like that?'

'Haven't you forgotten something?'

He looked flummoxed. 'What do you mean?'

'I don't actually recall you asking me to marry you, but if you did and I've forgotten, I don't actually recall my *accepting.' I was upsetting myself with being angry and when he opened his mouth to say something, I wouldn't let him. 'But if I did actually accept and I've forgotten that too, what use is a husband who isn't at home? How do I know that when you come back from Denmark you won't go running off to other places – places I've never even heard of.'*

I wanted to cry but then two of the guests appeared and as he was obliged to let them go by, I escaped at the same time. Of course, I did not want to walk with strangers so I set off in the opposite direction. The wind did its very best to push me back but I was determined.

'Wait, Silvia.' Salvo caught me up and, taking hold of my arm he steered me into a doorway out of the gale. 'You've forgotten your cloak. Here.'

'Oh.' I'd not even noticed the cold but found my teeth were chattering. I took it from his hand. Now, I knew the danger of cloaks; it was best I put it on myself. But as I tied the bow, Salvo pulled the hood from over my head. Holding either side he leaned down to look directly into my eyes.

'Please marry me, Silvia?' he said. 'You know I love you dearly.'

Of course, he proposed. I knew he would. Hadn't I thought of nothing else while sitting in the chapel all morning? So, now I had my choice. What would I decide?

Chapter Thirty-Three

I knew the days of a new Barbie outfit were well and truly over, but on the way home she didn't even want a hot chocolate in Costa. At least she couldn't escape into the ether with her bloody phone. Yes, I thoroughly approved of the school's policy of confiscation, which I discovered when Miss Price beckoned me from the school gate and handed it to me. Could she leave it at home in future?

You bet.

It had been found when Jon's email about Daniela pinged its arrival in class. I should have been cross with him too. It was Jon who backed up Mollie's insistence she had to have a smartphone.

'The thing is, Mollie,' I began, but she interrupted.

'I'll only do it if we can sing Jon's musical at school.'

'But it's just not suitable!'

God. It's bad enough sounding like Mum, but when did I start to sound like my ghastly grandmother?

Silence.

'What would your teachers at school think? They'd never let me near the choir again.'

More silence.

'Are you listening?'

'No.'

'Don't be rude.'

Silence.

Exeter High Street had never felt so long. I was even tempted to get the bus.

'I heard you coming up.' Mum opened the door before I could put the key in the lock. A moment later her beaming smile collapsed. 'What's happened?' she said to me. I felt too pissed off to say anything so she asked Mollie the same thing.

'Nothing,' she said, with a great sigh while swinging her rucksack off her shoulder and throwing it onto the floor in the middle of the hall. 'Can I have it back now?'

That was said to me. I still had her precious phone in my bag but wasn't ready to give it up.

'I think we have something to resolve first,' I said in Gran-speak. 'Put your stuff away and I'll make tea.'

'Why don't I do that?' Mum said, and she slunk away into the kitchen.

Mollie left her bag where it was and went into the lounge. The next thing I heard was the telly and when I went in she was clutching the remote with both hands.

I switched it off at the wall. Cue exploding Mollie.

'But you haven't *heard* it,' she yelled, her face puce.

'I don't need to,' I said, hideously reasonable. 'Even if Jon's musical was wonderful, he's made a mistake with the subject matter. It's completely unsuitable.'

'But it isn't, it *isn't*.'

Her crying came in loud ballooning, end-of-the-world sobs. I couldn't bear it when she sounded so tragic. Every sob pressed a finger on my tears button too. The memory of Jon's arms round me was fading. All I could think was that he'd been stupid to write a bloody musical.

'How can you say that, Mollie? It's the story of a horrible man murdering his wife and her … friend, in a very horrible way. It isn't a fairy story. There isn't a happy ending.'

A corner of the madrigal stuck out from the bottom of the heap on the table. Hateful thing. I kicked it.

'Goodness, look at you two.' Mum came in with the tea. 'Should I buy shares in Kleenex? Now then,' she said, putting down the tray and making herself comfortable on the sofa. 'Which one of you is going to tell me what the matter is? Mollie? Come and sit next to me, dear. Look. I bought these for you.'

She held one out and I realised, as Mollie dumped herself on the sofa, just how a pink wafer biscuit might resemble a carrot.

'Now then, what's your mum done that's so terrible?'

'It's what she *hasn't* done,' said Mollie. 'What she

won't let me do.'

'I can't …' I began, but Mollie would have none of it.

'You can, you can.'

Mum patted her knee. 'Now, now.'

Then she turned to me. 'What *is* all this about, Lisa?'

I explained briefly. She frowned a lot.

'But do you mean,' she said, when I'd finished, 'that you *haven't* heard any of Jon's musical?'

'She hasn't,' Mollie sniffed. 'She hasn't heard a single note.'

Their faces had the same look about them.

'Lisa,' said Mum, 'I'm surprised at you.'

What do you do when everyone is against you? Behave like an adult and consider carefully why this may be the case? Or be a toddler and storm off into your room to beat the pillow?

I stripped the whole bed afterwards, carried the bundle through to the kitchen and stuffed it in the washing machine. They were still sitting there and while Mum was managing a bland expression quite well, Mollie's quivered with suppressed triumph.

'It's on my phone,' she squeaked.

Of course it was, I should have realised. Oh Lord. She'd probably played it to half the school choir already. Would there be complaints from parents? Like that time in the Nativity play when an aggrieved Joseph piped up that he'd always worn a condom.

My pathetic siege was over, but at least I'd be proved right when we heard it.

When I handed her phone back, Mollie burst into action. 'Let's hear it through the speakers,' she said, shifting various bits of media kit with lightning skill. Was this part of the national curriculum for primary schools? Or had evolution hot-wired twenty-first century babies in the womb?

Mollie was far too wriggly to sit down so I made myself as comfortable as I could next to Mum.

'I'm sure it'll be all right, dear,' she whispered, patting my knee in exactly the same way she'd patted Mollie's. 'Jon wouldn't have done anything bad.'

'It isn't anything Jon's done,' I said. 'I've no doubt the music will be wonderful. It might even be a brilliant musical worthy of the West End or Broadway – God knows, he's talented enough – but we're talking a primary school choir, Mum. Gesualdo committed a gruesome murder—'

'Ready?' Mollie interrupted. She held out her phone. We nodded and she pressed Go.

Immediately, there was silence but then we heard the sort of familiar rustlings and coughs that home recordings always have. A note on the keyboard sounded and *Ready, Mollie?* Jon's voice took me by surprise and I stiffened. Repeated chords in a minor key followed, reminiscent of *Greensleeves*, but more miserable.

Singing along with the recording was soon irresistible to Mollie. She started by humming but whole lungfuls of air and words quickly followed and then, when she was completely carried away, actual *actions*.

Sad am I, she lamented, waving a Kleenex like a Morris dancer's hankie. Then she fell to her knees and sang in her best tragic voice:

My father died when I was small
And now my mother weeps all day
She had to wed a Prince who's cruel
They wouldn't let her have a say.

The castle where we live is cold
And I am forced to hide away.
My bedroom walls are thick with mould.
I have no friends with whom to play.

Oh, Mollie, I thought, already captivated by how she embraced the part, you are brilliant. The accompaniment was understated broken chords, the simplest of supports for such a strong melody. I sighed and Mum dug me in the side with her elbow.

The Prince writes lots of ghastly songs
His playing of the lute is bad
We have to listen all day long
I think that he is really mad.

When he is cross it's very frightening
Mummy hurries me to bed
But I lie and hear her pleading
Then I wish that he was ...

Mollie left us in no doubt what she wished for as she put her hands together in prayer. The music finished with an interrupted cadence, unresolved, like the line, and ready to lead into the next scene. But Mollie switched it off.

'See?' she said. 'What's the matter with that?'

'Nothing, darling,' said Mum, before I could get a word in. 'That was really lovely. Let's hear the next one.'

I wasn't going to say anything anyway, but I did smile and nod even if both were on the weak side. The song was lovely; Mollie's singing was lovely. No one could fail to be affected by it. What affected me was that Jon had chosen an entirely unexpected angle of approach. Maria d'Avalos did have a daughter called Margarita. If the whole story was from the her point of view then perhaps the more gruesome elements would be left out.

'Sure you're ready again?' Mollie said, looking at me.

'Yes, yes.'

She pressed *Go* and we heard applause. Clearly Jon and Mollie weren't the only people present. The next thing I heard was Daniela's voice congratulating Mollie. I could feel myself stiffen again but then Mum put her arm round me. Something she hadn't done for ages.

In the next song, Margarita is playing by herself in the castle courtyard. She watches as guests arrive for a party, which she cannot attend. Only one of them speaks to her and it is Fabrizio, the handsome duke. The Princess comes to wish her daughter goodnight and when she and Fabrizio meet it's love at first sight.

When that song ended, Mollie didn't stop the recording and we went straight into a love duet that she sang with Daniela. About halfway through, Mum reached for the tissues and we both took one. At first I thought I'd sniff a bit, that's all. Music has peaks and troughs of emotion in the same way as it has ups and downs in terms of volume, pitch and intensity. That's how it all works; variety makes for interest. But I wasn't experiencing any let up in what I felt.

One tissue wasn't enough. Over the next couple of numbers, I got through half the box even though they were rather upbeat and cheerful. Eventually, the Princess tells Fabrizio that even though she is being buried alive in her marriage to the mad Prince Carlo, it would be wrong to run away.

But then, just when we think it is all going to end unhappily with the lovers parting, in a reprieve of the opening number, Margarita overhears Don Carlo saying he is going to murder Princess Maria. Oh no! She warns Fabrizio and he rushes to save his true love. But would he get there in time?

After a rustling and footsteps the recording clicked off.

'That's all there is on here,' said Mollie. 'So? What do you think?'

I couldn't speak, but Mum said all the right things. Well done, Mollie. Well done, Jon. How marvellous.

'Mummy?'

That did it. Mollie calling me Mummy. She hadn't done that for ages. I nodded and kept on nodding.

'Yes,' I managed to feebly croak.

I didn't feel like crying anymore, but something was going on. Another demon was making itself known to me. I may have faced down Sneery and capitulated briefly to the Toddler Tantrum demon that beat up innocent pillows, but here was the sly Worm of Shame, and what it wanted me to do, was blame someone else for my folly. In my mind's eye, Daniela was first in line, then Jon. Even Mollie was presented as a candidate. But I had seen it, and although it tried to slither out of sight, I caught it by the tail. Never would I let it go underground again.

Both Mollie and Mum were looking at me, mystified. And I was mystified too. Where had all this emotional stuff come from? Wasn't I a rather calm and restrained individual? Once perhaps, but not any more.

'I'm so sorry,' I said, gasping from the effort of subduing a worm, bent on becoming a snake. 'I've been such an idiot,' I began.

'Oh, yes,' said Mollie, brightly. 'We know that.'

She came and sat between us, wriggling her little bottom to make room. She beamed and patted both our knees.

'So we can do it at school then?' she said to me.

What could I say? 'I'll have to run it past Miss Price, but I'm sure we can.'

'Yeaaay!' she squealed loud enough for Mum and me to cover our ears.

'But wait a minute,' I said, so taken with the music and Mollie's singing, I'd forgotten the central issue, 'what happens in the end?'

Mollie shrugged. 'I don't know. It wasn't written when we did the recording.'

'Surely,' said Mum. 'Jon wouldn't write anything unsuitable, would he?'

'I hope not,' I said. 'But the true story doesn't have a happy ending.'

'Who cares about the true story?' Mollie scoffed. 'It was *ages* ago.'

I was about to say you can't play fast and loose with the truth, but then I thought, hang on, if you only *base* your story on something, it doesn't matter a figgy leaf about the actual truth. 'That's right,' I said, changing my gambit. 'Jon didn't mean this to be the definitive story of Gesualdo's murdering of his wife and her lover. In fact, although he's named the wicked prince, Carlo, there's no mention of Gesualdo at all. Why have I got so het-uppity about it?'

'It's all the stupid frontispiece's fault,' said Mollie. 'And the madrigal that goes with it. I reckon someone put a spell on it.'

Mum laughed: 'What? Like the bad fairy at the christening?'

'Or the wicked queen with the mirror,' Mollie said.

'Or Beauty and the Beast.'

'Or the glass slipper.'

'The glass slipper?' Mum said. 'What's enchanted about that?'

Mollie thought about it for a bit. 'All right,' she said. 'Not the slipper, the pumpkin instead.'

They batted spells back and forth but I stopped listening. Even if there was a semi-quaver of truth in the existence of some kind of curse, I wasn't having anything to do with it. Once the concert was over, I'd never have another Gesualdo madrigal in the house.

'Do you think Jon's written the end?' I asked Mollie. 'I didn't put him off, did I?'

She looked at me with scorn. 'I wouldn't have thought so.'

'Will you ask him?'

'Oh, Lisa,' said Mum. 'Why don't you ask him? You haven't fallen out again, have you?'

'No. But I've had an idea. A good idea, I think.' I put my arm round Mollie and gave her a big squeeze. 'Ask him, will you, Mollie? But don't tell him it's for me. Now it's my turn to have a secret.'

Mum sighed. 'Haven't we all had enough of secrets? They never seem to come to any good.'

Chapter Thirty-Four

Napoli 1591

'I love you too, Salvo,' I whispered. 'But I don't think I can marry you.'

He was so close and his breath warmed my chilly face but I couldn't look at him.

'What was that?' he said as if he had not quite heard, as if the wind had taken my words and blown them away. 'What did you say?'

'I can't marry you, Salvo.' I said it more firmly.

He still held the corners of my hood but I felt his grip loosen.

'What do you mean, you can't?'

All the reasons I could give rushed into my head at once and I didn't know where to begin. Had all the threads in my workbox knotted themselves together, I would not have felt more in a tangle.

'I'm too busy,' I said. 'There's the altar—'

'Busy?' He almost choked on the word. 'How can you be too busy to get married? Silvia, what are you saying? Are you mad? This is me, Salvo. Remember?'

I nodded. Maybe I was mad. Certainly I felt sick, and my cloak could not keep out the cold or the fist that seemed to be gripping my insides. I turned away and he let go of my hood. The wind had risen still further and spots of rain began to fall. I didn't know where to go but set off anyway.

'Where are you going?' Salvo caught me up.

'Back to San Domenico,' I said, although it wasn't in that direction.

'Silvia, wait, please. You can't go without giving me some sort of an explanation. I always thought—' We'd reached the corner, where a sudden gust slapped us both about the face. I hesitated and Salvo put his hand on my arm. 'Look,' he said, holding up one of the keys that hung

from his belt. 'I have the key to the print shop. We can talk in there and be out of this rain.'

What would or could I say?

Salvo lit the lantern and at once tall shadows leapt about the room. There were two presses and between them ran washing lines pegged with many pieces of paper already printed and hung to dry. Title pages, some of them; others were illustrations of trees and flowers. All were beautiful, and I recognised his hand in most of them. The overpowering smell of resin, soot and vinegar stung my eyes. Had I climbed up a kitchen chimney, it would not be so strong. I put my handkerchief to my nose.

'It's the ink,' Salvo said. 'There's not much I can do about that. When my uncle is here, the doors are kept open. but I don't think we want an audience, do we? Besides, the wind will blow right in today. Now then,' he said, clearing a bench of several pieces of paper, 'sit down there and tell me what is going on. You've always been the one for me, Silvia, ever since I saw you sitting in your father's wood store. You must know that.'

'But I'm not that girl anymore,' I said, shaking my head, 'not since ... not since everything happened.'

Salvo stood up and began pacing up and down. Three steps in each direction. That was all the room he had between the presses. 'But that was a long time ago,' he said. 'You can forget about it now and look to the future – with me.' He knelt down and took my hand. 'Now what's all this about being busy?'

I thought of the serene calm of the convent and the beautiful singing. I thought of my own little cell, its white austerity and the less demanding and quieter Lady I was answerable to there. 'I'm to embroider a new altar cloth for the chapel.'

Salvo laughed. 'Why, that's wonderful! I always said you were the cleverest needlewoman there ever was – except when my mother was in the room, of course. But—' he hesitated and two little frown lines creased his forehead. 'What makes you think you can't do that if you marry me? Why, it will take you as long to do that as it will me to travel to Denmark and back. Then we can be happy together. See? See, Silvia?'

I looked up. How handsome he was! My heart leapt with longing for him. But then he reached up to push away a tumbled lock of hair, and I was reminded by the fall of the fabric from his wrist of the lettuce cuffs worn by Fabrizio on his last night on earth. Was it possible for love to bring lasting happiness? I had not seen it.

'You are very different too,' I said. 'You have been living another life. I can see that by your clothes, the dancing, and you must have been eating very well.' I found a handkerchief and wiped my eyes. It was coming in out of the cold wind that had made them water, I was sure of it. 'How do I know that you will come back?'

He stopped pacing and looked at me. 'Of course I'll come back. Why wouldn't I?'

'You don't know what will happen.'

'None of us knows the future, Silvia. We can't know it.'

He was right, of course. I opened my mouth to speak, but as I did so, another thought entered my head and immediately struck me as a solution.

'Oh,' I said, excitement making me sit up straight. 'I have a good idea! What if I come with you? If we were married, I could come. Then we wouldn't have to be apart. And I've always wanted to see other countries, France, Denmark, even England.' I imagined sailing away from Napoli on one of the tall ships down at the dock, leaving behind all my bad memories and worries about Don Carlo. I would fill my head with new places and new experiences, a whole new life. 'Could I come with you? Could I?'

What I wanted to hear was an answer as equally enthusiastic as my question, and I wanted him to say it straight away. Salvo certainly looked surprised and he did laugh, but it was an awkward laugh that turned into a cough.

'Oh, I wish you could, dearest Silvia, but I don't think that would be possible.'

'Whyever not? If I was your wife.'

'Because the invitations I've received are for a single man. One that does not have any special requirements.'

'What do you mean? What special requirements do I need?'

He looked embarrassed. 'I'm not sure, Silvia. I'm not a woman, but I know there'd be times when I'd have to leave you alone. Musicians can be strange and impetuous, as we well know. Signor Marenzio often keeps very late hours and I have no idea what the habits of Northern people are. I'd be constantly worried about you.'

Did I believe him? He sounded reasonable and had always been truthful with me. I remembered the pink-skinned Englishmen; they seemed civilised, but what did I know? I also remembered the long horrible silence when Salvo was away and couldn't help sighing.

'You will write to me this time, won't you?'

'Of course, I will, my darling, and I'm not going yet. We have weeks together. Why, we could go to Gesualdo. Your mother and father must agree before we can marry.'

'No,' I said, anxious at the mere thought of going to Gesualdo. 'We can send word instead. I'm quite sure they will be happy for us.'

'Is that a yes, then?' Salvo said. There was a change in his voice. The soft laughter returned, like the twinkling in his eyes. 'Do you trust me enough to marry me, Silvia Albana?'

He held out his hand for me to take. Trust him. That was all I had to do.

I don't know how he could have such warm hands when mine had got so cold, and I also wondered how he managed to raise me to my feet and enfold me in his arms so easily. But there I was, and his kisses played melodies on my lips until I could resist him no more.

'Yes,' I said. 'Oh, yes.'

We stayed drinking in each other's kisses for a long

time. All anxiety melted away. Why had I ever doubted him?

The noise of the lantern spluttering reminded us of the real world.

'I must light another,' said Salvo, 'or we'll be knocking everything over when it goes out. Stay there.'

An upset would certainly be a catastrophe. All the tools I remembered from my father's workshop lay higgledy-piggledy on trestle tables, and smaller tools for carving too. Pieces of wood of every sort and size were stacked up in corners, and on the walls were shelves of pots, jars and jugs of oils. Some of the labels I could make out and understand, like walnut, linseed and oak galls, but others were obliterated by thick black tears that had spilled down the outsides.

Salvo had only taken two steps when the lantern went out and we were in darkness.

'Damn,' he said.

I heard one more step and ... a huge crash and tumbling of I don't know what, but certainly glass was broken and metals jangled together.

The bench I sat on shivered. Salvo's curses were many times worse than before.

'Are you all right?' I said, peering into the black. 'Are you hurt?'

'No, I'm not hurt.' I heard him sigh then. 'But Heaven knows what we'll find when I get the lantern lit. Now where's my tinder box?'

'Do take care.' I said, but doubted he heard me over the crunch of glass under his boots. I swivelled round on the bench, following the sound of him as he slowly crossed the room. Gradually, my eyes accustomed to the dark. Grey moonlight seeped through the shutters but nothing was distinct in the gloom.

'Ah,' he said, 'here it is.'

After the familiar sound of the flint scraping, light flared across the room. I breathed out.

'That's better.'

'Yes, much.' Salvo laughed and snapped shut the door of the lantern. 'Now, my darling, where were we?'

'Don't you want to see what's got broken?'

'Oh, I don't think so, it can't be anything important.' He was holding the lantern so that the light didn't reach that far. I couldn't understand it.

'Don't you even want to make sure?' I asked. 'I can help you clear it up.'

'No, no. Let's not worry about it. Someone else will do it tomorrow.'

There was a note in his voice that rang contrary to the Salvo I knew, and it seemed so strange to me that he didn't care what had toppled over.

'But surely,' I persisted, 'we may be able to save something from further harm? It's always best to treat stained fabric straight away.'

Salvo put the lantern down on a low stool next to the door. It was the most odd place, for by putting it there, only the dimmest of light was cast. I knew there was a hook up above and so did Salvo because he'd warned me to avoid it when we first entered.

'If the ink has spilt, it's far too late to do anything about it now. Don't give it another thought, Silvia. Come, let me kiss your delicious lips again.'

He pulled me to my feet and kissed me with even more passion than previously. I thought his lips were very delicious too but for some reason, a voice in my head kept distracting me with a question.

'Salvo,' I said, reluctantly pushing myself away from him. 'Can I ask you something?'

'Of course,' he said. 'Does it have to be now though? I thought we were enjoying ourselves.'

'We were. We are ... I am, but—'

'But? My dear, Silvia, what is there to but about?'

He clasped me to his chest again and I had to push a little harder than the time before to free myself.

'No,' I said, firmly. 'Don't do this, Salvo. I've known you too long for this sort of deception. What is it that you *don't want me to see?'*

'What do you mean? There's nothing ... nothing at all.'
His laugh wasn't a bit convincing. It was as bad as the
note in his voice I didn't like, the one that rang with the
opposite of truth.

'Show me then,' I said. I tried not to let my voice
tremble although my heart had begun to thump in my
chest, and if someone had told me I had several spiders
crawling over the back of my neck, I wouldn't have been
surprised. Why was he behaving so strangely? What was
he hiding from me?

The lamp shone directly on my face, but his was in
shadow, and I could not see his expression. There was a
horrible silence, and where his hands gripped my
shoulders, I felt his strength.

But then they slackened and he dropped his arms to his
sides. 'No,' he said. 'I won't show you.' To my surprise he
sounded sad. 'Silvia,' he went on, 'if we are to be married
then one of the vows you will have to make is that you will
obey me. Will you obey me now, if I ask you not to look?'

Chapter Thirty-Five

'My go,' mouthed Mollie, as she poked my arm. I shook my head so she lifted one of the earphones away from my right ear and yelled: 'You can do that when I've gone to bed!'

'But I'm right in the middle ... oh, all right then.'

Time at the keyboard was precious. I hadn't had to transcribe such complex music since being at college.

When Mollie emailed Jon about the final song, he sent her the file straight away. She'd been admirably sly, suggesting that he shouldn't mention the musical while I was around as it might upset me. Humph.

Mollie sat at the keyboard and sang along to the accompaniments I'd already programmed in. I'd also recorded each part of the Gesualdo madrigal and both of us sang along with that. The madrigal sounded bizarre enough in its original state of two sopranos, alto, tenor and bass, but when I allocated the other three parts to the marimba and Mollie and I sang along with them, it cheered it up no end.

Miss Price hit ecstasy on her happiness scale.

'The headmistress wants a piece about the choir on the school website,' she gushed, when I arrived for the dress rehearsal. 'On the front page. With a photo.'

'Great,' I said. 'They'll love that.'

'And ...' she lowered her voice, so the whole world didn't have to hear, 'Mrs Brown has been informed – repeat, *informed* – that she would not be conducting the choir when she returned.'

'That's a shame.'

She batted an imaginary fly. 'No, no it isn't. It's because we really want *you* to stay on.'

'Oh?'

'Please say you will. I know the children would be heartbroken if you left us.'

'Well …' What can you say to such emotional blackmail? Robert had got used to me being away for an extra hour and the kids were really great.

'Besides,' Miss Price's brow knitted Fair Isle. 'There'll be nothing but ukuleles without you.'

That sounded as good a reason as any to stay.

Mollie insisted that she should host the *Noteworthy* dress rehearsal. If she was a member then she should have a turn. So, come the Sunday afternoon before the concert, we had tea and milkshakes instead of wine, and Mum made us cake. I wondered if I might find a blob of toffee icing on the cover of the Gesualdo afterwards. Perhaps things might have been different had we all been teetotal?

'When are we actually going to sing the Gesualdo on the day?' Sophie asked Jon. 'Have you got a running order?'

He fished about in his jacket pocket. 'Here,' he said, putting a piece of printed music on the table. I recognised it as the love duet straight away. 'Oh, no, sorry. Not that.' He turned it over to reveal a list in his chaotic handwriting. 'This is it so far.'

'What was that on the other side?' said Robert.

'Oh, nothing,' Jon said, keeping his hand firmly on the paper. 'Just something for work.'

Mollie and I glanced at each other. We both knew what it was and so did Sophie. I'd had to let her into the secret. Otherwise, when it came to voting, we'd have been in the minority.

Jon had given me a kiss when he arrived. A while ago, before Daniela, the Gesualdo and everything, he always did. It used to be a swift kiss, light, friendly and on the cheek. But today … I sighed and gave a little shiver. Today, his kiss had lingered a bit longer. Not massively longer, but enough for me to take in the deliciousness of him. If Jon were a cup of coffee he'd be a single estate espresso with a hint of chocolate, or perhaps cocoa. The French sort that wasn't sugary.

'Hello, Lisa? Are you receiving me?'

He was looking straight at me and smiling. A happy smile with no strain about it.

'Sorry, miles away.'

'Can I come next time?' he said. 'It looked like a good place to be.'

I'd forgotten how toes can curl with pleasure.

'Yaaawn,' Mollie said, and with a great deal of exaggeration, did so.

We all shuffled about on our chairs and coughed, as if it was the interval between movements in a concert. Sophie looked at me sideways with a twinkle in her eyes.

'Right then,' said Jon. 'I thought we'd start with the English things – Bennet, Orlando Gibbons … it's a pity we haven't got an Edward Gibbons madrigal really.'

'Edward Gibbons?' I said. 'Who was he? A son?'

'Brother,' Jon said, 'and choirmaster at Exeter.'

'Really?' I said. 'Wow.'

'Yes,' said Jon. 'It would have been nicely appropriate to have an Exeter composer in the concert.'

'Let's think about that for another time,' I said. 'What else have we got?'

Jon read out the rest: 'Wilbye, the Morley … oh, and the Byrd, of course, and then after the interval we can bring out the Italians – Banccieri and whatnot. Gesualdo second to last and then finish with *Il Bianco Dolce Cigno*. That'll balance nicely if we sing *The Silver Swan* at the end of the first half.'

I knew he would expect us to murmur our agreement as usual, so I nearly laughed at the way he jumped a little when Sophie said, cool as you like, 'Isn't it a bit long?'

'What?'

'The programme. Isn't it a bit too long?'

'I wouldn't have thought so.' He frowned, then looked at me. 'What do you think?'

'It is a bit,' I mused, as if I'd never thought about it before. 'Perhaps we ought to take one or two out.'

Mollie almost gave the game away. 'It's *miles* too

long,' she said. 'Who wants to sit through a load of old songs they don't understand?'

Jon looked at the three of us and I crossed my fingers under the table. He might smell a rat.

'Now now, Mollie,' I said. 'Don't get carried away. Lots of people like madrigals – that's why they're coming.' I turned to Jon. 'But I do think that while we might be happy to sing madrigals all night, it's a different experience for the audience. Shall we cut one or two?'

He shrugged. 'I wouldn't mind listening to them all night either. Okay, let's record everything on the list, have a listen, then decide what we don't want. Mollie, are you ready?'

Mollie had absorbed the entire programme almost on first hearing. It didn't bother her in the least that she wasn't singing the top line, her usual haunt. The Italian madrigals took her a little more time, and the Gesualdo more time than the rest combined, but that was the same for all of us.

Jon gave me another one of those kisses when we said goodbye.

The hall of my flat is quite generous considering the type of block it is. There's a cupboard for coats, another that houses the vacuum cleaner, light bulbs and my paltry collection of tools. Furniture-wise, I have a small chest of drawers, that's all. But I'd had to move it right into the corner to make room for Mum's walk-in suitcase and her shopping trolley – large enough to hold an aisle's worth from Sainsbury's.

So the whole business of conducting farewells took place in rather cramped conditions, and having a mother on one side and a daughter on the other wasn't exactly conducive to intimacy. Nevertheless, something happened between us when Jon kissed me. Definitely something and definitely delicious.

'What?' I said, when I turned round, having shut the door.

'Nothing,' they said, in unison.

'Don't even go there,' I said.

'Do you think everything's going to be all right now?' Mollie said, when I went in to say goodnight. In her faded pink pyjamas she looked much younger than the girl who had been singing with *Noteworthy* only hours beforehand.

'I don't see why not. You heard the recording. I like your voice better than Daniela's. With us, that is. You match in better.'

'I sound like you, that's why.'

'Yes, you do, although I was never a soprano, even at your age.' I smoothed the hair away from her forehead and she didn't complain.

'But I wasn't really thinking of the singing.'

'Oh?'

She pulled the duvet up under her chin. 'It's just that everything's been weird lately what with you being in hospital and not being friends with Jon. Dad said …' she hesitated and I felt an odd sensation in my stomach, like something scraping – a match maybe.

'Yes?'

'He said I could go and live with him if I wanted.'

'Oh, did he now?' Throws match in petrol tank.

Alarmed, she said hastily 'But I told him I didn't want to. Besides, even when you were bad, you still let me watch *Hollyoaks*.'

'Is that supposed to mollify me?'

She frowned 'I don't know what you mean, Mummy. Is that a joke?'

I hadn't meant it to be. 'No, darling, Not really. Everything's going to be fine, Mollie. Just you wait and see.'

'Will you and Jon get married?'

'Go to sleep.'

'Shouldn't these have gone back to the library by now?'

Mum had her arms full of the books I'd borrowed about

Gesualdo.

'God, yes,' I said. 'I'd forgotten all about them. How stupid. Here, give them to me, I'll take them tomorrow.'

When Mum's mobile rang, I assumed it would be Charles, but the call was short and, from the sound of it, formal.

'Guess what?' she said, afterwards. Her eyes were shining so I thought the worst.

'Charles is coming and you've invited him to stay here? There's a book missing. Have you seen it?'

'No he's not and have you looked under the sofa?'

I got down on my knees and peered into the gloom of under-the-sofa-land but couldn't see anything.

'Not there. That's a bugger.'

'No, even better. The tenants have given me notice.'

It took me a moment to twig what she was talking about.

'I'll have the flat back next week,' she said. 'Then you can have your room back.'

'Oh, that's good,' I said. Hallelujah!

'That's assuming they leave it okay, of course. I might have to stay here until I've cleaned it up.'

'Mollie and I will help,' I said, trying to sound level and not too jubilant.

'Although,' she said, with a sigh, 'it won't be in time for when Charles is coming.' She perched on the windowsill. 'You won't really mind if he stays, will you? I thought perhaps you and Mollie could share the sofa?'

'What? Are you kidding?' I thought she must be, but astonishingly, she was serious. 'No. Totally, no,' I said. 'Completely out of the question.'

'He's a very nice man. I'm sure he'd be no bother.'

'You're mad,' I said. 'He won't want to stay here. With any luck he'll whisk you off to a posh hotel. Give him the number of the Clarence.' I shooed her off the sill. 'You haven't come across an old blue hardback, have you?'

'I think it might be in Mollie's room.' She went and sat down at the other end of the sill. 'What about Duncan?'

'What about him?'

'Is he going to stay here?'

'Of course not. I don't know where he'll be staying.' I didn't know. In fact I'd forgotten all about him. The postcard was somewhere in the bottom of my bag. At least I thought it was. 'Excuse me,' I said. 'What were you doing looking in my bag?'

She looked aggrieved. 'I wasn't, dear. I knocked it off the table and everything fell out. I couldn't help catching sight of it. That's all.'

'Oh, really.'

'Really.'

'Does Jon know about Duncan?'

'Yes, of course he does. Err …' I'd said it much too quickly. He probably didn't know. A memory flashed up of Jon and I almost bashing our heads together in the hall. The postcard on the floor.

'I think you should tell him, Lisa,' said Mum. 'Otherwise he might get the wrong end of the stick.'

'Stick?' I said. 'There is no stick. Not unless you count Duncan's. He's a married man and miles too old for me. It's Charles that should be worried, not Jon.'

'If you say so, but I still think you should tell him.'

'I will, I will. Honestly, Mum. There's nothing to worry about on that score. Just you wait and see.'

Chapter Thirty-Six

Napoli 1591

The only thing that moved in the print shop was the flickering flame in the lantern. A draught from under the door; the wind was still strong. It wasn't so loud that it drowned the sound of our breathing, though, as we were standing close together. I couldn't see his face clearly, but Salvo's eyes glittered in the light.

Louder than both the wind and our breathing was the pounding of my heart.

'Salvo,' I whispered. 'I'm so afraid.'

I was not in fear of my life, but my love was in the greatest peril. They say that when you're about to die, all of your life spills before you in a moment. It seemed to me then that I remembered too much at once. A great jumble of memories, recent and from a long time ago, like a patchwork of all the fabrics I had ever worked, put together without a pattern.

Brightest of the memories was my looking down at Salvo's face from my seat in the wagon when I left Gesualdo. How he smiled, how his eyes twinkled, how much he cared for me. In my pocket I could feel the familiar sensation of the little wooden carvings. They had been with me ever since he placed them in my hands. Oh, Salvo! How had it come to this?

'I'm afraid too, Silvia,' he said, and I believed him, for his voice trembled. 'Shall we leave here now together? That would be my dearest wish.'

My mother's face appeared in my mind's eye. Why did I have a disobedient child, *she would say, whenever I went my own way.* She'll come to no good.

'How I wish,' I said, with an equal quiver of meaning in my voice, 'that you'd asked me to trust, rather than obey you, Salvo. I would not be your Silvia if I was a meek, compliant girl. Don't you remember how we played as

children? How curious we were?' I wiped away a tear that fell of its own accord. 'How disobedient?'

'I do, I do.' He groaned and stepped away from me to sit on the bench, head in hands. 'It is your choice, Silvia. It's all up to you.'

I could hardly bear to see him so unhappy. I looked into the darkness and then back at the curls on the top of his head. What did it matter that I didn't see whatever it was? I was never meant to. Why, if it hadn't been for a candle end, Salvo wouldn't have blundered about in the dark and knocked over whatever it was. We would still be happy. Did I really want my whole life to be changed because of a candle end?

'Let's go now, Salvo,' I said. 'I don't need to know, whatever it is.'

Slowly, he raised his head and because our places had changed about, his face was bright in the lamplight.

'Do you mean that?' he said, and when I nodded, saw the whole transformation from despair to joy. There was my Salvo again. The boy I remembered and the handsome man. He took hold of my hands and kissed them all over. Then he jumped to his feet, and once again I was enfolded in his velvet cloak.

'I love you very much, Silvia Albana,' he said. 'And don't you forget that while I'm away. I don't want you taking up with anyone else.'

I laughed and snuggled against his chest. Such relief I felt!

'Come then,' he said. 'Why don't we go back to my uncle's house? We'll tell him that we wish to wed very soon. If we're lucky, the musicians might still be there and I can teach you the sfessania.'

'What?' I said. 'Learn from someone as clumsy hoofed as you?'

His laughter rumbled against my ear. 'We'll see about that. Now, before we go.' And lifting my chin he pressed his lips to mine.

Eventually, he released me from my warm and

273

comfortable prison.

'We'll need this now it's dark,' he said, picking up the lantern and opening the door. We went out into the street. 'Here, hold it for me while I lock up.'

The wind had dropped to a breeze but the air was still cold. I took a deep breath, cleansing myself from the cloy of ink and soot. The lock complained for the lack of oiling and Salvo struggled with the key. I determined that if I could avoid it, I would never set foot in there again.

'Oh, damnation,' Salvo said, just when he had secured the door. 'I've only left my tinderbox in there. Sorry, Silvia, but I'd better get it. Wait there. I'll be very quick.'

He unlocked the door again amidst much cursing and then took the lantern from me. I resolved to stay by the door but a moment later from around the corner came a group of men, five or six of them, carrying torches and loud with jeers and drunken laughter. I did not want to be seen standing alone by a doorway in my best gown so I stepped inside and pulled the door closed behind me.

When I turned round I saw the tinderbox straight away. Salvo was holding the lantern up high and the metal shone in the light. It was on the trestle table just by where I'd been sitting on the bench. I couldn't understand why Salvo hadn't seen it, but then realised that he wasn't looking in that direction. His gaze was towards where the calamity had been.

I did not mean to look.

It wasn't much of a look even – more like a glance. A glimpse.

But it was enough for me to see.

Several printed pages had fallen to the floor as well as a bottle of ink. That had splashed about and the glass fragments too lay scattered, as if a jewel case had been upturned. But the pages were mostly unmarked. The images clear. The skill of the artist obvious. I knew an engraving by Salvo Carlino when I saw one.

I was not so feeble as to faint at the sight. Why, my lady was very free with her nakedness from the very first time I

274

saw her. Nor was I amazed by the acts of coupling so explicitly demonstrated.

But Salvo ... my Salvo. Where was the tender heart of my Salvo? The man I was to trust and obey. Where had he learned of such things – in such detail – and in such variation? Where, when and with whom? No wonder he looked so accomplished on the dance floor, so lavish in his dress. I thought of Don Carlo. Was Signor Marenzio similarly strange? Were all musicians debauched? Or had Salvo made these engravings for his own pleasure?

Although the air was cold, it was aflame compared to the inner chill I felt. Had all the workings of my body come to a standstill? Certainly I had no power of speech. My ears worked though. I heard the men outside go by and their voices recede, but my eyes were not my own, for they would not look away from the pages on the floor.

I must have made some small noise for Salvo turned then, saw me and knew at once what I had seen.

I did not cry or speak. What Salvo actually said, I do not remember, although he talked all the way back to San Domenico, pleading with me for forgiveness.

I left him at the door, closing it behind me without looking back. In the chapel the nuns were singing, their high, clear voices stretching into a distant tranquillity far away from all the tumult of the world.

For the second time I was seeking refuge at the convent. This time I would stay.

Chapter Thirty-Seven

The librarian checked in the books and then, to my surprise, winked at me. I took a step back.

'Good luck tonight,' he said, gesturing towards the wall where all the event posters were displayed. 'That is you, isn't it?'

I nodded. There we were. All in a frozen moment of terror. Except Mollie of course. *Sold Out* was scrawled in big black letters diagonally across the poster.

A large outside broadcast truck took up most of the museum car park, and cabling reminiscent of that in the London Underground snaked across the tarmac. Mollie's high-stepping, high spirits got spooked and she sidled past as if they were actual snakes. From then on, she remained quiet and glued to my side, in a way she hadn't done since she first went to school. The reality of an actual concert on the actual telly, singing in front of lots of actual people gave me the collywobbles too, but I wasn't going to admit that in front of my daughter.

We had an hour to go. I sent Jon a text.

I'd arranged to meet the curator at the rear entrance and she was standing at the top of the steps when we arrived. I was her best friend at last, if the smile was anything to go by. I was amazed her face could go that wide.

'Do call me Lorraine,' she whispered, with a coy look over her shoulder. There was nobody else about and I wondered whether Lorraine was a euphemism I should know about.

The staff at the museum had greeted my latest request with enthusiasm. In fact, they were cock-a-hoop. Something about reaching a wider demographic, being inclusive and altogether more accessible. In other words, more bums on seats.

'Oh, absolutely,' I'd agreed. 'That's exactly what I had in mind. Better for everyone.'

The additional subterfuge that was required proved to be no problem at all. It would be such excellent publicity. In what way could they help?

We were to sing in the new extension at the back. I thought that sounded rather like being asked to use the tradesman's entrance, but when we saw the transformation that had taken place inside, that idea fizzled into nothing, rather like the amaretti biscuit wrappers.

Although the front entrance retained its gothic staircase – albeit painted pink – and the statue of a rather stern Prince Albert, the back of the museum was entirely modern. A tall glass door swished slowly and silently open and once inside, we stood in a foreign land. Surely it wasn't bumbly old provincial Exeter. A London gallery or Paris maybe?

'Is this all right for you?' Lorraine led us to the corner of the first gallery.

How could it not be all right? The walls were lined with Renaissance masterpieces. Even Mollie gasped and I'd never reckoned art appreciation amongst her many attributes.

'There's a socket there,' Lorraine said, pointing at the far end of the gallery, 'and you won't have any late-comers barging in on top of you. You can put your stuff in …' we went through to the next gallery, 'here. Is that okay?'

'Lovely, thanks.'

She left us to it.

'Okay?' I said to Mollie.

She nodded but only very slowly. I saw her swallow.

'It'll be fine,' I said, giving her a hug. 'You'll be fine. We all will be.'

I looked at my watch. There was still another forty-five minutes to go. Too long really. When *Noteworthy* dressed up in costume, it was better. We could spend the time changing, but since appearing in our tableau outfits wasn't an option, we'd decided to stick to our safe black all over uniform and off-set it with a hint of pink: jewellery, scarves, shoes, something to jolly it up a bit. Mollie had quite a few pink accessories.

'No Jon then?' Sophie said, when she arrived with Robert.

'Not yet,' I said, checking my phone for a reply again. 'I know he had a work meeting this afternoon but that was ages ago.'

I'd not heard a thing from Duncan since the postcard. Oh, well. Perhaps Exeter was a step too far.

At five to seven I looked at my phone. Still nothing. Jon's phone went straight to voicemail.

The audience began to arrive. Dribs and drabs – quite a lot of people I knew of course, and I waved and nodded, but kept my distance. There's probably a doctorate to be had for someone on the behaviour of humans filling a hall full of chairs. What personality type sits where, etc. I didn't usually spend time checking out the audience before a concert, but I couldn't take my eye off the door.

Where was Jon? For a person who was late for almost everything else, I had never known him late for a gig. And by late, I meant less than half an hour before kick-off. I remembered him telling me he was pathologically early for concerts precisely because he tended to be late for everything else.

The make-up man came and powdered our noses at seven o'clock. I thought the extra eyebrow pencil made us all looked rather surprised, except Robert, who didn't need any.

At ten past seven we were checking our watches every few seconds when we thought the others couldn't see. Mollie didn't bother with her watch. She kept her gaze fixed on the door intoning the names of those we knew when they came in.

Shortly after she announced Mum and Charles, Mum put her head round the corner.

'Good lu—oh,' she said, frowning. 'Where's Jon?'

I shrugged.

'He'll be here,' she said. 'When has he ever let you down?'

I didn't say it, but Robert did. 'There's always a first.'

'He's here. He's here.' Mollie clapped her hands together and jumped in the air. A spring lamb suddenly. The rest of us breathed out. Sophie and Robert picked up their folders of music for a last minute check and Mollie actually agreed to let Mum brush her hair. The age of miracles had not passed

'Sorry, sorry,' he said. 'I've just had a smackeroo in the car.'

My hand was on his before I thought about it. 'Are you all right?'

'Yes, fine. I was only doing two miles an hour, thank God. Not my fault. Had to fiddle about with names and addresses though. My front wing's a goner. Here, can you do this for me?'

He fished his pink bow tie – it was pink even though he insisted it was maroon – out of his pocket. Why he didn't have the clip-on sort, I don't know. Sophie was much better at bow ties than me, but I wasn't going to let her do it. Besides I'd seen her tie Robert's and paid close attention.

I slid my hands round Jon's collar and stood it up straight before laying the bow tie flat against the shirt and folding the collar back down. I felt his breath on my forehead and the rise and fall of his chest as I positioned each end, one slightly further down than the other. I couldn't resist smoothing the fabric before tying the bow.

'We were beginning to worry,' I said.

'Really?'

'Yes, Mollie kept watch.'

'Did she?'

'Yes, I think she was more worried than any of us.'

'Oh, really?' He sounded ever so slightly disappointed. 'More than you?'

'Maybe.'

When I'd eased the bow through the loop and tweaked

each side to make them even, I did look up, straight into his eyes. Perhaps it was the halogen spot-lighting that made them so bright.

'Thanks,' he said, smiling.

Another elastane moment.

'Are we ready?' said Robert from far away.

Sigh. Shame about the concert really.

'Thanks,' said Jon again. And he leaned forward and kissed me. Only quickly, but not on the cheek. The name of my lipstick was *Pink Fizz*. I wondered if Jon felt a fizz like I did. Perhaps, but either way, it didn't suit him, so I brushed it from his lips with my finger. He kissed that too.

'Full house,' announced Lorraine. 'Are you all ready?'

And on we went. I had no idea that recording for the telly needed quite so much wattage. I offered up a little prayer to the god of performing musicians as we walked out into the light.

'There's an awful lot of kids in the audience,' said Jon, when we came off for the interval.

'That's because *I'm* singing,' said Mollie, all confidence returned. 'They've all come to see me.'

Had I created a monster? Possibly, but it didn't stop me giving her a huge hug and attempting a slobbery kiss, although she fought me off before I could succeed. We arranged a block of staging for her to stand on so that she didn't look too small but I was beginning to think that might have been a mistake. What she lacked in height, she made up for in a host of other ways.

'I suppose it's a good thing we cut the programme. Anyway,' said Jon. 'Well done us. I think we did Mr Gibbons and Wilbye proud.'

'And the rest,' Robert said.

'You were marvellous, darling,' said Sophie.

Both Robert and Mollie thought she meant them and I laughed. Pre-concert nerves were done with and the first half had been a success. Everything felt easier.

'Do you think,' Jon said, running his hands through his

hair so it stood up, 'that all those kids will start fidgeting soon? I wonder if we should have had the English lot in the second half and the Italians in the first.'

'Maybe,' I said, 'but it's too late now.'

Before we began again, Lorraine spoke about how mysterious it was that the Gesualdo manuscript had turned up in the museum archives. Don Carlo Gesualdo lived for most of his life in or near Naples. It wasn't unusual for musicians to travel widely at that time; the Cathedral churches and Royal Courts of the Renaissance often vied for the most talented musicians of the day; but even so, Exeter was certainly off the beaten track. It was her personal opinion, looking at the other manuscripts in the box, that it belonged in the Cathedral library. She made no mention of the frontispiece.

My eyes adjusted to the light during Lorraine's talk, which meant the audience was no longer a bright blur. At the back, near the door, I caught sight of Duncan. So he had made it after all.

Finally, Lorraine asked members of the audience not to leave their seats at the end as there was to be an additional item on the programme.

Jon, who'd been peering intently at the music, looked up, startled.

What? He mouthed silently at me from behind the fan of his folder. *What's she talking about?* I gave the tiniest shrug, but couldn't help smiling. His eyes narrowed. *What? What?*

There was no time to reply because Lorraine turned to us. Now for Gesualdo's madrigal. A few more minutes and it would be over. There are some madrigals that almost sing themselves, but with *Ite Sospiri Ardenti* we veered through a strange harmonic assault course. But we had mastered it, although it had taken us a while.

Jon would give us our cue, but I couldn't help glancing at Mollie. Would she be up to it? I needn't have worried. Her dear face showed no sign of fear as she looked with rapt attention at Jon. How I loved her. How I loved him too.

Then, as we all took a breath, under the hot lights and in front of so many, something new happened. Listening to, or performing any piece of music is a journey into an ephemeral world, and no two journeys can ever be exactly the same. The complexity of the Gesualdo and all the trouble that permeated my life since its discovery had made it difficult for me to sing. It had become a cerebral experience – do this here, breath there, watch out for that note, listen to Sophie at that point – but where was the heart?

With a rush of realisation that swept through my whole body, I knew the key to releasing the curse from the madrigal. Of course! The answer had been in the last line all along, but I hadn't truly understood its meaning. All madrigals are awash with torment and unrequited love, and Gesualdo himself certainly was, in both life and music. *Ite, ardenti sospiri* was no different.

> *Ite, ardenti sospiri,*
> *Nati del duol che mi consuma e strugge,*
> *Seguite, chi mi fugge*
> *E prend'in gioco i miei gravi martiri,*
> *Combattete quel core*
> *Finché rompa il suo ghiacchio il vostr'ardore.*

> *Go, burning sighs,*
> *born of the pain that consumes me,*
> *follow the one who flees me,*
> *and laughs at my heavy torments.*
> *Fight that heart until your warmth breaks its ice.*

I had never enjoyed singing this madrigal, let alone loved it, but as I sang my first phrase, all effort and previous misgivings dropped away. How sensual was the Italian language, how intense the pain of his torment, how delicately Sophie and Mollie sang their filigree semi-quavers, almost mocking the muscular harmonies of the men beneath. And my part, like the last gold thread, that completes a tapestry, and with its light brings warmth to an otherwise cold and austere picture.

It was as if, somehow, each note in its correct place was at last putting the world to rights.

The audience clapped very nicely and afterwards we finished with the Arcadelt *Il bianco e dolce cigno*. It was one of my favourites and much more agreeable to everyone, judging by the applause.

Then it was my turn to speak. I'd made a few notes and had slipped them into my folder. I'd agonised about whether to begin with Ladies and Gentleman, but it sounded so formal and then there were all the children. Should I address them too? I thought I should, so I stood up and said.

'Don Carlo Gesualdo, Prince of Venosa, born in 1560 probably, and died in 1613.' It wasn't the most arresting of beginnings, but nobody yawned. 'Not an A-list composer,' I went on, 'and probably not the first Italian nobleman to murder his wife and her lover. Evidently, murder was considered a fitting punishment for infidelity in those days. So, although lots of people assume he became mad as a result of his crime, it seems that he was probably mad all along. It's also not the case, although you'd be forgiven for thinking it, that madness inspired his music; other composers were writing the same sort of thing. It wasn't until the twentieth century, however, that the affirmation from Stravinsky really elevated Gesualdo's music to that of genius rather than lunatic.'

Under the lights I could feel my face getting hot. I took a sip of water.

'Since then,' I went on, 'both his life story and his music have been the source of inspiration for all manner of creative endeavours. I've discovered operas, novels, a ballet by Stravinsky, dance/dramas, documentaries and at least one movie. It was as if Stravinsky pressed *Go*!'

There was a ripple of appreciation for my small joke.

'So,' I said, 'it seems to me that bringing such a story

from the past to the present, via any medium, is like shining a light into darkness. What is fearful and troubling can be transformed.' I took a deep breath. That might be meaningless for the audience, but it meant a great deal to me. 'Now,' I began walking towards the keyboard, 'as far as I know, nobody has based a musical for children on his story. That is, until now.'

That was the cue for all the children in the school choir to stand up and come to the front. I couldn't bring myself to look at Jon.

Would he mind or would he be pleased? A glance said he looked stunned. But whether it was in a good way, I couldn't tell. Doubt, another hideous demon, jeered at me from the wings, but on stage, the choir neatened themselves into their usual rows. If I had misgivings, I certainly wasn't going to let them know, so I gave them my widest smile.

It was a shame we couldn't perform the whole thing, but the seats were hard and even the most padded of bottoms would resent them eventually. I'd chosen two choruses and the last love duet, which featured the chorus as well. Mollie I had no doubts about, but anxiety welled up in me when I caught sight of poor Jonah, who looked as if the Whale of Doom was swimming inexorably towards him.

I played the introduction. Jonah was about as far from the handsome and dashing hero, Fabrizio, as anyone could be, although in another ten years I could see he'd have a certain undernourished poet appeal. When I got to the chord where he was supposed to come in, I fixed him with my eye and nodded with all the determined encouragement I could muster.

Nothing happened. Well … something did. A cross between a croak and a cough.

I segued into the introduction again. The choir shuffled and Mollie looked alarmed. Some people wouldn't notice though, and if he came in the second time, all would be well.

He didn't, despite, or perhaps because of a dig in the side from Connor's elbow.

But someone did.

As he walked across the stage, Jon sang Fabrizio's opening line. Tears pricked at the corner of my eyes. He put a hand on the boy's shoulder, and Jonah found his voice and they sang together. Fabrizio stands between Maria and the mad Prince and declares he will die rather than see Maria hurt. Mollie, as Maria – and to some extent, Maria Callas – swears she will die if Fabrizio is hurt. I couldn't help but join in.

The Prince, aka the entire choir, swears they will both die, but in his madness waves his halberd rather too wildly and topples to his death from the battlements of his castle. The music ends in a fantastic descending cry for the choir at the same time as the two lovers ascend to the highest notes in their range. The accompaniment featured very many semiquavers all played at top speed and volume. It really deserved a full orchestra but in spite of that, the applause was thunderous as the audience rose to their feet. Then I did shed a tear, and was thankful for the emergency tissue I had up my sleeve.

After that everything got rather muddled. People milled. They always do after a concert, especially if parents and children are involved. I tried to see where Jon had got to but found Duncan standing in front of me instead.

'*Buona sera*, lovely Lisa,' he said, placing a large bouquet of pink roses in my arms and, with a gesture I associated with Italy rather than Scotland, he took hold of my hand and kissed it.

They were the most splendid roses. Honestly, they were. In a gesture that really was only one of pleasure and gratitude, I brought my hand and his up to my cheek. I was thanking a friend, that's all. Besides, behind him and obviously with him, stood a smiley woman of much more his age than mine. His wife, surely.

But as I gushed my thanks – I saw Jon. Right there,

with only a couple of people between us.

He wasn't looking in my direction but I could see he was frowning. Not crossly, more a quizzical sort of frown. One that asks a question. Where am I? Where are you?

Then he turned and he did see me. He saw the flowers too, and Duncan. I knew he was shocked. I saw the muscle in his jaw twitch and the awful cold and hostile expression I'd seen in the hospital returned. The next thing, he'd turned away and I lost sight of him.

Mum was at my elbow.

'Well, my girl,' she said. 'What are you going to do now?'

Chapter Thirty-Eight

Gesualdo 1611

I needed more than two hands to count the number of funerals I'd attended in my life. That's of the people I liked, rather than all the others who were ferried through the chapel.

Vitore, the cloth merchant, was found cold on the floor of his shop surrounded by roll upon roll of sumptuous fabrics. All his family were dead already, so San Domenico and surrounding churches were the beneficiaries of his riches. I placed one of my samples in his coffin, a small return.

Several sisters at the convent died of fever. In the year following the murder of my lady the summer's air was of poor quality. I took a walk to the sea most days in an attempt to breathe something less evil-smelling, but the sea stayed flat as if pressed down by the stench. Any waves made hard work of reaching the shore.

Rosa from Palazzo San Severo died in childbirth and the baby died too.

Some years weren't so bad and I'd been lucky. In winter there was pain in the tips of my fingers and the joint of my right hand thumb, but it was nothing much. My eyes had remained sharp and when I looked in the mirror I saw no sign of the fog that eventually blinded Salvo's mother. Perhaps if they were less sharp, I should not be able to see where little birds left their footprints round my eyes or where my hair was streaked grey. I sighed, and thought of the day at the market when I had first met Signora Carlino. It was a very long time ago. Twenty years now.

Agnola's letter should not have surprised me, but of course, it did. A great many people had died of fever in the city but somehow I didn't expect my mother to contract it up in the hills and in the spring too. She'd died quickly, a blessing for her, but too far away for me to get there while she still lived. I was glad Agnola had stayed and not been such a wilful daughter as me.

I looked down at my hands. In fact, my visits to Gesualdo were few enough for one. Four times I had made the journey, for my father's death, my sister's wedding and birth of her first baby, and now my mother. I could have gone more often, but even now, although the fear of Don Carlo had diminished considerably, when I looked up at the castle on the hill, I felt a pain in my heart that would never shift.

'Don Carlo won't leave the castle now,' Agnola said, as we walked back from the church together. 'They say he is under the spell of the witches, but from what I hear, he'd be mad with or without spells.'

'Witches? Really?'

'Yes,' she said, 'it's true. There's talk of the Inquisition and a trial. Do you remember Auralia, old Francesca's niece? She's one of them.'

I nodded, but my memory was of a child.

Agnola chatted on. She told me how Don Carlo mistreated his poor wife, how Auralia had become his mistress, even how he had to be whipped before going to stool ...

'Agnola!' I said, holding my hands up to my ears. 'Please don't tell me such things.'

'Oh, there's much worse than that,' she said, gaily. 'Laura told me that Auralia made Don Carlo drink her monthly blood.'

I stopped still and for a few paces Agnola didn't notice, so busy was she with her dreadful tales.

'Laura?' I said, 'not Laura Scala?'

'Yes, that's right. She's in charge of the laundry up there. She says the castle is full of the stuff of sorcery. Tokens and talismans, there are vials of different coloured potions. All the servants take their own bread to eat – they say the food made there is poisoned, not so that you'll die straight away, but slowly and very painfully. All your teeth turn black and fall out first.'

'Really,' I said. She was probably right. I doubted Laura had enough imagination to make up such a story. I sighed. How sheltered I'd been from the world and its gossip.

'Is it true,' Agnola asked, in a whisper even though no one was nearby, 'that Don Carlo threw the naked bodies down onto the church steps?'

I gasped. 'No! That's not true at all. I was there, Agnola. It was very terrible, but the rites were observed.'

'Ah well. That will be a disappointment to some. They say that she was so beautiful that even in death a priest could not resist her, and—'

Agnola talked on, but all I could think of was the last time I saw Laura from the window at San Severo. Had she betrayed us? Would Donna Maria be alive if she hadn't? The pain in my heart swelled and I had to force it away. Nothing that happened back then mattered anymore. Besides, I couldn't be more thankful for my life at the convent.

We'd reached the corner where we would turn into the track leading home. The castle hill would be behind us.

'You go on, Agnola,' I said. 'I'd like to walk a little further.'

Up ahead, I could see the shrine where I'd waited for Francesca the morning I went with her to market. I had it in my mind to leave a little posy in memory of my mother under the roundel of the Virgin. May is an abundant month for flowers and I picked daisies, lavender, a little late broom, and risked the prickles for a stem of the wild rose that rambled over the shrine itself.

The shrine was at the crossroads. To turn right and labour up the hill would eventually take the traveller to the castle. The track wound in amongst the olive trees where I first set eyes on Don Carlo from my hiding place. Ahead, the track led to Fontanarosa, and left and away down the hill and many hours away lay Napoli, Roma, Firenze and the rest of the world.

The shrine provided me with an excuse to linger. Two women with empty baskets nodded before heading for Fontanarosa. A horseman in Gesualdo livery rode at speed up the hill towards the castle. I stood back as he passed but still felt the quake in the ground from the horse's hooves. Once the noise of him passed, the bees' humming and twittering of little birds was all I could hear.

I sat down with my back against the warm stone of the shrine and pulled my knees up to my chest the way I used to as a girl. I was glad of my hat and pulled the brim down to keep the sun from my eyes.

So, Don Carlo had succumbed to the charms of a witch after all. I took a deep breath, full of the wild rose's sweet perfume. Perhaps it was that which made me smile.

The sound of movement in the undergrowth made me look up. A snake? I remembered the terror I used to feel at the sight of one and hoped for a mouse or a deer, but when the snake's eye glittered in the sunshine not an arm's length from me, I thought how beautiful it was. Like me, it was keen to enjoy a sunny spot. I kept very still as it curled its way, head down, into a spiral.

Was I afraid? Certainly, and even more so when I heard another noise. Fearful of taking my eyes from the snake for long, I glanced down the lane. A wagon approached, heavily laden I thought by the slow pace of the horse. I hoped the snake would slither away when it felt the clip-clop of hooves rattle its belly? Would it be startled and strike out if I moved?

The wagon came closer and closer. Still the snake did not move. Had they no ears? I felt the dart of something down the back of my neck and hoped it was a bead of sweat and not a spider. Why had I sat on the ground? What a foolish thing to do! I wasn't a girl anymore who could jump up with ease.

The snake shifted, its head reared up. Fear raced through me but I became as the stone on which I was seated. The wagon drew nearer until beneath the brim of my hat, I saw the horse. Perhaps the snake did too, for it shifted from the warm rut in which it lay towards the shrine and the place where I sat.

Over my shoes it slithered. The patterning of its skin rippled; a marvellous horror to see so close. Then, like a sinuous rope being drawn across my toes, I felt the solid weight of it. I watched as if from a long way away, even though I was not.

And then it was gone, and the wagon was almost upon me.

'Holy Mother of God!' said a voice. 'You were lucky there. Have you any idea how poisonous that snake was?'

For a moment I could not move. Perhaps, as serpents are wont to do, I had been tricked by it. The whole of Gesualdo was under a spell, not just Don Carlo. If I had been disbelieving of charms and spells then I was wrong. I was sorry.

The voice was too familiar.

'Are you hurt?'

Two boots appeared in my view, jumping down and landing with a thud that sent up a little cloud of dust. They began walking towards me.

This was more terrifying than even the snake. Please ... please ... had my heart stopped? My breath would not come, nor my voice.

'Are you all right?'

'Yes,' I whispered. 'Yes.'

'Here,' he said. 'Let me help you up. You must have had quite a fright then. It's a miracle you weren't bitten.'

A hand appeared and I reached towards it, knowing the grasp at once. In another moment, I was on my feet and thankful of my hat, for I couldn't bring myself to look at his face. But he saw mine.

'Silvia,' he said, his voice barely audible. 'Silvia, is that really you?' With a finger he lifted the brim of my hat and peered beneath.

I nodded and risked a glance. 'Yes, Salvo, it is.' Then I raised my eyes and looked at him directly.

Many things had changed in the twenty years since I'd seen him last, but not the way he looked at me then. Slowly, he raised my hand to his lips and kissed it tenderly, as if it were fragile.

'A miracle,' he said. 'This is a miracle.'

I had to laugh then. It was that or start sobbing like a child. 'Two miracles in such a short time, Salvo! After all these years. I must leave flowers at this shrine more often.'

Agnola thrust a baby in my arms as soon as I got back.

'If you keep this one quiet for half an hour,' she said, 'you can invite ten extra people to dinner.'

'I'll do my best,' I said, doubting my abilities would manage five minutes. 'But one extra guest is all I beg for.'

'Wasn't he...?' she trailed off, but searched my face as if all my secrets were written there for the reading. I blushed, which made her laugh.

'That was a long time ago,' I said. 'It was a surprise to see him again, that's all.'

'Really?'

'Yes, really.'

Of course, that wasn't all.

My sister shooed her family to bed earlier than I suspect they wished to go, which left Salvo and I sitting out under the stars. He asked me about my days at the convent and spent much time praising my success now that I was making robes for the cardinals.

'I always knew you were special, Silvia,' he said. 'I'm glad for you. My mother would have been very proud too.'

'She taught me all I know,' I said, almost truthfully, 'and I have only happy memories of those early days.'

'As I do,' he said. 'As I do.'

In the flickering light, I thought he could be the young Salvo I knew then. He was slim again and although the little birds had marched many times all over his face, still his eyes twinkled when he laughed and I loved him all over again.

But we had dark topics to discuss before love could be aired.

'It was a young man's folly, Silvia,' he said, 'and I was weak.' His jaw tightened as he talked about it. 'The money was the main thing. Not the women, although I know that's what you thought.' He sighed. 'Of course, you did.'

I didn't say anything. We were opening an old wound, plunging a knife right into the scar.

'Have you married since?' I asked, barely able to work my mouth round the words. I had to know.

There was a long pause. 'Yes,' he said, quietly, and in the torchlight his face was grim. The scar on the wound held. The flesh kept together somehow. 'But,' he said. 'I still have some money left and of course, all that I have earned since she died.'

'She died?' I whispered.

'Yes,' he said, 'and although I was sorry for the loss of a life, I could not mourn her, Silvia.'

'Oh?'

'Her family robbed me of all I had. Her brother was one of the men who paid ... paid for those engravings. I was a fool, Silvia. She had no interest in me. But my money? That was a different matter altogether.'

I did not know what to say.

'After you'd gone,' he went on, 'I did not care much what I did. My work paid well but there were demands for more and more ... oh, Silvia, once I saw it through your eyes, how it disgusted me! At first I blamed everyone else but myself for my stupidity.' He nodded in the direction of the castle. 'Especially him. He is a wicked man, there is no question of that, he was the at the root of all our troubles.'

I thought so too, but when I thought of Donna Maria and all the nightdresses I'd mended, Laura Scala and her betrayal to Uncle Giulio, I didn't blame him entirely. I couldn't help but blame myself for not warning my lady more fervently, although in my heart I knew she would take no notice of a servant, however much she raised me up when it suited her.

'Perhaps,' I said, 'in some way, we are all to blame. If the fabric of a garment has weakness in one place, it will affect the rest sooner or later.'

Salvo reached forward and covered my hand with his. 'No, Silvia,' he said. 'I would not have it that you are at fault for anything. You have always behaved in the most proper way, whereas I ...' He shook his head and groaned. 'There is something I must tell you.'

Had the night darkened? Were the owls, late singing blackbirds and all the small scurrying creatures holding their breath too? I felt his grip tighten on my hand as I tried to withdraw it.

'Please,' he said. 'Let me.'

I nodded. I wasn't young anymore and there wasn't much that could shock me, but disappointment was another matter? Could I bear it?

'There was a madrigal by Don Carlo, a single madrigal, not one of the collections. Perhaps it had got left out on purpose, I don't know, but there it was at my uncle's, moving from shelf to shelf. I think he was hoping the prince might die and he would be able to print it without any fuss.'

My hand relaxed a little. Anything about a Gesualdo madrigal wasn't likely to perturb me. I'd shut my ears to enough of them in the past.

'In secret,' he went on, 'I began an engraving for a frontispiece. It would be nothing like anything else I had done before. At first I thought it would reflect Don Carlo. Instead of the cherubs I had etched for Marenzio and the ... the other things.' He coughed and brought his other hand up to cover his mouth. 'I thought I would depict the Prince in Hell. That's where he is going, I told myself. He will suffer all the torments of a wicked man and with my chisel I will show the world.'

His voice shook with anger and I pulled my hand away for fear he might crush it, but then he turned to face me and I saw it wasn't anger at all. Tears fell down both cheeks and there was nothing but misery in his eyes.

'Is that so very bad, Salvo? You did not actually harm anyone ... did you?'

'Oh, my darling, Silvia. Harm? I don't know.' He wiped his tears away roughly.

'Surely—' I began but he interrupted.

'I cursed it, Silvia. The frontispiece. There was a woman in Firenze ... it was stupid of me. Stupid! She was a witch, I swear it and I was possessed with hatred for Don Carlo We called upon all the elements to rise up against the sound of his precious madrigal. Instead of bringing joy into the world like music should, I cursed its performance, desiring only trouble and worry should enter the ears of the listener.'

'But could you not destroy it, Salvo, if it was so very bad?'

'Oh, I did. I put the engraving in the brazier.'

'Well, then,' I said, relieved. 'Then there is nothing to worry about.'

'But not before I took a pressing.' He sighed. 'There is one copy which I dare not destroy.'

'Why ever not?'

'Because the pressing revealed to me my own wickedness. Once the ink had dried I could clearly see that the demons I had drawn were all my own. My face was on every one.'

'If that is the case, Salvo,' I said, slowly, 'then all the more reason to destroy it.'

'I'm sure I should not. It is a daily reminder of my sins. Gesualdo will not be tortured by my work, but innocent singers.' He shook his head. 'It is my penance.'

I did not know what to say.

'I'm fearful too, Silvia,' he went on, 'that if I destroy the frontispiece, I will soon be tortured by the flames of Hell.'

I could not make light of such a thing. Curses were curses, although I thought that apart from Sister Caterina, everyone I had ever met made judgements on each other.

'But that was a long time ago,' he said, sitting forward

and tipping the bench almost over. 'Many years now and since then, all that I have earned has been honest, if not well paid.' His laugh lacked humour. 'And here I am, back working for Don Carlo. There is some mirth there although I am not sure where.' He shook his head.

'Well, now,' I said. 'I think we may be able to find a little.'

He looked at me with surprise. 'Oh?'

'Look here,' I said, and I fished from my pouch the frontispiece that he had given me all those years ago. I unfolded and placed it before him. 'Do you remember this?'

There we were: our younger selves in the Garden of Eden.

Salvo gasped but neither of us said anything. He smoothed the paper, which was very creased from many unfoldings, and moved the lantern so that he could look at it closely.

'You've kept it all this time,' he said, softly.

I nodded. 'And you made it, Salvo Carlino. Just like you made the other. One bad and one good but both made by you.' I took his hand. 'Isn't that how people are? We're all both good and bad, not one thing or the other. Although,' I said, gesturing up the hill, 'we could be mad. I don't know what that means.'

Salvo laughed but not so grimly as before.

'Here,' I said, folding up and giving him the frontispiece. 'Put this with the other. I think they belong together. Now, tell me. Are you here long?'

For a while, Salvo didn't say anything. I think he was struggling to find words but he did pick up my hand and press it to his lips. I could see tears again but they weren't the unhappy sort, and I might well have been mistaken because of my own.

'A couple of months, I think,' he said, at last. 'Two books of madrigals, that's all, but it will be a great trial working for Don Carlo if he is so very mad.'

I agreed but didn't elaborate. The night air was too

warm and sweetly perfumed for such thoughts. There were nightingales in the valley too, and their song was so clear and beautiful we stopped talking in order to listen. After a little while Salvo leant across the table and took my hand.

'But if you are here,' he said, leaning closer still, 'then it will be no trial at all.' He laughed and pulled me so close towards him that it seemed likely we might kiss. 'And then, Silvia, I have an invitation from Mr Orlando Gibbons of London. I think he is more famous there than Signor Marenzio is here. At last, Silvia, to England! Do you remember how you wanted to go and see the Queen?'

He was so pleased with himself I began to laugh.

'But she died a long time ago now, Salvo.'

'Oh, did she?'

'I think you know she did, Salvo Carlino. There is a King there now, I've heard.'

'Really? Oh, well.' He laughed too and with a little tug pulled me close enough to kiss. But then he pulled away and the expression on his face was so serious suddenly that my heart almost stopped for fear of some further trouble.

'Come with me, Silvia,' he said. 'I have so many regrets in my life but none of them are so great as not taking you with me to Denmark.' He sighed. 'But wait!' He sat back and began looking through his purse. 'Ah, here it is. Look, my dear. I still have it. Believe me, I have thought of you every day since we parted.' He placed the carved swan in my hand. 'Do come to England. We will be so happy together. Let us not waste more years... please say you will.'

I thought of my white cell back at the convent, the gorgeous robes I was yet to sew and the serene singing of the chapel choir. I would never be hungry there, or afraid.

But neither would I see England or laugh with my lover and feel his caress. Certainly, I would never know the act of love.

I began to sigh, remembering how much I'd been afraid of lovemaking. But really, the night was so soft and *beautiful it was absurd to think of anything but happiness. Besides, I wasn't young anymore, and age had made me brave. I laughed then and although he didn't know why, Salvo did too.*

'Here,' I said, taking my swan from its velvet pouch and kissing it, 'let them be joined.'

Dear Salvo, in spite of being so deft, I saw his hands tremble as he fitted one to the other. 'There,' he said, placing the carvings on the table in the circle of lamplight. 'Two hearts become one at long, long last.'

How beautiful they looked together. I hoped our lives would be just as serene.

But that was ahead of us. In the warm, scented evening there was much kissing and laughing to be done. It was quite a while before we settled side by side in companionable silence.

A new moon was due to rise, and it seemed to me, in the burgeoning of its light, that from far across the valley, the song of the nightingales came to us more gloriously than ever before.

Chapter Thirty-Nine

I made it through the crowd to the door, but Jon was nowhere to be seen. I took a chance that he'd parked by the library so ran down the steps and took the cut through by the Phoenix.

In the car park? No.

But, yes … there! Out in the road.

'Jon … Jon!' I waved madly, both arms. Too late. The car turned the corner.

He didn't see me.

Or perhaps he did, and didn't stop. A cold gust hit me. It was December after all. I ran towards the High Street. I could get a bus to Jon's from there. By a miracle there was one at the stop and I accelerated, running faster than I had for years.

'Thank you,' I said, breathless and gasping.

The driver looked me up and down, at my dress, my unsuitable shoes, my lack of bag, phone, money.

'Please,' I said. 'I'm not drunk or mad, but I really need to get to the hospital.'

'You want the H bus then. I'm not going all the way.'

'That's all right, I'll get off at the nearest stop … and pay twice tomorrow. Honestly.'

'Of course you will, love,' said the driver, and he shut the doors behind me.

I gave him my best smile, then decided he thought I was mad after all. I glanced at my watch. Nine-fifteen.

By the time I reached his flat my teeth were having quite a conversation and my right shoe squeaked loudly in the suburban quiet. Jon's flat was the ground floor of a converted Victorian villa and the front garden had been turned into hard standing. The certainty of seeing his Golf parked there once I reached the end of the long yew hedge was so great, it never occurred to me that Jon might not have gone straight home.

I rang the bell, but knew it wouldn't be answered. The whole place was in darkness, even the flat upstairs. No cars were parked outside.

Shit. Idiot or what? I hugged myself and began to run on the spot. Perhaps he'd gone to the pub for a drink. Or more than one drink. He could be drowning his sorrows.

I wondered what the others were doing, back there in the warm, in their nice coats and comfortable cars. I hoped Mollie wasn't too vigorous with Duncan's bouquet of roses that I'd thrust into her arms. Mum would take charge. She was right, of course. If I'd only told Jon about Duncan. I groaned. Even though my lips were probably blue by then, I still felt the tingle of his kiss. Oh, Jon … had I blown it for good?

Left, *squeak* left, *squeak* left, *squeak*. The porch was no shelter at all. I'd walk home even if it meant dying of exposure on the way.

I was about to leave, when it occurred to me that Jon might have left a window open. It was about as unlikely as a pumpkin turning into a taxi, but I thought I'd give the handle on the side gate a go, just to see.

It did open but I couldn't see a thing, even the wheelie bins I walked into. Gradually, though, as I shuffled my way to the back, my eyes accustomed to the dark. Several times my heels squelched into something soft, but I remained upright. Only mud, I told myself, only mud. I was heading for the French windows and got to the corner without mishap, but one step on to the patio and a blinding security light came on.

'Shit,' I said, and for want of a better word said it several more times. There was no door or window open. Time for the long haul home. I'd have to ring him tomorrow.

The trouble with a security light is the dark next to it. The side of the house was even blacker than before. I put my hand against the wall and felt my way. At about halfway along I heard the sound of the side gate handle. It squeaked even more loudly than my shoe, cue for all of the unfrozen bits of me to give up the fight.

'J-J-Jon?'

'Who's there?'

'It's m-m-me.'

'Jesus Christ … *Lisa*?'

'Wait there,' he said, once we got inside. I stood in the hall, shivering – not just a bit of a quiver, great big trembly unstoppable wobbles. I felt wobbly inside too. Jon hadn't exactly looked delighted to see me. He'd taken the car to the garage ready for the repair work to be done and walked home from there.

A minute later he came back with a duvet, wrapped it round me then went away again without saying anything. I sat down on an old pew he'd rescued from the local church. There was a row of his shoes underneath with a space halfway along. I eased mine off and kicked them into the space, then rubbed my feet together in the hope of reminding the blood to pump that far.

I heard the sound of the kettle boiling but he appeared carrying a bottle of whisky and two glasses.

'Come in here,' he said, beckoning me to follow. 'I'll make tea, but I think you need a drop of this as well. I definitely do.'

I shuffled through to his sitting room. He took a gulp of his before handing me mine and sat himself in the armchair. Part of me felt like hiding, putting the duvet right over my head and hibernating until next spring. Fat chance. Besides, the better part of me had something it needed to say.

A quick swig and I opened my mouth ready to launch my apology.

'Sor—'

'I do hope you're not going to apologise,' he said.

Never has a word so rapidly evaporated. 'Oh. Err … no. Well, not really. Perhaps …'

'Only the thing is, Lisa,' he took another gulp of his whisky. 'The thing is, I used to think that we had, I dunno, a sort of thing. You know, we seemed to get on well. We laughed a lot. Mollie was great. I thought we ...' he trailed off and shook his head. 'But these last couple of months ...' I thought I knew every square centimetre of his handsome face but I'd never seen him look that bleak.

'I—'

He waved my response away. 'You've been so weird. So secretive. It was like you were turning into someone else. Someone I didn't know.'

'But—' He wouldn't let me speak.

'And then you came up with this curse business about the Gesualdo and I thought, okay, you've had a bump on the head. I even thought ...' he put his glass down on the table, stood up and began pacing around. 'I even thought there might be something in it. When you asked me round the other day and I had a look at the frontispiece again, I could almost see what you meant.'

He did that thing with his hair so that it stood up.

'But then, Lisa, then a mysterious postcard with kisses from Italy, a total stranger turns up with a bunch of roses and suddenly everything falls, plink, plinketty, plink ... into place. And then I get it.'

My heart was beating like a tom-tom but I'd half thawed by that time and put away most of my glass of whisky.

'No, stop,' I said, desperate to say something. 'No, you don't get it at all.'

He'd stopped pacing and instead kicked the rug as he stood with hands gripping either end of the mantelpiece.

'Please,' he said, 'don't take me for an idiot.' He took a deep breath. 'You still look frozen. I'll make that tea.'

In a gesture that turned out to be more theatrical than I meant, I cast off the duvet and stood up, barring his way out of the door.

'If all that's true, then what on earth do you think I'm doing here?'

He shrugged. 'Embarrassment? Guilt? God knows, Lisa. I certainly don't. One minute you're pulling a fantastic stunt with the choir and practically in my arms and the next … Christ almighty.'

I reached towards him but he side-stepped me and was out of the room before I could turn round. I grabbed the glass on the coffee table and downed the rest. I had things to say that needed fuel.

Right then, I told myself. Don't mess this up. It's your last chance. Look him in the eye and tell him straight.

And then the phone rang. A landline, cordless and on the arm of the sofa. Brrring, brrring. It vibrated as it rang, a high-pitched old-fashioned ambulance ring, but then it fell off the arm and buried itself in a cushion and all I heard was the brrr … brrr.

I thought for a moment he was going to ignore it but then it stopped ringing, and out in the kitchen I heard him laugh. Then nothing. Nothing apart from a few grunts and more laughs for quite a long time, until he said the one word that told me who he was talking to.

'*Arrivederci.*'

If there had been a wind to billow my sails, it dropped then, leaving them and me limp. So he was still in touch with Daniela. Part of me reasoned that she had probably phoned to find out how the concert went. But hadn't she done all the talking?

I put my glass down on the table. Time to go. It wasn't what was said that I found so painful but the fact that there'd been so much pleasure in his laughter. We didn't laugh like that anymore. He was right. We'd grown apart. The mammoth had got fed up and wandered off.

Waiting for the taxi felt like the worst ten minutes of my life. Jon insisted on lending me a jumper and spent a long time looking for one. In the warm taxi it exuded the musky, coffee smell of Jon and I had to wipe away tears on its sleeve.

At home, the bouquet of roses sat stiffly on the windowsill. Mum and Mollie were cuddled up on the sofa watching *Finding Nemo*, although I think they were both asleep before my opening the door woke them.

'Hello, love,' said Mum. 'I didn't expect to see …' She trailed off when she saw my face. 'What's happened?'

'Nothing,' I said. 'Absolutely nothing.'

That's what I felt too. Not miserable or upset. If I felt anything, it was anger. I wanted to kick something. Have a tantrum. But I had shut the lid on that too. And put a large imaginary rock on it with a notice that said: Danger. Do Not Open.

'What?' said Mollie, bleary-eyed. 'What's happened?'

'It's time you were in bed,' I said. 'You shouldn't be up this late.'

Everything's always in the tone, isn't it? A singer can have the best technique in the world but if their tone is unattractive, who wants to listen to them? It was the way Jon had laughed that got me and it was the way I spoke to Mollie that got her. Her chin trembled.

'What about Jon?' she said.

'Nothing about Jon. Go to bed.'

She frowned and I saw the telltale red spots on her cheeks that signalled an explosion. Her mouth opened but she obviously thought better of it and she shut it sharply. I caught a glimpse of grown-up Mollie then, although the way she ignored me, kissed Mum and stomped out of the room, sent the message anyway.

Mum was more circumspect. 'Do you want to talk about it?'

I shook my head.

'Can I get you a cup of tea? Cocoa? A large brandy?'

I shook my head again. 'You get to bed, Mum. I'll be fine.'

She brushed the hair from my eyes, like she used to when I was a child, then gave me a hug. 'Well, I don't know about that. But give me a shout if you want, won't you? Oh, by the way, I've arranged for us to meet your Duncan and his wife at the museum in the morning. I think he was a bit nonplussed when you rushed off like that, but I did my best to explain.'

Duncan. God, yes. I still didn't know what he wanted

304

to show me. Whatever it was, it didn't seem all that important.

After Mum shut the door, I looked out of the window although if the world had disappeared I might not have noticed. Jon's laughter rattled about in my mind. In the silence of the night it felt like torture. I wandered about picking things up and putting them down in the same place but when I saw Mollie's pink headphones lying on the kitchen table, I plugged them into my phone. Mozart was supposed to be soothing, but after a minute I changed it to Elisabeth Schwarzkopf singing Strauss's *Four Last Songs*.

I awoke with a stiff neck and where my head had been resting, a dead arm. It was quite some time after the last *Last Song*. The oven clock said half past midnight. Jon, Mollie, Daniela, memories of the evening all swirled about in my mind as painful as the pins and needles frothing through my arm.

It wouldn't be easy making my peace with Mollie. Jon was her friend. No, more than that, she wanted him to be another Dad. Oh, Mollie. Oh, dear. Big sigh. I pulled the headphones out of my ears and wound them round my fingers. It was surprising she hadn't taken them to bed with her. I knew she was cross but I'd never known her go to sleep without listening to something. Fancy.

I unravelled them.

Why hadn't she? Why not?

I was up in an instant.

'Mollie? *Mollie*?' I rushed into her room. The duvet was in a heap but Mollie wasn't underneath it. She wasn't in the bathroom either.

'Mum. *Mum*!' Maybe Mollie had gone into Mum for comfort. I shoved open the door, slamming my hand against the light switch.

No. No! She didn't. She wasn't there. Where was she?

'What?' Mum sat straight up. 'What is it, love?'

'Mollie's gone. She's not in bed. She was but not now.'

Mum blinked at me 'Are you sure?'

'Of course I'm bloody sure.' I ran back into Mollie's room to make sure even though I was. 'She's not here.' I could hear my voice rising. The terror in it.

Then I saw it. There, on the bedside cabinet.

'Her phone's here. Oh my God! She's not got her phone!' It was if my body belonged to someone else and I could see myself careering round her room, through the door bashing myself against the frame, into the hall. 'Her coat's gone. Her puffa jacket. And her boots!'

Mum was there. Opening the front door and looking out into the hall and down the stairs. She looked at me with an expression full of all the dread I felt, and shook her head.

'Where would she go?'

There was only one place. I ran back into the kitchen and grabbed my phone.

It rang and rang. Please, answer. Please. Would he? Four rings, five, six … I knew it went to message on the eighth.

On the seventh he picked up.

'Oh God! Jon, Jon, it's me.' I was almost screaming.

'Lisa?'

'She's not here. She's not here!'

'Lisa, what is it? Calm down. You need to calm down. Take a deep breath.'

I tried to but felt as if a vice had clamped my lungs together. 'Her bed's empty. Mollie … Mollie.'

'Mollie?' Now his voice was shot through with anxiety. 'What's happened?'

I managed to tell him. 'She's out there on her own, Jon. It's the middle of the night. Anyone could …who knows … they might … and there's the river …'

'Listen, Lisa,' he interrupted. 'Stop it. Don't think anything like that.'

'But—'

'No. You must listen to me. This is what you're going to do.'

306

A few minutes later, I left Mum phoning the police. I couldn't wait for them and neither could Jon. There was only one route Mollie would take to Jon's. She wouldn't go over the road bridge. Not in full sight. No. She would go along the river by the swings and cross at the pedestrian bridge by the quay. Jon and I would walk towards each other. Mollie would be somewhere in between.

She'd been sensible enough to leave her bright pink jacket on its hook and gone for the navy puffa but why hadn't she taken her phone? It was her best thing. Her very best thing.

Mostly I ran. Every now and then slowing to a quick walk. There was some traffic on the main road and I crossed over when I saw a man pushing a shopping trolley coming towards me. Why would anyone push a Sainsbury's trolley around at gone midnight? I looked across as he passed to check it was empty.

I gripped my phone so tight that I doubt it could have vibrated even if it wanted to. Please ring. I kept willing it to ring. To ring and be Jon saying she was found. I cut through to the river by the pub and when I couldn't see her, I ran back and round to the other side. From there I had a clear view along the river. The path by the water was lit but I could see perfectly well that it was empty.

Maybe she was at the end, near the bridge where I couldn't see. I ran faster. The water beside me was oily black and fast flowing. The boy with the needle surged into my mind, and although I knew it was impossible and probably a reflection of a distant light, I kept seeing his pale arm. Just before he drowned. He drowned. Drowned! Oh. Mollie. Mollie.

Then I saw Jon. He was running along the quay on the far side. It was dark over there but I would know Jon anywhere. I peered into the gloom for another figure. There? There? No. He reached the wooden footbridge over the leat. Then he was crossing the river. We met on my side. He looked like a ghost.

'No?' he said.

I shook my head. 'No. No … oh God, no … Mollie … Mollieeee.' I called out desperately, my voice echoing back a high-pitched whine. Only a dog barked in reply. Why had I been so short with her? Why?

'Phone home,' Jon said. 'The police should be there by now.'

As he said it, we heard the clack-clack-clack of the police helicopter.

Mum had no news. A policewoman was making tea in my kitchen. We shouldn't keep on the phone in case someone rang.

Someone? Please, someone, please ring. Please God.

'Nothing,' I said to Jon. I knew I was shaking because I could hardly keep the phone next to my ear but then I began to tremble. Really badly. I couldn't tell whether I was cold or not but I could hardly stand.

'Jon,' I whispered. His face was set, jaw clenched shut but he looked out across the river, along the quay and back to the path where we stood. Over and again. We both gazed into the darkest shadows, willing a small shape to reveal itself. But there was nothing.

'Oh, Jon. What have I done? Oh, Mollie, Mollie … if only …'

'Shh, Lisa,' he said. 'Don't say anything. Here,' he took off his jacket and wrapped it round me. 'She's a clever girl, your daughter. Let's not forget that.' He couldn't disguise the worry in his voice though. 'What about Michael? Wouldn't she go there?'

'He's away. Vienna or somewhere.'

'Does Mollie know?'

'Yes, of course she bloody knows. She was only there yesterday.'

He ignored my irritation. 'But has she got a key? Or does she know if there's one hidden somewhere?'

'Oh, I don't know. Maybe.' Hope blazed suddenly. Then I looked at the water; felt rain on my face. 'But we can't both go. What if she comes here and there's nobody?'

The helicopter was overhead and at the same time a blue light came flashing across the bridge, nearer and nearer as it came up Haven Road towards us. Then another blue light on the opposite side of the river, until the entire quay was illuminated.

We ran towards the police car. 'St David's Hill,' I said, having pulled open the back door and jumped in as if it was a taxi. 'She might be at her dad's. He's away, but she might know how to get in.'

So much that was familiar turned post-apocalyptic by the speed and blue light strobe of a police car. Both Jon and I sat forward on the back seat, as if in some hope that it would help us go faster. We peered through the windows for something, anything …

Michael's house was tucked away in an upmarket terrace behind the main drag.

'Here, here,' I said, as we reached the nearest place accessible by car. We jumped out and ran up the path but when we turned the corner into the square, I could see the house was in complete darkness.

'No, no, no!' I rang the bell and yelled through the letterbox but everything said she wasn't there. The gate was closed. The cat mewed round my ankles. A light went on next door and a window opened. No, they hadn't seen or heard anyone.

I'd been so sure. So *sure*. But then I'd been sure she was at Jon's and she wasn't. I don't remember walking back to the car. I do remember Jon's grim face, the policeman talking into his phone, in English, although I didn't understand what he said. It was late and apart from the even throb of the engine idling, there wasn't any noise.

Until the strange interjection of Mozart's 40th Symphony. My phone.

I was in such a state I could hardly get it out of my pocket. No caller ID. Oh my God, she'd been kidnapped. Jon put his arm round me.

'Hello, hello?'

'Mrs Barr?' A woman's voice.

'Yes?'

'This is the Royal Clarence Hotel.'

We arrived at the same time as Mum. Two police cars bumping over the cobbles in Cathedral Yard. At the Clarence, the receptionist was hopping from foot to foot outside the front door.

'Hello, hello,' she said, all smiles. 'How lovely. Go through. She's with my colleague, Donna. Do go through,' she shooed us towards the champagne bar. 'I wonder if you could keep the noise ...' She hesitated and looked at us. Mum, Jon, two policemen and me. 'Do you think you could be ... not too loud?'

But there was Mollie, and all my worries and fears, in one great surge, converted into relief.

'Mollie!' I yelled, laughing like an idiot and running towards her. 'Mollie, Mollie, Mollie!'

And she was down from the stool and in my arms.

'Oh Mum, Mummy ... I didn't mean ... I meant—'

'Shh, it's all right now.'

And for a few seconds it was perfectly all right. Nothing else mattered. I breathed in the scent of her and ran my hands through her hair, feeling its softness.

But then everything piled in. All the questions. What, where, how, why? They all came into my mind all jumbled up amidst lots of laughing and tears from all of us.

'I went to Dad's,' she said, her voice something between a sniff and sob. 'But halfway there, I remembered he was away. So I went to Jon's. But then he wasn't there.' She sniffed louder.

'I'm here now, Mollie.' Jon was just behind me. Next thing, he put his arms round her and me and squeezed us both tight. 'I'll always be here.'

His words went round and round in my head. Better than any applause, than any present. When we finally could bear to let go of each other, I was able to take in who was there and where we were.

'I'd walked all *over* the place by then,' said Mollie,

'and then I remembered Uncle Charles was staying here.'

Charles sat, wrapped in a hotel dressing gown, on a red velvet sofa next to my mum. He looked both pleased and embarrassed. 'I can't imagine what they thought at reception,' he said. 'A child asking for her granddad in the middle of the night.'

It was a funny but appalling thought. The two policemen shuffled. I thanked them for all their help, shaking their hands like a mad thing, but they were so relieved at such a happy outcome they didn't seem to mind at all. Mollie thanked them nicely without my prompting and I started to cry all over again.

It was quite a lot later that Mollie, Jon and I got back to the flat. The staff at the hotel offered us a nightcap and Mollie, the chocolate milkshake of her dreams. It came with a wiggly straw and a choice of umbrella and she chose turquoise over pink. Goodbye Barbie, hello Queen Elsa.

Quite when they decided it, I wasn't sure, but Mum looked very coy when I said we were going. I'm sure it wasn't merely curiosity about the Clarence's bedroom décor that prompted her to stay.

Mollie was asleep on her feet.

'I should go,' said Jon. He hovered at the door.

'Oh, please don't go,' I said. 'Wait while I put Mollie to bed.'

He smiled then, the sort that made my toes curl with deliciousness. Even more so when he lifted my chin and kissed me.

'I was wrong,' he said. 'What I said earlier. It's not true.' He kissed me again, then drew back. 'We're a family. Aren't we? Say we are, my lovely Lisa.'

Slowly, I nodded but then as he bent to kiss me again, I found my voice. 'We are. Yes, we are.'

'Hallelujah,' yawned Mollie, as she leaned against me. 'At long last.'

I didn't even insist she cleaned her teeth that night.

'Did you really think it was a fantastic stunt?' I said, over Coco Pops the next morning.

Jon laughed. 'I did. At least, until your Fabrizio failed to produce more than a squeak. But I was amazed. You were so against it. What was it you said? Terrible, horrible idea.'

'Don't,' I said. 'I'm so embarrassed about that. I spent much too long looking at that frontispiece and ended up with a head full of demons.'

'Sounds painful.'

'It was.' We sipped coffee in the rare quiet of a morning without Mollie singing at the top of her voice. She was still asleep, not surprisingly. I could hardly bear to look anywhere but at Jon. It was as if he was all new somehow, this handsome man I could touch, could kiss whenever I wanted to. I reached forward and put my hand on his.

'You know something?'

'What?'

'You look awesome in that vest.'

'Yeah?'

'You were a much better Fabrizio than Jonah.'

'Phew. That's good to hear. I was afraid the sexy princess might go off me.' He put down his coffee and caught hold of my hand in both of his. 'I really wrote it for you, Lisa. I wanted you to see I could write something substantial. Not exactly an opera, I know. But more than a jingle.'

God. How dumb I'd been. How utterly, utterly stupid.

'I had the idea when you started the coaching at Mollie's school. I thought, why not? It doesn't have to be gruesome. Stories can have happy and sad endings and it's not as if I'm some academic searching for "The Truth".' He frowned as he stressed the words. 'They were really good too.' His expression softened at the memory. 'Well, Mollie was.'

I laughed, in spite of everything. 'You saved the day. Poor Jonah, I wonder if he will get over it.'

'Oh, probably. Especially if you do it again.'

'But really, I should have told you beforehand. It was stupid and selfish of me not to. We could have worked on it together. Wouldn't that have been nice?'

'Yes, but it was nice anyway, Lisa. Don't beat yourself up about what wasn't.'

How lovely he was.

'I did think,' I said, 'that Mollie might burst keeping it a secret. I hadn't a clue what was going on. You didn't tell me what you were doing and were being all vague. Then there was the frontispiece. Did I imagine it? God, it *felt* so malevolent, I don't know, Jon. There were loads of times when I should have said things and didn't.'

'What things?'

'About Duncan for one and Daniela—'

'Daniela?'

I told him about the escape from Costa, how cross I was, how jealous.

'Why on earth were you jealous?' he said, with exactly the right tone of incredulity. 'She was entirely wrapped up in herself and not in the least bit funny. God, and she went on about singing at La Scala. How she'd come here because of some feckless bloke.'

'Is that what she said?' I snorted, piggily. Who knew?

'Yes, she … why? Didn't she?'

'She told me,' I said. 'She told me she'd auditioned for La Scala but not got in. That's why she came here and why she went back so quickly when they wanted her again.'

'Oh,' said Jon, and he nodded slowly. 'I see.'

'Mmm …' I said. 'Well, she lied to one or us. Either way, even if I had got it all wrong, she did almost break us up.'

In fact, I thought, but didn't say, she was the earthquake. We'd had fire, water and air but right at the beginning, when we first met together to sing the Gesualdo, that was the moment when everything began to shake. I couldn't have been more thankful that she'd gone.

'And this Duncan bloke?' Jon poured us both another

313

coffee. 'What's the story with him? Holiday fling?'

'No! Please, don't even go there.' I gave him a resume of the Naples trip. 'But why he's here I don't know yet. He's brought something for me to see. Oh shit! What's the time?' I leaned sideways so that I could see the oven clock behind Jon. 'Mum said we're all meeting at the museum this morning.'

'Oh yes? In that case, I'd better come along too.'

When it looked as if we were going to be shockingly late, we rushed about like mad things. Mollie was persuaded into clothes and began a campaign to be allowed a hot chocolate at the Clarence. It involved talking of almost nothing else.

'Damn,' I said, when we'd shut the door. 'Forgot the music.'

'Music?'

'Yeah, the Gesualdo. It's got to go back. And the sooner the better.' I went back for it. Of course, it wasn't where I thought it was, but why was I not surprised? As far as I was concerned, Mum or Mollie had emptied my music case and put the copies halfway down the pile under the coffee table. I wasn't going to entertain any other possibility. It was going, and that was bloody well that.

The entire population of Exeter seemed to be crammed into the museum but in the cafe, Mum and Mollie, Duncan and his lovely wife – hooray – had nabbed one of the big tables.

After the intros and congrats and a few sips of our chosen coffees, Duncan opened his briefcase and took out a folder.

'This is for you,' he said, handing it to me. 'We found it in Rome,' he said. 'Celia will tell you, we can't walk past an antiquarian book shop these days.'

Celia nodded; I got the impression she was equally keen.

'Why, thank you,' I said, not knowing what it was.

314

We all gasped when I laid the frontispiece on the table. Strange: the reaction was almost the same as when we'd first seen the one fronting Gesualdo's madrigal, but this one was entirely different. *Madrigal a cinque voci.* The composer was Luca Marenzio.

'Duncan,' I said, 'I don't know what to say. It's wonderful. Thank you.'

'It's a pleasure,' he said.

'It really is,' agreed Celia. What a lovely couple.

'Oh, cool,' said Mollie, pointing at the little row of singers. 'See the way the music they're holding is a mini version of the whole thing.'

'I'm sure,' said Duncan, 'that this is by the same engraver as yours. What was his name?'

'Salvo Carlino. The nephew of *Giovanni* Giacomo Carlino, the printer.'

'Yes, that's him. Look at the animals, the realism of the expressions on the faces of the people.'

'Wait a minute,' I said, delving into my bag. 'I've got the other one here. We can put them side by side.' I took out my old photocopy, that was rather crumpled, but I smoothed it out on the table, and we all leaned forward for a closer look.

'Do you know which one came first?' Sudden tears stung the corner of my eyes. There was a touching innocence to this new scene, and the thought that life could have gone so badly wrong for the artist felt almost unbearable.

Duncan shook his head. ' I don't know how we could ever know for sure, but I'd say this one was the earlier.' He tapped his forefinger on the one depicting the choir. 'Didn't you tell me that Gesualdo got ensconced with witchcraft in his later life and was very insane by the time he died?

'Yes,' I said. 'Although what's true and what's rumour, who knows? I hope it turned out well for Signor Carlino.' I stirred the froth on my cappuccino. There was no doubt in my mind they were by the same person. The endearing little vocal ensemble singing under the tree had such expressive faces, all so happy and joyful. The other one still made me shudder, but it was strange seeing the two engravings together.

The others chatted away while I kept stirring my coffee. I could hear them, the noise of the coffee machine making more cappuccinos and the clink of my spoon against the cup, but somehow I seemed to zone out of the present. It became shadowy and distant. I knew what it was. The gruesome frontispiece was pulling me in. But this time something was different.

'Oh, I see!' I said, rather more loudly that I meant. They all looked at me, and so did the family on the next table. I waved an apology. Everyone must have thought I was mad, because I began gabbling and laughing all at the same time. 'It's still,' I said, jabbing at the scene from Hell. 'It's all still. It isn't moving any more! Look!' I clutched hold of Jon's hand. He was the only one that knew what I was talking about. 'Do you see?'

We all held our breath. Certainly Mum and Mollie looked worried. Duncan and Celia more bemused.

But then Jon said the best three words in the world apart from, I love you, which he'd said to me only a couple of hours earlier.

'You're right, Lisa.' And he nodded and began to laugh when he saw the others' faces. 'She's absolutely right. I only wish I'd realised it sooner.'

He put his arm round me and kissed me, a big smackeroo on the lips. Mollie, always able to express her feelings, clapped and cheered.

'These two fontispieces belong together,' I said. 'If they're together, everything will be fine. I'll donate this to the museum, and you never know, maybe they might even put them on display. Is that okay, Duncan?'

'It sounds like a splendid idea to me.'

'Yay,' said Mollie, punching her fists in the air. 'Result!'

'I do wish,' I said, after finally managing a mouthful of

coffee, 'that we knew how the Gesualdo madrigal turned up here.'

'Musicians have always travelled,' Jon said. 'Look at John Dowland. He went as far as Ferrara. How do we know he didn't meet Gesualdo and bring a copy back to England himself?'

'I suppose so,' I said. 'And then Exeter?'

'Renaissance fax machine,' said Jon. 'Had Leonardo invented it by then?'

We all laughed, although I made a mental note to give Mollie a history lesson in case she argued with Miss Price.

'Oh, I know,' Jon said, sitting up smartly and knocking the table so that all the cups rattled in their saucers. 'It could easily have been Edward Gibbons. You know, the Cathedral Choirmaster, brother of Orlando. He went to London often enough. I reckon John Dowland gave it to Orlando Gibbons who then gave it to Edward. There. End of story.'

After a lot of surmising of this and that, we decided that was as near the truth as we were ever going to get. The frontispiece was hardly the sort of gift you'd be pleased with, although Gesualdo's madrigal might well have been.

'Oh, well,' I said. 'That'll have to do. There's so much we can't know.'

'But that means we can make something up instead,' Mollie said. 'Like Jon did. Then we can have a happy ending.'

'But you have to watch making stuff up, Mollie,' Jon said. 'If it's about what's going on now, then the best thing is to make sure everyone knows what's happening.' He put his hand on my knee and squeezed.

'Yes.' I laughed. 'Otherwise, it's very easy to jump to a whole lot of wrong conclusions.' Then with my super-strong piano player's hands, I squeezed his knee and to everyone's surprise, he swore rather loudly.

'I think,' said Duncan, 'we should make a move, so those

317

poor people can rest their legs.' The queue to get into the café extended beyond the door. 'Do you think it would be a good idea to visit your excellent looking Cathedral now?' He put his arm round Celia's shoulders. 'We're rather hoping that as it's so crowded in here, it might be quieter there.'

Mollie wasn't keen on the Cathedral. I could tell by the way she sagged around the knees when we all stood up. Mum was meeting Charles in the Royal Clarence for lunch, but in a fit of selflessness, she suggested she took Mollie with her.

Duncan was right. There weren't many people in the Cathedral. But he was also wrong; it certainly wasn't quiet. A choir was rehearsing the Monteverdi *Vespers*.

'Written in 1610,' said Jon. 'How very appropriate.'

Duncan and Celia sat down to listen, but Jon draped his arm round my shoulder and we wandered down the side aisle. There was no memorial to Edward Gibbons, only a list of the organists' name and dates.

I looked at the surrounding plaques. All musicians, and some I knew, but I was disappointed not to find Orlando's brother.

'There's probably stuff about him in the Cathedral Library,' Jon said.

'Yes,' I said. 'I expect there is.' I gestured at the memorials. 'Pity these aren't like the displays in the museum where you can press the button and up comes an information screen.'

'Mmm, shame,' said Jon. 'Tell you what, you can press my button later if you like. I do a great display ... oof.'

Well, I had to shut him up somehow.

Postscript

A few weeks later, I got a message from Lorraine to call in at the museum.

'Do you remember,' she said, tracing her finger down the front of a small wooden chest of drawers, 'asking me whether anything else had turned up with the manuscript?'

I felt a little pang of excitement. 'Yes, I do. Have you found something?'

'Some things, actually. I thought you should see them.' She opened a drawer. 'Here we are.'

She placed three plastic bags, similar to the sort used for coinage, on her desk, then removed from each a small wooden carving. Small enough to fit in the palm of a hand. A kitten and two swans.

'They're sweet, aren't they? And look, see what happens with the two swans?' She slotted them together, necks entwined and laid them on the desk. 'There.'

'Oh, how amazing. They're beautiful,' I whispered, 'and by the same man, aren't they?'

'We certainly think so.'

'He must have come here himself then.'

Lorraine shrugged. 'I have no idea. But I suppose it's possible.'

As I walked home, head burrowed in my hood out of the rain, I began to make up my own end to the story. In it Salvo Carlino fled from the wicked Prince who had accused him of murdering the Princess in order to exonerate himself. Hmm... not bad. But too simple.

Then, I thought, that maybe the wicked Prince had his eye on Salvo's wife and they both had to escape. Yes, I liked that version better. It had love interest and explained the little swans. I imagined Mrs Carlino as being rather like Silvia Albana. When I reached the bottom of the road, she was wearing my lovely dove grey dress. And by the time I put the key in the door, I didn't have to hope that

319

they lived happily ever after because I knew, as the rain from my coat puddled on the mat, that they did.

Yes, a good resolution. That's what was needed. Just like at the end of a good madrigal. Even those by the mysterious, mad murderer, Don Carlo Gesualdo, now considered works of genius. After the hey-nonny-nonnies, fa-la-laa's, the passion and the tears, when it comes to the end, there's always a harmonious resolution.

About the Author

Cathie Hartigan was brought up in London, but fell in love with Devon when she was a music student at Dartington College of Arts, and never left.

Cathie is a prize-winning short story writer, a three times finalist in the *Woman and Home* competition and her story, *Making the Grade*, was included in the Romantic Novelists' Association's latest anthology, *Truly, Madly, Deeply*. She has been published in several anthologies.

Cathie lectured in creative writing at Exeter College for nine years before establishing CreativeWritingMatters, which runs a range of author services and literary competitions including The Exeter Novel Prize.

She co-wrote the bestselling textbook *The Creative Writing Student's Handbook*, and *The Short Story Writer's Workbook* with Margaret James.

When she is not writing, Cathie plays the piano and sings in a small vocal ensemble. The beautiful Devon coastline provides plenty of distraction, although on a rainy day, if there's an opera or theatre screening at the cinema, she'll be there.

The *Secret of the Song* is her debut novel.

www.facebook.com/cathie.hartigan

www.twitter.com/cathiehartigan

www.creativewritingmatters.co.uk/cathie'sblog

13001771R00191

Printed in Great Britain
by Amazon.co.uk, Ltd.,
Marston Gate.